LEWIS CARROLL

The Annotated Alice

THE DEFINITIVE EDITION

Alice's Adventures in Wonderland
and Through the Looking-Glass

Original Illustrations by JOHN TENNIEL
With an Introduction and Notes by MARTIN GARDNER

PENGUIN BOOKS

PENGUIN BOOKS

Published by the Penguin Group
Penguin Books Ltd, 80 Strand, London WC2R 0RL, England
Penguin Putnam Inc., 375 Hudson Street, New York, New York 10014, USA
Penguin Books Australia Ltd, 250 Camberwell Road, Camberwell, Victoria 3124, Australia
Penguin Books Canada Ltd, 10 Alcorn Avenue, Toronto, Ontario, Canada M4V 3B2
Penguin Books India (P) Ltd, 11 Community Centre, Panchsheel Park, New Delhi – 110 017, India
Penguin Books (NZ) Ltd, Cnr Rosedale and Airborne Roads, Albany, Auckland, New Zealand
Penguin Books (South Africa) (Pty) Ltd, 24 Sturdee Avenue, Rosebank 2196, South Africa

Penguin Books Ltd, Registered Offices: 80 Strand, London WC2R 0RL, England

www.penguin.com

The Annotated Alice first published in the USA by Clarkson N. Potter Inc. 1960
First published in great Britain by Anthony Blond Ltd 1964
Published in Penguin Books 1965
revised edition 1970
More Annotated Alice first published in the USA by Random House Inc. 1990
The Annotated Alice: The definitive Edition first published in the USA
by W. W. Norton & Company Inc. 2000
First published in Great Britain by Allen Lane The Penguin Press 2000
Published in Penguin Books 2001

9

Copyright © Martin Gardner, 1960, 1970, 1988, 2000, 2001
All rights reserved

The moral right of the author has been asserted

Printed in England by Clays Ltd, St Ives plc

To the thousands of readers of my
Annotated Alice and *More Annotated Alice*
who took the time to send letters of appreciation,
and to offer corrections and suggestions
for new notes.

PENGUIN BOOKS

THE ANNOTATED ALICE

'All an annotated book should be – a classic text illuminated, a monument with windows in it . . . It memorializes the meeting of two remarkable eccentric minds at a particular moment in intellectual history' Adam Gopnik, *New Yorker*

'For nearly half a century, Martin Gardner's *Annotated Alice* has reigned supreme as the eccentric and engrossing commentary on manifold conundrums offered by Carroll's text' Robert McCrum, *Observer*

'Digresses into the most engrossing trivia, as fantastic and unexpected as Alice's adventures themselves . . . Much of what delighted Carroll's contemporaries . . . would have been lost to us, if it were not for Gardner's *Annotated Alice*' Jacques Guy, *The Times Higher Education Supplement*

'It is now hard to imagine Carroll without Gardner. A unique collaboration has produced, for once, a book that lives up to its name. As close to a definitive take on a classic work as anyone is likely to come' *Kirkus Reviews*

'Lewis Carroll and the *Alice* books, with their curiosity, their kindness, their gay, quizzical humour, and their glimpses of the beautiful and the sublime, were made for Gardner to be fascinated by, and for him to burnish up that fascination and convey it to us' Kenneth Wright, *Glasgow Herald*

'Readers will be delighted by Mr Gardner's glosses and his often pointed asides . . . We owe both Carroll and his annotator a great debt for keeping wonder alive' Rex Roberts, *Washington Times*

Lewis Carroll was the pen-name of the Reverend Charles Lutwidge Dodgson. Born in 1832, he was educated at Rugby School and Christ Church, Oxford, where he was appointed lecturer in mathematics in 1855, and where he spent the rest of his life. In 1861 he took deacon's orders, but shyness and a constitutional stammer prevented him from seeking the priesthood.

He wrote numerous satirical pamphlets on Oxford politics, including *Notes by an Oxford Chiel* (1874), and works on logic such as *Euclid and His Modern Rivals* and *Symbolic Logic* (1896). He also became a pioneering photographer, specializing in Victorian celebrities and children. Though Dodgson never married, children were the main interest of his life. After the publication of *Alice's Adventures in Wonderland* (1865) and *Through the Looking-Glass* (1871), both of which were originally written for Alice Liddell, the daughter of the dean of his college, he became the most famous children's writer of the day. In addition to his two nonsense classics, he also published several books of nonsense verse, including *Phantasmagoria and Other Poems* (1896), *The Hunting of the Snark* (1876) and *Rhyme? And Reason?* (1882); numerous books of puzzles and games such as *The Game of Logic* (1887); and towards the close of his life, a long children's novel in two parts, *Sylvie and Bruno* (1889, 1893). He died in 1898.

Martin Gardner was born in 1914 in Tulsa, Oklahoma. He worked as a journalist and publicity writer up to the outbreak of the Second World War, during which he served in the United States Navy. From 1957 to 1982 he wrote a monthly recreational mathematics column in *Scientific American*, which delighted a worldwide audience comprising mathematicians and dreamers, scientists and schoolchildren, computer programmers and poets. He is the author of many books, including, in Penguin, *Mathematical Puzzles and Diversions*, *Mathematical Carnival*, *Mathematical Circus*, *Mathematical Magic Show*, *The Ambidextrous Universe*, *The Night is Large* and *Visitors from Oz*, as well as *The Annotated Alice* and *The Hunting of the Snark*, of which he is editor. Gardner has been hailed by Douglas Hofstadter as 'one of the great intellects produced in this country in this century'. He lives in Hendersonville, North Carolina, and his main hobby is conjuring.

Contents

Alice, Where Art Thou?

Quaint child, old-fashioned Alice, lend your dream:
I would be done with modern story-spinners,
Follow with you the laughter and the gleam:
Weary am I, this night, of saints and sinners.
We have been friends since Lewis and old Tenniel
Housed you immortally in red and gold.
Come! Your naivete is a spring perennial:
Let me be young again before I'm old.

You are a glass of youth: this night I choose
Deep in your magic labyrinths to stray,
Where rants the Red Queen in her splendid hues
And the White Rabbit hurries on his way.
Let us once more adventure, hand in hand:
Give me belief again—in Wonderland!

—Vincent Starrett, in *Brillig* (Chicago: Dierkes Press, 1949)

Preface to the Definitive Edition of
The Annotated Alice

The Annotated Alice was first published in 1960 by Clarkson Potter. It went through many printings here and in England, in hardcover and paperback, and was translated into Italian, Japanese, Russian, and Hebrew. I was unable to persuade Crown, which took over Potter before Crown was in turn taken over by Random House, to let me do a major revision of the book by adding a raft of new notes that had accumulated in my files. I finally decided to put them in a sequel titled *More Annotated Alice*. Random House published it in 1990, thirty years after the previous book.

To distinguish the sequel from *The Annotated Alice* I substituted Peter Newell's 80 full-page illustrations for Tenniel's art. Michael Patrick Hearn contributed a fine essay on Newell. I also was able to add to *More Annotated Alice* the long-lost "Wasp in a Wig" episode that Carroll left out of his second *Alice* book after Tenniel strongly urged him to remove it, but one still had to open two separate *Alice* books simultaneously, which seemed a bit impractical.

In 1998 I was surprised and delighted when my editor at Norton, Robert Weil, suggested that the notes from both *Alice* books be combined in a single "definitive" edition. They are all here, some of them expanded, and many new notes have been added. Tenniel's pictures in *The Annotated Alice* were poorly reproduced, bristling with broken type and fuzzy lines. For this volume they have been faithfully copied in their original clarity.

The "Wasp in a Wig" episode is included in this book, along with the introduction and notes I wrote for its first publication by the Lewis Carroll Society of North America in a 1977 limited edition. I had the great pleasure of tracking down the New York City collector who had bought the original galleys at a London auction, and persuaded him to let me reprint them in a small book.

In addition to thanking Weil for making this edition possible, I also thank Justin Schiller, the nation's top seller and collector of rare books for children, for permission to include reproductions of Tenniel's preliminary sketches from Schiller's book *Alice's Adventures in Wonderland*, privately printed in 1990. Thanks, too, to David Schaefer for providing a checklist of film productions of *Alice*, based on his great collection of such films.

Introduction to *The Annotated Alice*

Let it be said at once that there is something preposterous
about an annotated *Alice*. Writing in 1932, on the hundred-
year anniversary of Lewis Carroll's birth, Gilbert K.
Chesterton voiced his "dreadful fear" that Alice's story had
already fallen under the heavy hands of the scholars and was
becoming "cold and monumental like a classic tomb."

"Poor, poor, little Alice!" bemoaned G.K. "She has not
only been caught and made to do lessons; she has been forced
to inflict lessons on others. Alice is now not only a schoolgirl
but a schoolmistress. The holiday is over and Dodgson is
again a don. There will be lots and lots of examination
papers, with questions like: (1) What do you know of the
following; mimsy, gimble, haddocks' eyes, treacle-wells,
beautiful soup? (2) Record all the moves in the chess game in
Through the Looking-Glass, and give diagram. (3) Outline
the practical policy of the White Knight for dealing with the
social problem of green whiskers. (4) Distinguish between
Tweedledum and Tweedledee."

There is much to be said for Chesterton's plea not to take
Alice too seriously. But no joke is funny unless you see the
point of it, and sometimes a point has to be explained. In the
case of *Alice* we are dealing with a very curious, complicated
kind of nonsense, written for British readers of another century, and we need to know a great many things that are not
part of the text if we wish to capture its full wit and flavor.
It is even worse than that, for some of Carroll's jokes could
be understood only by residents of Oxford, and other jokes,

still more private, could be understood only by the lovely daughters of Dean Liddell.

The fact is that Carroll's nonsense is not nearly as random and pointless as it seems to a modern American child who tries to read the *Alice* books. One says "tries" because the time is past when a child under fifteen, even in England, can read *Alice* with the same delight as is gained from, say, *The Wind in the Willows* or *The Wizard of Oz*. Children today are bewildered and sometimes frightened by the nightmarish atmosphere of Alice's dreams. It is only because adults—scientists and mathematicians in particular—continue to relish the *Alice* books that they are assured of immortality. It is only to such adults that the notes of this volume are addressed.

There are two types of notes I have done my best to avoid, not because they are difficult to do or should not be done, but because they are so exceedingly easy to do that any clever reader can write them out for himself. I refer to allegorical and psychoanalytic exegesis. Like Homer, the Bible, and all other great works of fantasy, the *Alice* books lend themselves readily to any type of symbolic interpretation—political, metaphysical, or Freudian. Some learned commentaries of this sort are hilarious. Shane Leslie, for instance, writing on "Lewis Carroll and the Oxford Movement" (in the *London Mercury*, July 1933), finds in *Alice* a secret history of the religious controversies of Victorian England. The jar of orange marmalade, for example, is a symbol of Protestantism (William of Orange; get it?). The battle of the White and Red Knights is the famous clash of Thomas Huxley and Bishop Samuel Wilberforce. The blue Caterpillar is Benjamin Jowett, the White Queen is Cardinal John Henry Newman, the Red Queen is Cardinal Henry Manning, the Cheshire Cat is Cardinal Nicholas Wiseman, and the Jabberwock "can only be a fearsome representation of the British view of the Papacy . . ."

In recent years the trend has naturally been toward psychoanalytic interpretations. Alexander Woollcott once expressed relief that the Freudians had left Alice's dreams unexplored; but that was twenty years ago and now, alas, we are all amateur head-shrinkers. We do not have to be told what it means to tumble down a rabbit hole or curl up inside a tiny house with one foot up the chimney. The rub is that any work of nonsense abounds with so many inviting symbols that you can start with any assumption you please about the author and easily build up an impressive case for it. Consider, for example, the scene in which Alice seizes the end of the White King's pencil and begins scribbling for him. In five minutes one can invent six different interpretations. Whether Carroll's unconscious had any of them in mind, however, is an altogether dubious matter. More pertinent is the fact that Carroll was interested in psychic phenomena and automatic writing, and the hypothesis must not be ruled out that it is only by accident that a pencil in this scene is shaped the way it is.

We must remember also that many characters and episodes in *Alice* are a direct result of puns and other linguistic jokes, and would have taken quite different forms if Carroll had been writing, say, in French. One does not need to look for an involved explanation of the Mock Turtle; his melancholy presence is quite adequately explained by mock-turtle soup. Are the many references to eating in *Alice* a sign of Carroll's "oral aggression," or did Carroll recognize that small children are obsessed by eating and like to read about it in their books? A similar question mark applies to the sadistic elements in *Alice*, which are quite mild compared with those of animated cartoons for the past seventy years. It seems unreasonable to suppose that all the makers of animated cartoons are sadomasochists; more reasonable to assume that they all made the same discovery about what children like to see on the screen. Carroll was a skillful storyteller, and we should give him credit for the ability to make a similar discovery. The point here is not that Carroll was not neurotic (we all know he was), but that books of nonsense fantasy for children are not such fruitful sources of psychoanalytic insight as one might suppose them to be. They are much too rich in symbols. The symbols have too many explanations.

Readers who care to explore the various conflicting

analytic interpretations that have been made of *Alice* will find useful the references cited in the bibliography at the back of this book. Phyllis Greenacre, a New York psychoanalyst, has made the best and most detailed study of Carroll from this point of view. Her arguments are most ingenious, possibly true, but one wishes that she were less sure of herself. There is a letter in which Carroll speaks of his father's death as "the greatest blow that has ever fallen on my life." In the *Alice* books the most obvious mother symbols, the Queen of Hearts and the Red Queen, are heartless creatures, whereas the King of Hearts and the White King, both likely candidates for father symbols, are amiable fellows. Suppose, however, we give all this a looking-glass reversal and decide that Carroll had an unresolved Oedipus complex. Perhaps he identified little girls with his mother so that Alice herself is the real mother symbol. This is Dr. Greenacre's view. She points out that the age difference between Carroll and Alice was about the same as the age difference between Carroll and his mother, and she assures us that this "reversal of the unresolved Oedipal attachment is quite common." According to Dr. Greenacre, the Jabberwock and Snark are screen memories of what analysts still persist in calling the "primal scene." Maybe so; but one wonders.

The inner springs of the Reverend Charles Lutwidge Dodgson's eccentricities may be obscure, but the outer facts about his life are well known. For almost half a century he was a resident of Christ Church, the Oxford college that was his alma mater. For more than half that period he was a teacher of mathematics. His lectures were humorless and boring. He made no significant contributions to mathematics, though two of his logical paradoxes, published in the journal *Mind*, touch on difficult problems involving what is now called metalogic. His books on logic and mathematics are written quaintly, with many amusing problems, but their level is elementary and they are seldom read today.

In appearance Carroll was handsome and asymmetric— two facts that may have contributed to his interest in mirror reflections. One shoulder was higher than the other, his smile was slightly askew, and the level of his blue eyes not quite the same. He was of moderate height, thin, carrying himself stiffly erect and walking with a peculiar jerky gait. He was afflicted with one deaf ear and a stammer that trembled his upper lip. Although ordained a deacon (by Bishop Wilberforce) he seldom preached because of his speech defect and he never went on to holy orders. There is no doubt about the depth and sincerity of his Church of England views. He was orthodox in all respects save his inability to believe in eternal damnation.

In politics he was a Tory, awed by lords and ladies and inclined to be snobbish toward inferiors. He objected strongly to profanity and suggestive dialogue on the stage, and one of his many unfinished projects was to bowdlerize Bowdler by editing an edition of Shakespeare suitable for young girls. He planned to do this by taking out certain passages that even Bowdler had found inoffensive. He was so shy that he could sit for hours at a social gathering and contribute nothing to the conversation, but his shyness and stammering "softly and suddenly vanished away" when he was alone with a child. He was a fussy, prim, fastidious, cranky, kind, gentle bachelor whose life was sexless, uneventful, and happy. "My life is so strangely free from all trial and trouble," he once wrote, "that I cannot doubt my own happiness is one of the talents entrusted to me to 'occupy' with, till the Master shall return, by doing something to make other lives happy."

So far so dull. We begin to catch glimpses of a more colorful personality when we turn to Charles Dodgson's hobbies. As a child he dabbled in puppetry and sleight of hand, and throughout his life enjoyed doing magic tricks, especially for children. He liked to form a mouse with his handkerchief then make it jump mysteriously out of his hand. He taught children how to fold paper boats and paper pistols that popped when swung through the air. He took up photography when the art was just beginning, specializing in portraits of children and famous people, and composing his pictures with remarkable skill and good taste. He enjoyed games of all sorts, especially chess, croquet, backgammon and billiards. He invented a great many mathematical and word puzzles, games, cipher methods, and a system for memorizing numbers (in his diary he mentions using his mnemonic system for memorizing *pi* to seventy-one decimal places). He was an enthusiastic patron of opera and the theater at a time when this was frowned upon by church officials. The famous actress Ellen Terry was one of his lifelong friends.

Ellen Terry was an exception. Carroll's principal hobby— the hobby that aroused his greatest joys—was entertaining little girls. "I am fond of children (except boys)," he once wrote. He professed a horror of little boys, and in later life avoided them as much as possible. Adopting the Roman symbol for a day of good fortune, he would write in his diary, "I mark this day with a white stone" whenever he felt it to be specially memorable. In almost every case his white-stone days were days on which he entertained a child-friend or made the acquaintance of a new one. He thought the naked bodies of little girls (unlike the bodies of boys) extremely beautiful. Upon occasion he sketched or photographed them in the nude, with the mother's permission, of course. "If I had the loveliest child in the world, to draw or photograph," he wrote, "and found she had a modest shrinking (however slight, and however easily overcome) from being taken nude, I should feel it was a solemn duty owed to God to drop the request *altogether*." Lest these undraped pictures later embarrass the girls, he requested that after his death they be destroyed or returned to the children or their parents. None seems to have survived.

In *Sylvie and Bruno Concluded* there is a passage that expresses poignantly Carroll's fixation upon little girls of all the passion of which he was capable. The narrator of the story, a thinly disguised Charles Dodgson, recalls that only once in his life did he ever see perfection. ". . . it was in a London exhibition, where, in making my way through a crowd, I suddenly met, face to face, a child of quite unearthly beauty." Carroll never ceased looking for such a child. He became adept at meeting little girls in railway carriages and on public beaches. A black bag that he always took with him on these seaside trips contained wire puzzles and other unusual gifts to stimulate their interest. He even carried a supply of safety pins for pinning up the skirts of little girls when they wished to wade in the surf. Opening gambits could be amusing. Once when he was sketching near the sea a little girl who had fallen into the water walked by with dripping clothes. Carroll tore a corner from a piece of blotting paper and said, "May I offer you this to blot yourself up?"

A long procession of charming little girls (we know they were charming from their photographs) skipped through Carroll's life, but none ever quite took the place of his first love, Alice Liddell. "I have had scores of child-friends since your time," he wrote to her after her marriage, "but they have been quite a different thing." Alice was the daughter of Henry George Liddell (the name rhymes with fiddle), the dean of Christ Church. Some notion of how attractive Alice must have been can be gained from a passage in *Praeterita*, a fragmentary autobiography by John Ruskin. Florence Becker Lennon reprints the passage in her biography of Carroll, and it is from her book that I shall quote.

Ruskin was at that time teaching at Oxford and he had given Alice drawing lessons. One snowy winter evening when Dean and Mrs. Liddell were dining out, Alice invited Ruskin over for a cup of tea. "I think Alice must have sent me a little note," he writes, "when the eastern coast of Tom Quad was clear." Ruskin had settled in an armchair by a roaring fire when the door burst open and "there was a sudden sense of some stars having been blown out by the wind." Dean and Mrs. Liddell had returned, having found the roads blocked with snow.

"How sorry you must be to see us, Mr. Ruskin!" said Mrs. Liddell.

"I was never more so," Ruskin replied.

The dean suggested that they go back to their tea. "And so we did," Ruskin continues, "but we couldn't keep papa and mamma out of the drawing-room when they had done dinner, and I went back to Corpus, disconsolate."

And now for the most significant part of the story. Ruskin *thinks* that Alice's sisters, Edith and Rhoda, were also present, but he isn't sure. "It is all so like a dream now," he writes. Yes, Alice must have been quite an attractive little girl.

There has been much argumentation about whether Carroll was in love with Alice Liddell. If this is taken to mean that he wanted to marry her or make love to her, there is not the slightest evidence for it. On the other hand, his attitude toward her was the attitude of a man in love. We do know that Mrs. Liddell sensed something unusual, took steps to discourage Carroll's attention, and later burned all of his early letters to Alice. There is a cryptic reference in Carroll's diary on October 28, 1862, to his being out of Mrs. Liddell's good graces "ever since Lord Newry's business." What business Lord Newry has in Carroll's diary remains to this day a tantalizing mystery.

There is no indication that Carroll was conscious of anything but the purest innocence in his relations with little girls, nor is there a hint of impropriety in any of the fond recollections that dozens of them later wrote about him. There was a tendency in Victorian England, reflected in the literature of the time, to idealize the beauty and virginal purity of little girls. No doubt this made it easier for Carroll to suppose that his fondness for them was on a high spiritual level, though of course this hardly is a sufficient explanation for that fondness. Of late Carroll has been compared with Humbert Humbert, the narrator of Vladimir Nabokov's novel *Lolita*. It is true that both had a passion for little girls, but their goals were exactly opposite. Humbert Humbert's "nymphets" were creatures to be used carnally. Carroll's little girls appealed to him precisely because he felt sexually safe with them. The thing that distinguishes Carroll from other writers who lived sexless lives (Thoreau, Henry James . . .) and from writers who were strongly drawn to little girls (Poe, Ernest Dowson . . .) was his curious combination, almost unique in literary history, of complete sexual innocence with a passion that can only be described as thoroughly heterosexual.

Carroll enjoyed kissing his child-friends and closing letters by sending them 10,000,000 kisses, or 4³/₄, or a two-millionth part of a kiss. He would have been horrified at the suggestion that a sexual element might be involved. There is one amusing record in his diary of his having kissed one little girl, only to discover later that she was seventeen. Carroll promptly wrote a mock apology to her mother, assuring her that it would never happen again, but the mother was not amused.

On one occasion a pretty fifteen-year-old actress named Irene Barnes (she later played the roles of White Queen and Knave of Hearts in the stage musical of *Alice*) spent a week with Charles Dodgson at a seaside resort. "As I remember him now," Irene recalls in her autobiography, *To Tell My Story* (the passage is quoted by Roger Green in Vol. 2, page 454, of Carroll's *Diary*), "he was very slight, a little under six foot, with a fresh, youngish face, white hair, and an impression of extreme cleanliness. . . . He had a deep love for children, though I am inclined to think not such a great understanding of them . . . His great delight was to teach me his Game of Logic [this was a method of solving syllogisms by placing black and red counters on a diagram of Carroll's own invention]. Dare I say this made the evening rather long, when the band was playing outside on the parade, and the moon shining on the sea?"

It is easy to say that Carroll found an outlet for his repressions in the unrestrained, whimsically violent visions of his *Alice* books. Victorian children no doubt enjoyed similar release. They were delighted to have at last some books without a pious moral, but Carroll grew more and more restive with the thought that he had not yet written a book for youngsters that would convey some sort of evangelistic Christian message. His effort in this direction was *Sylvie and Bruno*, a long, fantastic novel that appeared in two separately published parts. It contains some splendid comic scenes, and the Gardener's song, which runs like a demented fugue through the tale, is Carroll at his best. Here is the final verse, sung by the Gardener with tears streaming down his cheeks.

> He thought he saw an Argument
> That proved he was the Pope:
> He looked again, and found it was
> A Bar of Mottled Soap.
> "A fact so dread," he faintly said,
> "Extinguishes all hope!"

But the superb nonsense songs were not the features Carroll most admired about this story. He preferred a song sung by the two fairy children, Sylvie and her brother Bruno, the refrain of which went:

> For I think it is Love,
> For I feel it is Love,
> For I'm sure it is nothing but Love!

Carroll considered this the finest poem he had ever written. Even those who may agree with the sentiment behind it, and behind other portions of the novel that are heavily sugared with piety, find it difficult to read these portions today without embarrassment for the author. They seem to have been written at the bottom of treacle wells. Sadly one must conclude that, on the whole, *Sylvie and Bruno* is both an artistic and rhetorical failure. Surely few Victorian children, for whom the story was intended, were ever moved, amused, or elevated by it.

Ironically, it is Carroll's earlier and pagan nonsense that has, at least for a few modern readers, a more effective religious message than *Sylvie and Bruno*. For nonsense, as Chesterton liked to tell us, is a way of looking at existence that is akin to religious humility and wonder. The Unicorn thought Alice a fabulous monster. It is part of the philosophic dullness of our time that there are millions of rational monsters walking about on their hind legs, observing the world through pairs of flexible little lenses, periodically supplying themselves with energy by pushing organic substances through holes in their faces, who see nothing fabulous whatever about themselves. Occasionally the noses of these creatures are shaken by momentary paroxysms.

Kierkegaard once imagined a philosopher sneezing while recording one of his profound sentences. How could such a man, Kierkegaard wondered, take his metaphysics seriously?

The last level of metaphor in the *Alice* books is this: that life, viewed rationally and without illusion, appears to be a nonsense tale told by an idiot mathematician. At the heart of things science finds only a mad, never-ending quadrille of Mock Turtle Waves and Gryphon Particles. For a moment the waves and particles dance in grotesque, inconceivably complex patterns capable of reflecting on their own absurdity. We all live slapstick lives, under an inexplicable sentence of death, and when we try to find out what the Castle authorities want us to do, we are shifted from one bumbling bureaucrat to another. We are not even sure that Count West-West, the owner of the Castle, really exists. More than one critic has commented on the similarities between Kafka's *Trial* and the trial of the Jack of Hearts; between Kafka's *Castle* and a chess game in which living pieces are ignorant of the game's plan and cannot tell if they move of their own wills or are being pushed by invisible fingers.

This vision of the monstrous mindlessness of the cosmos ("Off with its head!") can be grim and disturbing, as it is in Kafka and the Book of Job, or lighthearted comedy, as in *Alice* or Chesterton's *The Man Who Was Thursday*. When Sunday, the symbol of God in Chesterton's metaphysical nightmare, flings little messages to his pursuers, they turn out to be nonsense messages. One of them is even signed Snowdrop, the name of Alice's White Kitten. It is a vision that can lead to despair and suicide, to the laughter that closes Jean-Paul Sartre's story "The Wall," to the humanist's resolve to carry on bravely in the face of ultimate darkness. Curiously, it can also suggest the wild hypothesis that there may be a light behind the darkness.

Laughter, declares Reinhold Niebuhr in one of his finest sermons, is a kind of no man's land between faith and despair. We preserve our sanity by laughing at life's surface absurdities, but the laughter turns to bitterness and derision if directed toward the deeper irrationalities of evil and death. "That is why," he concludes, "there is laughter in the vestibule of the temple, the echo of laughter in the temple itself, but only faith and prayer, and no laughter, in the holy of holies."

Lord Dunsany said the same thing this way in *The Gods of Pagana*. The speaker is Limpang-Tung, the god of mirth and melodious minstrels.

"I will send jests into the world and a little mirth. And while Death seems to thee as far away as the purple rim of hills, or sorrow as far off as rain in the blue days of summer, then pray to Limpang-Tung. But when thou growest old, or ere thou diest, pray not to Limpang-Tung, for thou becomest part of a scheme that he doth not understand.

"Go out into the starry night, and Limpang-Tung will dance with thee. . . . Or offer up a jest to Limpang-Tung; only pray not in thy sorrow to Limpang-Tung, for he saith of sorrow: 'It may be very clever of the gods, but he doth not understand.'"

Alice's Adventures in Wonderland and *Through the Looking-Glass* are two incomparable jests that the Reverend C. L. Dodgson, on a mental holiday from Christ Church chores, once offered up to Limpang-Tung.

Introduction to *More Annotated Alice*

Charles Lutwidge Dodgson, better known as Lewis Carroll, was a shy, eccentric bachelor who taught mathematics at Christ Church, Oxford. He had a great fondness for playing with mathematics, logic, and words, for writing nonsense, and for the company of attractive little girls. Somehow these passions magically fused to produce two immortal fantasies, written for his most-loved child-friend, Alice Liddell, daughter of the Christ Church dean. No one suspected at the time that those two books would become classics of English literature. And no one could have guessed that Carroll's fame would eventually surpass that of Alice's father and of all Carroll's colleagues at Oxford.

No other books written for children are more in need of explication than the *Alice* books. Much of their wit is interwoven with Victorian events and customs unfamiliar to American readers today, and even to readers in England. Many jokes in the books could be appreciated only by Oxford residents, and others were private jokes intended solely for Alice. It was to throw as much light as I could on these obscurities that forty years ago I wrote *The Annotated Alice*.

There was little in that volume that could not be found scattered among the pages of books about Carroll. My task then was not to do original research but to take all I could find from the existing literature that would make the *Alice* books more enjoyable to contemporary readers.

During the forty years that followed, public and scholarly interest in Lewis Carroll has grown at a remarkable rate. The Lewis Carroll Society was formed in England, and its lively periodical, *Jabberwocky* (now retitled *The Carrollian*), has appeared quarterly since its first issue in 1969. The Lewis Carroll Society of North America, under the leadership of Stan Marx, came into existence in 1974. New biographies of Carroll—and one of Alice Liddell!—as well as books about special aspects of Carroll's life and writings have been published. That indispensable guide for collectors, *The Lewis Carroll Handbook*, was revised and updated in 1962 by the late Roger Green, and updated again in 1979 by Denis Crutch. Papers about Carroll turned up with increasing frequency in academic journals. There were new collections of essays about Carroll, and new bibliographies. The two-volume *Letters of Lewis Carroll*, edited by Morton H. Cohen, was published in 1979. Michael Hancher's *The Tenniel Illustrations to the "Alice" Books* came out in 1985.

New editions of *Alice*, as well as reprintings of *Alice's Adventures Under Ground* (the original story hand-lettered and illustrated by Carroll as a gift to Alice Liddell), and *The Nursery "Alice"* (Carroll's retelling of the story for very young readers) rolled off presses around the world. Several editions of *Alice* were newly annotated—one by the British philosopher Peter Heath. Other editions were given new illustrations by distinguished graphic artists. Some notion of the vastness of this literature can be gained by leafing through the 253 pages of Edward Guiliano's *Lewis Carroll: An Annotated International Bibliography, 1960–77*, already more than two decades behind the times.

Since 1960 Alice has been the star of endless screen, television, and radio productions around the world. Poems and songs in the *Alice* books have been given new melodies by modern composers—one of them Steve Allen, for CBS's 1985 musical. David Del Tredici has been writing his brilliant symphonic works based on *Alice* themes. Glen Tetley's "Alice" ballet, featuring Del Tredici's music, was produced in Manhattan in 1986. Morton Cohen, who knows more about Dodgson than any other living person, published in 1995 his biography *Lewis Carroll*, which contained many startling revelations.

While all this was going on, hundreds of readers of *AA* sent me letters that called attention to aspects of Carroll's text I had failed to appreciate and that suggested where old notes could be improved and new ones added. When those letters reached the top of a large carton, I said to myself that the time had come to publish this new material. Should I try to revise and update the original book? Or should I write a sequel called *More Annotated Alice?* I finally decided that a sequel would be better. Readers who owned the original would not find it obsolete. There would be no need to compare its pages with those in a revised edition to see where fresh notes had been added. And it would have been a horrendous task to squeeze all the new notes into the marginal spaces of the original book.

A sequel also offered an opportunity to introduce readers to different illustrations. It is true that Tenniel's drawings are eternally part of the *Alice* "canon," but they are readily accessible in *The Annotated Alice*, as well as in scores of other editions currently in print. Peter Newell was not the first graphic artist after Tenniel to illustrate *Alice*, but he was the first to do so in a memorable way. An edition of the first *Alice* book with forty plates by Newell was published by Harper and Brothers in 1901, followed by the second *Alice* book, again with forty plates, in 1902. Both volumes are now costly collector's items. Whatever readers may think of Newell's art, I believe they will find it refreshing to see Alice and her friends through another artist's imagination.

Newell's fascinating article on his approach to *Alice* is reprinted here, followed by the latest and best of several essays about Newell and his work. I had planned to discuss Newell in this introduction until I discovered that my friend Michael Hearn, author of *The Annotated Wizard of Oz* and other books, had said everything in an essay that I could have said and much more.

The famous lost episode about a wasp in a wig—Carroll deleted it from the second *Alice* book after Tenniel complained that he couldn't draw a wasp and thought the book would be better without the episode—is included here at the back of the book, rather than in the chapter about the White Knight where Carroll had intended it to go. The episode was first published in 1977 as a chapbook by the Lewis Carroll Society of North America, with my introduction and notes. This book is now out of print, and I am pleased to have obtained permission to include the entire volume here.

A few errors in the introduction to *The Annotated Alice* need correcting. I spoke of Shane Leslie's essay, "Lewis Carroll and the Oxford Movement," as though it were serious criticism. Readers were quick to inform me it is no such thing. It was intended to spoof the compulsion of some scholars to search for improbable symbolism in *Alice*. I said that none of Carroll's photographs of naked little girls seemed to have survived. Four such pictures, hand colored, later turned up in the Carroll collection of the Rosenbach Foundation in Philadelphia. They are reproduced in *Lewis Carroll's Photographs of Nude Children*, a handsome monograph published by the foundation in 1979, with an introduction by Professor Cohen.

There has been considerable speculation among Carrollians about whether Carroll was "in love" with the real Alice. We know that Mrs. Liddell sensed something unusual in his attitude toward her daughter, took steps to discourage his attentions, and eventually burned all his early letters to Alice. My introduction mentioned a cryptic reference in Carroll's diary (October 28, 1862) to his being out of Mrs. Liddell's good graces "ever since Lord Newry's business." When Viscount Newry, age eighteen, was an undergraduate at Christ Church, Mrs. Liddell hoped he might marry one of her daughters. In 1862 Lord Newry wanted to give a ball, which was against college rules. He petitioned the faculty for permission, with Mrs. Liddell's support, but was turned down. Carroll had voted against him. Does this fully explain Mrs. Liddell's antagonism? Or was her anger reinforced by a feeling that Carroll himself wished someday to marry Alice? For Mrs. Liddell this was out of the question, not only because of the large age difference, but also because she considered Carroll too low on the social scale.

The page in Carroll's diary that covered the date of his break with Mrs. Liddell was cut from the volume by an unknown member of the Carroll family and was presumably destroyed. Alice's son Caryl Hargreaves is on record as having said he thought Carroll was romantically in love with his mother, and there are other indications, not yet made public, that Carroll may have expressed marital intentions to Alice's parents. Anne Clark, in her biographies of Carroll and of Alice, is convinced that some sort of proposal was made.

The question was thoroughly dealt with in Morton Cohen's biography of Carroll. Professor Cohen originally thought Carroll never considered marrying anyone, but Cohen later altered his opinion. Here is how he explained it in an interview published in *Soaring with the Dodo* (Lewis Carroll Society of North America, 1982), a collection of essays edited by Edward Guiliano and James Kincaid:

Actually, I didn't change my mind recently; I changed it in 1969 when I first got a photocopy of the diaries from the family. When I sat down and read through the diaries—the complete diaries not just the published excerpts—somewhere between 25 and 40% was never published, and naturally those unpublished bits and pieces are enormously significant. Those were the parts that the family decided should not be published. Roger Lancelyn Green, who edited the diaries, actually never even saw the full unpublished diaries because he worked from an edited typescript. When I first read through the unpublished portions of the diaries, however, I realized that another dimension to Lewis Carroll's "romanticism" existed. Of course it is pretty hard to reconcile the stern Victorian clergyman with the man who favored little girls to a point where he would want to propose marriage to one or more of them. I believe now that he made some sort of proposal of marriage to the Liddells, not saying "may I marry your eleven-year-old daughter," or anything like that, but perhaps advancing some meek suggestion that after six or eight years, if we feel the same way that we feel now, might some kind of alliance be possible? I believe also that he went on later on to think of the possibility of marrying other girls, and I think that he would have married. He was a marrying man.

I very firmly believe that he would have been happier married than as a bachelor, and I think one of the tragedies of his life was that he never managed to marry.

Some critics have likened Carroll to Humbert Humbert, the narrator of Vladimir Nabokov's novel *Lolita*. Both were indeed attracted to what Nabokov called nymphets, but their motives were quite different. Lewis Carroll's little girls may have appealed to him precisely because he felt sexually secure with them. There was a tendency in Victorian England, reflected in much of its literature and art, to idealize the beauty and virginal purity of little girls. This surely made it easier for Carroll to take for granted that his fondness for them was on a high spiritual plane. Carroll was a devout Anglican, and no scholar has suggested that he was conscious of anything but the noblest intentions, nor is there a hint of impropriety in the recollections of his many child-friends.

Although *Lolita* has many allusions to Edgar Allan Poe, who shared Humbert's sexual preferences, it contains no references to Carroll. Nabokov spoke in an interview about Carroll's "pathetic affinity" with Humbert, adding that "some odd scruple prevented me from alluding in *Lolita* to his wretched perversion and to those ambiguous photographs he took in dim rooms."

Nabokov was a great admirer of the *Alice* books. In his youth he translated *Alice's Adventures in Wonderland* into Russian—"not the first translation," he once remarked, "but the best." He wrote one novel about a chess player (*The Defense*) and another with a playing-card motif (*King, Queen, Knave*). Critics have also noticed the similarity of the endings of *Alice's Adventures in Wonderland* and Nabokov's *Invitation to a Beheading*.*

Several reviewers of *AA* complained that its notes ramble too far from the text, with distracting comments more suit-

---

*For the many allusions to *Alice* in Nabokov's fiction, see note 133 (pages 377–78, Chapter 29) of *The Annotated Lolita*, edited by Alfred Appel, Jr. (McGraw-Hill, 1970).

able for an essay. Yes, I often ramble, but I hope that at least some readers enjoy such meanderings. I see no reason why annotators should not use their notes for saying anything they please if they think it will be of interest, or at least amusing. Many of my long notes in *AA*—the one on chess as a metaphor for life, for example—were intended as mini-essays.

The names of readers who provided material for this book are given in the notes, but here I wish to acknowledge a special debt to Dr. Selwyn H. Goodacre, current editor of *Jabberwocky* and a noted Carrollian scholar. Not only did he provide numerous insights, but he also gave generously of his time in reading a first draft of my notes and offering valuable corrections and suggestions.

The Annotated Alice

THE DEFINITIVE EDITION

*Alice's Adventures
in Wonderland*

Contents

All in the golden afternoon[1]
  Full leisurely we glide;
For both our oars, with little skill,
  By little arms are plied,
While little hands make vain pretence
  Our wanderings to guide.[2]

Ah, cruel Three! In such an hour,
  Beneath such dreamy weather,
To beg a tale of breath too weak
  To stir the tiniest feather!
Yet what can one poor voice avail
  Against three tongues together?

Imperious Prima flashes forth
  Her edict "to begin it":
In gentler tones Secunda hopes
  "There will be nonsense in it!"
While Tertia interrupts the tale
  Not *more* than once a minute.

Anon, to sudden silence won,
  In fancy they pursue
The dream-child moving through a land
  Of wonders wild and new,
In friendly chat with bird or beast—
  And half believe it true.

And ever, as the story drained
  The wells of fancy dry,

1. In these prefatory verses Carroll recalls that "golden afternoon" in 1862 when he and his friend the Reverend Robinson Duckworth (then a fellow of Trinity College, Oxford, later canon of Westminster) took the three charming Liddell sisters on a rowing expedition up the Thames. "Prima" was the eldest sister, Lorina Charlotte, age thirteen. Alice Pleasance, age ten, was "Secunda," and the youngest sister, Edith, age eight, was "Tertia." Carroll was then thirty. The date was Friday, July 4, "as memorable a day in the history of literature," W. H. Auden has observed, "as it is in American history."

The trip was about three miles, beginning at Folly Bridge, near Oxford, and ending at the village of Godstow. "We had tea on the bank there," Carroll recorded in his diary, "and did not reach Christ Church again till quarter past eight, when we took them on to my rooms to see my collection of micro-photographs, and restored them to the Deanery just before nine." Seven months later he added to this entry the following note: "On which occasion I told them the fairy-tale of Alice's adventures underground . . ."

Twenty-five years later (in his article "*Alice* on the Stage," *The Theatre*, April 1887) Carroll wrote:

Many a day had we rowed together on that quiet stream—the three little maidens and I—and many a fairy tale had been extemporised for their benefit—whether it were at times when the narrator was "i' the vein," and fancies unsought came crowding thick upon him, or at times when the jaded Muse was goaded into action, and plodded meekly on, more because she had to say something than that she had something to say—yet none of these many tales got written down: they lived and died, like summer midges, each in its own golden afternoon until there came a day when, as it chanced, one of my little listeners petitioned that the tale might be written out for her. That was many a year ago, but I distinctly remember, now as I write, how, in a desperate attempt to strike out some new line of fairy-lore, I had sent my heroine straight down a rabbit-hole, to begin with, without the least idea what was to happen afterwards. And so, to please a child I loved (I don't remember any other motive), I printed in manuscript, and illustrated with my own crude designs—designs that rebelled against every law of Anatomy or Art (for I had never had a lesson in drawing)—the book which I have just had published in facsimile. In writing it out, I added many fresh ideas, which seemed to grow of themselves upon the original stock; and many more added themselves when, years afterwards, I wrote it all over again for publication . . .

Stand forth, then, from the shadowy past, "Alice," the child of my dreams. Full many a year has slipped away, since that "golden afternoon" that gave thee birth, but I can call it up almost as clearly as if it were yesterday—the cloudless blue above, the watery mirror below, the boat drifting idly on its way, the tinkle of the drops that fell from the oars, as they waved so sleepily to and fro, and (the one bright gleam of life in all the slumberous scene) the three eager faces, hungry for news of fairy-land, and who would not be said "nay" to: from whose lips "Tell us a story,

And faintly strove that weary one
 To put the subject by,
"The rest next time—" "It *is* next time!"
 The happy voices cry.

Thus grew the tale of Wonderland:
 Thus slowly, one by one,
Its quaint events were hammered out—
 And now the tale is done,
And home we steer, a merry crew,
 Beneath the setting sun.

Alice! A childish story take,
 And, with a gentle hand,
Lay it where Childhood's dreams are twined
 In Memory's mystic band,
Like pilgrim's wither'd wreath of flowers
 Pluck'd in a far-off land.[3]

please," had all the stern immutability of Fate!

Alice twice recorded her memories of the occasion. The following lines are quoted by Stuart Collingwood in *The Life and Letters of Lewis Carroll*:

Most of Mr. Dodgson's stories were told to us on river expeditions to Nuneham or Godstow, near Oxford. My eldest sister, now Mrs. Skene, was "Prima", I was "Secunda", and "Tertia" was my sister Edith. I believe the beginning of Alice was told one summer afternoon when the sun was so burning that we had landed in the meadows down the river, deserting the boat to take refuge in the only bit of shade to be found, which was under a new-made hayrick. Here from all three came the old petition of "Tell us a story," and so began the ever-delightful tale. Sometimes to tease us—and perhaps being really tired—Mr. Dodgson would stop suddenly and say, "And that's all till next time." "Ah, but it is next time," would be the exclamation from all three; and after some persuasion the story would start afresh. Another day, perhaps the story would begin in the boat, and Mr. Dodgson, in the middle of telling a thrilling adventure, would pretend to go fast asleep, to our great dismay.

Alice's son, Caryl Hargreaves, writing in the *Cornhill Magazine* (July 1932) quotes his mother as follows:

Nearly all of *Alice's Adventures Underground* was told on that blazing summer afternoon with the heat haze shimmering over the meadows where the party landed to shelter for a while in the shadow cast by the haycocks near Godstow. I think the stories he told us that afternoon must have been better than usual, because I have such a distinct recollection of the expedition, and also, on the next day I started to pester him to write down the story for me, which I had never done before. It was due to my "going on, going on" and importunity that, after saying he would think about it, he eventually gave the hesitating promise which started him writing it down at all.

Finally, we have the Reverend Duckworth's account, to be found in Collingwood's *The Lewis Carroll Picture Book*:

I rowed *stroke* and he rowed *bow* in the famous Long Vacation voyage to Godstow, when the three Miss Liddells were our passengers, and the story was actually composed and spoken *over my shoulder* for the benefit of Alice Liddell, who was acting as "cox" of our gig. I remember turning round and saying, "Dodgson, is this an extempore romance of yours?" And he replied, "Yes, I'm inventing as we go along." I also well remember how, when we had conducted the three children back to the Deanery, Alice said, as she bade us good-night, "Oh, Mr. Dodgson, I wish you would write out Alice's adventures for me." He said he should try, and he afterwards told me that he sat up nearly the whole night, committing to a MS. book his recollections of the drolleries with which he had enlivened the afternoon. He added illustrations of his own, and presented the volume, which used often to be seen on the drawing-room table at the Deanery.

It is with sadness I add that when a check was made in 1950 with the London meteorological office (as reported in Helmut Gernsheim's *Lewis Carroll: Photographer*) records indicated that the weather near Oxford on July 4, 1862, was "cool and rather wet."

This was later confirmed by Philip Stewart, of Oxford University's Department of Forestry. He informed me in a letter that the

Astronomical and Meteorological Observations Made at the Radcliffe Observatory Oxford, Vol. 23, gives the weather on July 4 as rain after two P.M., cloud cover 10/10, and maximum shade temperature of 67.9 degrees Fahrenheit. These records support the view that Carroll and Alice confused their memories of the occasion with similar boating trips made on sunnier days.

The question remains controversial, however. For a well-argued defense of the conjecture that the day may have been dry and sunny after all, see "The Weather on Alice in Wonderland Day, 4 July 1862," by H. B. Doherty, of the Dublin Airport, in *Weather*, Vol. 23 (February 1968), pages 75–78. The article was called to my attention by reader William Mixon.

2. Note how this stanza puns three times with the word "little." "Liddle" was pronounced to rhyme with "fiddle."

3. Pilgrims to the Holy Land often wore wreaths of flowers on their heads. Reader Howard Lees sent this quotation from the Prologue of Chaucer's *Canterbury Tales*, where the Summoner is described as follows:

*He wore a garland set upon his head
Large as the holly-bush upon a stake
Outside an ale house . . .*

Is not Carroll suggesting, Lees asks, "that Alice should store these tales in her childhood memory; the memory that, when she becomes an adult, is like a withered bunch of flowers plucked in the far-off land of childhood?"

A few years before writing this prefatory poem, Carroll photographed Alice with a wreath of flowers on her head. The picture is reproduced in Anne Clark's *Lewis Carroll: A Biography* (Schocken, 1979), opposite page 65, and in Morton Cohen's *Reflections in a Looking Glass* (Aperture, 1998), page 58.

I

Down the Rabbit-Hole

Alice[1] was beginning to get very tired of sitting by her sister on the bank, and of having nothing to do: once or twice she had peeped into the book her sister was reading, but it had no pictures or conversations in it, "and what is the use of a book," thought Alice, "without pictures or conversations?"

So she was considering, in her own mind (as well as she could, for the hot day made her feel very sleepy and stupid), whether the pleasure of making a daisy-chain would be worth the trouble of getting up and picking the daisies, when suddenly a White Rabbit with pink eyes ran close by her.

There was nothing so *very* remarkable in that; nor did Alice think it so *very* much out of the way to hear the Rabbit say to itself "Oh dear! Oh dear! I shall be too late!" (when she thought it over afterwards, it occurred to her that she ought to have wondered at this, but at the time it all seemed quite natural); but, when the Rabbit actually *took a watch out of its waistcoat-pocket*, and looked at it, and then hurried on, Alice started to her feet, for it flashed across her mind that she had never before seen a rabbit with either a waistcoat-pocket, or a watch to take out of it, and, burning with curiosity, she ran across the field after it, and was just in time

1. Tenniel's pictures of Alice are not pictures of Alice Liddell, who had dark hair cut short with straight bangs across her forehead. Carroll sent Tenniel a photograph of Mary Hilton Badcock, another child-friend, recommending that he use her for a model, but whether Tenniel accepted this advice is a matter of dispute. That he did not is strongly suggested by these lines from a letter Carroll wrote some time after both *Alice* books had been published (the letter is quoted by Mrs. Lennon in her book on Carroll):

Mr. Tenniel is the only artist, who has drawn for me, who has resolutely refused to use a model, and declared he no more needed one than I should need a multiplication table to work a mathematical problem! I venture to think that he was mistaken and that for want of a model, he drew several pictures of "Alice" entirely out of proportion—head decidedly too large and feet decidedly too small.

In "*Alice* on the Stage," an article cited in the first note on the prefatory poem, Carroll gave the following description of his heroine's personality:

What wert thou, dream-Alice, in thy foster-father's eyes? How shall he picture thee? Loving, first, loving and gentle: loving as a dog (forgive the prosaic simile, but I know no earthly love so pure and perfect), and gentle as a fawn: then courteous—courteous to *all*, high or low, grand or grotesque, King or Caterpillar, even as though she were herself a King's daughter, and her clothing of wrought gold: then trustful, ready to accept the wildest impossibilities with all that utter trust that only dreamers know; and lastly, curious—wildly curious, and with the eager enjoyment of Life that comes only in the happy hours of childhood, when all is new and fair, and when Sin and Sorrow are but names—empty words signifying nothing!

I agree with correspondent Richard Hammerud that it was Carroll's intention to begin his fantasy with the word "Alice."

The symbol at a lower corner, which you see on almost all of Tenniel's drawings, is a monogram of his initials, J. T.

to see it pop down a large rabbit-hole under the hedge.

In another moment down went Alice after it, never once considering how in the world she was to get out again.

The rabbit-hole went straight on like a tunnel for some way, and then dipped suddenly down, so suddenly that Alice had not a moment to think about stopping herself before she found herself falling down what seemed to be a very deep well.

Either the well was very deep, or she fell very slowly, for she had plenty of time as she went down to look about her, and to wonder what was going to happen next. First, she tried to look down and make out what she was coming to, but it was too dark to see anything: then she looked at the sides of the well, and noticed that they were filled with cupboards and book-shelves: here and there she saw maps and pictures hung upon pegs. She took down a jar from one of the shelves as she passed: it was labeled "ORANGE MARMALADE," but to her great disappointment it was empty: she did not like to drop the jar, for fear of killing somebody underneath, so managed to put it into one of the cupboards as she fell past it.[2]

"Well!" thought Alice to herself. "After such a fall as this, I shall think nothing of tumbling downstairs! How brave they'll all think me at home! Why, I wouldn't say anything about it, even if I fell off the top of the house!" (Which was very likely true.)[3]

Down, down, down. Would the fall *never* come to an end? "I wonder how many miles I've fallen by this time?" she said aloud. "I must be getting somewhere near the centre of the earth. Let me see: that would be four thousand miles down, I think—" (for, you see, Alice had learnt several things of this sort in her lessons in the school-room, and though this was not a *very* good opportunity for showing off her knowledge, as there was no one to listen to her, still it was good practice to say it over) "—yes, that's about the right distance—but then I wonder what Latitude or Longitude I've got to?" (Alice had not the slightest idea what Latitude was, or Longitude either, but she thought they were nice grand words to say.)

Presently she began again. "I wonder if I shall fall right *through* the earth![4] How funny it'll seem to come out among the people that walk with their heads downwards! The antipathies, I think—" (she was rather glad there *was* no one listening, this time, as it didn't sound at all the right word) "—but I shall have to ask them what the name of the country is, you know. Please, Ma'am, is this New Zealand? Or Australia?"

2. Carroll was aware, of course, that in a normal state of free fall Alice could neither drop the jar (it would remain suspended in front of her) nor replace it on a shelf (her speed would be too great). It is interesting to note that in his novel *Sylvie and Bruno*, Chapter 8, Carroll describes the difficulty of having tea inside a falling house, as well as in a house being pulled downward at an even faster acceleration; anticipating in some respects the famous "thought experiment" in which Einstein used an imaginary falling elevator to explain certain aspects of relativity theory.

3. William Empson has pointed out (in the section on Lewis Carroll in his *Some Versions of Pastoral*) that this is the first death joke in the Alice books. There are many more to come.

4. In Carroll's day there was considerable popular speculation about what would happen if one fell through a hole that went straight through the center of the earth. Plutarch had asked the question and many famous thinkers, including Francis Bacon and Voltaire, had argued about it. Galileo (*Dialogo dei Massimi Sistemi, Giornata Seconda*, Florence edition of 1842, Vol. 1, pages 251–52) gave the correct answer: the object would fall with increasing speed but decreasing acceleration until it reached the center of the earth, at which spot its acceleration would be zero. Thereafter it would slow down in speed, with increasing deceleration, until it reached the opening at the other end. Then it would fall back again. By ignoring air resistance and the coriolis force resulting from the earth's rotation (unless the hole ran from pole to pole), the object would oscillate back and forth forever. Air

resistance of course would eventually bring it to rest at the earth's center. The interested reader should consult "A Hole through the Earth," by the French astronomer Camille Flammarion, in *The Strand Magazine*, Vol. 38 (1909), page 348, if only to look at the lurid illustrations.

Carroll's interest in the matter is indicated by the fact that in Chapter 7 of his *Sylvie and Bruno Concluded*, there is described (in addition to a Möbius strip, a projective plane, and other whimsical scientific and mathematical devices) a remarkable method of running trains with gravity as the sole power source. The track runs through a perfectly straight tunnel from one town to another. Since the middle of the tunnel is necessarily nearer the earth's center than its ends, the train runs downhill to the center, acquiring enough momentum to carry it up the other half of the tunnel. Curiously, such a train would make the trip (ignoring air resistance and friction of the wheels) in exactly the same time that it would take an object to fall through the center of the earth—a little more than forty-two minutes. This time is constant regardless of the tunnel's length.

The fall into the earth as a device for entering a wonderland has been used by many other writers of children's fantasy, notably by L. Frank Baum in *Dorothy and the Wizard in Oz*, and Ruth Plumly Thompson in *The Royal Book of Oz*. Baum also used the tube through the earth as an effective plot gimmick in *Tik-Tok of Oz*.

5. The Liddell sisters were fond of the family's two tabby cats, Dinah and Villikens, named after a popular song, "Villikens and His Dinah." Dinah and her two kittens, Kitty and Snowdrop, reappear in the first chap-

(and she tried to curtsey as she spoke—fancy, *curtseying* as you're falling through the air! Do you think you could manage it?) "And what an ignorant little girl she'll think me for asking! No, it'll never do to ask: perhaps I shall see it written up somewhere."

Down, down, down. There was nothing else to do, so Alice soon began talking again. "Dinah'll miss me very much to-night, I should think!" (Dinah was the cat.)[5] "I hope they'll remember her saucer of milk at tea-time. Dinah, my dear! I wish you were down here with me! There are no mice in the air, I'm afraid, but you might catch a bat, and that's very like a mouse, you know. But do cats eat bats, I wonder?" And here Alice began to get rather sleepy, and went on saying to herself, in a dreamy sort of way, "Do cats eat bats? Do cats eat bats?" and sometimes "Do bats eat cats?" for, you see, as she couldn't answer either question, it didn't much matter which way she put it. She felt that she was dozing off, and had just begun to dream that she was walking hand in hand with Dinah, and was saying to her, very earnestly, "Now, Dinah, tell me the truth: did you ever eat a bat?" when suddenly, thump! thump! down she came upon a heap of sticks and dry leaves, and the fall was over.

Alice was not a bit hurt, and she jumped up on to her feet in a moment: she looked up, but it was all dark overhead: before her was another long passage, and the White Rabbit was still in sight, hurrying down it. There was not a moment to be lost: away went Alice like the wind, and was just in time to hear it say, as it turned a corner, "Oh my ears and whiskers, how late it's getting!" She was close behind it when she turned the corner, but the Rabbit was no longer to be

seen: she found herself in a long, low hall, which was lit up by a row of lamps hanging from the roof.

There were doors all round the hall, but they were all locked; and when Alice had been all the way down one side and up the other, trying every door, she walked sadly down the middle, wondering how she was ever to get out again.

Suddenly she came upon a little three-legged table, all made of solid glass: there was nothing on it but a tiny golden key, and Alice's first idea was that this might belong to one of the doors of the hall; but, alas! either the locks were too large, or the key was too small, but at any rate it would not open any of them. However, on the second time round, she came upon a low curtain she had not noticed before, and behind it was a little door about fifteen inches high: she tried the little golden key in the lock, and to her great delight it fitted![6]

Alice opened the door and found that it led into a small passage, not much larger than a rat-hole: she knelt down and looked along the

ter of the second *Alice* book, and later, in Alice's dream, as the Red and White Queens.

6. A gold key that unlocked mysterious doors was a common object in Victorian fantasy. Here is the second stanza of Andrew Lang's "Ballade of the Bookworm":

> One gift the fairies gave me (three
> They commonly bestowed of yore):
> The love of books, the golden key
> That opens the enchanted door.

In this notes for an Oxford edition of the *Alice* books, Roger Green links this gold key to the magic key to Heaven in George MacDonald's famous fantasy tale "The Golden Key." The story first appeared in an 1867 book, *Dealings with Fairies*, two years after the publication of *Alice in Wonderland*, but Carroll and MacDonald were good friends and it is possible, Green writes, that Carroll saw the story in manuscript. MacDonald also wrote a poem titled "The Golden Key" that was published early enough (1861) for Carroll to have read it. The story is reprinted in Michael Hearn's splendid anthology *The Victorian Fairy Tale Book* (Pantheon, 1988).

7. T. S. Eliot revealed to the critic Louis L. Martz that he was thinking of this episode when he wrote the following lines for "Burnt Norton," the first poem in his *Four Quartets*:

Time present and time past
Are both perhaps present in time future.
And time future contained in time past.
If all time is eternally present
All time is unredeemable.
What might have been is an abstraction
Remaining a perpetual possibility
Only in a world of speculation.
What might have been and what has been
Point to one end, which is always present.
Footfalls echo in the memory
Down the passage which we did not take
Towards the door we never opened
Into the rose-garden.

The little door to a secret garden also appears in Eliot's *The Family Reunion*. It was for him a metaphor for events that might have been, had one opened certain doors.

8. The Victorian medicine bottle had neither a screw top nor a label on the side. It was corked, with a paper label tied to the neck.

passage into the loveliest garden you ever saw.[7] How she longed to get out of that dark hall, and wander about among those beds of bright flowers and those cool fountains, but she could not even get her head through the doorway; "and even if my head *would* go through," thought poor Alice, "it would be of very little use without my shoulders. Oh, how I wish I could shut up like a telescope! I think I could, if I only knew how to begin." For, you see, so many out-of-the-way things had happened lately, that Alice had begun to think that very few things indeed were really impossible.

There seemed to be no use in waiting by the little door, so she went back to the table, half hoping she might find another key on it, or at any rate a book of rules for shutting people up like telescopes: this time she found a little bottle on it ("which certainly was not here before," said Alice), and tied round the neck of the bottle was a paper label, with the words "DRINK ME" beautifully printed on it in large letters.[8]

It was all very well to say "Drink me," but the wise little Alice was not going to do *that* in a hurry. "No, I'll look first," she said, "and see whether it's marked '*poison*' or not"; for she had read several nice little stories[9] about children who had got burnt, and eaten up by wild beasts, and other unpleasant things, all because they *would* not remember the simple rules their friends had taught them: such as, that a red-hot poker will burn you if you hold it too long; and that, if you cut your finger *very* deeply with a knife, it usually bleeds; and she had never forgotten that, if you drink much from a bottle marked "poison," it is almost certain to disagree with you, sooner or later.

However, this bottle was *not* marked "poison," so Alice ventured to taste it, and, finding it very nice (it had, in fact, a sort of mixed flavour of cherry-tart, custard, pine-apple, roast turkey, toffy, and hot buttered toast), she very soon finished it off.

          *   *   *   *
               *   *   *
          *   *   *   *

"What a curious feeling!" said Alice. "I must be shutting up like a telescope!"[10]

And so it was indeed: she was now only ten inches high, and her face brightened up at the thought that she was now the right size for going through the little door into that lovely garden. First, however, she waited for a few minutes to see if she was going to shrink any further: she felt a little nervous about this; "for it might end, you know," said Alice to herself, "in my going out altogether, like a candle.[11] I wonder what I should be like then?" And she tried to fancy what the flame of a candle looks like after the

9. The "nice little stories," Charles Lovett reminds me, were not so nice. They were the traditional fairy tales, filled with episodes of horror and usually containing a pious moral. By doing away with morals, the *Alice* books opened up a new genre of fiction for children.

10. This is the first of twelve occasions in the book on which Alice alters in size. Richard Ellmann has suggested that Carroll may have been unconsciously symbolizing the great disparity between the small Alice whom he loved but could not marry and the large Alice she would soon become. See "On Alice's Changes in Size in Wonderland," by Selwyn Goodacre, in *Jabberwocky* (Winter 1977), for many discrepancies in Tenniel's pictures with respect to Alice's size.

11. Note Tweedledum's use of the same candle-flame metaphor in the fourth chapter of the second *Alice* book.

12. "alas for poor Alice!": Did Carroll intend a pun on "alas"? It is hard to be sure, but there is no question about the intent in *Finnegans Wake* (Viking revised edition, 1959, page 528) when James Joyce writes: "Alicious, twinstreams twinestraines, through alluring glass or alas in jumboland?" And again (page 270): "Though Wonderlawn's lost us for ever. Alis, alas, she broke the glass! Liddell lokker through the leafery, ours is mistery of pain."

For the hundreds of references to Dodgson and the *Alice* books in *Finnegans Wake*, see Ann McGarrity Buki's excellent paper "Lewis Carroll in *Finnegans Wake*," in *Lewis Carroll: A Celebration* (Clarkson N. Potter, 1982), edited by Edward Guiliano, and J. S. Atherton's earlier paper "Lewis Carroll and *Finnegans Wake*," in *English Studies* (February 1952). Most of the allusions are not in dispute, though what is one to make of such oddities as the identical initial letters of the names Alice Pleasance Liddell and Anna Livia Plurabelle? Is it a coincidence, like the correspondences in the names of Carroll and Alice (noticed by reader Dennis Green) with respect to word lengths, and the positions of vowels, consonants, and double letters in the last names?

ALICE LIDDELL
LEWIS CARROLL

More letterplay: Consider the initial consonants of "Dear Lewis Carroll." Backwards they are the initials of Charles Lutwidge Dodgson.

Of more serious interest is the fact that Alice had a son named Caryl Liddell Hargreaves. Another coincidence? Alice's one major romance, before she married Reginald Hargreaves, was with England's Prince Leopold. They met when he was a Christ Church undergraduate. Queen

candle is blown out, for she could not remember ever having seen such a thing.

After a while, finding that nothing more happened, she decided on going into the garden at once; but, alas for poor Alice![12] when she got to the door, she found she had forgotten the little golden key, and when she went back to the table for it, she found she could not possibly reach it: she could see it quite plainly through the glass, and she tried her best to climb up one of the legs of the table, but it was too slippery; and when she had tired herself out with trying, the poor little thing sat down and cried.

"Come, there's no use in crying like that!" said Alice to herself rather sharply. "I advise you to leave off this minute!" She generally gave herself very good advice (though she very seldom followed it), and sometimes she scolded herself so severely as to bring tears into her eyes; and once she remembered trying to box her own ears for having cheated herself in a game of croquet she was playing against herself, for this curious child was very fond of pretending to be two people. "But it's no use now," thought poor Alice, "to pretend to be two people![13] Why, there's hardly enough of me left to make *one* respectable person."

Soon her eye fell on a little glass box that was lying under the table: she opened it, and found in it a very small cake, on which the words "EAT ME" were beautifully marked in currants. "Well, I'll eat it," said Alice, "and if it makes me grow larger, I can reach the key; and if it makes me grow smaller, I can creep under the door: so either way I'll get into the garden, and I don't care which happens!"

She ate a little bit, and said anxiously to herself "Which way? Which way?", holding her hand on the top of her head to feel which way it was growing; and she was quite surprised to find that she remained the same size. To be sure, this is what generally happens when one eats cake; but Alice had got so much into the way of expecting nothing but out-of-the-way things to happen, that it seemed quite dull and stupid for life to go on in the common way.

So she set to work, and very soon finished off the cake.

*　　*　　*　　*
　*　　*　　*
*　　*　　*　　*

Victoria considered unthinkable his marrying anyone other than a princess, and Mrs. Liddell agreed. Alice wore a gift from the prince on her wedding gown, and she named her second son Leopold. A few weeks later, Prince Leopold, married to a princess, named a daughter Alice. It is hard to believe that when Alice called her third son Caryl she did not have her old mathematician friend in mind, but according to Anne Clark, in her marvelous book *The Real Alice* (Stein & Day, 1982), Alice always insisted that the name came from a novel. The novel's identity is unknown.

13. There is no evidence, Denis Crutch and R. B. Shaberman maintain in their booklet *Under the Quizzing Glass* (Magpie Press, 1972), that Alice Liddell liked to pretend she was two people. However, in keeping with their contention that Carroll injected much of himself into his fictional Alice, they remind us that Carroll was always careful to keep separate Charles Dodgson, the Oxford mathematician, and Lewis Carroll, writer of children's books and lover of little girls.

The Pool of Tears

1. A fender is a low metal frame or screen, sometimes ornamental, between the hearthrug and an open fireplace.

Selwyn Goodacre suspects that when Alice addresses her right foot as "Esquire," Carroll may have intended a subtle English/French joke. The French word for "foot" is *pied*. Its gender is masculine regardless of the owner's sex.

"Curiouser and curiouser!" cried Alice (she was so much surprised, that for the moment she quite forgot how to speak good English). "Now I'm opening out like the largest telescope that ever was! Good-bye, feet!" (for when she looked down at her feet, they seemed to be almost out of sight, they were getting so far off). "Oh, my poor little feet, I wonder who will put on your shoes and stockings for you now, dears? I'm sure *I* sha'n't be able! I shall be a great deal too far off to trouble myself about you: you must manage the best way you can—but I must be kind to them," thought Alice, "or perhaps they wo'n't walk the way I want to go! Let me see. I'll give them a new pair of boots every Christmas."

And she went on planning to herself how she would manage it. "They must go by the carrier," she thought; "and how funny it'll seem, sending presents to one's own feet! And how odd the directions will look!

> *Alice's Right Foot, Esq.*
> *Hearthrug,*
> *near the Fender,*[1]
> *(with Alice's love).*

Oh dear, what nonsense I'm talking!"

Just at this moment her head struck against the roof of the hall: in fact she was now rather more than nine feet high, and she at once took up the little golden key and hurried off to the garden door:

Poor Alice! It was as much as she could do, lying down on one side, to look through into the garden with one eye; but to get through was more hopeless than ever: she sat down and began to cry again.

"You ought to be ashamed of yourself," said Alice, "a great girl like you," (she might well say this), "to go on crying in this way! Stop this moment, I tell you!" But she went on all the same, shedding gallons of tears, until there was a large pool all round her, about four inches deep, and reaching half down the hall.

After a time she heard a little pattering of feet in the distance, and she hastily dried her eyes to see what was coming. It was the White Rabbit returning, splendidly dressed, with a pair of white kid-gloves in one hand and a large fan in the other: he came trotting along in a great hurry, muttering to himself, as he came, "Oh! The Duchess, the Duchess! Oh! *Wo'n't* she be savage if I've kept her waiting!"

2. In his article "*Alice* on the Stage" (cited in the first note on the book's prefatory poem) Carroll wrote:

And the White Rabbit, what of *him*? Was *he* framed on the "Alice" lines, or meant as a contrast? As a contrast, distinctly. For *her* "youth," "audacity," vigour," and "swift directness of purpose," read "elderly," "timid," "feeble," and "nervously shilly-shallying," and you will get *something* of what I meant him to be. I *think* the White Rabbit should wear spectacles. I am sure his voice should quaver, and his knees quiver, and his whole air suggest a total inability to say "Bo" to a goose!

In *Alice's Adventures Under Ground*, the original manuscript, the rabbit drops a nosegay instead of a fan. Alice's subsequent shrinking is the result of smelling these flowers.

Alice felt so desperate that she was ready to ask help of any one: so, when the Rabbit came near her, she began, in a low, timid voice, "If you please, Sir—" The Rabbit started violently, dropped the white kid-gloves and the fan, and scurried away into the darkness as hard as he could go.[2]

Alice took up the fan and gloves, and, as the hall was very hot, she kept fanning herself all the time she went on talking. "Dear, dear! How queer everything is to-day! And yesterday things went on just as usual. I wonder if I've been changed in the night? Let me think: *was* I the same when I got up this morning? I almost think I can remember feeling a little different. But if I'm not the same, the next question is 'Who in the world am I?' Ah, *that's* the great puzzle!"

And she began thinking over all the children she knew that were of the same age as herself, to see if she could have been changed for any of them.

"I'm sure I'm not Ada," she said, "for her hair goes in such long ringlets, and mine doesn't go in ringlets at all; and I'm sure I ca'n't be Mabel,[3] for I know all sorts of things, and she, oh, she knows such a very little! Besides, *she's* she, and *I'm* I, and—oh dear, how puzzling it all is! I'll try if I know all the things I used to know. Let me see: four times five is twelve, and four times six is thirteen, and four times seven is—oh dear! I shall never get to twenty at that rate![4] However, the Multiplication-Table doesn't signify: let's try Geography. London is the capital of Paris, and Paris is the capital of Rome, and Rome—no, *that's* all wrong, I'm certain! I must have been changed for Mabel! I'll try and say 'How doth the little—', " and she crossed her hands on her lap, as if she were saying lessons, and began to repeat it, but her voice sounded hoarse and strange, and the words did not come the same as they used to do:—[5]

> "How doth the little crocodile
> Improve his shining tail,
> And pour the waters of the Nile
> On every golden scale!
>
> "How cheerfully he seems to grin,
> How neatly spreads his claws,
> And welcomes little fishes in,
> With gently smiling jaws!"

"I'm sure those are not the right words," said poor Alice, and her eyes filled with tears again as she went on, "I must be Mabel after all, and I shall have to go and live in that poky little house, and have next to no toys to play with, and oh,

3. In his original story, *Alice's Adventures Under Ground*, the names are Gertrude and Florence; these were cousins of Alice Liddell.

4. The simplest explanation of why Alice will never get to 20 is this: the multiplication table traditionally stops with the twelves, so if you continue this nonsense progression—4 times 5 is 12, 4 times 6 is 13, 4 times 7 is 14, and so on—you end with 4 times 12 (the highest she can go) is 19—just one short of 20.

A. L. Taylor, in his book *The White Knight*, advances an interesting but more complicated theory. Four times 5 actually is 12 in a number system using a base of 18. Four times 6 is 13 in a system with a base of 21. If we continue this progression, always increasing the base by 3, our products keep increasing by one until we reach 20, where for the first time the scheme breaks down. Four times 13 is not 20 (in a number system with a base of 42), but "1" followed by whatever symbol is adopted for "10."

For another interpretation of Alice's arithmetic, see "Multiplication in Changing Bases: A Note on Lewis Carroll," by Francine Abeles, in *Historia Mathematica*, Vol. 3 (1976), pages 183–84.

5. Most of the poems in the two *Alice* books are parodies of poems or popular songs that were well known to Carroll's contemporary readers. With few exceptions the originals have now been forgotten, their titles kept alive only by the fact that Carroll chose to poke fun at them. Because much of the wit of a burlesque is missed if one is not familiar with what is being caricatured, all the originals will be reprinted in this edition. Here we have a skillful parody of the best-known poem of Isaac

Watts (1674–1748), English theologian and writer of such well-known hymns as "O God, our help in ages past." Watts's poem, "Against Idleness and Mischief" (from his *Divine Songs for Children*, 1715), is reprinted below in its entirety.

> How doth the little busy bee
>   Improve each shining hour,
> And gather honey all the day
>   From every opening flower!
>
> How skillfully she builds her cell!
>   How neat she spreads the wax!
> And labours hard to store it well
>   With the sweet food she makes.
>
> In works of labour or of skill,
>   I would be busy too;
> For Satan finds some mischief still
>   For idle hands to do.
>
> In books, or work, or healthful play,
>   Let my first years be passed,
> That I may give for every day
>   Some good account at last.

Carroll has chosen the lazy, slow-moving crocodile as a creature far removed from the rapid-flying, ever-busy bee.

6. Alice's earlier expansions have been cited by cosmologists to illustrate aspects of the expanding-universe theory. Her narrow escape in this passage calls to mind a *diminishing*-universe theory once advanced in Carrollian jest by the eminent mathematician Sir Edmund Whittaker. Perhaps the total amount of matter in the universe is continually growing smaller, and eventually the entire universe will fade away into nothing at all. "This would have the recommendation," Whittaker said, "of supplying a very simple picture of the final destiny of the universe." (*Eddington's Principle in the Philosophy of Science*, a lecture by Whittaker published in 1951 by Cambridge University Press.) A

ever so many lessons to learn! No, I've made up my mind about it: if I'm Mabel, I'll stay down here! It'll be no use their putting their heads down and saying 'Come up again, dear!' I shall only look up and say 'Who am I, then? Tell me that first, and then, if I like being that person, I'll come up: if not, I'll stay down here till I'm somebody else'—but, oh dear!" cried Alice, with a sudden burst of tears, "I do wish they *would* put their heads down! I am so *very* tired of being all alone here!"

As she said this she looked down at her hands, and was surprised to see that she had put on one of the Rabbit's little white kid-gloves while she was talking. "How *can* I have done that?" she thought. "I must be growing small again." She got up and went to the table to measure herself by it, and found that, as nearly as she could guess, she was now about two feet high, and was going on shrinking rapidly: she soon found out that the cause of this was the fan she was holding, and she dropped it hastily, just in time to save herself from shrinking away altogether.

"That *was* a narrow escape!" said Alice, a good deal frightened at the sudden change, but very glad to find herself still in existence.[6] "And now for the garden!" And she ran with all speed back to the little door; but, alas! the little door was shut again, and the little golden key was lying on the glass table as before, "and things are worse than ever," thought the poor child, "for I never was so small as this before, never! And I declare it's too bad, that it is!"

As she said these words her foot slipped, and in another moment, splash! she was up to her chin in salt-water. Her first idea was that she had somehow fallen into the sea, "and in that case I can go back by railway," she said to herself.

(Alice had been to the seaside once in her life, and had come to the general conclusion that, wherever you go to on the English coast, you find a number of bathing-machines[7] in the sea, some children digging in the sand with wooden spades, then a row of lodging-houses, and behind them a railway station.) However, she soon made out that she was in the pool of tears which she had wept when she was nine feet high.

"I wish I hadn't cried so much!" said Alice, as she swam about, trying to find her way out. "I shall be punished for it now, I suppose, by being drowned in my own tears! That *will* be a queer thing, to be sure! However, everything is queer to-day."

Just then she heard something splashing about in the pool a little way off, and she swam nearer to make out what it was: at first she thought it must be a walrus or hippopotamus, but then she remembered how small she was now, and she soon made out that it was only a mouse, that had slipped in like herself.

"Would it be of any use, now," thought Alice, "to speak to this mouse? Everything is so out-of-the-way down here, that I should think very likely it can talk: at any rate, there's no harm in

similar vanish would occur if the universe has enough matter to stop expanding and go the other way toward a Big Crunch.

7. Bathing machines were small individual locker rooms on wheels. They were drawn into the sea by horses to the depth desired by the bather, who then emerged modestly through a door facing the sea. A huge umbrella in back of the machine concealed the bather from public view. On the beach the machines were of course used for privacy in dressing and undressing. This quaint Victorian contraption was invented about 1750 by Benjamin Beale, a Quaker who lived at Margate, and was first used on the Margate beach. The machines were later introduced at Weymouth by Ralph Allen, the original of Mr. Allworthy in Fielding's *Tom Jones*. In Smollett's *Humphry Clinker* (1771), a letter of Matt Bramble's describes a bathing machine at Scarborough. (See *Notes and Queries*, August 13, 1904, Series 10, Vol. 2, pages 130–31.)

The second "fit" of Carroll's great nonsense poem, *The Hunting of the Snark* (subtitled: *An Agony in Eight Fits*), tells us that a fondness for bathing machines is one of the "five unmistakable marks" by which a genuine snark can be recognized.

The fourth is its fondness for bathing-machines,
Which it constantly carries about,
And believes that they add to the beauty of scenes—
A sentiment open to doubt.

8. In his article "In Search of Alice's Brother's Latin Grammar," in *Jabberwocky* (Spring 1975), Selwyn Goodacre argues that the book may have been *The Comic Latin Grammar* (1840). It was anonymously written by Percival Leigh, a writer for *Punch*, with illustrations by *Punch* cartoonist John Leech. Carroll owned a first edition.

Only one noun in the book is declined in full: *musa*, the Latin word for "muse." Goodacre suggests that Alice, "looking over her brother's shoulder at his Latin Grammar, mistook *musa* for *mus*," the Latin word for "mouse." Further comments on this speculation appear in *Jabberwocky* (Spring 1977). Everett Bleiler notes that Alice's declining omits the ablative form.

9. Hugh O'Brien, writing on "The French Lesson Book" in *Notes and Queries* (December 1963), identified the book as *La Bagatelle: Intended to introduce children of three or four years old to some knowledge of the French language* (1804).

trying." So she began: "O Mouse, do you know the way out of this pool? I am very tired of swimming about here, O Mouse!" (Alice thought this must be the right way of speaking to a mouse: she had never done such a thing before, but she remembered having seen, in her brother's Latin Grammar,[8] "A mouse—of a mouse—to a mouse—a mouse—O mouse!") The mouse looked at her rather inquisitively, and seemed to her to wink with one of its little eyes, but it said nothing.

"Perhaps it doesn't understand English," thought Alice. "I daresay it's a French mouse, come over with William the Conqueror." (For, with all her knowledge of history, Alice had no very clear notion how long ago anything had happened.) So she began again: "Où est ma chatte?" which was the first sentence in her French lesson-book.[9] The Mouse gave a sudden leap out of the water, and seemed to quiver all over with fright. "Oh, I beg your pardon!" cried Alice hastily, afraid that she had hurt the poor animal's feelings. "I quite forgot you didn't like cats."

"Not like cats!" cried the Mouse in a shrill, passionate voice. "Would *you* like cats, if you were me?"

"Well, perhaps not," said Alice in a soothing tone: "don't be angry about it. And yet I wish I could show you our cat Dinah. I think you'd take a fancy to cats, if you could only see her. She is such a dear quiet thing," Alice went on, half to herself, as she swam lazily about in the pool, "and she sits purring so nicely by the fire, licking her paws and washing her face—and she is such a nice soft thing to nurse—and she's such a capital one for catching mice—oh, I beg your pardon!" cried Alice again, for this time the

Mouse was bristling all over, and she felt certain it must be really offended. "We wo'n't talk about her any more, if you'd rather not."

"We, indeed!" cried the Mouse, who was trembling down to the end of its tail. "As if *I* would talk on such a subject! Our family always *hated* cats: nasty, low, vulgar things! Don't let me hear the name again!"

"I wo'n't indeed!" said Alice, in a great hurry to change the subject of conversation. "Are you—are you fond—of—of dogs?" The Mouse did not answer, so Alice went on eagerly: "There is such a nice little dog, near our house, I should like to show you! A little bright-eyed terrier, you know, with oh, such long curly brown hair! And it'll fetch things when you throw them, and it'll sit up and beg for its dinner, and all sorts of things—I ca'n't remember half of them—and it belongs to a farmer, you know, and he says it's so useful, it's worth a hundred pounds! He says it kills all the rats and—oh dear!" cried Alice in a sorrowful tone. "I'm afraid I've offended it again!" For the Mouse was swimming away from her as hard as it could go, and making quite a commotion in the pool as it went.

So she called softly after it, "Mouse dear! Do

10. In two of Tenniel's illustrations for the next chapter, you will see the head of an ape. It has been suggested that Tenniel intended his ape to be a caricature of Charles Darwin. This seems unlikely. The face of Tenniel's ape, in his second picture, exactly duplicates his political cartoon in *Punch* (October 11, 1856), where the ape represents "King Bomba," the nickname for Ferdinand II, King of the Two Sicilies.

The flightless dodo became extinct about 1681. Charles Lovett informed me that the Oxford University Museum, which Carroll often visited with the Liddell children, contained (and still does) the remains of a dodo, and a famous painting of the bird by John Savory. The dodo was native to the island of Mauritius in the Indian Ocean. Dutch sailors and colonists killed the "disgusting birds," as they called them, for food, and their eggs (just one to a nest) were eaten by the farm animals of the early settlers. The dodo is one of the earliest examples of an animal species totally exterminated by the human species. See "The Dodo in the Caucus Race," by Stephen Jay Gould, in *Natural History* (November 1996).

Carroll's Dodo was intended as a caricature of himself—his stammer is said to have made him pronounce his name "Dodo-Dodgson." The Duck is the Reverend Robinson Duckworth, who often accompanied Carroll on boating expeditions with the Liddell sisters. The Lory, an Australian parrot, is Lorina, who was the eldest of the sisters (this explains why, in the second paragraph of the next chapter, she says to Alice, "I'm older than you, and must know better"). Edith Liddell is the Eaglet.

It is amusing to note that when his biography entered the *Encyclopaedia Britannica* it was inserted just before the entry on the Dodo. The indivi-

come back again, and we wo'n't talk about cats, or dogs either, if you don't like them!" When the Mouse heard this, it turned round and swam slowly back to her: its face was quite pale (with passion, Alice thought), and it said, in a low trembling voice, "Let us get to the shore, and then I'll tell you my history, and you'll understand why it is I hate cats and dogs."

It was high time to go, for the pool was getting quite crowded with the birds and animals that had fallen into it: there was a Duck and a Dodo, a Lory and an Eaglet, and several other curious creatures.[10] Alice led the way, and the whole party swam to the shore.

duals in this "queer-looking party" represent the participants in an episode entered in Carroll's diary on June 17, 1862. Carroll took his sisters, Fanny and Elizabeth, and his Aunt Lucy Lutwidge (the "other curious creatures"?) on a boating expedition, along with the Reverend Duckworth and the three Liddell girls.

June 17 (Tu). Expedition to Nuneham. Duckworth (of Trinity) and Ina, Alice and Edith came with us. We set out about 12.30 and got to Nuneham about 2: dined there, then walked in the park and set off for home about 4.30. About a mile above Nuneham heavy rain came on, and after bearing it a short time I settled that we had better leave the boat and walk: three miles of this drenched us all pretty well. I went on first with the children, as they could walk much faster than Elizabeth, and took them to the only house I knew in Sandford, Mrs. Broughton's, where Ranken lodges. I left them with her to get their clothes dried, and went off to find a vehicle, but none was to be had there, so on the others arriving, Duckworth and I walked on to Iffley, whence we sent them a fly.

In the original manuscript, *Alice's Adventures Under Ground*, a number of details appear relating to this experience that Carroll later deleted because he thought they would have little interest to anyone outside the circle of individuals involved. When the facsimile edition of the manuscript was published in 1886, Duckworth received a copy inscribed, "The Duck from the Dodo."

3

A Caucus-Race and
a Long Tale

They were indeed a queer-looking party that assembled on the bank—the birds with draggled feathers, the animals with their fur clinging close to them, and all dripping wet, cross, and uncomfortable.

The first question of course was, how to get dry again: they had a consultation about this, and after a few minutes it seemed quite natural to Alice to find herself talking familiarly with them, as if she had known them all her life. Indeed, she had quite a long argument with the Lory, who at last turned sulky, and would only say "I'm older than you, and must know better." And this Alice would not allow, without knowing how old it was, and, as the Lory positively refused to tell its age, there was no more to be said.

At last the Mouse, who seemed to be a person of some authority among them, called out "Sit down, all of you, and listen to me! *I'll* soon make you dry enough!" They all sat down at once, in a large ring, with the Mouse in the middle. Alice kept her eyes anxiously fixed on it, for she felt sure she would catch a bad cold if she did not get dry very soon.

"Ahem!" said the Mouse with an important air. "Are you all ready? This is the driest thing I know. Silence all round, if you please! 'William the Conqueror, whose cause was favoured by the pope, was soon submitted to by the English, who wanted leaders, and had been of late much accustomed to usurpation and conquest. Edwin and Morcar, the earls of Mercia and Northumbria—'"[1]

"Ugh!" said the Lory, with a shiver.

"I beg your pardon!" said the Mouse, frowning, but very politely. "Did you speak?"

"Not I!" said the Lory, hastily.

"I thought you did," said the Mouse. "I proceed. 'Edwin and Morcar, the earls of Mercia and Northumbria, declared for him; and even Stigand, the patriotic archbishop of Canterbury, found it advisable—'"

"Found *what?*" said the Duck.

"Found *it*," the Mouse replied rather crossly: "of course you know what 'it' means."

"I know what 'it' means well enough, when *I* find a thing," said the Duck: "it's generally a frog, or a worm. The question is, what did the archbishop find?"

The Mouse did not notice this question, but hurriedly went on, " '—found it advisable to go with Edgar Atheling to meet William and offer him the crown. William's conduct at first was moderate. But the insolence of his Normans—' How are you getting on now, my dear?" it continued, turning to Alice as it spoke.

"As wet as ever," said Alice in a melancholy tone: "it doesn't seem to dry me at all."

"In that case," said the Dodo solemnly, rising to its feet, "I move that the meeting adjourn, for the immediate adoption of more energetic remedies—"

"Speak English!" said the Eaglet. "I don't know the meaning of half those long words, and, what's more, I don't believe you do either!" And

1. Roger Lancelyn Green, editor of Carroll's diary, identifies this dusty passage as an actual quotation from Havilland Chepmell's *Short Course of History* (1862), pages 143–44. Carroll was distantly related to the earls Edwin and Morcar, but Green thinks it unlikely that Carroll knew this. (See *The Diaries of Lewis Carroll*, Vol. 1, page 2.) Chepmell's book was one of the lesson books studied by the Liddell children. Green elsewhere suggests that Carroll may have intended the Mouse to represent Miss Prickett, the children's governess.

2. The term *caucus* originated in the United States in reference to a meeting of the leaders of a faction to decide on a candidate or policy. It was adopted in England with a slightly different meaning, referring to a system of highly disciplined party organization by committees. It was generally used by one party as an abusive term for the organization of an opposing party. Carroll may have intended his caucus-race to symbolize the fact that committee members generally do a lot of running around in circles, getting nowhere, and with everybody wanting a political plum. It has been suggested that he was influenced by the caucus of crows in Chapter 7 of *Water Babies*, a scene that Charles Kingsley obviously intended as barbed political satire, but the two scenes have little in common.

The caucus-race does not appear in the original manuscript, *Alice's Adventures Under Ground*. It replaces the following deleted passage, based on the episode cited in Note 10 of the previous chapter.

"I only meant to say," said the Dodo in rather an offended tone, "that I know of a house near here, where we could get the young lady and the rest of the party dried, and then we could listen comfortably to the story which I think you were good enough to promise to tell us," bowing gravely to the mouse.

The mouse made no objection to this, and the whole party moved along the river bank, (for the pool had by this time begun to flow out of the hall, and the edge of it was fringed with rushes and forget-me-nots,) in a slow procession, the Dodo leading the way. After a time the Dodo became impatient, and, leaving the Duck to bring up the rest of the party, moved on at a quicker pace with Alice, the Lory and the Eaglet, and soon brought them to a little cottage, and there they sat snugly by

the Eaglet bent down its head to hide a smile: some of the other birds tittered audibly.

"What I was going to say," said the Dodo in an offended tone, "was, that the best thing to get us dry would be a Caucus-race."[2]

"What *is* a Caucus-race?" said Alice; not that she much wanted to know, but the Dodo had paused as if it thought that *somebody* ought to speak, and no one else seemed inclined to say anything.

"Why," said the Dodo, "the best way to explain it is to do it." (And, as you might like to try the thing yourself, some winter-day, I will tell you how the Dodo managed it.)

First it marked out a race-course, in a sort of circle, ("the exact shape doesn't matter," it said,) and then all the party were placed along the course, here and there. There was no "One, two, three, and away!" but they began running when they liked, and left off when they liked, so that it was not easy to know when the race was over. However, when they had been running half an hour or so, and were quite dry again, the Dodo suddenly called out "The race is over!" and they all crowded round it, panting, and asking "But who has won?"

This question the Dodo could not answer without a great deal of thought, and it stood for a long time with one finger pressed upon its forehead (the position in which you usually see Shakespeare, in the pictures of him), while the rest waited in silence. At last the Dodo said "*Everybody* has won, and *all* must have prizes."

"But who is to give the prizes?" quite a chorus of voices asked.

"Why, *she*, of course," said the Dodo, pointing to Alice with one finger; and the whole party

the fire, wrapped up in blankets, until the rest of the party had arrived, and they were all dry again.

The thimble, taken from Alice and then returned to her, may symbolize the way governments take taxes from the pockets of citizens, then return the money in the form of political projects. See "The Dodo and the Caucus-Race," by Narda Lacey Schwartz, in *Jabberwocky* (Winter 1977), and "The Caucus-Race in *Alice in Wonderland*: A Very Drying Exercise," by August Imholtz, Jr., in *Jabberwocky* (Autumn 1981). The running in the caucus-race, according to Alfreda Blanchard in *Jabberwocky* (Summer 1982), may signify the running of politicians for office.

In his drawing of this scene Tenniel was forced to put human hands under the Dodo's small, degenerate wings. How else could it hold a thimble?

3. Comfits are hard sweetmeats made by preserving dried fruits or seeds with sugar and covering them with a thin coating of syrup.

at once crowded round her, calling out, in a confused way, "Prizes! Prizes!"

Alice had no idea what to do, and in despair she put her hand in her pocket, and pulled out a box of comfits[3] (luckily the salt water had not got into it), and handed them round as prizes. There was exactly one a-piece, all round.

"But she must have a prize herself, you know," said the Mouse.

"Of course," the Dodo replied very gravely. "What else have you got in your pocket?" it went on, turning to Alice.

"Only a thimble," said Alice sadly.

"Hand it over here," said the Dodo.

Then they all crowded round her once more, while the Dodo solemnly presented the thimble, saying "We beg your acceptance of this elegant thimble"; and, when it had finished this short speech, they all cheered.

Alice thought the whole thing very absurd, but

4. The mouse's tale is perhaps the best-known example in English of emblematic, or figured, verse: poems printed in such a way that they resemble something related to their subject matter. The affectation goes back to ancient Greece. Practitioners have included such distinguished bards as Robert Herrick, George Herbert, Stéphane Mallarmé, Dylan Thomas, E. E. Cummings, and the modern French poet Guillaume Apollinaire. For a spirited if not convincing defense of emblematic verse as a serious art form, see Charles Boultenhouse's article, "Poems in the Shapes of Things," in the *Art News Annual* (1959). Other examples of the form will be found in *Portfolio* magazine (Summer 1950), C. C. Bombaugh's *Gleanings for the Curious* (1867, revised), William S. Walsh's *Handy-Book of Literary Curiosities* (1892), and Carolyn Wells's *A Whimsey Anthology* (1906).

Tennyson once told Carroll that he had dreamed a lengthy poem about fairies, which began with very long lines, then the lines got shorter and shorter until the poem ended with fifty or sixty lines of two syllables each. (Tennyson thought highly of the poem in his sleep, but forgot it completely when he awoke.) The opinion has been expressed (*The Diaries of Lewis Carroll*, Vol. I, page 146) that this may have given Carroll the idea for his mouse's tale.

In the original manuscript of the book, an entirely different poem appears as the tale; in a way a more appropriate one, for it fulfills the mouse's promise to explain why he dislikes cats and dogs, whereas the tale as it appears here contains no reference to cats. The original tale, as Carroll hand-lettered it, reads as follows:

they all looked so grave that she did not dare to laugh; and, as she could not think of anything to say, she simply bowed, and took the thimble, looking as solemn as she could.

The next thing was to eat the comfits: this caused some noise and confusion, as the large birds complained that they could not taste theirs, and the small ones choked and had to be patted on the back. However, it was over at last, and they sat down again in a ring, and begged the Mouse to tell them something more.

"You promised to tell me your history, you know," said Alice, "and why it is you hate—C and D," she added in a whisper, half afraid that it would be offended again.

"Mine is a long and a sad tale!" said the Mouse, turning to Alice, and sighing.

"It *is* a long tail, certainly," said Alice, looking down with wonder at the Mouse's tail; "but why do you call it sad?" And she kept on puzzling about it while the Mouse was speaking, so that her idea of the tale was something like this:—[4]

```
        "Fury said to
       a mouse, That
      he met in the
     house, 'Let
       us both go
         to law: I
          will prose-
          cute you.—
         Come, I'll
        take no
      denial: We
    must have
   the trial;
  For really
 this morn-
  ing I've
    nothing
      to do.'
        Said the
          mouse to
            the cur,
            'Such a
            trial, dear
          sir, With
        no jury
       or judge,
      would
     be wast-
      ing our
        breath.'
        'I'll be
          judge,
           I'll be
            jury,'
              said
              cun-
               ning
               old
              Fury:
            'I'll
             try
             the
            whole
           cause,
          and
         con-
        demn
       you to
     death.'5
```

"You are not attending!" said the Mouse to Alice, severely. "What are you thinking of?"

We lived beneath the mat,
Warm and snug and fat.
But one woe, and that
Was the cat!

To our joys a clog.
In our eyes a fog.
On our hearts a log
Was the dog!

When the cat's away,
Then the mice will play,
But, alas! one day;
(So they say)

Came the dog and cat,
Hunting for a rat,
Crushed the mice all flat,
Each one as he sat,

Underneath the mat,
Warm and snug and fat.
Think of that!

The American logician and philosopher Charles Peirce was much interested in the visual analogue of poetic onomatopoeia. Among his unpublished papers there is a copy of Poe's "The Raven," written with a technique that Peirce called "art chirography," the words formed so as to convey a visual impression of the poem's ideas. This is not as absurd as it seems. The technique is employed frequently today in the lettering of advertisements, book jackets, titles of magazine stories and articles, cinema and TV titles, and so on.

I did not know, until I read about it in *Under the Quizzing Glass*, by R. B. Shaberman and Denis Crutch, that Carroll once proposed an additional change in the poem's final quatrain. It was among thirty-seven corrections that he listed in his copy of the 1866 edition of the book. The revised stanza would have been:

Said the mouse to the cur. "Such a trial,
*   dear sir.*
With no jury or judge, would be tedious
*   and dry."*

"I'll be judge, I'll be jury," said cunning
old Fury:
"I'll try the whole cause, and condemn
you to die."

Fury was the name of a fox terrier
owned by Carroll's child-friend Eve-
line Hull. Morton Cohen, in a note
on page 358 of *The Letters of Lewis
Carroll* (Oxford, 1979), speculates
that the dog was named after the cur
in the mouse's tale. He quotes an
entry from Carroll's diary (omitted
from the published version) telling
how Fury developed hydrophobia
and had to be shot, which was done
in Carroll's presence.

'Fury said to the mouse,
That he met in the house,
"Let us both go to law: I will prosecute
you—

Come, I'll take no denial;
We must have the trial;
For really this morning I've nothing to
do."

Said the mouse to the cur,
"Such a trial, dear sir,
With no jury or judge, would be wasting
our breath."

"I'll be judge, I'll be jury,"
said cunning old Fury:
"I'll try the whole cause, and condemn
you to death".'

In 1989 two New York teenage
students at the Pennington School,
Gary Graham and Jeffrey Maiden,
made an unusual discovery. Carroll's
mouse poem has the structure of
what is known as a "tail rhyme"—a
rhyming couplet followed by a short
unrhymed line. By lengthening the
last line, Carroll turned his tail poem
into a pattern which, if printed in
traditional form as shown, resembles
a mouse with a long tail! For details
of the discovery, see "Tail in Tail(s):
A Study Worthy of Alice's Friends,"

"I beg your pardon," said Alice very humbly:
"you had got to the fifth bend, I think?"

"I had *not*!" cried the Mouse, sharply and
very angrily.

"A knot!" said Alice, always ready to make
herself useful, and looking anxiously about her
"Oh, do let me help to undo it!"[6]

"I shall do nothing of the sort," said the
Mouse, getting up and walking away. "You
insult me by talking such nonsense!"

"I didn't mean it!" pleaded poor Alice. "But
you're so easily offended, you know!"

The Mouse only growled in reply.

"Please come back, and finish your story!"
Alice called after it. And the others all joined in
chorus "Yes, please do!" But the Mouse only
shook its head impatiently, and walked a little
quicker.

"What a pity it wouldn't stay!" sighed the
Lory, as soon as it was quite out of sight. And an
old Crab took the opportunity of saying to her
daughter "Ah, my dear! Let this be a lesson to
you never to lose *your* temper!" "Hold your
tongue, Ma!" said the young Crab, a little snap-
pishly. "You're enough to try the patience of
an oyster!"

"I wish I had our Dinah here, I know I do!"
said Alice aloud, addressing nobody in particular. "*She'd* soon fetch it back!"

"And who is Dinah, if I might venture to ask
the question?" said the Lory.

Alice replied eagerly, for she was always ready
to talk about her pet: "Dinah's our cat. And she's
such a capital one for catching mice, you ca'n't
think! And oh, I wish you could see her after the
birds! Why, she'll eat a little bird as soon as look
at it!"

This speech caused a remarkable sensation

among the party. Some of the birds hurried off at once: one old Magpie began wrapping itself up very carefully, remarking "I really must be getting home: the night-air doesn't suit my throat!" And a Canary called out in a trembling voice, to its children, "Come away, my dears! It's high time you were all in bed!" On various pretexts they all moved off, and Alice was soon left alone.

"I wish I hadn't mentioned Dinah!" she said to herself in a melancholy tone. "Nobody seems to like her, down here, and I'm sure she's the best cat in the world! Oh, my dear Dinah! I wonder if I shall ever see you any more!" And here poor Alice began to cry again, for she felt very lonely and low-spirited. In a little while, however, she again heard a little pattering of footsteps in the distance, and she looked up eagerly, half hoping that the Mouse had changed his mind, and was coming back to finish his story.

in the *New York Times* (May 1, 1991, p. A23).

In 1995 David and Maxine Schaefer, of Silver Spring, Maryland, privately published a small hardcover book titled *The Tale of the Mouse's Tail*. Illustrated by Jonathan Dixon, this delightful volume reproduces all the different ways the mouse's tale has been pictured in editions of *Alice in Wonderland* throughout the world.

5. Cf. "The Barrister's Dream" (Fit 6 of *The Hunting of the Snark*), in which the Snark serves as judge and jury as well as counsel for the defense.

6. This line was later quoted by Carroll himself to head the answers for a series of ten mathematical brain-teasers (he called them "knots") that he contributed to *The Monthly Packet* in 1880. In 1885 they appeared in book form as *A Tangled Tale*.

4

The Rabbit Sends in a Little Bill

1. In *Alice's Adventures Under Ground* the White Rabbit exclaims: "The Marchioness! The Marchioness! oh my dear paws! oh my fur and whiskers! She'll have me executed as sure as ferrets are ferrets!" There is no Duchess in this first version of the story; we later learn from the White Rabbit: "The Queen's the Marchioness: didn't you know that?" And he adds: "Queen of Hearts and Marchioness of Mock Turtles."

We learn in the Pig and Pepper chapter that the White Rabbit's fear is justified, because the Duchess shouts at Alice, "Talking of axes, chop off her head!" Selwyn Goodacre thinks it out of character for a duchess to order executions. He suggests that Carroll introduced the Duchess's remark in an effort to harmonize the story with the White Rabbit's exclamation in the earlier version.

Ferrets are a semidomesticated variety of the English polecat, used mainly for hunting rabbits and mice. They are usually yellowish white, with pink eyes. The White Rabbit had good reason to refer to ferrets in his fear of being "executed." Here is a passage from Oliver Goldsmith's section on "The Ferret" in his *History of the Earth and Animated Nature*:

It is naturally such an enemy of the rabbit kind, that if a dead rabbit be presented to

It was the White Rabbit, trotting slowly back again, and looking anxiously about as it went, as if it had lost something; and she heard it muttering to itself, "The Duchess! The Duchess! Oh my dear paws! Oh my fur and whiskers! She'll get me executed, as sure as ferrets are ferrets![1] Where *can* I have dropped them, I wonder?" Alice guessed in a moment that it was looking for the fan and the pair of white kid-gloves, and she very good-naturedly began hunting about for them, but they were nowhere to be seen—everything seemed to have changed since her swim in the pool; and the great hall, with the glass table and the little door, had vanished completely.

Very soon the Rabbit noticed Alice, as she went hunting about, and called out to her, in an angry tone, "Why, Mary Ann,[2] what *are* you doing out here? Run home this moment, and fetch me a pair of gloves and a fan! Quick, now!"[3] And Alice was so much frightened that she ran off at once in the direction it pointed to, without trying to explain the mistake that it had made.

"He took me for his housemaid," she said to herself as she ran. "How surprised he'll be when he finds out who I am! But I'd better take him his fan and gloves—that is, if I can find them." As she said this, she came upon a neat little house, on the door of which was a bright brass plate with the name "W. RABBIT" engraved upon it. She went in without knocking, and hurried upstairs, in great fear lest she should meet the real Mary Ann, and be turned out of the house before she had found the fan and gloves.

"How queer it seems," Alice said to herself, "to be going messages for a rabbit![4] I suppose Dinah'll be sending me on messages next!" And she began fancying the sort of thing that would happen: " 'Miss Alice! Come here directly, and get ready for your walk!' 'Coming in a minute, nurse! But I've got to watch this mouse-hole till Dinah comes back, and see that the mouse doesn't get out.' Only I don't think," Alice went on, "that they'd let Dinah stop in the house if it began ordering people about like that!"

By this time she had found her way into a tidy little room with a table in the window, and on it (as she had hoped) a fan and two or three pairs of tiny white kid-gloves: she took up the fan and a pair of the gloves, and was just going to leave the room, when her eye fell upon a little bottle that stood near the looking-glass. There was no label this time with the words "DRINK ME," but nevertheless she uncorked it and put it to her lips. "I know *something* interesting is sure to happen," she said to herself, "whenever I eat or drink anything: so I'll just see what this bottle does. I do hope it'll make me grow large again, for really I'm quite tired of being such a tiny little thing!"

It did so indeed, and much sooner than she had expected: before she had drunk half the bottle, she found her head pressing against the ceiling, and had to stoop to save her neck from being broken. She hastily put down the bottle, saying to herself "That's quite enough—I hope I sha'n't grow any more—As it is, I ca'n't

a young ferret, although it has never seen one before, it instantly attacks and bites it with an appearance of rapacity. If the rabbit be living, the ferret is still more eager, seizes it by the neck, winds itself round it, and continues to suck its blood, till it be satiated.

In addition to the use of *ferret* as a verb, the word was colloquially applied in England to thieving moneylenders. According to Peter Heath's note in *The Philosopher's Alice* (St. Martin's, 1974), the phrase "as sure as ferrets are ferrets" was current in Carroll's day. Heath cites its use in one of Anthony Trollope's novels.

As Carroll notes in his *Nursery "Alice,"* Tenniel drew a ferret among the twelve jurors for the trial of the Knave of Hearts.

Owning a ferret in New York City, which is said to have ten thousand ferrets, is a health code violation. An Associated Press story (September 18, 1983) reported the formation of the New York City Friends of the Ferret, a group seeking to lift the city's injunction. Spokesmen for the group contended that ferrets "give you love and affection . . . know their names and can do tricks." During the previous summer the group held a "ferret festival" in Central Park. It was attended by two hundred people who brought along about seventy-five ferrets.

The *New York Times* (June 25, 1995) reported the founding of *Modern Ferret*, a glossy magazine devoted to praise of ferrets, published by Erie and Mary Shefferman of Massapequa Park, New York.

2. According to Roger Green, *Mary Ann* was at the time a British euphemism for "servant girl." Dodgson's friend Mrs. Julia Cameron, a passionate amateur photographer, actually had a fifteen-year-old house-

maid named Mary Anne, and there is a photograph of her in Anne Clark's biography of Carroll to prove it. Mary Anne Paragon was the dishonest servant who took care of David Copperfield's house (see Chapter 44 of the Dickens novel). Her nature, we are told, was "feebly expressed" by her last name.

Slang dictionaries give other meanings to *Mary Ann* that were current in Carroll's day. A dressmaker's dress stand was called a Mary Ann. Later the name became attached to women, especially in Sheffield, who attacked sweatshop owners. Still later it became a vulgar term for sodomites.

Before the French Revolution *Mary Anne* was a generic term for secret republican organizations, as well as a slang term for the guillotine. *Marianne* became and still is a mythic female symbol of republican virtues, a French symbol comparable to England's John Bull and our Uncle Sam. She is traditionally depicted, in political cartoons and statuettes, as wearing the red Phrygian, or liberty, bonnet worn by republicans in the French Revolution. It is probably coincidental that Carroll's use of the name anticipates the obsession with beheading shared by the Duchess and the Queen of Hearts.

3. Note how the White Rabbit's angry ordering about of his servants, here and elsewhere in the chapter, is in keeping with his timid character as described by Carroll in the passage quoted in Note 2 of Chapter 2.

4. *Going messages* is a phrase still used in England. It means "running errands."

5. In the Pennyroyal edition of *Alice in Wonderland* (University of

get out at the door—I do wish I hadn't drunk quite so much!"

Alas! It was too late to wish that! She went on growing, and growing, and very soon had to kneel down on the floor: in another minute there was not even room for this, and she tried the effect of lying down with one elbow against the door, and the other arm curled round her head. Still she went on growing, and, as a last resource, she put one arm out of the window, and one foot up the chimney, and said to herself "Now I can do no more, whatever happens. What *will* become of me?"

Luckily for Alice, the little magic bottle had now had its full effect, and she grew no larger: still it was very uncomfortable, and, as there seemed to be no sort of chance of her ever getting out of the room again, no wonder she felt unhappy.

"It was much pleasanter at home," thought poor Alice, "when one wasn't always growing larger and smaller, and being ordered about by mice and rabbits. I almost wish I hadn't gone down that rabbit-hole—and yet—and yet—it's rather curious, you know, this sort of life! I do wonder what *can* have happened to me! When I used to read fairy tales, I fancied that kind of thing never happened, and now here I am in the middle of one! There ought to be a book written about me, that there ought! And when I grow up, I'll write one—but I'm grown up now," she added in a sorrowful tone: "at least there's no room to grow up any more *here*."

"But then," thought Alice, "shall I *never* get any older than I am now? That'll be a comfort, one way—never to be an old woman—but then—always to have lessons to learn! Oh, I shouldn't like *that*!"[5]

"Oh, you foolish Alice!" she answered herself. "How can you learn lessons in here? Why, there's hardly room for *you*, and no room at all for any lesson-books!"

And so she went on, taking first one side and then the other, and making quite a conversation of it altogether; but after a few minutes she heard a voice outside, and stopped to listen.

"Mary Ann! Mary Ann!" said the voice. "Fetch me my gloves this moment!"[6] Then came a little pattering of feet on the stairs. Alice knew it was the Rabbit coming to look for her, and she trembled till she shook the house, quite forgetting that she was now about a thousand times as large as the Rabbit, and had no reason to be afraid of it.

Presently the Rabbit came up to the door, and tried to open it; but, as the door opened inwards, and Alice's elbow was pressed hard against it, that attempt proved a failure. Alice heard it say to itself "Then I'll go round and get in at the window."

"*That* you wo'n't!" thought Alice, and, after waiting till she fancied she heard the Rabbit just under the window, she suddenly spread out her

California, 1982), James Kincaid glosses Alice's remark this way:

> This is a double-edged line and perhaps a poignant one, given Carroll's feelings about his child-friends growing up. [His] letters are full of self-pitying jokes on the subject: "Some children have a most disagreeable way of getting grownup. I hope you won't do anything of that sort before we meet again."

In his "Confessions of a Corrupt Annotator" (*Jabberwocky*, Spring 1982), Kincaid defends the right of annotators to take off in any direction they like. He cites the above note as an example. "The historical context does not call for a gloss, but the passage provides an opportunity to point out the ambivalence that may attend the central figure and her desire to grow up." I thank Mr. Kincaid for supporting my own rambling.

6. This is the second time the White Rabbit has called for his gloves, but whether he ever obtained them we are not told. Gloves were as important to Carroll as they were to the Rabbit, both in reality and linguistically. "He was a little eccentric in his clothes," Isa Bowman writes in *The Story of Lewis Carroll* (J. M. Dent, 1899). "In the coldest weather he would never wear an overcoat, and he had a curious habit of always wearing, in all seasons of the year, a pair of grey and black cotton gloves."

Gloves are the topic of one of Carroll's most amusing letters, written to Isa Bowman's sister Maggie. Carroll pretended that when Maggie spoke of sending him "sacks full of love and baskets full of kisses," she really meant to write "a sack full of *gloves* and a basket full of *kittens*!" A sack full of 1,000 gloves arrived, he goes on, and a basket of 250 kittens. He was thus able to put four gloves on each kitten to prevent their paws from scratching the schoolgirls to whom he gave the kittens:

So the little girls went dancing home again, and the next morning they came dancing back to school. The scratches were all healed, and they told me "The kittens *have* been good!" And, when any kitten wants to catch a mouse, it just takes off *one* of its gloves; and if it wants to catch *two* mice, it takes off two gloves; and if it wants to catch *three* mice, it takes off *three* gloves; and if it wants to catch *four* mice, it takes off all its gloves. But the moment they've caught the mice, they pop their gloves on again, because they know we can't love them without their gloves. For, you see, "gloves" have got "love" *inside* them—there's none *outside*.

7. A cucumber frame is a glass frame that provides heat for growing cucumbers by trapping solar radiation.

Carrollians have noticed that in Tenniel's illustration of this scene the White Rabbit's vest, white in an earlier picture, has become checked like his jacket.

8. Is this another French joke? As reader Michael Bergmann points out in a letter, "apple" is *pomme* in French, and "potato" is *pomme de terre*, or "apple of the earth." No, it is an Irish joke. Pat is an Irish name and he speaks in an Irish brogue. As Everett Bleiler informs me, *Irish apples* was a nineteenth-century slang term for Irish potatoes.

What kind of animal is Pat, the apple digger? Carroll doesn't say. Denis Crutch and R. B. Shaberman, in *Under the Quizzing Glass*, conjecture that Pat is one of the two guinea pigs who revive Bill after he has been kicked out of the chimney. During the trial of the Knave of Hearts both guinea pigs are in the courtroom, where they are "suppressed" for cheering.

hand, and made a snatch in the air. She did not get hold of anything, but she heard a little shriek and a fall, and a crash of broken glass, from which she concluded that it was just possible it had fallen into a cucumber-frame,[7] or something of the sort.

Next came an angry voice—the Rabbit's—"Pat! Pat! Where are you?" And then a voice she had never heard before, "Sure then I'm here! Digging for apples, yer honour!"[8]

'Digging for apples, indeed!" said the Rabbit angrily. "Here! Come and help me out of *this*!" (Sounds of more broken glass.)

"Now tell me, Pat, what's that in the window?"

"Sure, it's an arm, yer honour!" (He pronounced it "arrum.")

"An arm, you goose! Who ever saw one that size? Why, it fills the whole window!"

"Sure, it does, yer honour: but it's an arm for all that."

"Well, it's got no business there, at any rate: go and take it away!"

There was a long silence after this, and Alice could only hear whispers now and then; such as "Sure, I don't like it, yer honour, at all, at all!" "Do as I tell you, you coward!", and at last she spread out her hand again, and made another snatch in the air. This time there were *two* little shrieks, and more sounds of broken glass. "What a number of cucumber-frames there must be!" thought Alice. "I wonder what they'll do next! As for pulling me out of the window, I only wish they *could*! I'm sure *I* don't want to stay in here any longer!"

She waited for some time without hearing anything more: at last came a rumbling of little cart-wheels, and the sound of a good many voices all talking together: she made out the words: "Where's the other ladder?—Why, I hadn't to bring but one. Bill's got the other—Bill! Fetch it here, lad!—Here, put 'em up at this corner—No, tie 'em together first—they don't reach half high enough yet—Oh, they'll do well enough. Don't be particular—Here, Bill! Catch hold of this rope—Will the roof bear?—Mind that loose slate—Oh, it's coming down! Heads below!" (a loud crash)—"Now, who did that?—It was Bill, I fancy—Who's to go down the chimney?—Nay, *I* sha'n't! *You* do it!—*That* I wo'n't, then!—Bill's got to go down—Here, Bill! The master says you've got to go down the chimney!"

"Oh! So Bill's got to come down the chimney, has he?" said Alice to herself. "Why, they seem to put everything upon Bill! I wouldn't be in Bill's place for a good deal: this fireplace is narrow, to be sure; but I *think* I can kick a little!"

She drew her foot as far down the chimney as she could, and waited till she heard a little animal (she couldn't guess of what sort it was) scratching and scrambling about in the chimney close above her: then, saying to herself "This is Bill," she gave one sharp kick, and waited to see what would happen next.

The first thing she heard was a general chorus of "There goes Bill!" then the Rabbit's voice alone —"Catch him, you by the hedge!" then silence, and then another confusion of voices—"Hold up his head—Brandy now—Don't choke him—How was it, old fellow? What happened to you? Tell us all about it!"

Last came a little feeble, squeaking voice ("That's Bill," thought Alice), "Well, I hardly know—No more, thank ye; I'm better now—but I'm a deal too flustered to tell you—all I know is, something comes at me like a Jack-in-the-box, and up I goes like a sky-rocket!"

"So you did, old fellow!" said the others.

"We must burn the house down!" said the Rabbit's voice. And Alice called out, as loud as she could, "If you do, I'll set Dinah at you!"

There was a dead silence instantly, and Alice thought to herself "I wonder what they *will* do next! If they had any sense, they'd take the roof off." After a minute or two, they began moving about again, and Alice heard the Rabbit say "A barrowful will do, to begin with."

"A barrowful of *what*?" thought Alice. But she had not long to doubt, for the next moment a shower of little pebbles came rattling in at the window, and some of them hit her in the face. "I'll put a stop to this," she said to herself, and shouted out "You'd better not do that again!", which produced another dead silence.

Alice noticed, with some surprise, that the pebbles were all turning into little cakes as they lay on the floor, and a bright idea came into her head. "If I eat one of these cakes," she thought, "it's sure to make *some* change in my size; and, as it ca'n't possibly make me larger, it must make me smaller, I suppose."

So she swallowed one of the cakes, and was delighted to find that she began shrinking directly. As soon as she was small enough to get through the door, she ran out of the house, and found quite a crowd of little animals and birds waiting outside. The poor little Lizard, Bill, was in the middle, being held up by two guinea-pigs, who were giving it something out of a bottle. They all made a rush at Alice the moment she appeared; but she ran off as hard as she could, and soon found herself safe in a thick wood.

"The first thing I've got to do," said Alice to herself, as she wandered about in the wood, "is to grow to my right size again; and the second thing is to find my way into that lovely garden. I think that will be the best plan."

It sounded an excellent plan, no doubt, and very neatly and simply arranged: the only difficulty was, that she had not the smallest idea how to set about it; and, while she was peering about anxiously among the trees, a little sharp bark just over her head made her look up in a great hurry.

An enormous puppy was looking down at her with large round eyes, and feebly stretching out one paw, trying to touch her.[9] "Poor little thing!" said Alice, in a coaxing tone, and she tried hard to whistle to it; but she was terribly frightened all the time at the thought that it might be hungry, in which case it would be very likely to eat her up in spite of all her coaxing.

Hardly knowing what she did, she picked up a little bit of stick, and held it out to the puppy: whereupon the puppy jumped into the air off all its feet at once, with a yelp of delight, and rushed at the stick, and made believe to worry it: then Alice dodged behind a great thistle, to keep her-

self from being run over; and, the moment she appeared on the other side, the puppy made another rush at the stick, and tumbled head over heels in its hurry to get hold of it: then Alice, thinking it was very like having a game of play with a cart-horse, and expecting every moment to be trampled under its feet, ran round the thistle again: then the puppy began a series of short charges at the stick, running a very little way forwards each time and a long way back, and barking hoarsely all the while, till at last it sat down a good way off, panting, with its tongue hanging out of its mouth, and its great eyes half shut.

This seemed to Alice a good opportunity for making her escape: so she set off at once, and ran till she was quite tired and out of breath, and till the puppy's bark sounded quite faint in the distance.

"And yet what a dear little puppy it was!" said Alice, as she leant against a buttercup to rest herself, and fanned herself with one of the leaves. "I should have liked teaching it tricks very much, if—if I'd only been the right size to do it! Oh dear! I'd nearly forgotten that I've got to grow up again! Let me see—how *is* it to be managed? I suppose I ought to eat or drink something or other; but the great question is 'What?'"

The great question certainly was "What?" Alice looked all round her at the flowers and the blades of grass, but she could not see anything that looked like the right thing to eat or drink under the circumstances. There was a large mushroom growing near her, about the same height as herself; and, when she had looked under it, and on both sides of it, and behind it, it occurred to her that she might as well look and see what was on the top of it.

She stretched herself up on tiptoe, and peeped over the edge of the mushroom, and her eyes immediately met those of a large blue caterpillar, that was sitting on the top, with its arms folded, quietly smoking a long hookah, and taking not the smallest notice of her or of anything else.

5

Advice from a Caterpillar

The Caterpillar[1] and Alice looked at each other for some time in silence: at last the Caterpillar took the hookah out of its mouth, and addressed her in a languid, sleepy voice.

"Who are *you*?" said the Caterpillar.

This was not an encouraging opening for a conversation. Alice replied, rather shyly, "I—I hardly know, Sir, just at present—at least I know who I *was* when I got up this morning, but I think I must have been changed several times since then."

"What do you mean by that?" said the Caterpillar, sternly. "Explain yourself!"

"I ca'n't explain *myself*, I'm afraid, Sir," said Alice, "because I'm not myself, you see."

"I don't see," said the Caterpillar.

"I'm afraid I ca'n't put it more clearly," Alice replied, very politely, "for I ca'n't understand it myself, to begin with; and being so many different sizes in a day is very confusing."

"It isn't," said the Caterpillar.

"Well, perhaps you haven't found it so yet," said Alice; "but when you have to turn into a chrysalis—you will some day, you know—and then after that into a butterfly, I should think you'll feel it a little queer, wo'n't you?"

"Not a bit," said the Caterpillar.

1. In *The Nursery "Alice,"* Carroll calls attention to the Caterpillar's nose and chin in Tenniel's drawing and explains that they are really two of its legs. Ned Sparks took the role of the Caterpillar in Paramount's 1933 movie production of *Alice*, and Richard Haydn supplied the Caterpillar's voice in Walt Disney's 1951 animation of the tale. One of the most striking visual effects in the Disney film was obtained by having the Caterpillar illustrate his words by blowing multicolored smoke rings that assumed the shapes of letters and objects.

2. Fred Madden, in *Jabberwocky* (Summer/Autumn 1988), calls attention to a chapter titled "Popular Follies of Great Cities," in Charles Mackay's classic work, *Extraordinary Popular Delusions and the Madness of Crowds* (1841). Mackay tells of various catch phrases which sprang up suddenly in London. One such phrase was "*Who* are *you*," spoken with emphasis on the first and last words. It appeared suddenly, "like a mushroom . . . One day it was unheard, unknown, uninvented; the next day it pervaded London. . . . Every new comer into an alehouse tap room was asked unceremoniously 'Who are you?'"

In "Who Are You: A Reply" (*Jabberwocky*, Winter/Spring 1990), John Clark points out that Carroll owned Mackay's book and probably heard the question shouted at him when it was a short-lived London rage. Did he have this craze in mind when he had his blue Caterpillar, sitting on a mushroom, ask Alice, "Who are *you*?" It certainly seems possible. I first learned about the Mackay reference in a letter from Teller, of the Penn and Teller comedy/magic team.

"Well, perhaps *your* feelings may be different," said Alice: "all I know is, it would feel very queer to *me*."

"You!" said the Caterpillar contemptuously. "Who are *you*?"[2]

Which brought them back again to the beginning of the conversation. Alice felt a little irritated at the Caterpillar's making such *very* short remarks, and she drew herself up and said, very gravely, "I think you ought to tell me who *you* are, first."

"Why?" said the Caterpillar.

Here was another puzzling question; and, as Alice could not think of any good reason, and the Caterpillar seemed to be in a very unpleasant state of mind, she turned away.

"Come back!" the Caterpillar called after her.

"I've something important to say!"

This sounded promising, certainly. Alice turned and came back again.

"Keep your temper," said the Caterpillar.

"Is that all?" said Alice, swallowing down her anger as well as she could.

"No," said the Caterpillar.

Alice thought she might as well wait, as she had nothing else to do, and perhaps after all it might tell her something worth hearing. For some minutes it puffed away without speaking; but at last it unfolded its arms, took the hookah out of its mouth again, and said "So you think you're changed, do you?"

"I'm afraid I am, Sir," said Alice. "I ca'n't remember things as I used—and I don't keep the same size for ten minutes together!"

"Ca'n't remember *what* things?" said the Caterpillar.

"Well, I've tried to say '*How doth the little busy bee,*' but it all came different!" Alice replied in a very melancholy voice.

"Repeat '*You are old, Father William,*'" said the Caterpillar.

Alice folded her hands,[3] and began:—

3. Selwyn Goodacre (in *Jabberwocky*, Spring 1982) has an interesting comment on Alice's folded hands here, and her crossed hands in Chapter 2 ("as if she were saying lessons") when she repeated "How doth the little crocodile . . .":

I discussed these passages with a retired primary school headmaster . . . and he confirmed to me that that is *exactly* how children were taught—i.e., they had to repeat their lessons (note that the word is not "recite"—that refers to house parties and home entertainment), this means learning by rote; she would have been expected to know the lessons by heart—and to cross her hands if sitting, to fold them if standing, both systems intended to concentrate the mind and prevent fidgeting.

"You are old, father William," one of the undisputed masterpieces of nonsense verse, is a clever parody of Robert Southey's (1774–1843) long-forgotten didactic poem, "The Old Man's Comforts and How He Gained Them."

"You are old, father William," the young
 man cried,
 "The few locks which are left you are
  grey;
You are hale, father William, a hearty old
 man;
 Now tell me the reason, I pray."

"In the days of my youth," father William
 replied,
 "I remember'd that youth would fly
  fast,
And abus'd not my health and my vigour
 at first,
 That I never might need them at last."

"You are old, father William," the young
 man cried,
 "And pleasures with youth pass away.
And yet you lament not the days that are
 gone;
 Now tell me the reason, I pray."

"In the days of my youth," father William replied,
  "I remember'd that youth could not last;
I thought of the future, whatever I did,
  "That I never might grieve for the past."

"You are old, father William," the young man cried,
  "And life must be hast'ning away;
You are cheerful and love to converse upon death;
  Now tell me the reason, I pray."

"I am cheerful, young man," father William replied,
  "Let the cause thy attention engage;
In the days of my youth I remember'd my God!
  And He hath not forgotten my age."

Although Southey had an enormous literary output of both prose and poetry, he is little read today except for a few short poems such as "The Inchcape Rock" and "The Battle of Blenheim," and for his version of the immortal folktale about Goldilocks and the three bears.

4. In the original version of this poem, in *Alice's Adventures Under Ground*, the price of the ointment is five shillings.

"You are old, Father William," the young man said,
  "And your hair has become very white;
And yet you incessantly stand on your head—
  Do you think, at your age, it is right?"

"In my youth," Father William replied to his son,
  "I feared it might injure the brain;
But, now that I'm perfectly sure I have none,
  Why, I do it again and again."

"You are old," said the youth, "as I mentioned before,
  And have grown most uncommonly fat;
Yet you turned a back-somersault in at the door—
  Pray, what is the reason of that?"

"In my youth," said the sage, as he shook his grey locks,
  "I kept all my limbs very supple
By the use of this ointment—one shilling the box—[4]
  Allow me to sell you a couple?"

"You are old," said the youth, "and your jaws are too weak
  For anything tougher than suet;

Yet you finished the goose, with the bones and the
    beak—
    Pray, how did you manage to do it?"

"In my youth," said his father, "I took to the
    law,
    And argued each case with my wife;
And the muscular strength, which it gave to
    my jaw
    Has lasted the rest of my life."

5. In Tenniel's illustration for this line you see in the background what looks like a bridge. Philip Benham, writing in *Jabberwocky* (Winter 1970), says: "The 'bridge' is in fact an eel trap, built across a stream or river, and consists of a barrier of conical baskets woven out of rushes or sometimes willow."

Robert Wakeman adds that one made of iron still exists near Guildford. "A small hole at the end of each basket enables the eels to escape into a separate pond, while other types of fish are unable to go through the holes." For more details and other pictures of eel traps, see Michael Hancher's *The Tenniel Illustrations to the "Alice" Books* (Ohio State University Press, 1985).

"You are old," said the youth, "one would hardly
suppose
That your eye was as steady as ever;
Yet you balanced an eel on the end of your nose—[5]
What made you so awfully clever?"

"I have answered three questions, and that is
enough,"
Said his father. "Don't give yourself airs!
Do you think I can listen all day to such stuff?
Be off, or I'll kick you down-stairs!"

"That is not said right," said the Caterpillar.

"Not *quite* right, I'm afraid," said Alice, timidly: "some of the words have got altered."

"It is wrong from beginning to end," said the Caterpillar, decidedly; and there was silence for some minutes.

The Caterpillar was the first to speak.

"What size do you want to be?" it asked.

"Oh, I'm not particular as to size," Alice hastily replied; "only one doesn't like changing so often, you know."

"I *don't* know," said the Caterpillar.

Alice said nothing: she had never been so much contradicted in all her life before, and she felt that she was losing her temper.

"Are you content now?" said the Caterpillar.

"Well, I should like to be a *little* larger, Sir, if you wouldn't mind," said Alice: "three inches is such a wretched height to be."

"It is a very good height indeed!" said the Caterpillar angrily, rearing itself upright as it spoke (it was exactly three inches high).

"But I'm not used to it!" pleaded poor Alice in a piteous tone. And she thought to herself "I wish the creatures wouldn't be so easily offended!"

"You'll get used to it in time," said the

Caterpillar; and it put the hookah into its mouth, and began smoking again.

This time Alice waited patiently until it chose to speak again. In a minute or two the Caterpillar took the hookah out of its mouth, and yawned once or twice, and shook itself. Then it got down off the mushroom, and crawled away into the grass, merely remarking, as it went, "One side will make you grow taller, and the other side will make you grow shorter."[6]

"One side of *what*? The other side of *what*?" thought Alice to herself.

"Of the mushroom," said the Caterpillar, just as if she had asked it aloud;[7] and in another moment it was out of sight.

Alice remained looking thoughtfully at the mushroom for a minute, trying to make out which were the two sides of it; and, as it was perfectly round, she found this a very difficult question. However, at last she stretched her arms round it as far as they would go, and broke off a bit of the edge with each hand.

"And now which is which?" she said to herself, and nibbled a little of the right-hand bit to try the effect. The next moment she felt a violent blow underneath her chin: it had struck her foot!

She was a good deal frightened by this very sudden change, but she felt that there was no time to be lost, as she was shrinking rapidly: so she set to work at once to eat some of the other bit. Her chin was pressed so closely against her foot, that there was hardly room to open her mouth; but she did it at last, and managed to swallow a morsel of the left-hand bit.

      *   *   *   *
          *   *   *
      *   *   *   *

6. In *Alice's Adventures Under Ground* the Caterpillar tells Alice that the *top* of the mushroom will make her grow taller and the *stalk* will make her grow shorter.

Many readers have referred me to old books, which Carroll could have read, that describe the hallucinogenic properties of certain mushrooms. *Amanita muscaria* (or fly agaric) is most often cited. Eating it produces hallucinations in which time and space are distorted. However, as Robert Hornback makes clear in his delightful "Garden Tour of Wonderland," in *Pacific Horticulture* (Fall 1983), this cannot be the mushroom drawn by Tenniel:

Amanita muscaria has bright red caps that appear to be splattered with bits of cottage cheese. The Caterpillar's perch is, instead, a smooth-capped species, very like *Amanita fulva*, which is nontoxic and rather tasty. We might surmise that neither Tenniel nor Carroll wanted children to emulate Alice and end up eating poisonous mushrooms.

7. The Caterpillar has read Alice's mind. Carroll did not believe in spiritualism, but he did believe in the reality of ESP and psychokinesis. In an 1882 letter (see Morton Cohen's *The Letters of Lewis Carroll*, Vol. 1, pages 471–72) he speaks of a pamphlet on "thought reading," published by the Society for Psychical Research, which strengthened his conviction that psychic phenomena are genuine. "All seems to point to the existence of a natural force, allied to electricity and nerve-force, by which brain can act on brain. I think we are close on the day when this shall be classed among the known natural forces, and its laws tabulated, and when the scientific sceptics, who always shut their eyes till the last moment to any evidence that seems to

point beyond materialism, will have to accept it as a proved fact in nature."

Carroll was an enthusiastic charter member all his life of the Society for Psychical Research, and his library contained dozens of books on the occult. See "Lewis Carroll and the Society for Psychical Research," by R. B. Shaberman, in *Jabberwocky* (Summer 1972).

"Come, my head's free at last!" said Alice in a tone of delight, which changed into alarm in another moment, when she found that her shoulders were nowhere to be found: all she could see, when she looked down, was an immense length of neck, which seemed to rise like a stalk out of a sea of green leaves that lay far below her.

"What *can* all that green stuff be?" said Alice. "And where *have* my shoulders got to? And oh, my poor hands, how is it I ca'n't see you?" She was moving them about, as she spoke, but no result seemed to follow, except a little shaking among the distant green leaves.

As there seemed to be no chance of getting her hands up to her head, she tried to get her head down to *them*, and was delighted to find that her neck would bend about easily in any direction, like a serpent. She had just succeeded in curving it down into a graceful zigzag, and was going to dive in among the leaves, which she found to be nothing but the tops of the trees under which she had been wandering, when a sharp hiss made her draw back in a hurry: a large pigeon had flown into her face, and was beating her violently with its wings.

"Serpent!" screamed the Pigeon.

"I'm *not* a serpent!" said Alice indignantly. "Let me alone!"

"Serpent, I say again!" repeated the Pigeon, but in a more subdued tone, and added, with a kind of sob, "I've tried every way, but nothing seems to suit them!"

"I haven't the least idea what you're talking about," said Alice.

"I've tried the roots of trees, and I've tried banks, and I've tried hedges," the Pigeon went on, without attending to her; "but those serpents! There's no pleasing them!"

Alice was more and more puzzled, but she thought there was no use in saying anything more till the Pigeon had finished.

"As if it wasn't trouble enough hatching the eggs," said the Pigeon; "but I must be on the look-out for serpents, night and day! Why, I haven't had a wink of sleep these three weeks!"

"I'm very sorry you've been annoyed," said Alice, who was beginning to see its meaning.

"And just as I'd taken the highest tree in the wood," continued the Pigeon, raising its voice to a shriek, "and just as I was thinking I should be free of them at last, they must needs come wriggling down from the sky! Ugh, Serpent!"

"But I'm *not* a serpent, I tell you!" said Alice. "I'm a—I'm a—"

"Well! *What* are you?" said the Pigeon. "I can see you're trying to invent something!"

"I—I'm a little girl," said Alice, rather doubt-fully, as she remembered the number of changes she had gone through, that day.

"A likely story indeed!" said the Pigeon, in a tone of the deepest contempt. "I've seen a good many little girls in my time, but never *one* with such a neck as that! No, no! You're a serpent; and there's no use denying it. I suppose you'll be telling me next that you never tasted an egg!"

"I *have* tasted eggs, certainly," said Alice, who was a very truthful child; "but little girls eat eggs quite as much as serpents do, you know."

"I don't believe it," said the Pigeon; "but if they do, why, then they're a kind of serpent: that's all I can say."

This was such a new idea to Alice, that she was quite silent for a minute or two, which gave the Pigeon the opportunity of adding "You're looking for eggs, I know *that* well enough; and what does it matter to me whether you're a little girl or a serpent?"

"It matters a good deal to *me*," said Alice hastily; "but I'm not looking for eggs, as it happens; and, if I was, I shouldn't want *yours*: I don't like them raw."

"Well, be off, then!" said the Pigeon in a sulky tone, as it settled down again into its nest. Alice crouched down among the trees as well as she could, for her neck kept getting entangled among the branches, and every now and then she had to stop and untwist it. After a while she remembered that she still held the pieces of mushroom in her hands, and she set to work very carefully, nibbling first at one and then at the other, and growing sometimes taller, and sometimes shorter, until she had succeeded in bringing herself down to her usual height.

It was so long since she had been anything near the right size, that it felt quite strange at first; but she got used to it in a few minutes, and began talking to herself, as usual, "Come, there's half my plan done now! How puzzling all these changes are! I'm never sure what I'm going to be, from one minute to another! However, I've got back to my right size: the next thing is, to get into that beautiful garden—how *is* that to be done, I wonder?" As she said this, she came suddenly upon an open place, with a little house in it about four feet high. "Whoever lives there," thought Alice, "it'll never do to come upon them *this* size: why, I should frighten them out of their wits!" So she began nibbling at the right-hand bit again, and did not venture to go near the house till she had brought herself down to nine inches high.

6

Pig and Pepper

For a minute or two she stood looking at the
house, and wondering what to do next, when
suddenly a footman in livery came running out
of the wood—(she considered him to be a footman because he was in livery: otherwise, judging
by his face only, she would have called him a
fish)—and rapped loudly at the door with his
knuckles. It was opened by another footman in
livery, with a round face, and large eyes like a
frog; and both footmen, Alice noticed, had pow-
dered hair that curled all over their heads. She
felt very curious to know what it was all about,
and crept a little way out of the wood to listen.

The Fish-Footman began by producing from
under his arm a great letter, nearly as large as
himself, and this he handed over to the other,
saying, in a solemn tone, "For the Duchess. An
invitation from the Queen to play croquet." The
Frog-Footman repeated, in the same solemn
tone, only changing the order of the words a
little, "From the Queen. An invitation for the
Duchess to play croquet."

Then they both bowed low, and their curls got
entangled together.

Alice laughed so much at this, that she had to
run back into the wood for fear of their hearing
her; and, when she next peeped out, the Fish-
Footman was gone, and the other was sitting on

the ground near the door, staring stupidly up into the sky.

Alice went timidly up to the door, and knocked.

"There's no sort of use in knocking," said the Footman, "and that for two reasons. First, because I'm on the same side of the door as you are: secondly, because they're making such a noise inside, no one could possibly hear you." And certainly there *was* a most extraordinary noise going on within—a constant howling and sneezing, and every now and then a great crash, as if a dish or kettle had been broken to pieces.

"Please, then," said Alice, "how am I to get in?"

"There might be some sense in your knocking," the Footman went on, without attending to her, "if we had the door between us. For instance, if you were *inside*, you might knock, and

I could let you out, you know." He was looking up into the sky all the time he was speaking, and this Alice thought decidedly uncivil. "But perhaps he ca'n't help it," she said to herself; "his eyes are so *very* nearly at the top of his head. But at any rate he might answer questions.—How am I to get in?" she repeated, aloud.

"I shall sit here," the Footman remarked, "till tomorrow—"

At this moment the door of the house opened, and a large plate came skimming out, straight at the Footman's head: it just grazed his nose, and broke to pieces against one of the trees behind him.

"—or next day, maybe," the Footman continued in the same tone, exactly as if nothing had happened.

"How am I to get in?" asked Alice again, in a louder tone.

"*Are* you to get in at all?" said the Footman. "That's the first question, you know."

It was, no doubt: only Alice did not like to be told so. "It's really dreadful," she muttered to herself, "the way all the creatures argue. It's enough to drive one crazy!"

The Footman seemed to think this a good opportunity for repeating his remark, with variations. "I shall sit here," he said, "on and off, for days and days."

"But what am *I* to do?" said Alice.

"Anything you like," said the Footman, and began whistling.

"Oh, there's no use in talking to him," said Alice desperately: "he's perfectly idiotic!" And she opened the door and went in.

The door led right into a large kitchen, which was full of smoke from one end to the other: the Duchess[1] was sitting on a three-legged stool in

1. Not until Chapter 9, when Alice and the Duchess meet again, are we told that Alice tried to keep her distance from the Duchess because she "was *very* ugly," and because the Duchess kept prodding her shoulder with her "sharp little chin." The sharp chin is mentioned two more times in this episode. The whereabouts of the Duke, if living, is left in mystery.

The chin of Tenniel's Duchess is not very little or sharp, but she is certainly ugly. It seems likely that he copied a painting attributed to the sixteenth-century Flemish artist Quentin Matsys (his name has variant spellings). The portrait is popularly regarded as one of the fourteenth-century duchess Margaret of Carinthia and Tyrol. She had the reputation of being the ugliest woman in history. (Her nickname, "Maultasche," means "pocket-mouthed.") Lion Feuchtwanger's novel *The Ugly Duchess* is about her sad life. See also "A Portrait of the Ugliest Princess in History," by W. A. Baillie-Grohman, *Burlington Magazine* (April 1921).

QUENTIN MATSYS'S PAINTING OF THE "UGLY DUCHESS."
(National Gallery, London)

On the other hand, there are numerous engravings and drawings almost identical with Matsys's painting, including a drawing by Francesco Melzi, a pupil of Leonardo da Vinci. Part of the Royal Collection at Buckingham Palace, it is said to be a copy of a lost original by da Vinci! For the confusing history of these pictures, which may have no connection whatever with Duchess Margaret, see Chapter 4 of Michael Hancher's, *The Tenniel Illustrations to the "Alice" Books*.

2. The pepper in the soup and in the air suggests the peppery ill temper of the Duchess. Was it the custom in Victorian England for lower classes to put excessive pepper in their soup to mask the taste of slightly spoiled meat and vegetables?

For Savile Clarke's stage production of *Alice*, Carroll provided the following lines to be spoken by the cook while she stirs the soup: "There's nothing like pepper, says I. . . . Not half enough yet. Nor a quarter enough." The cook then recites, like a witch chanting a charm:

> Boil it so easily,
> Mix it so greasily,
> Stir it so sneezily,
> One! Two!! Three!!!

"One for the Missus, two for the cat, and three for the baby," the cook continues, striking the baby's nose.

I quote from Charles C. Lovett's valuable book *Alice on Stage: A History of the Early Theatrical Productions of Alice in Wonderland* (Meckler, 1990). The lines appeared both in the stage production and in the script's published version.

3. "Grin like a Cheshire cat" was a common phrase in Carroll's day. Its origin is not known. The two leading

the middle, nursing a baby: the cook was leaning over the fire, stirring a large cauldron which seemed to be full of soup.

"There's certainly too much pepper in that soup!"[2] Alice said to herself, as well as she could for sneezing.

There was certainly too much of it in the *air*. Even the Duchess sneezed occasionally; and as for the baby, it was sneezing and howling alternately without a moment's pause. The only two creatures in the kitchen, that did *not* sneeze, were the cook, and a large cat, which was lying on the hearth and grinning from ear to ear.

"Please would you tell me," said Alice, a little timidly, for she was not quite sure whether it was good manners for her to speak first, "why your cat grins like that?"

"It's a Cheshire-Cat,"[3] said the Duchess, "and that's why. Pig!"

She said the last word with such sudden violence that Alice quite jumped; but she saw in another moment that it was addressed to the baby, and not to her, so she took courage, and went on again:—

"I didn't know that Cheshire-Cats always grinned; in fact, I didn't know that cats *could* grin."

"They all can," said the Duchess; "and most of 'em do."

"I don't know of any that do," Alice said very politely, feeling quite pleased to have got into a conversation.

"You don't know much," said the Duchess; "and that's a fact."

Alice did not at all like the tone of this remark, and thought it would be as well to introduce some other subject of conversation. While she was trying to fix on one, the cook took the cauldron of soup off the fire, and at once set to work throwing everything within her reach at the Duchess and the baby—the fire-irons came first; then followed a shower of saucepans, plates, and dishes. The Duchess took no notice of them even when they hit her; and the baby was howling so much already, that it was quite impossible to say whether the blows hurt it or not.

"Oh, *please* mind what you're doing!" cried Alice, jumping up and down in an agony of terror. "Oh, there goes his *precious* nose!", as an unusually large saucepan flew close by it, and very nearly carried it off.

"If everybody minded their own business," the Duchess said, in a hoarse growl, "the world would go round a deal faster than it does."

"Which would *not* be an advantage," said Alice, who felt very glad to get an opportunity of showing off a little of her knowledge. "Just think what work it would make with the day and night! You see the earth takes twenty-four hours to turn round on its axis—"

"Talking of axes," said the Duchess, "chop off her head!"

theories are: (1) A sign painter in Cheshire (the county, by the way, where Carroll was born) painted grinning lions on the signboards of inns in the area (see *Notes and Queries*, No. 130, April 24, 1852, page 402); (2) Cheshire cheeses were at one time molded in the shape of a grinning cat (see *Notes and Queries*, No. 55, Nov. 16, 1850, page 412). "This has a peculiar Carrollian appeal," writes Dr. Phyllis Greenacre in her psychoanalytic study of Carroll, "as it provokes the fantasy that the cheesy cat may eat the rat that would eat the cheese." The Cheshire Cat is not in the original manuscript, *Alice's Adventures Under Ground*.

David Greene sent me this quotation from an 1808 letter of Charles Lamb: "I made a pun the other day, and palmed it upon Holcroft, who grinned like a Cheshire cat. Why do cats grin in Cheshire? Because it was once a county palatine and the cats cannot help laughing whenever they think of it, though I see no great joke in it."

Hans Haverman wrote to suggest that Carroll's vanishing cat might derive from the waning of the moon—the moon has long been associated with lunacy—as it slowly turns into a fingernail crescent, resembling a grin, before it finally disappears.

Did T. S. Eliot have the Cheshire Cat in mind when he concluded "Morning at the Window" with this couplet?

An aimless smile that hovers in the air
And vanishes along the level of the roofs.

For more on the grin, see "The Cheshire-Cat and Its Origins," by Ken Oultram, in *Jabberwocky* (Winter 1973).

A 1989 pamphlet published in Japan, *Lewis Carroll and His*

World—*Cheshire Cat*, by Katsuko Kasai, quotes the following lines from Thackeray's novel *Newcomes* (1855): "That woman grins like a Cheshire cat. . . . Who was the naturalist who first discovered that peculiarity of the cats in Cheshire?" Kasai also quotes from Captain Gosse's *A Dictionary of the Buckish Slang, University Wit and Pickpocket Eloquence* (1811): "He grins like a Cheshire cat; said of any one who shews his teeth and gums in laughing." Other quotes and various theories about the phrase's origin are discussed by Kasai. In a 1995 letter to me, Kasai makes an interesting conjecture. We know that Cheshire cheese was once sold in the shape of a grinning cat. One would tend to slice off the cheese at the cat's tail end until finally only the grinning head would remain on the plate.

Knight Letter, the official organ of The Lewis Carroll Society of North America, published Joel Birenbaum's article (Summer 1992), "Have We Finally Found the Cheshire Cat?" Birenbaum reports on his tour of St. Peter's Church, in Croft-on-Tees, where Carroll's father was rector. On the chancel's east wall he noticed a stone carving of a cat's head, floating in the air a few feet above the floor. When he got on his knees for closer inspection and looked up, the cat's mouth appeared as a broad grin. His discovery made the front page of the *Chicago Tribune* (July 13, 1992).

Whoopi Goldberg was the Cheshire Cat in NBC's undistinguished, boring television version of *Alice in Wonderland* that aired on February 28, 1999.

4. The original of this burlesque is "Speak Gently," a happily unremembered poem attributed by some authorities to one G. W. Langford

Alice glanced rather anxiously at the cook, to see if she meant to take the hint; but the cook was busily stirring the soup, and seemed not to be listening, so she went on again: "Twenty-four hours, I *think*; or is it twelve? I—"

"Oh, don't bother *me*!" said the Duchess. "I never could abide figures!" And with that she began nursing her child again, singing a sort of lullaby to it as she did so, and giving it a violent shake at the end of every line:—[4]

> *"Speak roughly to your little boy,*
> *And beat him when he sneezes:*
> *He only does it to annoy,*
> *Because he knows it teases."*

CHORUS

(in which the cook and the baby joined):—
"Wow! wow! wow!"

While the Duchess sang the second verse of the song, she kept tossing the baby violently up and down, and the poor little thing howled so, that Alice could hardly hear the words:—

> *"I speak severely to my boy,*
> *I beat him when he sneezes;*
> *For he can thoroughly enjoy*
> *The pepper when he pleases!"*

CHORUS

"Wow! wow! wow!"

"Here! You may nurse it a bit, if you like!" the Duchess said to Alice, flinging the baby at her as she spoke. "I must go and get ready to play croquet with the Queen," and she hurried out of the room. The cook threw a frying-pan after her as she went, but it just missed her.

Alice caught the baby with some difficulty, as it was a queer-shaped little creature, and held out its arms and legs in all directions, "just like a star-fish," thought Alice. The poor little thing was snorting like a steam-engine when she caught it, and kept doubling itself up and straightening itself out again, so that altogether, for the first minute or two, it was as much as she could do to hold it.

As soon as she had made out the proper way of nursing it (which was to twist it up into a sort of knot, and then keep tight hold of its right ear and left foot, so as to prevent its undoing itself), she carried it out into the open air. "If I don't take this child away with me," thought Alice, "they're sure to kill it in a day or two. Wouldn't it be murder to leave it behind?" She said the last words out loud, and the little thing grunted in reply (it had left off sneezing by this time). "Don't grunt," said Alice; "that's not at all a proper way of expressing yourself."

The baby grunted again, and Alice looked very anxiously into its face to see what was the matter with it. There could be no doubt that it had a *very* turn-up nose, much more like a snout than a real nose: also its eyes were getting extremely small for a baby: altogether Alice did not like the look of the thing at all. "But perhaps it was only sobbing," she thought, and looked into its eyes again, to see if there were any tears.

No, there were no tears. "If you're going to turn into a pig, my dear," said Alice, seriously, "I'll have nothing more to do with you. Mind now!" The poor little thing sobbed again (or grunted, it was impossible to say which), and they went on for some while in silence.

Alice was just beginning to think to herself, "Now, what am I to do with this creature, when I get it home?" when it grunted again, so violently,

and by other authorities to David Bates, a Philadelphia broker.

John M. Shaw, in *The Parodies of Lewis Carroll and their Originals* (the catalog and notes of an exhibition at the Florida State University Library, December 1960), reports that he was unsuccessful in his search for Langford's version; in fact he failed to find Langford himself. Shaw did find the poem on page 15 of *The Eolian*, a book of verse published by Bates in 1849. Shaw points out that Bates's son, in a preface to his father's *Poetical Works* (1870), states that his father had indeed written this widely quoted poem.

Speak gently! It is better far
To rule by love than fear;
Speak gently; let no harsh words mar
The good we might do here!

Speak gently! Love doth whisper low
The vows that true hearts bind;
And gently Friendship's accents flow;
Affection's voice is kind.

Speak gently to the little child!
Its love be sure to gain;
Teach it in accents soft and mild;
It may not long remain.

Speak gently to the young, for they
Will have enough to bear;
Pass through this life as best they may,
'Tis full of anxious care!

Speak gently to the aged one,
Grieve not the care-worn heart;
Whose sands of life are nearly run,
Let such in peace depart!

Speak gently, kindly, to the poor;
Let no harsh tone be heard;
They have enough they must endure,
Without an unkind word!

Speak gently to the erring; know
They may have toiled in vain;
Perchance unkindness made them so;
Oh, win them back again!

Speak gently! He who gave his life
To bend man's stubborn will,
When elements were in fierce strife,
Said to them, "Peace, be still."

Speak gently! 'tis a little thing
Dropped in the heart's deep well;
The good, the joy, that it may bring,
Eternity shall tell.

The Langford family tradition is that George wrote the poem while visiting his birthplace in Ireland in 1845. All British printings of the poem prior to 1900 are either anonymous or credited to Langford. No known printing of the poem in England predates 1848.

Bates's case was strongly boosted by the discovery in 1986 that the poem, signed "D.B.," appeared on the second page of the *Philadelphia Inquirer*, July 15, 1845. Unless an earlier printing can be found in a British or Irish newspaper, it seems highly improbable that Langford could have written it, although a capital mystery remains. How did his name become so firmly attached to the poem in England?

For a detailed history of the controversy, see my essay "Speak Gently," in *Lewis Carroll Observed* (Clarkson N. Potter, 1976), edited by Edward Guiliano, and reprinted with additions in my *Order and Surprise*.

5. It was surely not without malice that Carroll turned a male baby into a pig, for he had a low opinion of little boys. In *Sylvie and Bruno Concluded* an unpleasant child named Uggug ("a hideous fat boy . . . with the expression of a prize-pig") finally turns into a porcupine. Carroll now and then made an effort to be friendly with a little boy, but usually only when the lad had sisters that Carroll wanted to meet. In one of his concealed-rhyme letters (a letter that seems to be prose

that she looked down into its face in some alarm. This time there could be *no* mistake about it: it was neither more nor less than a pig, and she felt that it would be quite absurd for her to carry it any further.[5]

So she set the little creature down, and felt quite relieved to see it trot away quietly into the wood. "If it had grown up," she said to herself, "it would have made a dreadfully ugly child: but it makes rather a handsome pig, I think." And she began thinking over other children she knew, who might do very well as pigs, and was just saying to herself "if one only knew the right way to change them—" when she was a little startled by seeing the Cheshire-Cat sitting on a bough of a tree a few yards off.[6]

The Cat only grinned when it saw Alice. It looked good-natured, she thought: still it had *very* long claws and a great many teeth, so she felt that it ought to be treated with respect.

"Cheshire-Puss," she began, rather timidly, as

she did not at all know whether it would like the name: however, it only grinned a little wider. "Come, it's pleased so far," thought Alice, and she went on. "Would you tell me, please, which way I ought to go from here?"

"That depends a good deal on where you want to get to," said the Cat.

"I don't much care where—" said Alice.

"Then it doesn't matter which way you go," said the Cat.[7]

"—so long as I get *somewhere*," Alice added as an explanation.

"Oh, you're sure to do that," said the Cat, "if you only walk long enough."

Alice felt that this could not be denied, so she tried another question. "What sort of people live about here?"

"In *that* direction," the Cat said, waving its right paw round, "lives a Hatter: and in *that* direction," waving the other paw, "lives a March Hare. Visit either you like: they're both mad."[8]

but on closer inspection turns out to be verse) he closed a P.S. with these lines:

My best love to yourself,—to your
    Mother
My kindest regards—to your small,
Fat, impertinent, ignorant brother
My hatred—I think that is all.

(Letter 21, to Maggie Cunnynghame, in *A Selection from the Letters of Lewis Carroll to His Child-friends*, edited by Evelyn M. Hatch.)

Tenniel's picture of Alice holding the pig-baby appears, with the baby redrawn as a human one, on the front of the envelope holding the Wonderland Postage-Stamp Case. This was a cardboard case designed to hold postage stamps, invented by Carroll and sold by a firm in Oxford. When you slip the case out of its envelope, you find on the front of it the same picture except that the baby has become a pig, as in Tenniel's original drawing. The back of the envelope and case provide a similar transformation from Tenniel's picture of the grinning Cheshire Cat to the picture in which the cat has mostly faded away. Slipped into the case was a tiny booklet titled *Eight or Nine Words about Letter Writing*. This delightfully written essay by Carroll opens as follows:

Some American writer has said "the snakes in this district may be divided into one species—the venomous." The same principle applies here. Postage-Stamp-Cases may be divided into one species, the "Wonderland." Imitations of it will soon appear, no doubt: but they cannot include the two Pictorial Surprises, which are copyright.

You don't see why I call them "Surprises"? Well, take the Case in your left hand, and regard it attentively. You see Alice nursing the Duchess's Baby? (An entirely new combination, by the way: it doesn't occur in the book.) Now, with your right thumb and forefinger, lay hold of the little book, and suddenly pull it out. *The Baby has turned into a Pig!* If *that* doesn't surprise you, why, I suppose you wouldn't be surprised if your own Mother-in-law suddenly turned into a Gyroscope!

Frankie Morris, in *Jabberwocky* (Autumn 1985), suggests that the baby's transformation into a pig may derive from a famous prank played on James I by the Countess of Buckingham. She arranged for His Majesty to witness the baptism of what he thought was an infant in arms but was actually a pig, an animal that James I particularly loathed.

6. In *The Nursery "Alice"* Carroll calls attention to the Fox Glove showing in the background of Tenniel's drawing for this scene (it can be seen also in the previous illustration). Foxes do not wear gloves, Carroll explains to his young readers. "The right word is 'Folk's-Gloves.' Did you ever hear that Fairies used to be called 'the good *Folk*'?"

7. These remarks are among the most quoted passages in the *Alice* books. An echo is heard in Jack Kerouac's novel *On the Road*:

". . . we gotta go and never stop going till we get there."

"Where we going, man?"

"I don't know but we gotta go."

John Kemeny places Alice's question, and the Cat's famous answer, at the head of his chapter on science and values in *A Philosopher Looks at Science*, 1959. In fact each chapter of Kemeny's book is preceded by an appropriate quote from *Alice*. The Cat's answer expresses very precisely the eternal cleavage between science and ethics. As Kemeny makes clear, science cannot tell us where to go,

"But I don't want to go among mad people," Alice remarked.

"Oh, you ca'n't help that," said the Cat: "we're all mad here. I'm mad. You're mad."[9]

"How do you know I'm mad?" said Alice.

"You must be," said the Cat, "or you wouldn't have come here."

Alice didn't think that proved it at all: however, she went on: "And how do you know that you're mad?"

"To begin with," said the Cat, "a dog's not mad. You grant that?"

"I suppose so," said Alice.

"Well, then," the Cat went on, "you see a dog growls when it's angry, and wags its tail when it's pleased. Now *I* growl when I'm pleased, and wag my tail when I'm angry. Therefore I'm mad."

"*I* call it purring, not growling," said Alice.

"Call it what you like," said the Cat. "Do you play croquet with the Queen to-day?"

"I should like it very much," said Alice, "but I haven't been invited yet."

"You'll see me there," said the Cat, and vanished.

Alice was not much surprised at this, she was getting so well used to queer things happening. While she was still looking at the place where it had been, it suddenly appeared again.

"By-the-bye, what became of the baby?" said the Cat. "I'd nearly forgotten to ask."

"It turned into a pig," Alice answered very quietly, just as if the Cat had come back in a natural way.

"I thought it would," said the Cat, and vanished again.

Alice waited a little, half expecting to see it again, but it did not appear, and after a minute

or two she walked on in the direction in which the March Hare was said to live. "I've seen hatters before," she said to herself: "the March Hare will be much the most interesting, and perhaps, as this is May, it wo'n't be raving mad—at least not so mad as it was in March." As she said this, she looked up, and there was the Cat again, sitting on a branch of a tree.[10]

"Did you say 'pig', or 'fig'?" said the Cat.

"I said 'pig'," replied Alice; "and I wish you wouldn't keep appearing and vanishing so suddenly: you make one quite giddy!"

"All right," said the Cat; and this time it vanished quite slowly, beginning with the end of the tail, and ending with the grin, which remained some time after the rest of it had gone.

"Well! I've often seen a cat without a grin," thought Alice; "but a grin without a cat! It's the most curious thing I ever saw in all my life!"[11]

She had not gone much farther before she came in sight of the house of the March Hare: she thought it must be the right house, because the chimneys were shaped like ears and the roof was thatched with fur. It was so large a house, that she did not like to go nearer till she had nibbled some more of the left-hand bit of mush-

but after this decision is made on other grounds, it *can* tell us the best way to get there.

I am told there is a passage in the Talmud that says: "If you don't know where you are going, any road will take you there."

8. The phrases "mad as a hatter" and "mad as a March hare" were common at the time Carroll wrote, and of course that was why he created the two characters. "Mad as a hatter" may have been a corruption of the earlier "mad as an adder" but more likely owes its origin to the fact that until recently hatters actually did go mad. The mercury used in curing felt (there are now laws against its use in most states and in parts of Europe) was a common cause of mercury poisoning. Victims developed a tremor called "hatter's shakes," which affected their eyes and limbs and addled their speech. In advanced stages they developed hallucinations and other psychotic symptoms.

"Did the Mad Hatter Have Mercury Poisoning?" is the title of an article by H. A. Waldron in *The British Medical Journal* (December 24–31, 1983). Dr. Waldron argues that the Mad Hatter was not such a victim, but Dr. Selwyn Goodacre and two other physicians dispute this in the January 28, 1984, issue.

Two British scientists, Anthony Holley and Paul Greenwood, reported (in *Nature*, June 7, 1984) on extensive observations that fail to support a folk belief that male hares go into a frenzy during the March rutting season. The main behavior of hares throughout their entire eight-month breeding period consists in males chasing females, then getting into boxing matches with them. March is no different from any other month. It was Erasmus who wrote

"Mad as a marsh hare." The scientists think "marsh" got corrupted to "March" in later decades.

When Tenniel drew the March Hare he showed wisps of straw on the hare's head. Carroll does not mention this, but at the time it was a symbol, both in art and on the stage, of madness. In *The Nursery "Alice"* Carroll writes, "That's the March Hare with the long ears, and straws mixed up with his hair. The straws showed he was mad—I don't know why." For more on this, see Michael Hancher's chapter on straw as a sign of insanity in *The Tenniel Illustrations to the "Alice" Books*. In Harry Furniss's drawings of the Mad Gardener in Carroll's *Sylvie and Bruno* books you'll see similar straw in the Gardener's hair and clothing.

The Hatter and the Hare appear at least twice in *Finnegans Wake*: "Hatters hares" (page 83, line 1, of the Viking revised edition, 1959), and "hitters hairs" (page 84, line 28).

9. Compare the Cheshire Cat's remarks with the following entry, of February 9, 1856, in Carroll's diary:

Query: when we are dreaming and, as often happens, have a dim consciousness of the fact and try to wake, do we not say and do things which in waking life would be insane? May we not then sometimes define insanity as an inability to distinguish which is the waking and which the sleeping life? We often dream without the least suspicion of unreality: "Sleep hath its own world," and it is often as lifelike as the other.

In Plato's *Theaetetus*, Socrates and Theaetetus discuss this topic as follows:

THEAETETUS: I certainly cannot undertake to argue that madmen or dreamers think truly, when they imagine, some of

room, and raised herself to about two feet high: even then she walked up towards it rather timidly, saying to herself "Suppose it should be raving mad after all! I almost wish I'd gone to see the Hatter instead!"

them that they are gods, and others that they can fly, and are flying in their sleep.

SOCRATES: Do you see another question which can be raised about these phenomena, notably about dreaming and waking?

THEAETETUS: What question?

SOCRATES: A question which I think that you must often have heard persons ask: how can you determine whether at this moment we are sleeping, and all our thoughts are a dream; or whether we are awake, and talking to one another in the waking state?

THEAETETUS: Indeed, Socrates, I do not know how to prove the one any more than the other, for in both cases the facts precisely correspond; and there is no difficulty in supposing that during all this discussion we have been talking to one another in a dream; and when in a dream we seem to be narrating dreams, the resemblance of the two states is quite astonishing.

SOCRATES: You see, then, that a doubt about the reality of sense is easily raised, since there may even be a doubt whether we are awake or in a dream. And as our time is equally divided between sleeping and waking, in either sphere of existence the soul contends that the thoughts which are present to our minds at the time are true; and during one half of our lives we affirm the truth of the one, and, during the other half, of the other; and are equally confident of both.

THEAETETUS: Most true.

SOCRATES: And may not the same be said of madness and the other disorders?

The difference is only that the times are not equal.

(Cf. Chapter 12, Note 9, and *Through the Looking-Glass*, Chapter 4, Note 10.)

10. Selwyn Goodacre has observed that although Alice had "walked on," Tenniel shows the Cheshire Cat, when it reappears, sitting in the same tree as before. This enabled Carroll, in his *Nursery "Alice,"* to add a bit of paper-folding whimsy. Tenniel's two pictures were placed on left-hand pages so that (in Carroll's words) "if you turn up the corner of this leaf, you'll have Alice looking at the Grin: and she doesn't look a bit more frightened than when she was looking at the Cat, *does* she?"

11. The phrase "grin without a cat" is not a bad description of pure mathematics. Although mathematical theorems often can be usefully applied to the structure of the external world, the theorems themselves are abstractions that belong in another realm "remote from human passions," as Bertrand Russell once put it in a memorable passage, "remote even from the pitiful facts of Nature . . . an ordered cosmos, where pure thought can dwell as in its natural home, and where one, at least, of our nobler impulses can escape from the dreary exile of the actual world."

7

A Mad Tea-Party

1. There is good reason to believe that Tenniel adopted a suggestion of Carroll's that he draw the Hatter to resemble one Theophilus Carter, a furniture dealer near Oxford (and no grounds whatever for the widespread belief at the time that the Hatter was a burlesque of Prime Minister Gladstone). Carter was known in the area as the Mad Hatter, partly because he always wore a top hat and partly because of his eccentric ideas. His invention of an "alarm clock bed" that woke the sleeper by tossing him out on the floor (it was exhibited at the Crystal Palace in 1851) may help explain why Carroll's Hatter is so concerned with time as well as with arousing a sleepy dormouse. One notes also that items of furniture—table, armchair, writing desk—are prominent in this episode.

The Hatter, Hare, and Dormouse do not appear in *Alice's Adventures Under Ground*; the entire chapter was a later addition to the tale. The Hare and Hatter reappear as the King's messengers, Haigha and Hatta, in Chapter 6 of *Through the Looking-Glass*. In Paramount's 1933 motion picture of *Alice*, Edward Everett Horton was the Hatter, Charles Ruggles the March Hare. Ed Wynn supplied the Hatter's voice in Walt Disney's 1951 animation, and Jerry Colonna spoke the part of the Hare.

There was a table set out under a tree in front of the house, and the March Hare and the Hatter[1] were having tea at it: a Dormouse[2] was sitting between them, fast asleep, and the other two were using it as a cushion, resting their elbows on it, and talking over its head. "Very uncomfortable for the Dormouse," thought Alice; "only as it's asleep, I suppose it doesn't mind."

The table was a large one, but the three were all crowded together at one corner of it. "No room! No room!" they cried out when they saw Alice coming. "There's *plenty* of room!" said Alice indignantly, and she sat down in a large arm-chair at one end of the table.

"Have some wine," the March Hare said in an encouraging tone.

Alice looked all round the table, but there was nothing on it but tea.[3] "I don't see any wine," she remarked.

"There isn't any," said the March Hare.

"Then it wasn't very civil of you to offer it," said Alice angrily.

"It wasn't very civil of you to sit down without being invited," said the March Hare.

"I didn't know it was *your* table," said Alice: "it's laid for a great many more than three."

"Your hair wants cutting,"[4] said the Hatter. He had been looking at Alice for some time with great curiosity, and this was his first speech.

"You should learn not to make personal remarks," Alice said with some severity: "it's very rude."

The Hatter opened his eyes very wide on hearing this; but all he *said* was "Why is a raven like a writing-desk?"[5]

"Come, we shall have some fun now!" thought Alice. "I'm glad they've begun asking riddles—I believe I can guess that," she added aloud.

"Do you mean that you think you can find out the answer to it?" said the March Hare.

"Exactly so," said Alice.

"Then you should say what you mean," the March Hare went on.

"I do," Alice hastily replied; "at least—at least I mean what I say—that's the same thing, you know."

"Not the same thing a bit!" said the Hatter. "Why, you might just as well say that 'I see what I eat' is the same thing as 'I eat what I see'!"

"You might just as well say," added the

"It is impossible to describe Bertrand Russell," writes Norbert Wiener in Chapter 14 of his autobiography *Ex-Prodigy*, "except by saying that he looks like the Mad Hatter . . . the caricature of Tenniel almost argues an anticipation on the part of the artist." Wiener goes on to point out the likenesses of philosophers J. M. E. McTaggart and G. E. Moore, two of Russell's fellow dons at Cambridge, to the Dormouse and March Hare respectively. The three men were known in the community as the Mad Tea Party of Trinity.

Ellis Hillman, writing on "Who Was the Mad Hatter?" in *Jabberwocky* (Winter 1973), provides a new candidate: Samuel Ogden, a Manchester hatter known as "Mad Sam," who in 1814 designed a special hat for the czar of Russia when he visited London.

Hillman also conjectures that "Mad Hatter," if the *H* is dropped, sounds like "Mad Adder." This, he writes, could be taken as describing a mathematician, such as Carroll himself, or perhaps Charles Babbage, a Cambridge mathematician widely regarded as slightly mad in his efforts to build a complicated mechanical calculating machine.

Hugh Rawson, in *Devious Derivations* (1994) writes that Thackeray used the phrase "mad as a hatter" in *Pendennis* (1849). So did Thomas Chandler Haliburton, a Nova Scotia judge, in *The Clockmaker* (1837): "Sister Sal . . . walked out of the room, as mad as a hatter."

2. The British dormouse is a tree-living rodent that resembles a small squirrel much more than it does a mouse. The name is from the Latin *dormire*, to sleep, and has reference to the animal's habit of winter hibernation. Unlike the squirrel, the dormouse is nocturnal, so that even

in May (the month of Alice's adventure) it remains in a torpid state throughout the day. In *Some Reminiscences of William Michael Rossetti* (1906) we are told that the dormouse may have been modeled after Dante Gabriel Rossetti's pet wombat, which had a habit of sleeping on the table. Carroll knew all the Rossettis and occasionally visited them.

Dr. Selwyn Goodacre noticed that the dormouse is sexless at the tea party, but is revealed as male in Chapter 11.

A British correspondent, J. Little, sent me the stamp shown below which pictures the British dormouse as an endangered species. The stamp was issued in January 1998.

Decline in distribution

20 **ENDANGERED SPECIES**
Common dormouse
Muscardinus avellanarius

3. Both Carroll and Tenniel apparently forgot that a milk jug was also on the table. We know this because later on in the tea party the Dormouse upsets it.

4. In *Under the Quizzing Glass*, R. B. Shaberman and Denis Crutch point out that no one would tell a Victorian little girl that her hair was too long, but the remark *would* apply to Carroll. In Isa Bowman's *The Story of Lewis Carroll* (J. M. Dent, 1899), the actress and former child-friend

March Hare, "that 'I like what I get' is the same thing as 'I get what I like'!"

"You might just as well say," added the Dormouse, which seemed to be talking in its sleep, "that 'I breathe when I sleep' is the same thing as 'I sleep when I breathe'!"

"It *is* the same thing with you," said the Hatter, and here the conversation dropped, and the party sat silent for a minute, while Alice thought over all she could remember about ravens and writing-desks, which wasn't much.

The Hatter was the first to break the silence. "What day of the month is it?" he said, turning to Alice: he had taken his watch out of his pocket, and was looking at it uneasily, shaking it every now and then, and holding it to his ear.

Alice considered a little, and then said "The fourth."[6]

"Two days wrong!" sighed the Hatter. "I told you butter wouldn't suit the works!" he added, looking angrily at the March Hare.

"It was the *best* butter," the March Hare meekly replied.

"Yes, but some crumbs must have got in as well," the Hatter grumbled: "you shouldn't have put it in with the bread-knife."

The March Hare took the watch and looked at it gloomily: then he dipped it into his cup of tea, and looked at it again: but he could think of nothing better to say than his first remark, "It was the *best* butter, you know."

Alice had been looking over his shoulder with some curiosity. "What a funny watch!"[7] she remarked. "It tells the day of the month, and doesn't tell what o'clock it is!"

"Why should it?" muttered the Hatter. "Does *your* watch tell you what year it is?"

"Of course not," Alice replied very readily:

"but that's because it stays the same year for such a long time together."

"Which is just the case with *mine*," said the Hatter.

Alice felt dreadfully puzzled. The Hatter's remark seemed to her to have no sort of meaning in it, and yet it was certainly English. "I don't quite understand you," she said, as politely as she could.

"The Dormouse is asleep again," said the Hatter, and he poured a little hot tea upon its nose.

The Dormouse shook its head impatiently, and said, without opening its eyes, "Of course, of course: just what I was going to remark myself."

"Have you guessed the riddle yet?" the Hatter said, turning to Alice again.

"No, I give it up," Alice replied. "What's the answer?"

"I haven't the slightest idea," said the Hatter.

"Nor I," said the March Hare.

Alice sighed wearily. "I think you might do something better with the time," she said, "than wasting it in asking riddles that have no answers."

"If you knew Time as well as I do," said the Hatter, "you wouldn't talk about wasting *it*. It's *him*."

"I don't know what you mean," said Alice.

"Of course you don't!" the Hatter said, tossing his head contemptuously. "I dare say you never even spoke to Time!"

"Perhaps not," Alice cautiously replied; "but I know I have to beat time when I learn music."

"Ah! That accounts for it," said the Hatter. "He wo'n't stand beating. Now, if you only kept on good terms with him, he'd do almost

recalls: "Lewis Carroll was a man of medium height. When I knew him his hair was silvery-grey, rather longer than it was the fashion to wear, and his eyes were a deep blue."

5. The Mad Hatter's famous unanswered riddle was the object of much parlor speculation in Carroll's time. His own answer (given in a new preface that he wrote for the 1896 edition) is as follows:

Enquiries have been so often addressed to me, as to whether any answer to the Hatter's Riddle can be imagined, that I may as well put on record here what seems to me to be a fairly appropriate answer, viz: "Because it can produce a few notes, tho they are *very* flat; and it is never put with the wrong end in front!" This, however, is merely an afterthought; the Riddle, as originally invented, had no answer at all.

Other answers have been proposed, notably by Sam Loyd, the American puzzle genius, in his posthumous *Cyclopedia of Puzzles* (1914), page 114. In keeping with Carroll's alliterative style Loyd offers as his best solution: because the notes for which they are noted are not noted for being musical notes. Other Loyd suggestions: because Poe wrote on both; bills and tales are among their characteristics; because they both stand on their legs, conceal their steels (steals), and ought to be made to shut up.

In 1989 England's Lewis Carroll Society announced a contest for new answers, to be published eventually in the society's newsletter, *Bandersnatch*.

Aldous Huxley, writing on "Ravens and Writing Desks" (*Vanity Fair*, September 1928), supplies two nonsense answers: because there's a *b* in both, and because there's an *n* in neither. James Michie sent a similar answer: because each begins with *e*.

Huxley defends the view that such metaphysical questions as: Does God exist? Do we have free will? Why is there suffering? are as meaningless as the Mad Hatter's question—"nonsensical riddles, questions not about reality but about words."

"Both have quills dipped in ink" was suggested by reader David B. Jodrey, Jr. Cyril Pearson, in his undated *Twentieth Century Standard Puzzle Book*, suggests, "Because it slopes with a flap."

Denis Crutch (*Jabberwocky*, Winter 1976) reported an astonishing discovery. In the 1896 edition of *Alice*, Carroll wrote a new preface in which he gave what he considered the best answer to the riddle: "Because it can produce a few notes, tho they are *very* flat; and it is nevar put with the wrong end in front." Note the spelling of "never" as "nevar." Carroll clearly intended to spell "raven" backwards. The word was corrected to "never" in all later printings, perhaps by an editor who fancied he had caught a printer's error. Because Carroll died soon after this "correction" destroyed the ingenuity of his answer, the original spelling was never restored. Whether Carroll was aware of the damage done to his clever answer is not known.

In 1991 *The Spectator*, in England, asked for answers to the Hatter's riddle as its competition No. 1683. The winners, listed on July 6, are as follows:

Because without them both *Brave New World* could not have been written.
(Roy Davenport)

Because one has flapping fits and the other fitting flaps. (Peter Veale)

Because one is good for writing books and the other better for biting rooks.
(George Simmers)

anything you liked with the clock. For instance, suppose it were nine o'clock in the morning, just time to begin lessons: you'd only have to whisper a hint to Time, and round goes the clock in a twinkling! Half-past one, time for dinner!"

("I only wish it was," the March Hare said to itself in a whisper.)

"That would be grand, certainly," said Alice thoughtfully; "but then—I shouldn't be hungry for it, you know."

"Not at first, perhaps," said the Hatter: "but you could keep it to half-past one as long as you liked."

"Is that the way *you* manage?" Alice asked.

The Hatter shook his head mournfully. "Not I!" he replied. "We quarrelled last March—just before *he* went mad, you know—" (pointing with his teaspoon at the March Hare,) "—it was at the great concert given by the Queen of Hearts, and I had to sing[8]

'Twinkle, twinkle, little bat!
How I wonder what you're at!'

You know the song, perhaps?"

"I've heard something like it," said Alice.

"It goes on, you know," the Hatter continued, "in this way:—

> 'Up above the world you fly
> Like a tea-tray in the sky.
>   Twinkle, twinkle—'"

Here the Dormouse shook itself, and began singing in its sleep "*Twinkle, twinkle, twinkle, twinkle—*" and went on so long that they had to pinch it to make it stop.

"Well, I'd hardly finished the first verse," said the Hatter, "when the Queen bawled out 'He's murdering the time![9] Off with his head!'"

"How dreadfully savage!" exclaimed Alice.

"And ever since that," the Hatter went on in a mournful tone, "he wo'n't do a thing I ask! It's always six o'clock now."

A bright idea came into Alice's head. "Is that the reason so many tea-things are put out here?" she asked.

"Yes, that's it," said the Hatter with a sigh: "it's always tea-time,[10] and we've no time to wash the things between whiles."

"Then you keep moving round, I suppose?" said Alice.

"Exactly so," said the Hatter: "as the things get used up."

"But what happens when you come to the beginning again?" Alice ventured to ask.

"Suppose we change the subject," the March Hare interrupted, yawning. "I'm getting tired of this. I vote the young lady tells us a story."

"I'm afraid I don't know one," said Alice, rather alarmed at the proposal.

"Then the Dormouse shall!" they both cried.

Because a writing-desk is a rest for pens and a raven is a pest for wrens.

(Tony Weston)

Because "raven" contains five letters, which you might equally well expect to find in a writing-desk. (Roger Baresel)

Because they are both used to carri-on decomposition. (Noel Petty)

Because they both tend to present unkind bills. (M.R. Macintyre)

Because they both have a flap in oak.

(J. Tebbutt)

Here are two more answers by Francis Huxley, author of *The Raven and the Writing Desk* (1976):

Because it bodes ill for owed bills.
Because they each contain a river—Neva and Esk.

6. Alice's remark that the day is the fourth, coupled with the previous chapter's revelation that the month is May, establishes the date of Alice's underground adventure as May 4. May 4, 1852, was Alice Liddell's birthday. She was ten in 1862, the year Carroll first told and recorded the story, but her age in the story is almost certainly seven (see Chapter 1, Note 1, of *Through the Looking-Glass*). On the last page of the hand-lettered manuscript, *Alice's Adventures Under Ground*, which Carroll gave to Alice, he pasted a photograph of her that he had taken in 1859, when she was seven.

In his book *The White Knight*, A. L. Taylor reports that on May 4, 1862, there was exactly two days' difference between the lunar and calendar months. This, Taylor argues, suggests that the Mad Hatter's watch ran on lunar time and accounts for his remark that his watch is "two days wrong." If Wonderland is near the earth's center, Taylor points out, the position of the sun would be useless for time-telling, whereas phases of the moon remain unambiguous. The conjecture is also supported by the close connection of "lunar" with "lunacy," but it is hard to believe that Carroll had all this in mind.

7. An even funnier watch is the Outlandish Watch owned by the German professor in Chapter 23 of *Sylvie and Bruno*. Setting its hands back in time has the result of setting events themselves back to the time indicated by the hands; an interesting anticipation of H. G. Wells's *The Time Machine*. But that is not all. Pressing a "reversal peg" on the Outlandish Watch starts events moving *backward*; a kind of looking-glass reversal of time's linear dimension.

One is reminded also of an earlier piece by Carroll in which he proves that a stopped clock is more accurate than one that loses a minute a day. The first clock is exactly right twice every twenty-four hours, whereas the other clock is exactly right only once in two years. "You *might* go on to ask," Carroll adds, "'How am I to know when eight o'clock *does* come? My clock will not tell me.' Be patient: you know that when eight o'clock comes your clock is right; very good; then your rule is this: keep your eyes fixed on the clock and the *very moment it is right* it will be eight o'clock."

8. The Hatter's song parodies the first verse of Jane Taylor's well-known poem, "The Star."

Twinkle, twinkle, little star,
How I wonder what you are!
Up above the world so high,
Like a diamond in the sky.

"Wake up, Dormouse!" And they pinched it on both sides at once.

The Dormouse slowly opened its eyes. "I wasn't asleep," it said in a hoarse, feeble voice, "I heard every word you fellows were saying."

"Tell us a story!" said the March Hare.

"Yes, please do!" pleaded Alice.

"And be quick about it," added the Hatter, "or you'll be asleep again before it's done."

"Once upon a time there were three little sisters," the Dormouse began in a great hurry; "and their names were Elsie, Lacie, and Tillie;[11] and they lived at the bottom of a well—"

"What did they live on?" said Alice, who always took a great interest in questions of eating and drinking.

"They lived on treacle,"[12] said the Dormouse, after thinking a minute or two.

"They couldn't have done that, you know," Alice gently remarked. "They'd have been ill."

"So they were," said the Dormouse; "*very* ill."

Alice tried a little to fancy to herself what such an extraordinary way of living would be like, but it puzzled her too much: so she went on: "But why did they live at the bottom of a well?"

"Take some more tea," the March Hare said to Alice, very earnestly.

"I've had nothing yet," Alice replied in an offended tone: "so I ca'n't take more."

"You mean you ca'n't take *less*," said the Hatter: "it's very easy to take *more* than nothing."

"Nobody asked *your* opinion," said Alice.

"Who's making personal remarks now?" the Hatter asked triumphantly.

Alice did not quite know what to say to this: so she helped herself to some tea and bread-and-butter, and then turned to the Dormouse, and repeated her question. "Why did they live at the bottom of a well?"

The Dormouse again took a minute or two to think about it, and then said "It was a treacle-well."

"There's no such thing!" Alice was beginning very angrily, but the Hatter and the March Hare went "Sh! Sh!" and the Dormouse sulkily remarked "If you ca'n't be civil, you'd better finish the story for yourself."

"No, please go on!" Alice said very humbly. "I wo'n't interrupt you again. I dare say there may be *one*."

"One, indeed!" said the Dormouse indignantly. However, he consented to go on. "And so these three little sisters—they were learning to draw, you know—"

"What did they draw?" said Alice, quite forgetting her promise.

"Treacle," said the Dormouse, without considering at all, this time.

"I want a clean cup," interrupted the Hatter: "let's all move one place on."

He moved on as he spoke, and the Dormouse followed him: the March Hare moved into the Dormouse's place, and Alice rather unwillingly took the place of the March Hare. The Hatter was the only one who got any advantage from the change; and Alice was a good deal worse off than before, as the March Hare had just upset the milk-jug into his plate.

Alice did not wish to offend the Dormouse again, so she began very cautiously: "But I don't understand. Where did they draw the treacle from?"

"You can draw water out of a water-well," said the Hatter; "so I should think you could draw treacle out of a treacle-well—eh, stupid?"

When the blazing sun is gone,
When he nothing shines upon,
Then you show your little light,
Twinkle, twinkle, all the night.

Then the traveller in the dark
Thanks you for your tiny spark:
He could not see which way to go,
If you did not twinkle so.

In the dark blue sky you keep,
And often through my curtains peep,
For you never shut your eye
Till the sun is in the sky.

As your bright and tiny spark
Lights the traveller in the dark,
Though, I know not what you are,
Twinkle, twinkle, little star.

Carroll's burlesque may contain what professional comics call an "inside joke." Bartholomew Price, a distinguished professor of mathematics at Oxford and a good friend of Carroll's, was known among his students by the nickname "The Bat." His lectures no doubt had a way of soaring high above the heads of his listeners.

Carroll's parody may also owe something to an incident that Helmut Gernsheim recounts in *Lewis Carroll: Photographer* (Chanticleer, 1949):

At Christ Church the usually staid don relaxed in the company of little visitors to his large suite of rooms—a veritable children's paradise. There was a wonderful array of dolls and toys, a distorting mirror, a clockwork bear, and a flying bat made by him. This latter was the cause of much embarrassment when, on a hot summer afternoon, after circling the room several times, it suddenly flew out of the window and landed on a tea-tray which a college servant was just carrying across Tom Quad. Startled by this strange apparition, he dropped the tray with a great clatter.

9. "Murdering the time": Mangling the song's meter.

10. This was written before five-o'clock tea had become the general custom in England. It was intended to refer to the fact that the Liddells sometimes served tea at six o'clock, the children's suppertime. Arthur Stanley Eddington, as well as less distinguished writers on relativity theory, have compared the Mad Tea Party, where it is always six o'clock, with that portion of De Sitter's model of the cosmos in which time stands eternally still. (See Chapter 10 of Eddington's *Space Time and Gravitation*.)

11. The three little sisters are the three Liddell sisters. Elsie is L.C. (Lorina Charlotte), Tillie refers to Edith's family nickname Matilda, and Lacie is an anagram of Alice.

This is the second time that Carroll has punned on the word "Liddell." His first play with the sound similarity of "Liddell" and "little" is in the first stanza of his prefatory poem where "little" is used three times to refer to the "cruel Three" of the next stanza. We know how "Liddell" was pronounced because in Carroll's day the students at Oxford composed the following couplet:

I am the Dean and this is Mrs. Liddell.
She plays the first, and I the second fiddle.

For some reason Tenniel did not draw the three sisters. Peter Newell's picture of them at the bottom of the well is on page 90 of my *More Annotated Alice*.

12. *Treacle* is British for "molasses." Vivien Greene (wife of novelist Graham Greene), who lives in Oxford, was the first to inform me—later Mrs. Henry A. Morss, Jr.,

"But they were *in* the well," Alice said to the Dormouse, not choosing to notice this last remark.

"Of course they were," said the Dormouse: "well in."

This answer so confused poor Alice, that she let the Dormouse go on for some time without interrupting it.

"They were learning to draw," the Dormouse went on, yawning and rubbing its eyes, for it was getting very sleepy; "and they drew all manner of things—everything that begins with an M—"

"Why with an M?" said Alice.

"Why not?" said the March Hare.[13]

Alice was silent.

The Dormouse had closed its eyes by this time, and was going off into a doze; but, on being pinched by the Hatter, it woke up again with a little shriek, and went on: "—that begins with an M, such as mouse-traps, and the moon, and memory, and muchness—you know you say things are 'much of a muchness'[14]—did you ever see such a thing as a drawing of a muchness!"

"Really, now you ask me," said Alice, very much confused, "I don't think—"

"Then you shouldn't talk," said the Hatter.

This piece of rudeness was more than Alice could bear: she got up in great disgust, and walked off: the Dormouse fell asleep instantly, and neither of the others took the least notice of her going, though she looked back once or twice, half hoping that they would call after her: the last time she saw them, they were trying to put the Dormouse into the teapot.[15]

"At any rate I'll never go *there* again!" said Alice, as she picked her way through the wood. "It's the stupidest tea-party I ever was at in all my life!"[16]

Just as she said this, she noticed that one of the trees had a door leading right into it. "That's very curious!" she thought. "But everything's curious today. I think I may as well go in at once." And in she went.

Once more she found herself in the long hall, and close to the little glass table. "Now, I'll manage better this time," she said to herself, and began by taking the little golden key, and unlocking the door that led into the garden. Then she set to work nibbling at the mushroom (she had kept a piece of it in her pocket) till she was about a foot high: then she walked down the little passage: and *then*—she found herself at last in the beautiful garden, among the bright flower-beds and the cool fountains.

of Massachusetts, sent similar information—that what was called a "treacle well" actually existed in Carroll's time in Binsey, near Oxford. *Treacle* originally referred to medicinal compounds given for snakebites, poisons and various diseases. Wells believed to contain water of medicinal value were sometimes called "treacle wells." This adds of course to the meaning of the Dormouse's remark, a few lines later, that the sisters were "very ill."

Mavis Batey, in *Alice's Adventures in Oxford* (A Pitkin Pictorial Guide, 1980), tells the eighth-century legend of the Binsey well. It seems that God struck King Algar blind because he pursued the princess Frideswide with the intent to marry her. Her prayer to Saint Margaret for mercy on the king was answered by the appearance of a well at Binsey with miraculous waters that cured Algar's blindness. Saint Frideswide returned to Oxford, where she supposedly founded a nunnery at the spot where Christ Church now stands. The treacle well was a popular healing spot throughout the Middle Ages.

An amusing instance of the earlier meaning of *treacle* is provided by a famous "Curious Bible" printed in 1568 and known as the Treacle Bible. (*Curious Bible* is a generic term for Bibles that contain peculiar printer's errors or strange choices of words made by an editor. In the King James Bible, Jeremiah 8:22 begins: "Is there no balm in Gilead . . .?" In the Treacle Bible it reads: "Is there not treacle at Gilead?"

In the Latin Chapel of Christ Church Cathedral, a stained-glass window (reproduced in color in Mrs. Batey's booklet) depicts a group of ailing persons on their way to the Binsey treacle well.

13. Henry Holiday, who illustrated Carroll's *Hunting of the Snark*, recalled in a letter asking Carroll why all the names of the ship's crew members begin with *B*. Carroll replied, "Why not?"

Note that it is the March Hare, not the Dormouse, who answers Alice's question. As Selwyn Goodacre has pointed out, "his own name begins with an *M* as well, and he wanted to be part of the story."

Selwyn Goodacre also called my attention to the fact that because "molasses" begins with *m*, it was appropriate that the girls "draw" treacle from the well.

14. "Much of a muchness" is still a colloquial British phrase meaning that two or more things are very much alike, or have the same value; or it may refer to any sort of all-pervading sameness in a situation.

15. I am indebted to Roger Green for the surprising information that Victorian children actually had dormice as pets, keeping them in old teapots filled with grass or hay.

16. A scene based on the Mad Tea Party was one of the earliest to be constructed for a rapidly developing new technology called "virtual reality." A person puts on a helmet with goggles that provide each eye with a video screen connected to a computer program. The subject also wears headphones, and a special suit and gloves fitted with fiber-optic sensors that tell the computer how one's body and hands are moving, and how those motions alter the visual scene. One is thus able to see and move about in a three-dimensional artificial "space." A person can take the role of Alice, or any of the other characters at the Mad Tea Party, and, as the technology improves, should even be able to interact with the characters. See "On the Road to the Global Village," by Karen Wright (*Scientific American*, March 1990), and "Artificial Reality," by G. Pascal Zachary (*Wall Street Journal*, January 23, 1990, page 1).

8

The Queen's Croquet-Ground

A large rose-tree stood near the entrance of the garden: the roses growing on it were white, but there were three gardeners at it, busily painting them red. Alice thought this a very curious thing, and she went nearer to watch them, and, just as she came up to them, she heard one of them say "Look out now, Five! Don't go splashing paint over me like that!"

"I couldn't help it," said Five, in a sulky tone. "Seven jogged my elbow."

On which Seven looked up and said "That's right, Five! Always lay the blame on others!"

"*You'd* better not talk!" said Five. "I heard the Queen say only yesterday you deserved to be beheaded."

"What for?" said the one who had spoken first.

"That's none of *your* business, Two!" said Seven.

"Yes, it *is* his business!" said Five. "And I'll tell him—it was for bringing the cook tulip-roots instead of onions."[1]

Seven flung down his brush, and had just begun "Well, of all the unjust things—" when his eye chanced to fall upon Alice, as she stood watching them, and he checked himself suddenly: the others looked round also, and all of them bowed low.

1. Bruce Bevan wrote to say that Carroll may have had in mind here an incident described in the chapter on tulip mania in Charles Mackay's 1841 work *Extraordinary Popular Delusions and the Madness of Crowds*. An English traveler in Holland, unaware of the high prices then being paid for rare species of tulips, picked up a tulip root, thinking it an onion, and began to peel it. As it happened, the root was worth four thousand florins. The poor man was arrested and sent to prison until he found the means to pay this sum to the tulip root's owner.

"Would you tell me, please," said Alice, a little timidly, "why you are painting those roses?"

Five and Seven said nothing, but looked at Two. Two began, in a low voice, "Why, the fact is, you see, Miss, this here ought to have been a *red* rose-tree, and we put a white one in by mistake; and, if the Queen was to find it out, we should all have our heads cut off, you know. So you see, Miss, we're doing our best, afore she comes, to—" At this moment, Five, who had been anxiously looking across the garden, called out "The Queen! The Queen!" and the three gardeners instantly threw themselves flat upon their faces. There was a sound of many footsteps, and Alice looked round, eager to see the Queen.

First came ten soldiers carrying clubs: these were all shaped like the three gardeners, oblong and flat, with their hands and feet at the corners: next the ten courtiers: these were ornamented all over with diamonds, and walked two and two, as the soldiers did. After these came the royal children: there were ten of them, and the little dears came jumping merrily along, hand in hand, in couples: they were all ornamented with hearts.[2] Next came the guests, mostly Kings and Queens, and among them Alice recognized the White Rabbit: it was talking in a hurried nervous manner, smiling at everything that was said, and went by without noticing her. Then followed the Knave of Hearts, carrying the King's crown on a crimson velvet cushion; and, last of all this grand procession, came THE KING AND THE QUEEN OF HEARTS.[3]

Alice was rather doubtful whether she ought not to lie down on her face like the three gardeners, but she could not remember ever having heard of such a rule at processions; "and besides, what would be the use of a procession," thought she, "if people had all to lie down on their faces, so that they couldn't see it?" So she stood where she was, and waited.

When the procession came opposite to Alice, they all stopped and looked at her, and the Queen said, severely, "Who is this?" She said it to the Knave of Hearts, who only bowed and smiled in reply.

"Idiot!" said the Queen, tossing her head impatiently; and, turning to Alice, she went on: "What's your name, child?"

"My name is Alice, so please your Majesty," said Alice very politely; but she added, to herself, "Why, they're only a pack of cards, after all. I needn't be afraid of them!"

"And who are *these*?" said the Queen, pointing to the three gardeners who were lying round the rose-tree; for, you see, as they were lying on their faces, and the pattern on their backs was the same as the rest of the pack, she could not tell

2. Among the spot cards the spades are the gardeners, the clubs are soldiers, diamonds are courtiers, and the hearts are the ten royal children. The court cards are of course members of the court. Note how cleverly throughout this chapter Carroll has linked the behavior of his animated cards with the behavior of actual playing cards. They lie flat on their faces, they cannot be identified from their backs, they are easily turned over, and they bend themselves into croquet arches.

Mrs. Dave Alexander, reading my *More Annotated Alice*, noticed that Peter Newell made the mistake of showing the gardeners as hearts instead of spades.

3. Tenniel's illustration of this garden scene is admirably analyzed in Michael Hancher's book on Tenniel. The Knave, his nose slightly shaded (see Chapter 12, Note 7), is carrying England's official St. Edward's crown. The heads of the King of Hearts and the Knave of Hearts (one of the two one-eyed jacks, as they are known to cardplayers) are of course based on playing cards. Left of the King of Hearts you see the faces of the King of Spades and the King of Clubs, and the one-eyed King of Diamonds, facing east instead of his customary west.

The Queen of Hearts wears a dress patterned like the dress of a queen of spades. Was Tenniel, Hancher asks, identifying her with a card traditionally associated with death? Note the glass dome of a conservatory in the far background.

Puzzle: Find the White Rabbit in the picture.

4. "I pictured to myself the Queen of Hearts," Carroll wrote in his article "*Alice* on the Stage" (cited in previous notes), "as a sort of embodiment of ungovernable passion—a blind and aimless Fury." Her constant orders for beheadings are shocking to those modern critics of children's literature who feel that juvenile fiction should be free of all violence and especially violence with Freudian undertones. Even the Oz books of L. Frank Baum, so singularly free of the horrors to be found in Grimm and Andersen, contain many scenes of decapitation. As far as I know, there have been no empirical studies of how children react to such scenes and what harm if any is done to their psyche. My guess is that the normal child finds it all very amusing and is not damaged in the least, but that books like *Alice's Adventures in Wonderland* and *The Wizard of Oz* should not be allowed to circulate indiscriminately among adults who are undergoing analysis.

In Tenniel's illustration for this scene, in *The Nursery "Alice,"* the Queen's face is a bright red.

whether they were gardeners, or soldiers, or courtiers, or three of her own children.

"How should *I* know?" said Alice, surprised at her own courage. "It's no business of *mine*."

The Queen turned crimson with fury,[4] and, after glaring at her for a moment like a wild beast, began screaming "Off with her head! Off with—"

"Nonsense!" said Alice, very loudly and decidedly, and the Queen was silent.

The King laid his hand upon her arm, and timidly said "Consider, my dear: she is only a child!"

The Queen turned angrily away from him, and said to the Knave "Turn them over!"

The Knave did so, very carefully, with one foot.

"Get up!" said the Queen in a shrill, loud

voice, and the three gardeners instantly jumped up, and began bowing to the King, the Queen, the royal children, and everybody else.

"Leave off that!" screamed the Queen. "You make me giddy." And then, turning to the rose-tree, she went on "What *have* you been doing here?"

"May it please your Majesty," said Two, in a very humble tone, going down on one knee as he spoke, "we were trying—"

"*I* see!" said the Queen, who had meanwhile been examining the roses. "Off with their heads!" and the procession moved on, three of the soldiers remaining behind to execute the unfortunate gardeners, who ran to Alice for protection.

"You sha'n't be beheaded!" said Alice, and she put them into a large flower-pot that stood near. The three soldiers wandered about for a minute or two, looking for them, and then quietly marched off after the others.

"Are their heads off?" shouted the Queen.

"Their heads are gone, if it please your Majesty!" the soldiers shouted in reply.

"That's right!" shouted the Queen. "Can you play croquet?"

The soldiers were silent, and looked at Alice, as the question was evidently meant for her.

"Yes!" shouted Alice.

"Come on, then!" roared the Queen, and Alice joined the procession, wondering very much what would happen next.

"It's—it's a very fine day!" said a timid voice at her side. She was walking by the White Rabbit, who was peeping anxiously into her face.

"Very," said Alice. "Where's the Duchess?"

"Hush! Hush!" said the Rabbit in a low hurried tone. He looked anxiously over his shoulder

5. In Carroll's original manuscript of *Alice* as well as in the sketches he made for it, the mallets are ostriches instead of flamingoes.

Carroll spent a great deal of time inventing new and unusual ways of playing familiar games. Of some two hundred pamphlets that he privately printed, about twenty deal with original games. His rules for Castle Croquet, a complicated game he often played with the Liddell sisters, is reprinted, along with his other game pamphlets, in my *Universe in a Handkerchief: Lewis Carroll's Mathematical Recreations, Games, Puzzles, and Word Play* (1996).

as he spoke, and then raised himself upon tiptoe, put his mouth close to her ear, and whispered "She's under sentence of execution."

"What for?" said Alice.

"Did you say 'What a pity!'?" the Rabbit asked.

"No, I didn't," said Alice. "I don't think it's at all a pity. I said 'What for?'"

"She boxed the Queen's ears—" the Rabbit began. Alice gave a little scream of laughter. "Oh, hush!" the Rabbit whispered in a frightened tone. "The Queen will hear you! You see she came rather late, and the Queen said—"

"Get to your places!" shouted the Queen in a voice of thunder; and people began running about in all directions, tumbling up against each other: however; they got settled down in a minute or two, and the game began.

Alice thought she had never seen such a curious croquet-ground in her life: it was all ridges and furrows: the croquet balls were live hedgehogs, and the mallets live flamingoes,[5] and the soldiers had to double themselves up and stand on their hands and feet, to make the arches.

The chief difficulty Alice found at first was in managing her flamingo: she succeeded in getting its body tucked away, comfortably enough, under her arm, with its legs hanging down, but generally, just as she had got its neck nicely straightened out, and was going to give the hedgehog a blow with its head, it *would* twist itself round and look up in her face, with such a puzzled expression that she could not help bursting out laughing; and, when she had got its head down, and was going to begin again, it was very provoking to find that the hedgehog had unrolled itself, and was in the act of crawling away: besides all this, there was generally a ridge or a furrow in the way wherever she wanted to send the hedgehog to, and, as the doubled-up soldiers were always getting up and walking off to other parts of the ground, Alice soon came to the conclusion that it was a very difficult game indeed.

The players all played at once, without waiting for turns, quarrelling all the while, and fighting for the hedgehogs; and in a very short time the Queen was in a furious passion, and went stamping about, and shouting "Off with his head!" or "Off with her head!" about once in a minute.

Alice began to feel very uneasy: to be sure, she had not as yet had any dispute with the Queen, but she knew that it might happen any minute, "and then," thought she, "what would become of me? They're dreadfully fond of beheading people here: the great wonder is, that there's any one left alive!"

She was looking about for some way of escape, and wondering whether she could get

away without being seen, when she noticed a curious appearance in the air: it puzzled her very much at first, but after watching it a minute or two she made it out to be a grin, and she said to herself "It's the Cheshire-Cat: now I shall have somebody to talk to."

"How are you getting on?" said the Cat, as soon as there was mouth enough for it to speak with.

Alice waited till the eyes appeared, and then nodded. "It's no use speaking to it," she thought, "till its ears have come, or at least one of them." In another minute the whole head appeared, and then Alice put down her flamingo, and began an account of the game, feeling very glad she had some one to listen to her. The Cat seemed to think that there was enough of it now in sight, and no more of it appeared.

"I don't think they play at all fairly," Alice began, in rather a complaining tone, "and they all quarrel so dreadfully one ca'n't hear oneself speak—and they don't seem to have any rules in particular: at least, if there are, nobody attends to them—and you've no idea how confusing it is all the things being alive: for instance, there's the arch I've got to go through next walking about at the other end of the ground—and I should have croqueted the Queen's hedgehog just now, only it ran away when it saw mine coming!"

"How do you like the Queen?" said the Cat in a low voice.

"Not at all," said Alice: "she's so extremely—" Just then she noticed that the Queen was close behind her, listening: so she went on "—likely to win, that it's hardly worth while finishing the game."

The Queen smiled and passed on.

"Who *are* you talking to?" said the King,

coming up to Alice, and looking at the Cat's head with great curiosity.

"It's a friend of mine—a Cheshire-Cat," said Alice: "allow me to introduce it."

"I don't like the look of it at all," said the King: "however, it may kiss my hand, if it likes."

"I'd rather not," the Cat remarked.

"Don't be impertinent," said the King, "and don't look at me like that!" He got behind Alice as he spoke.

"A cat may look at a king," said Alice. "I've read that in some book, but I don't remember where."[6]

"Well, it must be removed," said the King very decidedly; and he called to the Queen, who was passing at the moment, "My dear! I wish you would have this cat removed!"

The Queen had only one way of settling all difficulties, great or small. "Of with his head!" she said without even looking round.

"I'll fetch the executioner myself," said the King eagerly, and he hurried off.

Alice thought she might as well go back and see how the game was going on, as she heard the Queen's voice in the distance, screaming with passion. She had already heard her sentence three of the players to be executed for having missed their turns, and she did not like the look of things at all, as the game was in such confusion that she never knew whether it was her turn or not. So she went off in search of her hedgehog.

The hedgehog was engaged in a fight with another hedgehog, which seemed to Alice an excellent opportunity for croqueting one of them with the other: the only difficulty was, that her flamingo was gone across to the other side of the garden, where Alice could see it trying in a helpless sort of way to fly up into a tree.

6. Frankie Morris suggests in *Jabberwocky* (Autumn 1985) that the book Alice read could have been *A Cat May Look Upon a King* (London, 1652), a slashing attack on English kings by Sir Archibald Weldon. "A cat may look at a king" is a familiar proverb implying that inferiors have certain privileges in the presence of superiors.

By the time she had caught the flamingo and brought it back, the fight was over, and both the hedgehogs were out of sight: "but it doesn't matter much," thought Alice, "as all the arches are gone from this side of the ground." So she tucked it away under her arm, that it might not escape again, and went back to have a little more conversation with her friend.

When she got back to the Cheshire-Cat, she was surprised to find quite a large crowd collected round it: there was a dispute going on between the executioner, the King, and the Queen, who were all talking at once, while all the rest were quite silent, and looked very uncomfortable.[7]

The moment Alice appeared, she was appealed

to by all three to settle the question, and they repeated their arguments to her, though, as they all spoke at once, she found it very hard to make out exactly what they said.

The executioner's argument was, that you couldn't cut off a head unless there was a body to cut it off from: that he had never had to do such a thing before, and he wasn't going to begin at *his* time of life.

The King's argument was that anything that had a head could be beheaded, and that you weren't to talk nonsense.

The Queen's argument was that, if something wasn't done about it in less than no time, she'd have everybody executed, all round. (It was this last remark that had made the whole party look so grave and anxious.)

Alice could think of nothing else to say but "It belongs to the Duchess: you'd better ask *her* about it."

"She's in prison," the Queen said to the executioner: "fetch her here." And the executioner went off like an arrow.

The Cat's head began fading away the moment he was gone, and, by the time he had come back with the Duchess, it had entirely disappeared: so the King and the executioner ran wildly up and down, looking for it, while the rest of the party went back to the game.

9

The Mock Turtle's Story

"You ca'n't think how glad I am to see you again, you dear old thing!" said the Duchess, as she tucked her arm affectionately into Alice's, and they walked off together.

Alice was very glad to find her in such a pleasant temper, and thought to herself that perhaps it was only the pepper that had made her so savage when they met in the kitchen.

"When *I'm* a Duchess," she said to herself (not in a very hopeful tone, though), "I wo'n't have any pepper in my kitchen *at all*. Soup does very well without—Maybe it's always pepper that makes people hot-tempered," she went on, very much pleased at having found out a new kind of rule, "and vinegar that makes them sour—and camomile[1] that makes them bitter—and—and barley-sugar[2] and such things that make children sweet-tempered. I only wish people knew *that*: then they wouldn't be so stingy about it, you know—"

She had quite forgotten the Duchess by this time, and was a little startled when she heard her voice close to her ear. "You're thinking about something, my dear, and that makes you forget to talk. I ca'n't tell you just now what the moral of that is, but I shall remember it in a bit."

"Perhaps it hasn't one," Alice ventured to remark.

"Tut, tut, child!" said the Duchess. "Every thing's got a moral, if only you can find it."[3] And she squeezed herself up closer to Alice's side as she spoke.

Alice did not much like her keeping so close to her: first, because the Duchess was *very* ugly; and secondly, because she was exactly the right height to rest her chin on Alice's shoulder, and it was an uncomfortably sharp chin. However, she did not like to be rude: so she bore it as well as she could.

"The game's going on rather better now," she said, by way of keeping up the conversation a little.

" 'Tis so," said the Duchess: "and the moral of that is—'Oh, 'tis love, 'tis love, that makes the world go round!' "[4]

3. M. J. C. Hodgart calls my notice to the following statement in Charles Dickens's novel *Dombey and Son* (Chapter 2): "There's a moral in everything, if we would only avail ourselves of it." James Kincaid, in one of his notes for the Pennyroyal edition of *Through the Looking-Glass* (1983), illustrated by Barry Moser, quotes from Carroll's monograph *The New Belfry of Christ Church, Oxford*: "Everything has a moral if you choose to look for it. In Wordsworth a good half of every poem is devoted to the Moral: in Byron, a smaller proportion: in Tupper, the whole."

4. A popular French song of the time contains the lines "C'est l'amour, l'amour, l'amour/Qui fait le monde à la ronde," but Roger Green thinks the Duchess is quoting the first line of an equally old English song, "The Dawn of Love." He calls attention to the similar statement that closes Dante's *Paradiso*.

" 'Tis love that makes the world go round, my baby," writes Dickens (*Our Mutual Friend*, Book 4, Chapter 4), and there are endless other expressions of the sentiment in English literature.

5. The "somebody" was the Duchess herself, in Chapter 6.

6. Surely few American readers have recognized this for what it is, an extremely ingenious switch on the British proverb, "Take care of the pence and the pounds will take care of themselves." The Duchess's remark is sometimes quoted as a good rule to follow in writing prose or even poetry. Unsound, of course.

7. Carroll seems to have invented this proverb. It describes what in modern game theory is called a two-person zero-sum game—a game in which the payoff to the winner exactly equals the losses of the loser. Poker is a many-person * zero-sum game because the total amount of money won equals the total amount of money lost.

8. Alice has gone from animal to mineral to vegetable. As reader Jane Parker writes in a letter, we have here a reference to the popular Victorian parlor game "animal, vegetable, mineral," in which players tried to guess what someone was thinking of. The first questions asked were traditionally: Is it animal? Is it vegetable? Is it mineral? Answers had to be yes or no, and the object was to guess correctly in twenty or fewer questions. A more explicit reference to the game can be found in Chapter 7 of the second *Alice* book.

"Somebody said,"[5] Alice whispered, "that it's done by everybody minding their own business!"

"Ah, well! It means much the same thing," said the Duchess, digging her sharp little chin into Alice's shoulder as she added "and the moral of *that* is—'Take care of the sense, and the sounds will take care of themselves.' "[6]

"How fond she is of finding morals in things!" Alice thought to herself.

"I dare say you're wondering why I don't put my arm round your waist," the Duchess said, after a pause: "the reason is, that I'm doubtful about the temper of your flamingo. Shall I try the experiment?"

"He might bite," Alice cautiously replied, not feeling at all anxious to have the experiment tried.

"Very true," said the Duchess: "flamingoes and mustard both bite. And the moral of that is—'Birds of a feather flock together.' "

"Only mustard isn't a bird," Alice remarked.

"Right, as usual," said the Duchess: "what a clear way you have of putting things!"

"It's a mineral, I *think*," said Alice.

"Of course it is," said the Duchess, who seemed ready to agree to everything that Alice said: "there's a large mustard-mine near here. And the moral of that is—'The more there is of mine, the less there is of yours.' "[7]

"Oh, I know!" exclaimed Alice, who had not attended to this last remark. "It's a vegetable.[8] It doesn't look like one, but it is."

"I quite agree with you," said the Duchess; "and the moral of that is—'Be what you would seem to be'—or, if you'd like it put more simply—'Never imagine yourself not to be otherwise than what it might appear to others that what you were or might have been was not otherwise than what you had been would have appeared to them to be otherwise.'"

"I think I should understand that better," Alice said very politely, "if I had it written down: but I ca'n't quite follow it as you say it."

"That's nothing to what I could say if I chose," the Duchess replied, in a pleased tone.

"Pray don't trouble yourself to say it any longer than that," said Alice.

"Oh, don't talk about trouble!" said the Duchess. "I make you a present of everything I've said as yet."

"A cheap sort of present!" thought Alice. "I'm glad people don't give birthday-presents like that!" But she did not venture to say it out loud.

"Thinking again?" the Duchess asked, with another dig of her sharp little chin.

"I've a right to think," said Alice sharply, for she was beginning to feel a little worried.

"Just about as much right," said the Duchess, "as pigs have to fly[9] and the m—"

But here, to Alice's great surprise, the Duchess's voice died away, even in the middle of her favourite word "moral", and the arm that was linked into hers began to tremble. Alice looked up, and there stood the Queen in front of them, with her arms folded, frowning like a thunderstorm.

"A fine day, your Majesty!" the Duchess began in a low, weak voice.

"Now, I give you fair warning," shouted the Queen, stamping on the ground as she spoke; "either you or your head must be off, and that in about half no time! Take your choice!"

The Duchess took her choice, and was gone in a moment.

"Let's go on with the game," the Queen said to Alice; and Alice was too much frightened to

9. A reference to flying pigs occurs in Tweedledee's song in the second *Alice* book when the Walrus wonders if pigs have wings. "Pigs may fly," so goes an old Scottish proverb, "but it's not likely." You'll see winged pigs in Henry Holiday's illustration of the Beaver's lesson in *The Hunting of the Snark*.

10. Mock turtle soup is an imitation of green turtle soup, usually made from veal. This explains why Tenniel drew his Mock Turtle with the head, hind hoofs, and tail of a calf.

11. The gryphon, or griffin, is a fabulous monster with the head and wings of an eagle and the lower body of a lion. In the *Purgatorio*, Canto 29, of Dante's *Divine Comedy* (that lesser-known tour of Wonderland by way of a hole in the ground), the chariot of the Church is pulled by a gryphon. The beast was a common medieval symbol for the union of God and man in Christ. Here both the Gryphon and Mock Turtle are obvious satires on the sentimental college alumnus, of which Oxford has always had an unusually large share.

I am indebted to Vivien Greene for informing me that the gryphon is the emblem of Oxford's Trinity College. It appears on Trinity's main gate; a fact surely familiar to Carroll and the Liddell sisters.

Reader James Bethune thinks there is satirical significance in the Gryphon's sleeping. Griffins were supposed to guard fiercely the gold mines of ancient Scythia, and this led to their becoming heraldic emblems of extreme vigilance. See Anne Clark's article "The Griffin and the Gryphon," in *Jabberwocky* (Winter 1977).

say a word, but slowly followed her back to the croquet-ground.

The other guests had taken advantage of the Queen's absence, and were resting in the shade: however, the moment they saw her, they hurried back to the game, the Queen merely remarking that a moment's delay would cost them their lives.

All the time they were playing the Queen never left off quarreling with the other players, and shouting "Off with his head!" or "Off with her head!" Those whom she sentenced were taken into custody by the soldiers, who of course had to leave off being arches to do this, so that, by the end of half an hour or so, there were no arches left, and all the players, except the King, the Queen, and Alice, were in custody and under sentence of execution.

Then the Queen left off, quite out of breath, and said to Alice "Have you seen the Mock Turtle yet?"

"No," said Alice. "I don't even know what a Mock Turtle is."

"It's the thing Mock Turtle Soup[10] is made from," said the Queen.

"I never saw one, or heard of one," said Alice.

"Come on, then," said the Queen, "and he shall tell you his history."

As they walked off together, Alice heard the King say in a low voice, to the company generally, "You are all pardoned." "Come, *that's* a good thing!" she said to herself, for she had felt quite unhappy at the number of executions the Queen had ordered.

They very soon came upon a Gryphon,[11] lying fast asleep in the sun. (If you don't know what a Gryphon is, look at the picture.) "Up, lazy thing!" said the Queen, "and take this young

12. If the Gryphon's "nobody" is never executed, then Alice may well have seen nobody on the road in Chapter 7 of the second *Alice* book.

lady to see the Mock Turtle, and to hear his history. I must go back and see after some executions I have ordered;" and she walked off, leaving Alice alone with the Gryphon. Alice did not quite like the look of the creature, but on the whole she thought it would be quite as safe to stay with it as to go after that savage Queen: so she waited.

The Gryphon sat up and rubbed its eyes: then it watched the Queen till she was out of sight: then it chuckled. "What fun!" said the Gryphon, half to itself, half to Alice.

"What *is* the fun?" said Alice.

"Why, *she*," said the Gryphon. "It's all her fancy, that: they never executes nobody, you know.[12] Come on!"

"Everybody says 'come on!' here," thought Alice, as she went slowly after it: "I never was so ordered about before, in all my life, never!"

They had not gone far before they saw the Mock Turtle in the distance, sitting sad and lonely on a little ledge of rock, and, as they came nearer, Alice could hear him sighing as if his heart would break. She pitied him deeply. "What is his sorrow?" she asked the Gryphon. And the Gryphon answered, very nearly in the same

13. In Alice's day the word *tortoise* was usually given to land turtles to distinguish them from turtles that lived in the sea.

14. Carroll used this pun again in his article "What the Tortoise said to Achilles," in *Mind* (April 1895). After explaining a disconcerting logical paradox to Achilles, the tortoise remarks: "And *would* you mind, as a personal favor—considering what a lot of instruction this colloquy of ours will provide for the Logicians of the Nineteenth Century—*would* you mind adopting a pun that my cousin the Mock-Turtle will then make, and allowing yourself to be re-named Taught-Us?"

Achilles buries his face in his hands, then in low tones of despair he counters with another pun: "As you please! Provided that *you*, for *your* part, will adopt a pun the Mock-Turtle never made, and allow yourself to be renamed A Kill-Ease!"

words as before, "It's all his fancy, that: he hasn't got no sorrow, you know. Come on!"

So they went up to the Mock Turtle, who looked at them with large eyes full of tears, but said nothing.

"This here young lady," said the Gryphon, "she wants for to know your history, she do."

"I'll tell it her," said the Mock Turtle in a deep, hollow tone. "Sit down, both of you, and don't speak a word till I've finished."

So they sat down, and nobody spoke for some minutes. Alice thought to herself "I don't see how he can *ever* finish, if he doesn't begin." But she waited patiently.

"Once," said the Mock Turtle at last, with a deep sigh, "I was a real Turtle."

These words were followed by a very long silence, broken only by an occasional exclamation of "Hjckrrh!" from the Gryphon, and the constant heavy sobbing of the Mock Turtle. Alice was very nearly getting up and saying "Thank you, Sir, for your interesting story," but she could not help thinking there *must* be more to come, so she sat still and said nothing.

"When we were little," the Mock Turtle went on at last, more calmly, though still sobbing a little now and then, "we went to school in the sea. The master was an old Turtle—we used to call him Tortoise—"

"Why did you call him Tortoise, if he wasn't one?"[13] Alice asked.

"We called him Tortoise because he taught us,"[14] said the Mock Turtle angrily. "Really you are very dull!"

"You ought to be ashamed of yourself for asking such a simple question," added the Gryphon; and then they both sat silent and looked at poor Alice, who felt ready to sink into the earth. At last the Gryphon said to the Mock Turtle "Drive on, old fellow! Don't be all day about it!" and he went on in these words:—

"Yes, we went to school in the sea, though you mayn't believe it—"

"I never said I didn't!" interrupted Alice.

"You did," said the Mock Turtle.[15]

"Hold your tongue!" added the Gryphon, before Alice could speak again. The Mock Turtle went on.

"We had the best of educations—in fact, we went to school every day—"

"*I've* been to a day-school, too," said Alice. "You needn't be so proud as all that."

"With extras?" asked the Mock Turtle, a little anxiously.

"Yes," said Alice: "we learned French and music."

15. As Peter Heath has pointed out in *The Philosopher's Alice*, the Mock Turtle is telling Alice that she has just said "I didn't." Heath reminds us of how Humpty, in the next book, catches Alice in a similar verbal trap by referring to something she *didn't* say.

16. The phrase "French, music and washing—extra" often appeared on boarding-school bills. It meant, of course, that there was an extra charge for French and music, and for having one's laundry done by the school.

17. Needless to say, all the Mock Turtle's subjects are puns (reading, writing, addition, subtraction, multiplication, division, history, geography, drawing, sketching, painting in oils, Latin, Greek). In fact, this chapter and the one to follow fairly swarm with puns. Children find puns very funny, but most contemporary authorities on what children are supposed to like believe that puns lower the literary quality of juvenile books.

18. The "Drawling-master" who came once a week to teach "Drawling, Stretching, and Fainting in Coils" is a reference to none other than the art critic John Ruskin. Ruskin came once a week to the Liddell home to teach drawing, sketching, and painting in oils to the children. They were taught well. It takes only a glance at Alice's many watercolors and those of her brother Henry, and at an oil painting of Alice by her younger sister Violet, to appreciate the talent for art that they inherited from their father. See Colin Gordon's *Beyond the Looking Glass* (Harcourt Brace Jovanovich, 1982) for reproductions, many in color, of works of art produced by the Liddells.

Photographs of Ruskin at the time, and a caricature by Max Beerbohm, show him tall and thin, and strongly resembling a conger eel. Like Carroll, he was attracted to little girls precisely because of their sexual purity. His marriage to Euphemia ("Effie") Gray, ten years his junior, was annulled after six miserable years on grounds of "incurable impo-

"And washing?" said the Mock Turtle.

"Certainly not!" said Alice indignantly.

"Ah! Then yours wasn't a really good school," said the Mock Turtle in a tone of great relief. "Now, at *ours*, they had, at the end of the bill, 'French, music, *and washing*—extra.'"[16]

"You couldn't have wanted it much," said Alice; "living at the bottom of the sea."

"I couldn't afford to learn it," said the Mock Turtle, with a sigh. "I only took the regular course."

"What was that?" inquired Alice.

"Reeling and Writhing,[17] of course, to begin with," the Mock Turtle replied; "and then the different branches of Arithmetic—Ambition, Distraction, Uglification, and Derision."

"I never heard of 'Uglification,'" Alice ventured to say. "What is it?"

The Gryphon lifted up both its paws in surprise. "Never heard of uglifying!" it exclaimed. "You know what to beautify is, I suppose?"

"Yes," said Alice doubtfully: "it means—to—make—anything—prettier."

"Well, then," the Gryphon went on, "if you don't know what to uglify is, you *are* a simpleton."

Alice did not feel encouraged to ask any more questions about it: so she turned to the Mock Turtle, and said "What else had you to learn?"

"Well, there was Mystery," the Mock Turtle replied, counting off the subjects on his flappers,—"Mystery, ancient and modern, with Seaography: then Drawling—the Drawling-master was an old conger-eel, that used to come once a week: *he* taught us Drawling, Stretching, and Fainting in Coils."[18]

"What was *that* like?" said Alice.

"Well, I ca'n't show it you, myself," the Mock

Turtle said: "I'm too stiff. And the Gryphon never learnt it."

"Hadn't time," said the Gryphon: "I went to the Classical master, though. He was an old crab, *he* was."

"I never went to him," the Mock Turtle said with a sigh. "He taught Laughing and Grief, they used to say."

"So he did, so he did," said the Gryphon, sighing in his turn; and both creatures hid their faces in their paws.

"And how many hours a day did you do lessons?" said Alice, in a hurry to change the subject.

"Ten hours the first day," said the Mock Turtle: "nine the next, and so on."

"What a curious plan!" exclaimed Alice.

"That's the reason they're called lessons," the Gryphon remarked: "because they lessen from day to day."

This was quite a new idea to Alice, and she thought it over a little before she made her next remark. "Then the eleventh day must have been a holiday?"

"Of course it was," said the Mock Turtle.

"And how did you manage on the twelfth?" Alice went on eagerly.[19]

"That's enough about lessons," the Gryphon interrupted in a very decided tone. "Tell her something about the games now."

tency." Effie promptly married young John Millais, whose Pre-Raphaelite paintings Ruskin greatly admired. She bore him eight children, one of whom was the little girl pictured in Millais's famous *My First Sermon*. (See Chapter 3, Note 4, of the second *Alice* book.)

Four years later Ruskin fell passionately in love with Rosie La Touche, daughter of an Irish banker, whose wife admired Ruskin's writings. She was then ten, and he was forty-seven. He proposed marriage when she was eighteen, but she turned him down. It was a crushing blow. Ruskin continued to fall in love with little girls as virginal as himself, proposing marriage to one girl when he was seventy. In 1900 he died after ten years of severe manic-depression. An autobiography speaks of his admiration for Alice Liddell, but there is no mention of Lewis Carroll.

19. Alice's excellent question rightly puzzles the Gryphon because it introduces the possibility of mysterious negative numbers (a concept that also puzzled early mathematicians), which seem to have no application to hours of lessons in the "curious" educational scheme. On the twelfth day and succeeding days did the pupils start teaching their teacher?

10

The Lobster-Quadrille

1. The quadrille, a kind of square dance in five figures, was one of the most difficult of the ballroom dances fashionable at the time Carroll wrote his tale. The Liddell children had been taught the dance by a private tutor.

In one of his letters to a little girl, Carroll described his own dancing technique as follows:

As to dancing, my dear, I *never* dance, unless I am allowed to do it *in my own peculiar way*. There is no use trying to describe it: it has to be seen to be believed. The last house I tried it in, the floor broke through. But then it was a poor sort of floor—the beams were only six inches thick, hardly worth calling beams at all: stone arches are much more sensible, when any dancing, *of my peculiar kind*, is to be done. Did you ever see the Rhinoceros, and the Hippopotamus, at the Zoological Gardens, trying to dance a minuet together? It is a touching sight.

"Lobster Quadrille" could be an intended play on "Lancers Quadrille," a walking square dance for eight to sixteen couples that was enormously popular in English ballrooms at the time Carroll wrote his *Alice* books. A variant of the quadrille, it consisted of five figures, each in a different meter. According to *The Grove Dictionary of Music and Musicians*, the Lancers (as both the dance and its music were called) was

The Mock Turtle sighed deeply, and drew the back of one flapper across his eyes. He looked at Alice and tried to speak, but, for a minute or two, sobs choked his voice. "Same as if he had a bone in his throat," said the Gryphon; and it set to work shaking him and punching him in the back. At last the Mock Turtle recovered his voice, and, with tears running down his cheeks, he went on again:—

"You may not have lived much under the sea—" ("I haven't," said Alice)—"and perhaps you were never even introduced to a lobster—" (Alice began to say "I once tasted—" but checked herself hastily, and said "No, never") "—so you can have no idea what a delightful thing a Lobster-Quadrille is!"[1]

"No, indeed," said Alice. "What sort of a dance is it?"

"Why," said the Gryphon, "you first form into a line along the sea-shore—"

"Two lines!" cried the Mock Turtle. "Seals, turtles, salmon, and so on: then, when you've cleared all the jelly-fish out of the way—"

"*That* generally takes some time," interrupted the Gryphon.

"—you advance twice—"

"Each with a lobster as a partner!" cried the Gryphon.

"Of course," the Mock Turtle said: "advance twice, set to partners—"[2]

"—change lobsters, and retire in same order," continued the Gryphon.

"Then, you know," the Mock Turtle went on, "you throw the—"

"The lobsters!" shouted the Gryphon, with a bound into the air.

"—as far out to sea as you can—"

"Swim after them!" screamed the Gryphon.

"Turn a somersault in the sea!" cried the Mock Turtle, capering wildly about.

"Change lobsters again!" yelled the Gryphon at the top of its voice.

"Back to land again, and—that's all the first figure," said the Mock Turtle, suddenly dropping his voice; and the two creatures, who had been jumping about like mad things all this time, sat

invented by a Dublin dancing master and achieved an international following in the 1850s after being introduced in Paris. The Liddell children were taught the dance by a private tutor. The last stanza of the Mock Turtle's song may reflect the popularity of the Lancers in France, and the tossing of the lobsters may allude to the tossing of lances in combat. Whether such tossing played a role in the dance I do not know.

2. A British correspondent who signed her letter "R. Reader" points out that "set to partners" means to face your partner, hop on one foot, then on the other.

3. The Mock Turtle's song parodies the first line and adopts the meter of Mary Howitt's poem (in turn based on an older song) "The Spider and the Fly." The first stanza of Mrs. Howitt's version reads:

"Will you walk into my parlour?" said
the spider to the fly.
" 'Tis the prettiest little parlour that ever
you did spy.
The way into my parlour is up a winding
stair,
And I've got many curious things to show
when you are there."
"Oh, no, no," said the little fly, "to ask
me is in vain,
For who goes up your winding stair can
ne'er come down again."

In Carroll's original manuscript the Mock Turtle sings a different song:

Beneath the waters of the sea
Are lobsters thick as thick can be—
They love to dance with you and me.
My own, my gentle Salmon!

CHORUS

Salmon, come up! Salmon, go down!
Salmon, come twist your tail around!
Of all the fishes of the sea
There's none so good as Salmon!

Here Carroll is parodying a Negro minstrel song, the chorus of which begins:

Sally come up! Sally go down!
Sally come twist your heel around!

An entry in Carroll's diary on July 3, 1862 (the day before the famous expedition up the river Thames), mentions hearing the Liddell sisters (at a rainy-day get-together in the Deanery) sing this minstrel song "with great spirit." Roger Green, in a note on this entry, provides the song's second verse and chorus:

down again very sadly and quietly, and looked at Alice.

"It must be a very pretty dance," said Alice timidly.

"Would you like to see a little of it?" said the Mock Turtle.

"Very much indeed," said Alice.

"Come, let's try the first figure!" said the Mock Turtle to the Gryphon. "We can do it without lobsters, you know. Which shall sing?"

"Oh, *you* sing," said the Gryphon. "I've forgotten the words."

So they began solemnly dancing round and round Alice, every now and then treading on her toes when they passed too close, and waving their fore-paws to mark the time, while the Mock Turtle sang this, very slowly and sadly:—[3]

"Will you walk a little faster?" said a whiting[4] to a
snail,
"There's a porpoise close behind us, and he's treading
on my tail.
See how eagerly the lobsters and the turtles all
advance!
They are waiting on the shingle[5]—will you come and
join the dance?
  Will you, wo'n't you, will you, wo'n't you, will
  you join the dance?
  Will you, wo'n't you, will you, wo'n't you, wo'n't
  you join the dance?

"You can really have no notion how delightful it will
be
When they take us up and throw us, with the
lobsters, out to sea!"
But the snail replied "Too far, too far!", and gave a
look askance—
Said he thanked the whiting kindly, but he would not
join the dance.

Would not, could not, would not, could not,
  would not join the dance.
Would not, could not, would not, could not,
  could not join the dance.

"What matters it how far we go?" his scaly friend
  replied.
"There is another shore, you know, upon the other
  side.
The further off from England the nearer is to
  France—
Then turn not pale, beloved snail, but come and join
  the dance.
Will you, wo'n't you, will you, wo'n't you, will
  you join the dance?
Will you, wo'n't you, will you, wo'n't you,
  wo'n't you join the dance?"

"Thank you, it's a very interesting dance to
watch," said Alice, feeling very glad that it was
over at last: "and I do so like that curious song
about the whiting!"

"Oh, as to the whiting," said the Mock Turtle,
"they—you've seen them, of course?"

"Yes," said Alice, "I've often seen them at
dinn—" she checked herself hastily.

"I don't know where Dinn may be," said the
Mock Turtle; "but, if you've seen them so often,
of course you know what they're like?"

"I believe so," Alice replied thoughtfully.
"They have their tails in their mouths[6]—and
they're all over crumbs."

"You're wrong about the crumbs," said the
Mock Turtle: "crumbs would all wash off in the
sea. But they *have* their tails in their mouths; and
the reason is—" here the Mock Turtle yawned
and shut his eyes. "Tell her about the reason and
all that," he said to the Gryphon.

"The reason is," said the Gryphon, "that they

Last Monday night I gave a ball,
And I invite de Niggers all,
The thick, the thin, the short, the tall,
  But none came up to Sally!

Sally come up! Sally go down!
Sally come twist your heel around!
De old man he's gone down to town—
  Oh Sally come down de middle!

Some verses end "Dar's not a gal like
Sally!" In a letter (1886) to Henry
Savile Clarke, who adapted the *Alice*
books to the stage operetta, Carroll
urged that his songs that parodied
old nursery rhymes be sung to the
traditional tunes, not set to new
music. He singled out this song in
particular. "It would take a very good
composer to write anything better
than the old sweet air of 'Will you
walk into my parlor, said the Spider
to the Fly.'"

Tenniel's political cartoon in
Punch (March 8, 1899), captioned
"Alice in Bumbleland," features the
same trio of Alice, Gryphon, and
Mock Turtle. Alice is the conservative
politician Arthur James Balfour, the
Gryphon is London, and the weeping
Mock Turtle is the city of West-
minister: Alice, the Gryphon, and an
ordinary turtle appear in Tenniel's
earlier cartoon "Alice in Blunderland" (*Punch*, October 30, 1880).
Other appearances of Alice in *Punch*
are in Tenniel's February 1, 1868,
cartoon (Alice represents the United
States), and in Tenniel's frontispiece
to the bound Volume 46 (1864).

4. A whiting is a food fish in the cod
family.

5. *Shingle* is a word, more common
in England than the United States,
for that portion of the seaside where
the beach is covered with large
rounded stones and pebbles.

6. "When I wrote that," Carroll is quoted as saying (in Stuart Collingwood's *The Life and Letters of Lewis Carroll*, page 402), "I believed that whiting really did have their tails in their mouths, but I have since been told that fishmongers put the tail through the eye, not in the mouth at all."

A reader who signed her name only with "Alice" sent me a clipping of a letter from Craig Claiborne that appeared in *The New Yorker* (February 15, 1993). He describes a French dish known as *merlan en colere* or "whiting in anger," prepared by "twisting the fish into a circle and tying or otherwise securing the tail in its mouth. It is then deep-fried (not boiled) and served with parsley, lemon, and tartar sauce. When it is served hot, it has a distinctly choleric, or irascible, appearance."

would go with the lobsters to the dance. So they got thrown out to sea. So they had to fall a long way. So they got their tails fast in their mouths. So they couldn't get them out again. That's all."

"Thank you," said Alice, "it's very interesting. I never knew so much about a whiting before."

"I can tell you more than that, if you like," said the Gryphon. "Do you know why it's called a whiting?"

"I never thought about it," said Alice. "Why?"

"*It does the boots and shoes*," the Gryphon replied very solemnly.

Alice was thoroughly puzzled. "Does the boots and shoes!" she repeated in a wondering tone.

"Why, what are *your* shoes done with?" said the Gryphon. "I mean, what makes them so shiny?"

Alice looked down at them, and considered a little before she gave her answer. "They're done with blacking, I believe."

"Boots and shoes under the sea," the Gryphon went on in a deep voice, "are done with whiting. Now you know."

"And what are they made of?" Alice asked in a tone of great curiosity.

"Soles and eels, of course," the Gryphon replied, rather impatiently: "any shrimp could have told you that."

"If I'd been the whiting," said Alice, whose thoughts were still running on the song, "I'd have said to the porpoise 'Keep back, please! We don't want *you* with us!'"

"They were obliged to have him with them," the Mock Turtle said. "No wise fish would go anywhere without a porpoise."

"Wouldn't it, really?" said Alice, in a tone of great surprise.

"Of course not," said the Mock Turtle. "Why, if a fish came to *me*, and told me he was going a journey, I should say 'With what porpoise?'"

"Don't you mean 'purpose'?" said Alice.

"I mean what I say," the Mock Turtle replied, in an offended tone. And the Gryphon added "Come, let's hear some of *your* adventures."

"I could tell you my adventures—beginning from this morning," said Alice a little timidly; "but it's no use going back to yesterday, because I was a different person then."

"Explain all that," said the Mock Turtle.

"No, no! The adventures first," said the Gryphon in an impatient tone: "explanations take such a dreadful time."

So Alice began telling them her adventures from the time when she first saw the White Rabbit. She was a little nervous about it, just at first, the two creatures got so close to her, one on each side, and opened their eyes and mouths so *very* wide; but she gained courage as she went on. Her listeners were perfectly quiet till she got to the part about her repeating "*You are old, Father William,*" to the Caterpillar, and the words all coming different, and then the Mock Turtle drew a long breath, and said "That's very curious!"

"It's all about as curious as it can be," said the Gryphon.

"It all came different!" the Mock Turtle repeated thoughtfully. "I should like to hear her try and repeat something now. Tell her to begin." He looked at the Gryphon as if he thought it had some kind of authority over Alice.

"Stand up and repeat '*'Tis the voice of the sluggard,*'" said the Gryphon.

7. The first line of this poem calls to mind the Biblical phrase "the voice of the turtle" (Song of Songs 2:12); actually it is a parody of the opening lines of "The Sluggard," a dismal poem by Isaae Watts (see Note 5 of Chapter 2), which was well known to Carroll's readers.

*'Tis the voice of the sluggard; I heard him
    complain,*
"You have wak'd me too soon, I must
    slumber again."
As the door on its hinges, so he on his
    bed,
Turns his sides and his shoulders and his
    heavy head.

"A little more sleep, and a little more
    slumber;"
Thus he wastes half his days, and his
    hours without number,
And when he gets up, he sits folding his
    hands,
Or walks about sauntering, or trifling he
    stands.

I pass'd by his garden, and saw the wild
    brier,
The thorn and the thistle grow broader
    and higher;
The clothes that hang on him are turning
    to rags;
And his money still wastes till he starves
    or he begs.

I made him a visit, still hoping to find
That he took better care for improving his
    mind:
He told me his dreams, talked of eating
    and drinking;
But he scarce reads his Bible, and never
    loves thinking.

Said I then to my heart, "Here's a lesson
    for me,"
This man's but a picture of what I might
    be:
But thanks to my friends for their care in
    my breeding,
Who taught me betimes to love working
    and reading.

"How the creatures order one about, and make one repeat lessons!" thought Alice. "I might just as well be at school at once." However, she got up, and began to repeat it, but her head was so full of the Lobster-Quadrille, that she hardly knew what she was saying; and the words came very queer indeed:—[7]

" *'Tis the voice of the Lobster: I heard him declare
  'You have baked me too brown, I must sugar my
    hair.'
As a duck with its eyelids, so he with his nose
Trims his belt and his buttons, and turns out his toes.
When the sands are all dry, he is gay as a lark,
And will talk in contemptuous tones of the Shark:
But, when the tide rises and sharks are around,
His voice has a timid and tremulous sound."*

"That's different from what *I* used to say when I was a child," said the Gryphon.

"Well, *I* never heard it before," said the Mock Turtle; "but it sounds uncommon nonsense."

Alice said nothing: she had sat down with her face in her hands, wondering if anything would *ever* happen in a natural way again.

"I should like to have it explained," said the Mock Turtle.

"She ca'n't explain it," said the Gryphon hastily. "Go on with the next verse."

"But about his toes?" the Mock Turtle persisted. "How *could* he turn them out with his nose, you know?"

"It's the first position in dancing,"[8] Alice said; but she was dreadfully puzzled by the whole thing, and longed to change the subject.

"Go on with the next verse," the Gryphon repeated: "it begins '*I passed by his garden.*'"

Alice did not dare to disobey, though she felt sure it would all come wrong, and she went on in a trembling voice:—

"I passed by his garden, and marked, with one eye,
How the Owl and the Panther were sharing a pie:
The Panther took pie-crust, and gravy, and meat,
While the Owl had the dish as its share of the treat.
When the pie was all finished, the Owl, as a boon,
Was kindly permitted to pocket the spoon:
While the Panther received knife and fork with a
*   growl,*
And concluded the banquet by—"[9]

"What *is* the use of repeating all that stuff?" the Mock Turtle interrupted, "if you don't explain it as you go on? It's by far the most confusing thing *I* ever heard!"

"Yes, I think you'd better leave off," said the Gryphon, and Alice was only too glad to do so.

Carroll's burlesque of Watts's doggerel underwent a good many changes. Before 1886 all editions of *Alice* had a first verse of four lines and a second verse that was interrupted after the second line. Carroll supplied the missing two lines for William Boyd's *Songs from Alice in Wonderland*, a book published in 1870. The full stanza then read:

I passed by his garden, and marked, with
*   one eye,*
How the owl and the oyster were sharing
*   a pie,*
While the duck and the Dodo, the lizard
*   and cat*
Were swimming in milk round the brim
*   of a hat.*

In 1886 Carroll revised and enlarged the poem to sixteen lines for the stage musical of *Alice*. This is the final version, which appears in editions of *Alice* after 1886. It is hard to believe, but an Essex vicar actually wrote a letter to *The St. James' Gazette* accusing Carroll of irreverence because of the Biblical allusion in the first line of his parody.

8. Selwyn Goodacre passed on to me his daughter's observation that Tenniel carefully followed Alice's remark by drawing the lobster with its feet in the first position in ballet.

9. The grim final words, "eating the owl," appear in the 1886 printed edition of Savile Clarke's operetta. Another and probably earlier version of the last couplet, given in Stuart Collingwood's biography, runs:

But the panther obtained both the fork
    and the knife,
So, when *he* lost his temper, the owl lost
    its life.

Carrollians have amused themselves by replacing "eating the owl" with other phrases, which are reported from time to time in the Lewis Carroll Society's newsletter, *Bandersnatch*. Here are some proposed endings: "taking a prowl," "wiping his jowl," "giving a howl," "taking a trowel," "kissing the fowl," "giving a scowl," and "donning a cowl."

10. On August 1, 1862, Carroll records in his diary that the Liddell sisters sang for him the popular song "Star of the Evening." The words and music were by James M. Sayles.

> Beautiful star in heav'n so bright,
> Softly falls thy silv'ry light,
> As thou movest from earth afar,
> Star of the evening, beautiful star.

CHORUS

> Beautiful star,
> Beautiful star,
> Star of the evening, beautiful star.

> In Fancy's eye thou seem'st to say,
> Follow me, come from earth away.
> Upward thy spirit's pinions try,
> To realms of love beyond the sky.

> Shine on, oh star of love divine,
> And may our soul's affection twine
> Around thee as thou movest afar,
> Star of the twilight, beautiful star.

Carroll's second stanza, with its E. E. Cummings-like partition of "pennyworth," does not appear in the original manuscript. The divisions of "beautiful," "soup," and "evening" suggest the manner in which the original song was sung. Cary Grant sobbed through the song in his role of the Mock Turtle in Paramount's undistinguished 1933 movie version of Alice.

Several readers have informed me that marine turtles often appear to weep copiously—especially females, when they make nocturnal egg-laying visits to the shore. One reader, Henry Smith, explains why: Reptilian kid-

"Shall we try another figure of the Lobster-Quadrille?" the Gryphon went on. "Or would you like the Mock Turtle to sing you another song?"

"Oh, a song, please, if the Mock Turtle would be so kind," Alice replied, so eagerly that the Gryphon said, in a rather offended tone, "Hm! No accounting for tastes! Sing her '*Turtle Soup*,' will you, old fellow?"

The Mock Turtle sighed deeply, and began, in a voice choked with sobs, to sing this:—[10]

> "Beautiful Soup, so rich and green,
> Waiting in a hot tureen!
> Who for such dainties would not stoop?
> Soup of the evening, beautiful Soup!
> Soup of the evening, beautiful Soup!
> Beau—ootiful Soo—oop!
> Beau—ootiful Soo—oop!
> Soo—oop of the e—e—evening,
> Beautiful, beautiful Soup!

> "Beautiful Soup! Who cares for fish,
> Game, or any other dish?
> Who would not give all else for two p
> ennyworth only of beautiful Soup?
> Pennyworth only of beautiful Soup?
> Beau—ootiful Soo—oop!
> Beau—ootiful Soo—oop!
> Soo—oop of the e—e—evening,
> Beautiful, beauti—FUL SOUP!"

"Chorus again!" cried the Gryphon, and the Mock Turtle had just begun to repeat it, when a cry of "The trial's beginning!" was heard in the distance.

"Come on!" cried the Gryphon, and, taking Alice by the hand, it hurried off, without waiting for the end of the song.

"What trial is it?" Alice panted as she ran; but the Gryphon only answered "Come on!" and ran the faster, while more and more faintly came, carried on the breeze that followed them, the melancholy words:—

> *"Soo—oop of the e—e—evening,*
> *Beautiful, beautiful Soup!"*

neys are not made to deal efficiently with removing salt from water. Marine turtles are equipped with a special gland that discharges salty water through a duct at the outside corners of each eye. Underwater the secretion washes away, but when the turtle is on land the secretion resembles a flood of tears. Carroll, who had a lively interest in zoology, undoubtedly knew of this phenomenon.

11

Who Stole the Tarts?

The King and Queen of Hearts were seated on their throne when they arrived, with a great crowd assembled about them—all sorts of little birds and beasts, as well as the whole pack of cards: the Knave was standing before them, in chains, with a soldier on each side to guard him; and near the King was the White Rabbit, with a trumpet in one hand, and a scroll of parchment in the other. In the very middle of the court was a table, with a large dish of tarts upon it: they looked so good, that it made Alice quite hungry to look at them—"I wish they'd get the trial done," she thought, "and hand round the refreshments!" But there seemed to be no chance of this; so she began looking at everything about her to pass away the time.

Alice had never been in a court of justice before, but she had read about them in books, and she was quite pleased to find that she knew the name of nearly everything there. "That's the judge," she said to herself, "because of his great wig."

The judge, by the way, was the King; and, as he wore his crown over the wig (look at the frontispiece if you want to see how he did it), he did not look at all comfortable, and it was certainly not becoming.

"And that's the jury-box," thought Alice;

"and those twelve creatures," (she was obliged to say "creatures," you see, because some of them were animals, and some were birds,) "I suppose they are the jurors." She said this last word two or three times over to herself, being rather proud of it: for she thought, and rightly too, that very few little girls of her age knew the meaning of it at all. However, "jurymen" would have done just as well.

The twelve jurors were all writing very busily on slates. "What are they doing?" Alice whispered to the Gryphon. "They ca'n't have anything to put down yet, before the trial's begun."

"They're putting down their names," the Gryphon whispered in reply, "for fear they should forget them before the end of the trial."

"Stupid things!" Alice began in a loud indignant voice; but she stopped herself hastily, for the White Rabbit cried out "Silence in the court!", and the King put on his spectacles and looked anxiously round, to make out who was talking.

Alice could see, as well as if she were looking over their shoulders, that all the jurors were writing down "Stupid things!" on their slates, and she could even make out that one of them didn't know how to spell "stupid," and that he had to ask his neighbour to tell him. "A nice muddle their slates'll be in, before the trial's over!" thought Alice.

One of the jurors had a pencil that squeaked. This, of course, Alice could *not* stand, and she went round the court and got behind him, and very soon found an opportunity of taking it away. She did it so quickly that the poor little juror (it was Bill, the Lizard) could not make out at all what had become of it; so, after hunting all about for it, he was obliged to write with one finger for the rest of the day; and this was

1. As William and Ceil Baring-Gould note in their *Annotated Mother Goose* (Clarkson N. Potter, 1962, p. 149), the White Rabbit reads only the first lines of a four-stanza poem that originally appeared in *The European Magazine* (April 1782). The first stanza found its way into a collection of "Mother Goose" rhymes and probably owes its present fame, as the Baring-Goulds suggest, to its use by Carroll.

Here is the entire poem:

*The Queen of Hearts
She made some tarts,
All on a summer's day;
The Knave of Hearts
He stole the tarts,
And took them clean away.
The King of Hearts
Called for the tarts,
And beat the Knave full sore;
The Knave of Hearts
Brought back the tarts,
And vow'd he'd steal no more.*

*The King of Spades
He kissed the maids,
Which made the Queen full sore;
The Queen of Spades
She beat those maids,
And turned them out of door;
The Knave of Spades
Grieved for those jades,
And did for them implore;
The Queen so gent
She did relent
And vow'd she'd ne'er strike more.*

*The King of Clubs
He often drubs
His loving Queen and wife;
The Queen of Clubs
Returns his snubs,
And all is noise and strife;
The Knave of Clubs
Gives winks and rubs,
And swears he'll take her part;
For when our kings
Will do such things,
They should be made to smart.*

of very little use, as it left no mark on the slate.

"Herald, read the accusation!" said the King.

On this the White Rabbit blew three blasts on the trumpet, and then unrolled the parchment-scroll, and read as follows:—[1]

"*The Queen of Hearts, she made some tarts,
    All on a summer day:
The Knave of Hearts, he stole those tarts
    And took them quite away!*"

"Consider your verdict," the King said to the jury.

"Not yet, not yet!" the Rabbit hastily interrupted. "There's a great deal to come before that!"

"Call the first witness," said the King; and the White Rabbit blew three blasts on the trumpet, and called out "First witness!"

The first witness was the Hatter. He came in

with a teacup in one hand and a piece of bread-and-butter in the other. "I beg pardon, your Majesty," he began, "for bringing these in; but I hadn't quite finished my tea when I was sent for."

"You ought to have finished," said the King. "When did you begin?"

The Hatter looked at the March Hare, who had followed him into the court, arm-in-arm with the Dormouse. "Fourteenth of March, I *think* it was," he said.

"Fifteenth," said the March Hare.

"Sixteenth," said the Dormouse.

"Write that down," the King said to the jury; and the jury eagerly wrote down all three dates on their slates, and then added them up, and reduced the answer to shillings and pence.

"Take off your hat," the King said to the Hatter.

"It isn't mine," said the Hatter.

"*Stolen!*" the King exclaimed, turning to the jury, who instantly made a memorandum of the fact.

"I keep them to sell," the Hatter added as an explanation. "I've none of my own. I'm a hatter."

Here the Queen put on her spectacles, and began staring hard at the Hatter, who turned pale and fidgeted.

"Give your evidence," said the King; "and don't be nervous, or I'll have you executed on the spot."

This did not seem to encourage the witness at all: he kept shifting from one foot to the other, looking uneasily at the Queen, and in his confusion he bit a large piece out of his teacup instead of the bread-and-butter.[2]

Just at this moment Alice felt a very curious

The Diamond King
I fain would sing,
And likewise his fair Queen;
But that the Knave,
A haughty slave,
Must needs step in between;
Good Diamond King,
With hempen string,
The haughty Knave destroy!
Then may your Queen
With mind serene,
Your royal bed enjoy.

Tenniel's original drawing of the White Rabbit blowing the horn differs in many respects from the one printed.

2. It has been noticed that the Hatter's bow tie, in Tenniel's illustration for this scene, has its pointed end on his right, as in Newell's pictures. In two earlier Tenniel illustrations the tie points to the Hatter's left. Michael Hancher, in his book on Tenniel, cites this as one of several amusing inconsistencies in Tenniel's art.

3. The Queen is recalling the occasion, described in Chapter 7, on which the Hatter murdered the time by singing "'Twinkle, twinkle, little bat!'"

sensation, which puzzled her a good deal until she made out what it was: she was beginning to grow larger again, and she thought at first she would get up and leave the court; but on second thoughts she decided to remain where she was as long as there was room for her.

"I wish you wouldn't squeeze so," said the Dormouse, who was sitting next to her. "I can hardly breathe."

"I ca'n't help it," said Alice very meekly: "I'm growing."

"You've no right to grow *here*," said the Dormouse.

"Don't talk nonsense," said Alice more boldly: "you know you're growing too."

"Yes, but *I* grow at a reasonable pace," said the Dormouse: "not in that ridiculous fashion." And he got up very sulkily and crossed over to the other side of the court.

All this time the Queen had never left off staring at the Hatter, and, just as the Dormouse crossed the court, she said, to one of the officers of the court, "Bring me the list of the singers in the last concert!" on which the wretched Hatter trembled so, that he shook off both his shoes.[3]

"Give your evidence," the King repeated angrily, "or I'll have you executed, whether you're nervous or not."

"I'm a poor man, your

Majesty," the Hatter began, in a trembling voice, "and I hadn't begun my tea—not above a week or so—and what with the bread-and-butter getting so thin—and the twinkling of the tea—"[4]

"The twinkling of *what*?" said the King.

"It *began* with the tea," the Hatter replied.

"Of course twinkling *begins* with a T!" said the King sharply. "Do you take me for a dunce? Go on!"

"I'm a poor man," the Hatter went on, "and most things twinkled after that—only the March Hare said—"

"I didn't!" the March Hare interrupted in a great hurry.

"You did!" said the Hatter.

"I deny it!" said the March Hare.

"He denies it," said the King: "leave out that part."

"Well, at any rate, the Dormouse said—" the Hatter went on, looking anxiously round to see if he would deny it too; but the Dormouse denied nothing, being fast asleep.

"After that," continued the Hatter, "I cut some more bread-and-butter—"

"But what did the Dormouse say?" one of the jury asked.

"That I ca'n't remember," said the Hatter.

"You *must* remember," remarked the King, "or I'll have you executed."

The miserable Hatter dropped his teacup and bread-and-butter, and went down on one knee. "I'm a poor man, your Majesty," he began.

"You're a *very* poor *speaker*," said the King.

Here one of the guinea-pigs cheered, and was immediately suppressed by the officers of the court. (As that is rather a hard word, I will just explain to you how it was done. They had a large canvas bag, which tied up at the mouth with

4. If the Hatter had not been interrupted he would have said "tea tray." He is thinking of the song he sang at the Mad Tea Party about the bat that twinkled in the sky like a tea tray.

strings: into this they slipped the guinea-pig, head first, and then sat upon it.)

"I'm glad I've seen that done," thought Alice. "I've so often read in the newspapers, at the end of trials, 'There was some attempt at applause, which was immediately suppressed by the officers of the court,' and I never understood what it meant till now."

"If that's all you know about it, you may stand down," continued the King.

"I ca'n't go no lower," said the Hatter: "I'm on the floor, as it is."

"Then you may *sit* down," the King replied.

Here the other guinea-pig cheered, and was suppressed.

"Come, that finishes the guinea-pigs!" thought Alice. "Now we shall get on better."

"I'd rather finish my tea," said the Hatter, with an anxious look at the Queen, who was reading the list of singers.

"You may go," said the King, and the Hatter hurriedly left the court, without even waiting to put his shoes on.

"—and just take his head off outside," the

Queen added to one of the officers; but the Hatter was out of sight before the officer could get to the door.

"Call the next witness!" said the King.

The next witness was the Duchess's cook. She carried the pepper-box in her hand, and Alice guessed who it was, even before she got into the court, by the way the people near the door began sneezing all at once.

"Give your evidence," said the King.

"Sha'n't," said the cook.

The King looked anxiously at the White Rabbit, who said, in a low voice, "Your Majesty must cross-examine *this* witness."

"Well, if I must, I must," the King said with a melancholy air, and, after folding his arms and frowning at the cook till his eyes were nearly out of sight, he said, in a deep voice, "What are tarts made of?"

"Pepper, mostly," said the cook.

"Treacle," said a sleepy voice behind her.

"Collar that Dormouse!" the Queen shrieked out. "Behead that Dormouse! Turn that Dormouse out of court! Suppress him! Pinch him! Off with his whiskers!"

For some minutes the whole court was in confusion, getting the Dormouse turned out, and, by the time they had settled down again, the cook had disappeared.

"Never mind!" said the King, with an air of great relief. "Call the next witness." And, he added, in an undertone to the Queen, "Really, my dear, *you* must cross-examine the next witness. It quite makes my forehead ache!"

Alice watched the White Rabbit as he fumbled over the list, feeling very curious to see what the next witness would be like, "—for they haven't got much evidence *yet*," she said to herself. Imagine her surprise, when the White Rabbit read out, at the top of his shrill little voice, the name "Alice!"

of course," he said, in a very respectful tone, but frowning and making faces at him as he spoke.

"*Un*important, of course, I meant," the King hastily said, and went on to himself in an under-tone, "important—unimportant—unimportant—important—" as if he were trying which word sounded best.

Some of the jury wrote it down "important," and some "unimportant." Alice could see this, as she was near enough to look over their slates; "but it doesn't matter a bit," she thought to herself.

At this moment the King, who had been for some time busily writing in his note-book, called out "Silence!", and read out from his book, "Rule Forty-two.² *All persons more than a mile high to leave the court.*"

Everybody looked at Alice.

"*I'm* not a mile high," said Alice.

"You are," said the King.

"Nearly two miles high," added the Queen.

"Well, I sha'n't go, at any rate," said Alice: "besides, that's not a regular rule: you invented it just now."

"It's the oldest rule in the book," said the King.

"Then it ought to be Number One," said Alice.

The King turned pale, and shut his note-book hastily. "Consider your verdict," he said to the jury, in a low trembling voice.

"There's more evidence to come yet, please your Majesty," said the White Rabbit, jumping up in a great hurry: "this paper has just been picked up."

"What's in it?" said the Queen.

"I haven't opened it yet," said the White Rabbit; "but it seems to be a letter, written by the prisoner to—to somebody."

2. The number forty-two held a spe-cial meaning for Carroll. The first *Alice* book had forty-two illustra-tions. An important nautical rule, Rule 42, is cited in Carroll's preface to *The Hunting of the Snark*, and in Fit 1, stanza 7, the Baker comes aboard the ship with forty-two care-fully packed boxes. In his poem "Phantasmagoria," Canto 1, stanza 16, Carroll gives his age as forty-two although he was five years younger at the time. In *Through the Looking-Glass* the White King sends 4,207 horses and men to restore Humpty Dumpty, and seven is a factor of forty-two. Alice's age in the second book is seven years and six months, and seven times six equals forty-two. It is probably coincidental, but (as Philip Benham has observed) each *Alice* book has twelve chapters, or twenty-four in all, and twenty-four is forty-two backwards.

For more numerology about forty-two—in Carroll's life, in the Bible, in the Sherlock Holmes canon, and elsewhere—see the forty-second issue of *Bandersnatch*, the newsletter of England's Lewis Carroll Society. (The issue was published in January 1942 plus 42.) See also Edward Wakeling's "What I Tell You Forty-two Times Is True!" (*Jabberwocky*, Autumn 1977), his "Further Find-ings About the Number Forty-two" (*Jabberwocky*, Winter/Spring 1988) and Note 32 of my *Annotated Snark* as it appears in *The Hunting of the Snark* (William Kaufmann, Inc., 1981). In Douglas Adams's popular science-fiction novel *The Hitch-hiker's Guide to the Galaxy*, forty-two is said to be the answer to the "Ultimate Question about Every-thing." See Chapter 1, Note 4, for still another forty-two.

3. If the Knave didn't write it, asks Selwyn Goodacre, how did he know it wasn't signed?

"It must have been that," said the King, "unless it was written to nobody, which isn't usual, you know."

"Who is it directed to?" said one of the jurymen.

"It isn't directed at all," said the White Rabbit: "in fact, there's nothing written on the *outside*." He unfolded the paper as he spoke, and added "It isn't a letter, after all: it's a set of verses."

"Are they in the prisoner's handwriting?" asked another of the jurymen.

"No, they're not," said the White Rabbit, "and that's the queerest thing about it." (The jury all looked puzzled.)

"He must have imitated somebody else's hand," said the King. (The jury all brightened up again.)

"Please your Majesty," said the Knave, "I didn't write it, and they ca'n't prove that I did: there's no name signed at the end."[3]

"If you didn't sign it," said the King, "that only makes the matter worse. You *must* have meant some mischief, or else you'd have signed your name like an honest man."

There was a general clapping of hands at this: it was the first really clever thing the King had said that day.

"That *proves* his guilt, of course," said the Queen: "so, off with—."

"It doesn't prove anything of the sort!" said Alice. "Why, you don't even know what they're about!"

"Read them," said the King.

The White Rabbit put on his spectacles. "Where shall I begin, please your Majesty?" he asked.

"Begin at the beginning," the King said, very

gravely, "and go on till you come to the end: then stop."

There was dead silence in the court, whilst the White Rabbit read out these verses:—[4]

> *"They told me you had been to her,*
> *   And mentioned me to him;*
> *She gave me a good character,*
> *   But said I could not swim.*
>
> *He sent them word I had not gone*
> *   (We know it to be true):*
> *If she should push the matter on,*
> *   What would become of you?*
>
> *I gave her one, they gave him two,*
> *   You gave us three or more;*
> *They all returned from him to you,*
> *   Though they were mine before.*
>
> *If I or she should chance to be*
> *   Involved in this affair,*
> *He trusts to you to set them free,*
> *   Exactly as we were.*
>
> *My notion was that you had been*
> *   (Before she had this fit)*
> *An obstacle that came between*
> *   Him, and ourselves, and it.*
>
> *Don't let him know she liked them best,*
> *   For this must ever be*
> *A secret, kept from all the rest,*
> *   Between yourself and me."*

"That's the most important piece of evidence we've heard yet," said the King, rubbing his hands; "so now let the jury—"

"If any one of them can explain it," said Alice, (she had grown so large in the last few minutes that she wasn't a bit afraid of interrupting him,)

4. The White Rabbit's evidence consists of six verses with confused pronouns and very little sense. They are taken in considerably revised form from Carroll's eight-verse nonsense poem, "She's All My Fancy Painted Him," which first appeared in *The Comic Times* of London in 1855. The first line of the original copies the first line of "Alice Gray," a sentimental song by William Mee that was popular at the time. The rest of the poem has no resemblance to the song except in meter.

Carroll's earlier version, with his introductory note, follows:

This affecting fragment was found in MS. among the papers of the well-known author of "Was it You or I?" a tragedy, and the two popular novels, "Sister and Son," and "The Niece's Legacy, or the Grateful Grandfather."

> *She's all my fancy painted him*
> *   (I make no idle boast);*
> *If he or you had lost a limb,*
> *   Which would have suffered most?*
>
> *He said that you had been to her,*
> *   And seen me here before;*
> *But, in another character,*
> *   She was the same of yore.*
>
> *There was not one that spoke to us,*
> *   Of all that thronged the street:*
> *So he sadly got into a bus,*
> *   And pattered with his feet.*
>
> *They sent him word I had not gone*
> *   (We know it to be true);*
> *If she should push the matter on,*
> *   What would become of you?*
>
> *They gave her one, they gave me two,*
> *   They gave us three or more;*
> *They all returned from him to you,*
> *   Though they were mine before.*
>
> *If I or she should chance to be*
> *   Involved in this affair,*
> *He trusts to you to set them free,*
> *   Exactly as we were.*

It seemed to me that you had been
    (Before she had this fit)
An obstacle, that came between
    Him, and ourselves, and it.

Don't let him know she liked them best,
    For this must ever be
A secret, kept from all the rest,
    Between yourself and me.

Did Carroll introduce this poem into his story because the song behind it tells of the unrequited love of a man for a girl named Alice? I quote from John M. Shaw's booklet (cited in Note 4 of Chapter 6) the song's opening stanzas:

She's all my fancy painted her,
    She's lovely, she's divine,
But her heart it is another's,
    She never can be mine.

Yet loved I as man never loved,
    A love without decay,
O, my heart, my heart is breaking
    For the love of Alice Gray.

5. "A statement that is a measure of her increasing confidence," comments Selwyn Goodacre (*Jabberwocky*, Spring 1982), "because *we* know she hasn't a coin in her pocket—she told the Dodo she only had the thimble."

"I'll give him sixpence.[5] *I* don't believe there's an atom of meaning in it."

The jury all wrote down, on their slates, "*She* doesn't believe there's an atom of meaning in it," but none of them attempted to explain the paper.

"If there's no meaning in it," said the King, "that saves a world of trouble, you know, as we needn't try to find any. And yet I don't know," he went on, spreading out the verses on his knee, and looking at them with one eye; "I seem to see some meaning in them, after all. '—*said I could not swim*—' you ca'n't swim, can you?" he added, turning to the Knave.

The Knave shook his head sadly. "Do I look like it?" he said. (Which he certainly did *not*, being made entirely of cardboard.)

"All right, so far," said the King; and he went on muttering over the verses to himself: "'*We know it to be true*'—that's the jury, of course—'*If she should push the matter on*'—that must be the Queen—'*What would become of you?*'—What, indeed!—'*I gave her one, they gave him*

two'—why, that must be what he did with the tarts, you know—"

"But it goes on '*they all returned from him to you,*'" said Alice.

"Why, there they are?" said the King triumphantly, pointing to the tarts on the table. "Nothing can be clearer than *that*. Then again—'*before she had this fit*'—you never had *fits*, my dear, I think?" he said to the Queen.

"Never!" said the Queen, furiously, throwing an inkstand at the Lizard as she spoke. (The unfortunate little Bill had left off writing on his slate with one finger, as he found it made no mark; but he now hastily began again, using the ink, that was trickling down his face, as long as it lasted.)[6]

"Then the words don't *fit* you," said the King, looking round the court with a smile. There was a dead silence.[7]

"It's a pun!" the King added in an angry tone, and everybody laughed. "Let the jury consider their verdict," the King said, for about the twentieth time that day.

"No, no!" said the Queen. "Sentence first—verdict afterwards."

"Stuff and nonsense!" said Alice loudly. "The idea of having the sentence first!"

"Hold your tongue!" said the Queen, turning purple.

"I wo'n't!" said Alice.

"Off with her head!" the Queen shouted at the top of her voice. Nobody moved.

"Who cares for *you*?" said Alice (she had grown to her full size by this time). "You're nothing but a pack of cards!"

At this the whole pack rose up into the air, and came flying down upon her;[8] she gave a little scream, half of fright and half of anger, and tried

6. This is the first of two references to throwing ink on someone's face. In the first chapter of *Through the Looking-Glass*, Alice intends to revive the White King by tossing ink on his face.

7. A similar reaction to a pun is one of the five characteristic traits of a snark, as we learn in the second "fit" of Carroll's *The Hunting of the Snark*:

> The third is its slowness in taking a jest;
>   Should you happen to venture on one,
> It will sigh like a thing that is deeply distressed;
>   And it always looks grave at a pun.

Tenniel's illustration of the King looking around with a faint smile was clearly intended to show the King only a moment after the scene that appeared in the book's frontispiece. The Knave has not altered his defiant stance, although the King (as Selwyn Goodacre noticed) has managed to change his crown, put on spectacles, and discard his orb and scepter, and the three court officials have fallen asleep. Observe that in both pictures Tenniel shaded the Knave's nose to suggest that he is a lush. Victorians thought of criminals as heavy drinkers, and shading noses was a convention among cartoonists then, as it is now, to signify boozers. In *The Nursery "Alice,"* whose illustrations were hand-colored by Tenniel, the tip of the Knave's nose is a rosy color in the frontispiece as well as in the picture in Chapter 8 where the Knave is presenting the King with his crown.

CHARLES BENNETT'S FRONTISPIECE
FOR *The Fables of Aesop and Others*.

Jeffrey Stern, in *Jabberwocky* (Spring 1978), calls attention to many similarities between this frontispiece and the frontispiece of *The Fables of Aesop and Others Translated into Human Nature* (1857), illustrated by Tenniel's fellow *Punch* artist Charles Henry Bennett:

The Court clerk (the owl) has the stunned look of the King, and the Lion has an identical scowl to the Queen's (she is even looking the same way). Some of the jurors and the bewigged bird/lawyers are in similar pose, and the pleading dog is in something of the same position as the Knave. All this would not mean very much but for the fact that Bennett's book appeared in 1857—eight years before *Wonderland*. The fable illustrated, incidentally, is "Man tried at the Court of the Lion for the Ill-treatment of a Horse."

8. In Tenniel's illustration of this scene the cards have become ordinary playing cards, though three have retained vestigial noses. In Peter Newell's version some even have heads, arms, and legs.

In many editions of *Alice in Wonderland* (I have not checked first

to beat them off, and found herself lying on the bank, with her head in the lap of her sister, who was gently brushing away some dead leaves that had fluttered down from the trees upon her face.

"Wake up, Alice dear!" said her sister. "Why, what a long sleep you've had!"

"Oh, I've had such a curious dream!" said Alice. And she told her sister, as well as she could remember them, all these strange Adventures of hers that you have just been reading about; and, when she had finished, her sister kissed her, and said "It *was* a curious dream, dear, certainly; but now run in to your tea: it's getting late." So Alice got up and ran off, thinking while she ran, as well she might, what a wonderful dream it had been.

But her sister sat still just as she left her, leaning her head on her hand, watching the setting sun, and thinking of little Alice and all her wonderful Adventures, till she too began dreaming after a fashion, and this was her dream:—

First, she dreamed about little Alice herself: once again the tiny hands were clasped upon her knee, and the bright eager eyes were looking up into hers—she could hear the very tones of her voice, and see that queer little toss of her head to keep back the wandering hair that *would* always get into her eyes—and still as she listened, or seemed to listen, the whole place around her became alive with the strange creatures of her little sister's dream.[9]

The long grass rustled at her feet as the White Rabbit hurried by—the frightened Mouse splashed his way through the neighbouring pool—she could hear the rattle of the teacups as the March Hare and his friends shared their never-ending meal, and the shrill voice of the Queen ordering off her unfortunate guests to execution—once more the pig-baby was sneezing on the Duchess's knee, while plates and dishes crashed around it—once more the shriek of the Gryphon, the squeaking of the Lizard's slate-pencil, and the choking of the suppressed guinea-pigs, filled the air, mixed up with the distant sob of the miserable Mock Turtle.

So she sat on, with closed eyes, and half believed herself in Wonderland, though she knew she had but to open them again, and all would change to dull reality—the grass would be only rustling in the wind, and the pool rippling to the waving of the reeds—the rattling teacups would change to tinkling sheep-bells, and the Queen's shrill cries to the voice of the shepherd-boy—and the sneeze of the baby, the shriek of the

editions), the card hidden by the six of spades has on its left margin the mysterious letters "B. ROLLITZ." Perhaps he was an employee of the Dalziel brothers, who made the wood engravings.

To underscore the return from dream to reality, as Richard Kelly notes in his contribution to *Lewis Carroll: A Celebration*, edited by Edward Guiliano, Tenniel has undressed the White Rabbit.

9. This dream-within-a-dream motif (Alice's sister dreaming of Alice's dream) reoccurs in a more complicated form in the sequel. See *Through the Looking-Glass*, Chapter 4, Note 10.

10. On the last page of Carroll's hand-lettered manuscript of *Alice's Adventures Under Ground*, which he gave to Alice Liddell, he pasted an oval photograph of her face that he had taken in 1859 when she was seven, the age of Alice in the story. It was not until 1977 that Morton Cohen discovered concealed underneath this photograph a drawing of Alice's face. It is the only known sketch Dodgson ever made of the real Alice.

Gryphon, and all the other queer noises, would change (she knew) to the confused clamour of the busy farm-yard—while the lowing of the cattle in the distance would take the place of the Mock Turtle's heavy sobs.

Lastly, she pictured to herself how this same little sister of hers would, in the after-time, be herself a grown woman; and how she would keep, through all her riper years, the simple and loving heart of her childhood; and how she would gather about her other little children, and make *their* eyes bright and eager with many a strange tale, perhaps even with the dream of Wonderland of long ago; and how she would feel with all their simple sorrows, and find a pleasure in all their simple joys, remembering her own child-life, and the happy summer days.[10]

Through the Looking-Glass
and
What Alice Found There

Contents

White Pawn (Alice) to play, and win in eleven moves.

RED

WHITE

1. Alice meets R. Q.
2. Alice through Q's 3d (*by railway*) to Q's 4th (*Tweedledum and Tweedledee*)
3. Alice meets W. Q. (*with shawl*)
4. Alice to Q's 5th (*shop, river, shop*)
5. Alice to Q's 6th (*Humpty Dumpty*)
6. Alice to Q's 7th (*forest*)
7. W. Kt. takes R. Kt.
8. Alice to Q's 8th (*coronation*)
9. Alice becomes Queen
10. Alice castles (*feast*)
11. Alice takes R. Q. & wins

1. R. Q. to K. R's 4th
2. W. Q. to Q. B's 4th (*after shawl*)
3. W. Q. to Q. B's 5th (*becomes sheep*)
4. W. Q. to K. B's 8th (*leaves egg on shelf*)
5. W. Q. to Q. B's 8th (*flying from R. Kt.*)
6. R. Kt. to K's 2nd (ch.)
7. W. Kt. to K. B's 5th
8. R. Q. to K's sq. (*examination*)
9. Queens castle
10. W. Q. to Q. R's 6th (*soup*)

Preface to the 1897 Edition

As the chess-problem, given on the previous page, has puzzled some of my readers, it may be well to explain that it is correctly worked out, so far as the *moves* are concerned. The *alternation* of Red and White is perhaps not so strictly observed as it might be, and the "castling" of the three Queens is merely a way of saying that they entered the palace:[1] but the "check" of the White King at move 6, the capture of the Red Knight at move 7, and the final "checkmate" of the Red King, will be found, by any one who will take the trouble to set the pieces and play the moves as directed, to be strictly in accordance with the laws of the game.[2]

The new words, in the poem "Jabberwocky," have given rise to some differences of opinion as to their pronunciation: so it may be well to give instructions on *that* point also. Pronounce "slithy" as if it were the two words "sly, the": make the "g" *hard* in "gyre" and "gimble": and pronounce "rath" to rhyme with "bath."

For this sixty-first thousand, fresh electrotypes have been taken from the wood-blocks (which, never having been used for printing from, are in as good condition as when first cut in 1871), and the whole book has been set up fresh with new type. If the artistic qualities of this re-issue fall short, in any particular, of those possessed by the

1. There is no chess move in which queens castle. Carroll is here explaining that when the three Queens (the Red Queen, the White Queen, and Alice) have entered the "castle," they have moved to the eighth row, where pawns become queens.

2. Carroll's description of the chess problem, which underlies the book's action, is accurate. One is at loss to account for the statement on page 48 of *A Handbook of the Literature of the Rev. C. L. Dodgson*, by Sidney Williams and Falconer Madan, that "no attempt" is made to execute a normal checkmate. The final mate is completely orthodox. It is true, however, as Carroll himself points out, that red and white do not alternate moves properly, and some of the "moves" listed by Carroll are not represented. by actual movements of the pieces on the board (for example, Alice's first, third, ninth and tenth "moves," and the "castling" of the queens).

The most serious violation of chess rules occurs near the end of the problem, when the White King is placed in check by the Red Queen without either side taking account of the fact. "Hardly a move has a sane purpose, from the point of view of chess," writes Mr. Madan. It is true that both sides play an exceedingly careless game, but what else could one expect from the mad creatures behind the mirror? At two points the White Queen passes up a chance to checkmate and on another occasion she flees from the Red Knight when she could have captured him. Both oversights, however, are in keeping with her absent-mindedness.

Considering the staggering difficulties involved in dovetailing a chess game with an amusing nonsense fantasy, Carroll does a remarkable job. At no time, for example, does Alice exchange words with a piece that is not then on a square alongside her own. Queens bustle about doing things while their husbands remain relatively fixed and impotent, just as in actual chess games. The White Knight's eccentricities fit admirably the eccentric way in which Knights move; even the tendency of the Knights to fall off their horses, on one side or the other, suggests the knight's move, which is two squares in one direction followed by one square to the right or left. In order to assist the reader in integrating the chess moves with the story, each move will be noted in the text at the precise point where it occurs.

The rows of the giant chessboard are separated from each other by brooks. The columns are divided by hedges. Throughout the problem Alice remains on the queen's file except for her final move when (as queen) she captures the Red Queen to checkmate the dozing Red King. It is amusing to note that it is the Red Queen who persuades Alice to advance along her file to the eighth square. The Queen is protecting herself with this advice, for white has at the outset an easy, though inelegant, checkmate in three moves. The White Knight first checks at KKt. 3. If the Red King moves to either Q6 or Q5, white can mate with the Queen at QB3. The only alternative

original issue, it will not be for want of painstaking on the part of author, publisher, or printer.

I take this opportunity of announcing that the Nursery "Alice," hitherto priced at four shillings, net, is now to be had on the same terms as the ordinary shilling picture-books—although I feel sure that it is, in every quality (except the *text* itself, on which I am not qualified to pronounce), greatly superior to them. Four shillings was a perfectly reasonable price to charge, considering the very heavy initial outlay I had incurred: still, as the Public have practically said "We will *not* give more than a shilling for a picture-book, however artistically got-up," I am content to reckon my outlay on the book as so much dead loss, and, rather than let the little ones, for whom it was written, go without it, I am selling it at a price which is, to me, much the same thing as *giving* it away.

Christmas, 1896

Child of the pure unclouded brow[3]
    And dreaming eyes of wonder!
Though time be fleet, and I and thou
    Are half a life asunder,
Thy loving smile will surely hail
The love-gift of a fairy-tale.

I have not seen thy sunny face,
    Nor heard thy silver laughter:
No thought of me shall find a place
    In thy young life's hereafter—[4]
Enough that now thou wilt not fail
To listen to my fairy-tale.

A tale begun in other days,
    When summer suns were glowing—
A simple chime, that served to time
    The rhythm of our rowing—
Whose echoes live in memory yet,
Though envious years would say "forget."

Come, hearken then, ere voice of dread,
    With bitter tidings laden,
Shall summon to unwelcome bed[5]
    A melancholy maiden!
We are but older children, dear,
Who fret to find our bedtime near.

Without, the frost, the blinding snow,
    The storm-wind's moody madness—
Within, the firelight's ruddy glow,
    And childhood's nest of gladness.
The magic words shall hold thee fast:
Thou shalt not heed the raving blast.

is for the Red King to move to K4. The White Queen then checks on QB5, forcing the Red King to K3. The Queen then mates on Q6. This calls, of course, for an alertness of mind not possessed by either the Knight or Queen.

Attempts have been made to work out a better sequence of chess moves that would both fit the narrative and at the same time conform to all the rules of the game. The most ambitious attempt of this sort that I have come across is to be found in the *British Chess Magazine* (Vol. 30, May 1910, page 181). Donald M. Liddell presents an entire chess game, starting with the Bird Opening and ending with a mate by Alice when she enters the eighth square on her sixty-sixth move! The choice of opening is appropriate, for no chess expert ever had a more hilarious and eccentric style of play than the Englishman H. E. Bird. Whether Donald Liddell is related to *the* Liddells I have not been able to determine.

In the Middle Ages and Renaissance chess games were sometimes played with human pieces on enormous fields (see Rabelais's *Gargantua and Pantagruel*, Book 5, Chapters 24 and 25), but I know of no earlier attempt than Carroll's to base a fictional narrative on animated chess pieces. It has been done many times since, mostly by science-fiction writers. A recent example is Poul Anderson's fine short story *The Immortal Game (Fantasy and Science Fiction*, February 1954).

For many reasons chess pieces are singularly appropriate to the second *Alice* book. They complement the playing cards of the first book, permitting the return of kings and queens; the loss of knaves is more than offset by the acquisition of knights. Alice's bewildering changes of size in the first book are replaced by equally bewildering changes of place, occasioned of course by the movements of chess pieces over the board. By a happy accident chess also ties in beautifully with the mirror-reflection motif. Not only do rooks, bishops, and knights come in pairs, but the asymmetric arrangement of one player's pieces at the start of a game (asymmetric because of the positions of king and queen) is an exact mirror reflection of his opponent's pieces. Finally, the mad quality of the chess game conforms to the mad logic of the looking-glass world.

DRAMATIS PERSONAE
(*As arranged before commencement of game.*)

WHITE		RED	
PIECES	PAWNS	PAWNS	PIECES
Tweedledee	Daisy	Daisy	Humpty Dumpty
Unicorn	Haigha	Messenger	Carpenter
Sheep	Oyster	Oyster	Walrus
W. Queen	"Lily"	Tiger-Lily	R. Queen
W. King	Fawn	Rose	R. King
Aged man	Oyster	Oyster	Crow
W. Knight	Hatta	Frog	R. Knight
Tweedledum	Daisy	Daisy	Lion

The above list of dramatis personae appeared in early editions of the book before Carroll replaced it with his 1896 preface. Removing it was wise because it only adds confusion to the chess game. I will cite only one instance. If the Tweedle brothers are the two white rooks, asked Denis Crutch in a lecture on the chess game (published in *Jabberwocky*, Summer 1972), then who is the white rook on the first row of Carroll's diagram?

The arrangement of the words in the starting position of a chess game makes it easy to identify each piece

And, though the shadow of a sigh
  May tremble through the story,
For "happy summer days"[6] gone by,
  And vanish'd summer glory—
It shall not touch, with breath of bale,[7]
The pleasance[8] of our fairy-tale.

and pawn. Observe that the bishops, never mentioned in the story, are here linked to the Sheep, Aged man, Walrus, and Crow, though for no discernible reason.

3. Proofs of the prefatory poem have survived with alterations in Carroll's handwriting. The changes made for the first edition are listed on page 60 of *The Lewis Carroll Handbook* (Oxford, 1931) by Sidney Williams and Falconer Madan. In stanza 4, line 4, "A melancholy maiden" replaced "A wilful weary maiden." In stanza 5, line 1, "Without, the frost, the blinding snow" replaced "Without, the whirling wind and snow," and the next line, "The storm-wind's moody madness" replaced "That lash themselves to madness."

4. Although the majority of Carroll's child-friends broke off contact with him (or he with them) after their adolescence, the sad presentment of these lines proved groundless. Among the finest tributes ever paid to Carroll are the recollections of him expressed by Alice in her later years.

5. "unwelcome bed": A reference to the melancholy maiden's death, with the Christian implication that it will be merely a bedtime slumber, and, as Freudian critics never tire of pointing out, perhaps with subconscious overtones of the marriage bed.

6. The three words in quotation marks are the last three words of *Alice's Adventures in Wonderland*.

7. "breath of bale": breath of sorrow.

8. "pleasance": The word was "pleasures" in proofs of the book. Carroll cleverly changed it to the archaic "pleasance" so he could introduce Alice Liddell's middle name.

I

Looking-Glass House

One thing was certain, that the *white* kitten had had nothing to do with it—it was the black kitten's fault entirely. For the white kitten had been having its face washed by the old cat for the last quarter of an hour (and bearing it pretty well, considering): so you see that it *couldn't* have had any hand in the mischief.

The way Dinah washed her children's faces was this: first she held the poor thing down by its ear with one paw, and then with the other paw she rubbed its face all over, the wrong way, beginning at the nose: and just now, as I said, she was hard at work on the white kitten, which was lying quite still and trying to purr—no doubt feeling that it was all meant for its good.

But the black kitten had been finished with earlier in the afternoon, and so, while Alice was sitting curled up in a corner of the great arm-chair, half talking to herself and half asleep, the kitten had been having a grand game of romps with the ball of worsted Alice had been trying to wind up, and had been rolling it up and down till it had all come undone again; and there it was, spread over the hearth-rug, all knots and tangles, with the kitten running after its own tail in the middle.

"Oh, you wicked wicked little thing!" cried Alice, catching up the kitten, and giving it a little

1. It was characteristic of Carroll, with his love of sharp contrast, to open his sequel on an indoor, midwinter scene. (The previous book opens out of doors on a warm May afternoon.) The wintry weather also harmonizes with the wintry symbols of age and approaching death that enter into his prefatory and terminal poems. The preparation for a bonfire and Alice's remark "Do you know what tomorrow is, Kitty?" suggest that the date was November 4, the day before Guy Fawkes Day. (The holiday was annually celebrated at Christ Church with a huge bonfire in Peckwater Quadrangle.) This is supported by Alice's statement to the White Queen (Chapter 5) that she is *exactly* seven and one half years old, for Alice Liddell's birthday was May 4, and the previous trip to Wonderland occurred on May 4, when Alice presumably was exactly seven (see Note 6, Chapter 7 of the previous book). As Robert Mitchell says in a letter, May 4 and November 4, being six months apart, are two dates that could not be further separated.

This leaves open the question of whether the year is 1859 (when Alice actually was seven), 1860, 1861, or 1862 when Carroll told and wrote down the story of Alice's first adventure. November 4, 1859, was a Friday. In 1860 it was Sunday, in 1861 Monday, and in 1862 Tuesday. The last date seems the most plausible in view of Alice's remark to the kitten (in the next paragraph but one) that she is saving up her punishments until a week from Wednesday.

Mrs. Mavis Baitey, in her booklet *Alice's Adventures in Oxford* (A Pitkin Pictorial Guide, 1980), argues that the day was March 10, 1863, the wedding day of the Prince of Wales. The occasion was celebrated at Oxford with bonfires and fireworks, and in his diary Carroll tells of taking

kiss to make it understand that it was in disgrace. "Really, Dinah ought to have taught you better manners! You *ought*, Dinah, you know you ought!" she added, looking reproachfully at the old cat, and speaking in as cross a voice as she could manage—and then she scrambled back into the arm-chair, taking the kitten and the worsted with her, and began winding up the ball again. But she didn't get on very fast, as she was talking all the time, sometimes to the kitten, and sometimes to herself. Kitty sat very demurely on her knee, pretending to watch the progress of the winding, and now and then putting out one paw and gently touching the ball, as if it would be glad to help if it might.

"Do you know what to-morrow is, Kitty?" Alice began. "You'd have guessed if you'd been up in the window with me—only Dinah was making you tidy, so you couldn't. I was watching the boys getting in sticks for the bonfire[1]—and it wants plenty of sticks, Kitty! Only it got so cold, and it snowed so, they had to leave off. Never mind, Kitty, we'll go and see the bonfire to-morrow." Here Alice wound two or three turns of the worsted round the kitten's neck, just to see how it would look: this led to a scramble, in which the ball rolled down upon the floor, and yards and yards of it got unwound again.

"Do you know, I was so angry, Kitty," Alice went on, as soon as they were comfortably settled again, "when I saw all the mischief you had been doing, I was very nearly opening the window, and putting you out into the snow! And you'd have deserved it, you little mischievous darling! What have you got to say for yourself? Now don't interrupt me!" she went on, holding up one finger. "I'm going to tell you all your faults. Number one: you squeaked twice while Dinah was washing your face this morning. Now you ca'n't deny it, Kitty: I heard you! What's that you say?" (pretending that the kitten was speaking). "Her paw went into your eye? Well, that's *your* fault, for keeping your eyes open—if you'd shut them tight up, it wouldn't have happened. Now don't make any more excuses, but listen! Number two: you pulled Snowdrop[2] away by the tail just as I had put down the saucer of milk

Alice on an evening tour through the university: "It was delightful to see the thorough abandonment with which Alice enjoyed the whole thing." However, Carroll's diary for March 9 and 10 makes no mention of the snow Alice speaks of. However, Mrs. Baitey's conjecture is supported by the fact that in England snow is very rare in early November and quite common in March.

2. Snowdrop was the name of a kitten belonging to one of Carroll's early child-friends, Mary MacDonald. Mary was the daughter of Carroll's good friend George MacDonald, the Scottish poet and novelist, and author of such well-known children's fantasies as *The Princess and the Goblin* and *At the Back of the North Wind.* The MacDonald children were in part responsible for Carroll's decision to publish *Alice's Adventures in Wonderland.* To test the story's general appeal, he asked Mrs. MacDonald to read the manuscript to her children. The reception was enthusiastic. Greville, age six (who later recalled the occasion in his book *George MacDonald and His Wife*), declared that there ought to be sixty thousand copies of it.

Kitty and Snowdrop, the black and white kittens, reflect the chessboard's black and white squares, and the red and white pieces of the book's chess game.

before her! What, you were thirsty, were you? How do you know she wasn't thirsty too? Now for number three: you unwound every bit of the worsted while I wasn't looking!

"That's three faults, Kitty, and you've not been punished for any of them yet. You know I'm saving up all your punishments for Wednesday week[3]—Suppose they had saved up all *my* punishments?" she went on, talking more to herself than the kitten. "What *would* they do at the end of a year? I should be sent to prison, I suppose, when the day came. Or—let me see— suppose each punishment was to be going without a dinner: then, when the miserable day came, I should have to go without fifty dinners at once! Well, I shouldn't mind *that* much! I'd far rather go without them than eat them!

"Do you hear the snow against the window-panes, Kitty? How nice and soft it sounds! Just as if some one was kissing the window all over outside. I wonder if the snow *loves* the trees and fields, that it kisses them so gently? And then it covers them up snug, you know, with a white quilt; and perhaps it says 'Go to sleep, darlings, till the summer comes again.' And when they wake up in the summer, Kitty, they dress themselves all in green, and dance about—whenever the wind blows—oh, that's very pretty!" cried Alice, dropping the ball of worsted to clap her hands. "And I do so *wish* it was true! I'm sure the woods look sleepy in the autumn, when the leaves are getting brown.

"Kitty, can you play chess? Now, don't smile, my dear, I'm asking it seriously. Because, when we were playing just now, you watched just as if you understood it: and when I said 'Check!' you purred! Well, it *was* a nice check, Kitty, and really I might have won, if it hadn't been for that nasty Knight, that came wriggling[4] down among my pieces. Kitty, dear, let's pretend—" And here I wish I could tell you half the things Alice used to say, beginning with her favourite phrase "Let's pretend." She had had quite a long argument with her sister only the day before—all because Alice had begun with "Let's pretend we're kings and queens"; and her sister, who liked being very exact, had argued that they couldn't, because there were only two of them, and Alice had been reduced at last to say "Well, *you* can be one of them, then, and *I'll* be all the rest." And once she had really frightened her old nurse by shouting suddenly in her ear, "Nurse! Do let's pretend that I'm a hungry hyæna, and you're a bone!"

But this is taking us away from Alice's speech to the kitten. "Let's pretend that you're the Red Queen, Kitty! Do you know, I think if you sat up and folded your arms, you'd look exactly like her. Now do try, there's a dear!" And Alice got the Red Queen off the table, and set it up before the kitten as a model for it to imitate: however, the thing didn't succeed, principally, Alice said, because the kitten wouldn't fold its arms properly. So, to punish it, she held it up to the Looking-glass, that it might see how sulky it was, "—and if you're not good directly," she added, "I'll put you through into Looking-glass House. How would you like *that*?

"Now, if you'll only attend, Kitty, and not talk so much, I'll tell you all my ideas about Looking-glass House. First, there's the room you can see through the glass—that's just the same as our drawing-room, only the things go the other way.[5] I can see all of it when I get upon a chair— all but the bit just behind the fireplace. Oh! I do so wish I could see *that* bit! I want so much to

4. "Wriggling" is a good description of how the knight moves across a chessboard.

5. The looking-glass theme seems to have been a late addition to the story. We have the word of Alice Liddell that a good part of the book was based on chess tales that Carroll told the Liddell girls at a time when they were learning excitedly how to play the game. It was not until 1868 that another Alice, Carroll's distant cousin Alice Raikes, played a role in suggesting the mirror motif. This is how she told the story in the London *Times*, January 22, 1932:

As children, we lived in Onslow Square and used to play in the garden behind the houses. Charles Dodgson used to stay with an old uncle there, and walk up and down, his hands behind him, on the strip of lawn. One day, hearing my name, he called me to him saying, "So you are another Alice. I'm very fond of Alices. Would you like to come and see something which is rather puzzling?" We followed him into his house which opened, as ours did, upon the garden, into a room full of furniture with a tall mirror standing across one corner.

"Now," he said, giving me an orange, "first tell me which hand you have got that in." "The right," I said. "Now," he said, "go and stand before that glass, and tell me which hand the little girl you see there has got it in." After some perplexed contemplation, I said, "The left hand." "Exactly," he said, "and how do you explain that?" I couldn't explain it, but seeing that some solution was expected, I ventured, "If I was on the *other* side of the glass, wouldn't the orange still be in my right hand?" I can remember his laugh. "Well done, little Alice," he said. "The best answer I've had yet."

I heard no more then, but in after years was told that he said that had given him his first idea for *Through the Looking-Glass*, a copy of which, together with each of his other books, he regularly sent me.

In a mirror all asymmetrical objects (objects not superposable on their mirror images) "go the other way." There are many references in the book to such left-right reversals. Tweedledee and Tweedledum are, as we shall see, mirror-image twins; the White Knight sings of squeezing a right foot into a left shoe; and it may not be accidental that there are several references to corkscrews, for the helix is an asymmetric structure with distinct right and left forms. If we extend the mirror-reflection theme to include the reversal of any asymmetric relation, we hit upon a note that dominates the entire story. It would take too much space to list here all the instances, but the following examples make the point. To approach the Red Queen, Alice walks backward; in the railway carriage the Guard tells her she is traveling the wrong way; the King has two messengers, "one to come, and one to go." The White Queen explains the advantages of living backward in time; the looking-glass cake is handed around first, then sliced. Odd and even numbers, the combinatorial equivalent of left and right, are worked into the story at several points (e.g., the White Queen requests jam every other day). In a sense, nonsense itself is a sanity-insanity inversion. The ordinary world is turned upside down and backward; it becomes a world in which things go every way expect the way they are supposed to.

Inversion themes occur, of course, throughout all of Carroll's nonsense writing. In the first *Alice* book Alice wonders if cats eat bats or bats eat cats, and she is told that to say what she means is not the same as meaning what she says. When she eats the left side of the mushroom, she grows large; the right side has the reverse effect. These changes in size, which take place so often in the first book,

know whether they've a fire in the winter: you never *can* tell, you know, unless our fire smokes, and then smoke comes up in that room too—but that may be only pretence, just to make it look as if they had a fire. Well then, the books are something like our books, only the words go the wrong way: I know *that*, because I've held up one of our books to the glass, and then they hold up one in the other room.

"How would you like to live in Looking-glass House, Kitty? I wonder if they'd give you milk in there? Perhaps Looking-glass milk isn't good to drink[6]—but oh, Kitty! now we come to the passage. You can just see a little *peep* of the passage in Looking-glass House, if you leave the door of our drawing-room wide open: and it's very like our passage as far as you can see, only you know

it may be quite different on beyond. Oh, Kitty, how nice it would be if we could only get through into Looking-glass House! I'm sure it's got, oh! such beautiful things in it! Let's pretend there's a way of getting through into it, somehow, Kitty. Let's pretend the glass has got all soft like gauze, so that we can get through. Why, it's turning into a sort of mist now, I declare! It'll be easy enough to get through—" She was up on the chimney-piece[7] while she said this, though she hardly knew how she had got there. And certainly the glass *was* beginning to melt away, just like a bright silvery mist.

In another moment Alice was through the glass,[8] and had jumped lightly down into the Looking-glass room. The very first thing she did was to look whether there was a fire in the fireplace, and she was quite pleased to find that

are in themselves reversals (e.g., instead of a large girl and small puppy we have a large puppy and small girl). In *Sylvie and Bruno* we learn about "imponderal," an antigravity wool that can be stuffed into parcel-post packages to make them weigh less than nothing; a watch that reverses time; black light; Fortunatus's purse, a projective plane with outside inside and inside outside. We learn that E-V-I-L is simply L-I-V-E backward.

In real life also Carroll milked the notion of inversion as much as he could to amuse his child-friends. One of his letters speaks of a doll whose right hand becomes "left" when the left hand drops off; another letter tells how he sometimes goes to bed so soon after getting up that he finds himself back in bed *before* he gets up. He wrote letters in mirror writing that had to be held to a mirror to be read. He wrote letters that had to be read by starting at the last word and reading to the first. He had a collection of music boxes and one of his favorite stunts was to play them backward. He drew funny pictures that changed to different pictures when you turned them upside down.

Even in serious moments Carroll's mind, like that of the White Knight, seemed to function best when he was seeing things upside down. He invented a new method of multiplication in which the multiplier is written backward and *above* the multiplicand. *The Hunting of the Snark*, he tells us, was actually composed backward. The final line, "For the Snark *was* a Boojum, you see," came into his head as a sudden inspiration, then he fashioned a stanza to fit the line and finally a poem to fit the stanza.

Closely related to Carroll's inversion humor is his humor of logical contradiction. The Red Queen knows of a hill so large that, compared to it, this hill is a valley; dry biscuits are eaten to quench thirst; a messenger whispers by shouting; Alice runs as fast as she can to stay in the same place. It is not surprising to learn that Carroll was fond of the Irish bull, of which logical contradiction is the essence. He once wrote to his sister: "Please analyze logically the following piece of reasoning: *Little Girl*: 'I'm *so* glad I don't like asparagus.' *Friend*: 'Why, my dear?' *Little Girl*: 'Because if I *did* like it, I should have to eat it—and I can't bear it!'" One of Carroll's acquaintances recalled hearing him speak about a friend he knew whose feet were so big that he had to put his trousers on over his head.

Treating a "null class" (a set with no members) as though it were an existing thing is another rich source of Carrollian logical nonsense. The March Hare offers Alice some nonexistent wine; Alice wonders where the flame of a candle is when the candle is not burning; the map in *The Hunting of the Snark* is "a perfect and absolute blank"; the King of Hearts thinks it unusual to write letters to nobody, and the White King compliments Alice on having keen enough eyesight to see nobody at a great distance down the road.

Why was Carroll's humor so interwoven with logical twists of these sorts? We shall not enter here into the question of whether Carroll's interest in logic and mathematics is a sufficient explanation, or whether there were unconscious compulsions that made it necessary for him to be forever warping and stretching, compressing and inverting, reversing and distorting the familiar world. Surely the thesis advanced by Florence Becker Lennon in her otherwise admirable biography *Victoria Through the Looking Glass* is hardly adequate. She argues that Carroll was born left-handed but forced to

there was a real one, blazing away as brightly as the one she had left behind. "So I shall be as warm here as I was in the old room," thought Alice: "warmer; in fact, because there'll be no one here to scold me away from the fire. Oh, what fun it'll be, when they see me through the glass in here, and ca'n't get at me!"

Then she began looking about, and noticed that what could be seen from the old room was quite common and uninteresting, but that all the rest was as different as possible. For instance, the pictures on the wall next the fire seemed to be all alive, and the very clock on the chimney-piece (you know you can only see the back of it in the Looking-glass) had got the face of a little old man, and grinned at her.

"They don't keep this room so tidy as the other," Alice thought to herself, as she noticed several of the chessmen down in the hearth among the cinders; but in another moment, with a little "Oh!" of surprise, she was down on her hands and knees watching them. The chessmen were walking about, two and two!

"Here are the Red King and the Red Queen,"

Alice said (in a whisper, for fear of frightening them), "and there are the White King and the White Queen sitting on the edge of the shovel—and here are two Castles walking arm in arm[9]—I don't think they can hear me," she went on, as she put her head closer down, "and I'm nearly sure they ca'n't see me. I feel somehow as if I was getting invisible—"

Here something began squeaking on the table behind Alice, and made her turn her head just in time to see one of the White Pawns roll over and begin kicking; she watched it with great curiosity to see what would happen next.

"It is the voice of my child!" the White Queen cried out, as she rushed past the King, so violently that she knocked him over among the cinders. "My precious Lily! My imperial kitten!" and she began scrambling wildly up the side of the fender.

"Imperial fiddlestick!" said the King, rubbing his nose, which had been hurt by the fall. He had a right to be a *little* annoyed with the Queen, for he was covered with ashes from head to foot.

Alice was very anxious to be of use, and, as the poor little Lily was nearly screaming herself into a fit, she hastily picked up the Queen and set her on the table by the side of her noisy little daughter.

The Queen gasped, and sat down: the rapid journey through the air had quite taken away her breath, and for a minute or two she could do nothing but hug the little Lily in silence. As soon as she had recovered her breath a little, she called out to the White King, who was sitting sulkily among the ashes, "Mind the volcano!"

"What volcano?" said the King, looking up anxiously into the fire, as if he thought that was the most likely place to find one.

use his right hand, and that "he took his revenge by doing a little reversing himself." Unfortunately there is only the flimsiest, most unconvincing evidence that Carroll was born left-handed. Even if true, it seems a woefully inadequate explanation for the origin of Carrollian nonsense.

R. B. Shaberman, writing on the influence of George MacDonald on Carroll (*Jabberwocky*, Summer 1976), quotes the following passage from Chapter 13 of MacDonald's 1858 novel, *Phantastes*:

What a strange thing a mirror is! And what a wondrous affinity exists between it and a man's imagination! For this room of mine, as I behold it in the glass, is the same and yet not the same. It is not the mere representation of the room I live in, but it looks just as if I were reading about it in a story I like. All its commonness has disappeared. The mirror has lifted it out of the region of fact into the realms of art ... I should like to live in that room if I could only get into it.

6. Alice's speculation about looking-glass milk has a significance greater than Carroll suspected. It was not until several years after the publication of *Through the Looking-Glass* that stereochemistry found positive evidence that organic substances had an asymmetric arrangement of atoms. Isomers are substances that have molecules composed of exactly the same atoms, but with these atoms linked together in structures that are topologically quite different. Stereoisomers are isomers that are identical even in topological structure, but, owing to the asymmetric nature of this structure, they come in mirror-image pairs. Most substances that occur in living organisms are stereoisometric. Sugar is a common example; in right-handed form it is called dextrose, in left-handed form,

levulose. Because the intake of food involves complicated chemical reactions between asymmetric food and asymmetric substances in the body, there often are marked differences in the taste, smell, and digestibility of left- and right-handed forms of the same organic substance. No laboratory or cow has yet produced reversed milk, but if the asymmetric structure of ordinary milk were to be reflected, it is a safe bet that this looking-glass milk would *not* be good to drink.

In this judgment on looking-glass milk only a reversal of the structure by which the milk's atoms are linked to each other is considered. Of course a true mirror reflection of milk would also reverse the structure of the elementary particles themselves. In 1957 two Chinese-American physicists, Tsung Dao Lee and Chen Ning Yang, received the Nobel Prize for theoretical work that led to the "gay and wonderful discovery" (in Robert Oppenheimer's happy phrase) that some elementary particles are asymmetric. It now appears likely that particles and their antiparticles (that is, identical particles with opposite charges) are, like stereoisomers, nothing more than mirror-image forms of the same structure. If this is true, then looking-glass milk would be composed of "anti-matter," which would not even be drinkable by Alice; both milk and Alice would explode as soon as they came in contact. Of course an anti-Alice, on the other side of the looking-glass, would find anti-milk as tasty and nourishing as usual.

Readers who would like to learn more about the philosophical and scientific implications of left- and right-handedness are referred to Hermann Weyl's delightful little book on *Symmetry* (1952) and Philip Morrison's article "The Overthrow of Parity," in *Scientific American*

"Blew—me—up," panted the Queen, who was still a little out of breath. "Mind you come up—the regular way—don't get blown up!"

Alice watched the White King as he slowly struggled up from bar to bar,[10] till at last she said "Why, you'll be hours and hours getting to the table, at that rate. I'd far better help you, hadn't I?" But the King took no notice of the question: it was quite clear that he could neither hear her nor see her.

So Alice picked him up very gently, and lifted him across more slowly than she had lifted the Queen, that she mightn't take his breath away; but, before she put him on the table, she thought she might as well dust him a little, he was so covered with ashes.

She said afterwards that she had never seen in all her life such a face as the King made, when he found himself held in the air by an invisible hand, and being dusted: he was far too much astonished to cry out, but his eyes and his mouth went on getting larger and larger; and rounder and rounder, till her hand shook so with laughing that she nearly let him drop upon the floor.

"Oh! *please* don't make such faces, my dear!" she cried out, quite forgetting that the King couldn't hear her: "You make me laugh so that I can hardly hold you! And don't keep your mouth so wide open! All the ashes will get into it—there, now I think you're tidy enough!" she added, as she smoothed his hair, and set him upon the table near the Queen.

The King immediately fell flat on his back,[11] and lay perfectly still; and Alice was a little alarmed at what she had done, and went round the room to see if she could find any water to throw over him. However, she could find nothing but a bottle of ink, and when she got back with it she found he had recovered, and he and the Queen were talking together in a frightened whisper—so low, that Alice could hardly hear what they said.

The King was saying "I assure you, my dear, I turned cold to the very ends of my whiskers!"

To which the Queen replied "You haven't got any whiskers."[12]

"The horror of that moment," the King went on, "I shall never, *never* forget!"

"You will, though," the Queen said, "if you don't make a memorandum of it."

Alice looked on with great interest as the King took an enormous memorandum-book out of his pocket, and began writing. A sudden thought struck her, and she took hold of the end of the pencil, which came some way over his shoulder, and began writing for him.[13]

The poor King looked puzzled and unhappy, and struggled with the pencil for some time without saying anything; but Alice was too strong for him, and at last he panted out "My dear! I really

(April 1957). On the lighter side there is my discussion of left-right topics in the last chapter of *The Scientific American Book of Mathematical Puzzles and Diversions* (1959) and my story "Left or Right?" in *Esquire* (February 1951). The classic science-fiction tale involving left-right reversal is "The Plattner Story" by H. G. Wells. And one must not overlook *The New Yorker's* Department of Amplification, December 15, 1956, page 164, in which Dr. Edward Teller comments with Carrollian wit on a previously published *New Yorker* poem (November 10, 1956, page 52) that describes the explosion that occurred when Dr. Teller shook hands with Dr. Edward Anti-Teller.

Recent nontechnical references on the symmetry and asymmetry of space and time include *Reality's Mirror: Exploring the Mathematics of Symmetry*, by Bryan Bunch (Wiley, 1989); my *New Ambidextrous Universe* (W. H. Freeman, 1990); and "The Handedness of the Universe," by Roger Hegstrom and Dilip Kondepudi, in *Scientific American* (January 1990).

There is considerable speculation among atomic scientists about the possibility of creating antimatter in the laboratory, keeping it suspended in space by magnetic forces, then combining it with matter to achieve a total conversion of nuclear mass into energy (in contrast to both fusion and fission in which only a small portion of mass is so converted). The road to ultimate nuclear power may, therefore, lie on the other side of the looking glass.

7. For American readers: the chimneypiece is the mantel. A number of science-fiction writers have used the mirror as a device for joining our world to a parallel world: Henry S. Whitehead's "The Trap," Donald

Wandrei's "The Painted Mirror," and Fritz Leiber's "Midnight in the Mirror World" are three such stories.

8. Tenniel's pictures of Alice passing through the mirror are worth studying. Observe that in the second illustration he added a grinning face to the back of the clock and to the lower part of the vase. It was a Victorian custom to put clocks and artificial flowers under glass bell jars. Less obvious is the gargoyle, sticking out its tongue, in the ornament at the top of the fireplace.

The pictures also show that Alice is not reversed on the other side of the glass. She continues to raise her right arm and to kneel on her right leg.

Note the name "Dalziel" at the bottom of both pictures, as well as on most of Tenniel's illustrations in both *Alice* books. The Dalziel brothers were the wood engravers for all of Tenniel's drawings. Observe also that Tenniel has reversed his monogram in the second picture.

We are told later on that the pictures on the wall near the fire seem to be alive. Peter Newell indicated this in his illustration of Alice emerging from the mirror. In the 1933 Paramount motion picture the pictures on the wall come alive and talk to Alice.

In all standard editions, the two pictures are on opposite sides of a leaf, as if the leaf itself was the mirror Alice passed through. A Puffin edition (1948) puts the pictures on its front and back covers, making the book the mirror.

9. Notice how Tenniel has suggested mirror reflections in his pairing of chess pieces in the illustration for this scene. Although Carroll never mentions bishops (perhaps out of deference to the clergy), they can be seen

must get a thinner pencil. I ca'n't manage this one a bit: it writes all manner of things that I don't intend—"

"What manner of things?" said the Queen, looking over the book (in which Alice had

put "*The White Knight is sliding down the poker. He balances very badly*".[14] "That's not a memorandum of *your* feelings!"

There was a book lying near Alice on the table, and while she sat watching the White King (for she was still a little anxious about him, and had the ink all ready to throw over him, in case he fainted again), she turned over the leaves, to find some part that she could read, "—for it's all in some language I don't know," she said to herself.

It was like this.

ʎʞɔoɯɹǝqqɐſ

'Twas brillig, and the slithy toves
Did gyre and gimble in the wabe:
All mimsy were the borogoves,
And the mome raths outgrabe.

She puzzled over this for some time, but at last a bright thought struck her. "Why, it's a Looking-glass book, of course! And, if I hold it up to a glass, the words will all go the right way again."[15]

This was the poem that Alice read.

Jabberwocky[16]

'Twas brillig, and the slithy[17] toves[18]
    Did gyre[19] and gimble[20] in the wabe:
All mimsy[21] were the borogoves,[22]
    And the mome[23] raths[24] outgrabe.[25]

"Beware the Jabberwock,[26] my son!
    The jaws that bite, the claws that catch!
Beware the Jubjub[27] bird, and shun
    The frumious[28] Bandersnatch!"[29]

He took his vorpal[30] sword in hand:
    Long time the manxome[31] foe he sought—
So rested he by the Tumtum[32] tree,
    And stood awhile in thought.

clearly in Tenniel's drawing. Isaac Asimov's mystery story "The Curious Omission," in his *Tales of the Black Widowers*, derives from Carroll's curious omission of chess bishops.

10. The White King's slow struggle up the fender, from bar to bar, reflects the fact that although a chess king can move in any direction like a queen, it is allowed to move only from one square to the next. A queen can go as far as seven cells in one move, which explains the ability of queens later on to fly through the air, but it takes a king seven moves to go from one side of a chessboard to the other.

11. In chess play the loser often signifies defeat by turning his king flat on its back. As we soon learn, this is a moment of horror for the King, who naturally turns cold, like a person slain in combat. The Queen's suggestion about making a memorandum of the event suggests the practice of recording chess moves so that a player won't forget the game.

12. American readers have been puzzled by the Queen's remark because Tenniel's illustrations show the White King, both here and in Chapter 7, with mustache and beard. As Denis Crutch has pointed out, the Queen meant that the King has no sideburns. Crutch quotes a remark in Carroll's *Sylvie and Bruno* (Chapter 18) about a man's face being "bounded on the North by a fringe of hair, on the East and West by a fringe of whiskers, and on the South by a fringe of beard." In England, *whiskers* customarily means sideburns.

13. Automatic writing, as it was called, was a major aspect of the

spiritualist craze in the nineteenth century. A disembodied spirit was believed to seize the hand of a psychic—Conan Doyle's wife was an accomplished automatic writer—and produce messages from the Great Beyond. For my comments about Carroll's interest in the occult, see *Alice in Wonderland*, Chapter 5, Note 7.

14. The poor balance of the White Knight on the poker foreshadows his poor balance on horseback when Alice meets him later in Chapter 8.

15. Carroll originally intended to print the entire "Jabberwocky" in reversed form, but later decided to limit this to the first verse. The fact that the printing appeared reversed to Alice is evidence that she herself was not reversed by her passage through the mirror. As explained earlier, there are now scientific reasons for suspecting that an unreversed Alice could not exist for more than a fraction of a second in a looking-glass world. (See also Chapter 5, Note 10.)

There are other reasons for assuming Alice was not mirror reflected. Many of Tenniel's pictures in the first book show her right-handed, and she continues to be right-handed in his pictures for the second book. Peter Newell's art is ambiguous on this point, though in Chapter 9 his Alice holds a scepter in her left hand, not in her right as Tenniel has it.

Alice has no difficulty reading the Wasp's newspaper in the long-lost "Wasp in a Wig" episode, so presumably, unlike "Jabberwocky," it was not reversed. Also unreversed are "DUM" and "DEE" on the collars of the Tweedle brothers, the label on the Mad Hatter's top hat, and "Queen Alice" over the door in Chapter 9. Brian Kirshaw sent a detailed analysis

And, as in uffish[33] *thought he stood,*
    The Jabberwock, with eyes of flame,
Came whiffling[34] *through the tulgey wood,*
    And burbled[35] *as it came!*

One, two! One, two! And through and through
    The vorpal blade went snicker-snack![36]
He left it dead, and with its head
    He went galumphing[37] *back.*

"And hast thou slain the Jabberwock?[38]
    Come to my arms, my beamish[39] *boy!*
O frabjous day! Callooh![40] *Callay!"*
    He chortled[41] *in his joy.*

'Twas brillig, and the slithy toves
    Did gyre and gimble in the wabe:
All mimsy were the borogoves,
    And the mome raths outgrabe.

"It seems very pretty," she said when she had finished it, "but it's *rather* hard to understand!" (You see she didn't like to confess, even to herself, that she couldn't make it out at all.) "Somehow it seems to fill my head with ideas—only I don't exactly know what they are! However, *somebody* killed *something*: that's clear, at any rate—"[42]

"But oh!" thought Alice, suddenly jumping up, "if I don't make haste, I shall have to go back through the Looking-glass, before I've seen what the rest of the house is like! Let's have a look at the garden first!" She was out of the room in a moment, and ran down stairs—or, at least, it wasn't exactly running, but a new invention for getting down stairs quickly and easily, as Alice said to herself. She just kept the tips of her fingers on the hand-rail, and floated gently down without even touching the stairs with her feet: then she floated on through the hall, and would have gone straight out at the door in the same way, if she hadn't caught hold of the door-post. She was getting a little giddy with so much floating in the air, and was rather glad to find herself walking again in the natural way.

of the left-right aspects of the book, all of which lead to the conclusion that neither Tenniel nor Carroll was consistent about who or what was mirror-reflected behind the looking glass.

16. The opening stanza of "Jabberwocky" first appeared in *Mischmasch*, the last of a series of private little "periodieals" that young Carroll wrote, illustrated and handlettered for the amusement of his brothers and sisters. In an issue dated 1855 (Carroll was then twenty-three), under the heading "Stanza of Anglo-Saxon Poetry," the following "curious fragment" appears:

Carroll then proceeds to interpret the words as follows:

BRYLLYG (derived from the verb TO BRYL or BROIL), "the time of broiling dinner, i.e. the close of the afternoon."

SLYTHY (compounded of SLIMY and LITHE). "Smooth and active."

TOVE. A species of Badger. They had smooth white hair, long hind legs, and short horns like a stag; lived chiefly on cheese.

GYRE, verb (derived from GYAOUR or GIAOUR, "a dog"). To scratch like a dog.

GYMBLE (whence GIMBLET). "To screw out holes in anything."

WABE (derived from the verb TO SWAB or SOAK). "The side of a hill" (from its being *soaked* by the rain).

MIMSY (whence MIMSERABLE and MISERABLE). "UNHAPPY."

BOROGOVE. An extinct kind of Parrot. They had no wings, beaks turned up, and made their nests under sundials: lived on veal.

MOME (hence SOLEMOME, SOLEMONE, and SOLEMN). "Grave."

RATH. A species of land turtle. Head

erect: mouth like a shark: forelegs curved out so that the animal walked on its knees: smooth green body: lived on swallows and oysters.

OUTGRABE, past tense of the verb to OUTGRIBE (It is connected with old verb to GRIKE, or SHRIKE, from which are derived "shriek" and "creak"). "Squeaked."

Hence the literal English of the passage is: "It was evening, and the smooth active badgers were scratching and boring holes in the hill-side; all unhappy were the parrots; and the grave turtles squeaked out."

There were probably sundials on the top of the hill, and the "borogoves" were afraid that their nests would be undermined. The hill was probably full of the nests of "raths", which ran out, squeaking with fear, on hearing the "toves" scratching outside. This is an obscure, but yet deeply-affecting, relic of ancient Poetry.

It is interesting to compare these explanations with those given by Humpty Dumpty in Chapter 6.

Few would dispute the fact that "Jabberwocky" is the greatest of all nonsense poems in English. It was so well known to English school-boys in the late nineteenth century that five of its nonsense words appear casually in the conversation of students in Rudyard Kipling's *Stalky & Co.* Alice herself, in the paragraph following the poem, puts her finger on the secret of the poem's charm: ". . . it seems to fill my head with ideas—only I don't know exactly what they are." Although the strange words have no precise meaning, they chime with subtle overtones.

There is an obvious similarity between nonsense verse of this sort and an abstract painting. The realistic artist is forced to copy nature, imposing on the copy as much as he can in the way of pleasing forms and colors; but the abstract artist is free to romp with the paint as much as he pleases. In similar fashion the nonsense poet does not have to search for ingenious ways of combining pattern and sense; he simply adopts a policy that is the opposite of the advice given by the Duchess in the previous book (see Chapter 9, Note 6)—he takes care of the sounds and allows the sense to take care of itself. The words he uses may suggest vague meanings, like an eye here and a foot there in a Picasso abstraction, or they may have no meaning at all—just a play of pleasant sounds like the play of nonobjective colors on a canvas.

Carroll was not, of course, the first to use this technique of double-talk in humorous verse. He was preceded by Edward Lear, and it is a curious fact that nowhere in the writings or letters of these two undisputed leaders of English nonsense did either of them refer to the other, nor is there evidence that they ever met. Since the time of Lear and Carroll there have been attempts to produce a more serious poetry of this sort—poems by the Dadaists, the Italian futurists, and Gertrude Stein, for example—but somehow when the technique is taken too seriously the results seem tiresome. I have yet to meet someone who could recite one of Miss Stein's poetic efforts, but I have known a good many Carrollians who found that they knew the "Jabberwocky" by heart without ever having made a conscious effort to memorize it. Ogden Nash produced a fine piece of nonsense in his poem "Geddondillo" ("The Sharrot scudders nights in the quastran now,/The dorlim slinks undeceded in the grost . . ."), but even here there seems to be a bit too much straining for effect, whereas "Jabberwocky" has a careless lilt and perfection that makes it the unique thing it is.

"Jabberwocky" was a favorite of the British astronomer Arthur Stanley Eddington and is alluded to several times in his writings. In *New Pathways in Science* he likens the abstract syntactical structure of the poem to that modern branch of mathematics known as group theory. In *The Nature of the Physical World* he points out that the physicist's description of an elementary particle is really a kind of Jabberwocky; words applied to "something unknown" that is "doing we don't know what." Because the description contains numbers, science is able to impose a certain amount of order on the phenomena and to make successful predictions about them.

"By contemplating eight circulating electrons in one atom and seven circulating electrons in another," Eddington writes,

we begin to realize the difference between oxygen and nitrogen. Eight slithy toves gyre and gimble in the oxygen wabe; seven in nitrogen. By admitting a few numbers even "Jabberwocky" may become scientific. We can now venture on a prediction; if one of its toves escapes, oxygen will be masquerading in a garb properly belonging to nitrogen. In the stars and nebulae we do find such wolves in sheep's clothing which might otherwise have startled us. It would not be a bad reminder of the essential unknownness of the fundamental entities of physics to translate it into "Jabberwocky"; provided all numbers—all metrical attributes—are unchanged, it does not suffer in the least.

"Jabberwocky" has been translated skillfully into several languages. There are two Latin versions. One by Augustus A. Vansittart, fellow of Trinity College, Cambridge, was issued as a pamphlet by the Oxford University Press in 1881 and will be found on page 144 of Stuart Collingwood's biography of Carroll. The other version, by Carroll's uncle, Hassard H. Dodgson, is in *The Lewis Carroll Picture Book* on page 364. (The Gaberbocchus Press, a whimsical London publishing house, derives its name from Uncle Hassard's Latin word for Jabberwock.)

The following French translation by Frank L. Warrin first appeared in *The New Yorker* (January 10, 1931). (I quote from Mrs. Lennon's book, where it is reprinted.)

Le Jaseroque

Il brilgue: les tôves lubricilleux
Se gyrent en vrillant dans le guave,
Enmîmés sont les gougebosqueux,
Et le mômerade horsgrave.

Garde-toi du Jaseroque, mon fils!
La gueule qui mord; la griffe qui prend!
Garde-toi de l'oiseau Jube, évite
Le frumieux Band-à-prend.

Son glaive vorpal en main il va-
T-à la recherche du fauve manscant;
Puis arrivé à l'arbre Té-Té,
Il y reste, réfléchissant.

Pendant qu'il pense, tout uffusé,
Le Jaseroque, à l'œil flambant,
Vient siblant par le bois tullegeais,
Et burbule en venant.

Un deux, un deux, par le milieu,
Le glaive vorpal fait pat-à-pan!
La bête défaite, avec sa tête,
Il rentre gallomphant.

As-tu tué le Jaseroque?
Viens à mon cœur, fils rayonnais!
O jour frabbejeais! Calleau! Callai!
Il cortule dans sa joie.

Il brilgue: les tôves lubricilleux
Se gyrent en vrillant dans le guave,
Enmîmés sont les gougebosqueux,
Et le mômerade horsgrave.

A magnificent German translation was made by Robert Scott, an eminent Greek scholar who had collaborated with Dean Liddell (Alice's father) on a Greek lexicon. It first appeared in an article, "The Jabberwock Traced to Its True Source," *Macmillan's Magazine* (February 1872). Using the pseudonym of Thomas Chatterton, Scott tells of attending a séance at which the spirit of one Hermann von Schwindel insists that Carroll's poem is simply an English translation of the following old German ballad:

Der Jammerwoch

Es brillig war. Die schlichte Toven
  Wirrten und wimmelten in Waben;
Und aller-mümsige Burggoven
  Die mohmen Räth' ausgraben.

Bewahre doch vor Jammerwoch!
  Die Zähne knirschen, Krallen
    kratzen!
Bewahr' vor Jubjub—Vogel, vor
  Frumiösen Banderschnätzchen!

Er griff sein vorpals Schwertchen zu,
  Er suchte lang das manchsam' Ding;
Dann, stehend unten Tumtum Baum,
  Er an-zu-denken-fing.

Als stand er tief in Andacht auf,
  Des Jammerwochen's Augen-feuer
Durch tulgen Wald mit wiffek kam
  Ein burbelnd ungeheuer!

Eins, Zwei! Eins, Zwei!
  Und durch und durch
Sein vorpals Schwert
  zerschnifer-schnück,
Da blieb es todt! Er, Kopf in Hand,
  Geläumfig zog zurück.

Und schlugst Du ja den Jammerwoch?
  Umarme mich, mien Böhm' sches
    Kind!
O Freuden-Tag! O Halloo-Schlag!
  Er chortelt froh-gesinnt.

Es brillig war, &c!

New translations of the *Alice* books keep appearing; there must be at least fifty different versions of "Jabberwocky" in fifty different languages. See my *More Annotated Alice* for a second French translation, and versions in Latin, Italian, Spanish, Russian, and Welsh.

Endless parodies of "Jabberwocky" have been attempted. Three of the best will be found on pages 36 and 37 of Carolyn Wells's anthology, *Such Nonsense* (1918); "Somewhere-in-Europe Wocky," "Footballwocky," and "The Jabberwocky of the Publishers" ("'Twas Harpers and the Little Browns/Did Houghton Mifflin the book . . ."). But I incline toward Chesterton's dim view (expressed in his article on Carroll mentioned in the introduction) of all such efforts to do humorous imitations of something humorous.

In "Mimsy Were the Borogoves," one of the best-known science fiction tales by Lewis Padgett (pen name for the collaborated work of the late Henry Kuttner and his wife, Catherine L. More), the words of "Jabberwocky" are revealed as symbols from a future language. Rightly understood, they explain a technique for entering a four-dimensional continuum. A similar notion is found in Fredric Brown's magnificently funny mystery novel, *Night of the Jabberwock.* Brown's narrator is an enthusiastic Carrollian. He learns from Yehudi Smith, apparently a member of a society of Carroll admirers called The Vorpal Blades, that Carroll's fantasies are not fiction at all, but realistic reporting about another plane of existence. The clues of the fantasies are cleverly concealed in Carroll's mathematical treatises, especially *Curiosa Mathematica*, and in his nonacrostic poems, which are really acrostics of a subtler kind. No Carrollian can afford to miss *Night of the Jabberwock*. It is an outstanding work of fiction that has close ties to the *Alice* books.

17. The *Oxford English Dictionary* lists *slithy* as a variant of *sleathy*, an obsolete word meaning slovenly, but in Chapter 6 Humpty Dumpty gives *slithy* a different interpretation.

18. *Toves* should be pronounced to rhyme with *groves*, Carroll tells us in his preface to *The Hunting of the Snark*.

19. The *Oxford English Dictionary* traces *gyre* back to 1420 as a word meaning to turn or whirl around. This agrees with Humpty Dumpty's interpretation.

20. According to the *Oxford English Dictionary, gimble* is a variant spelling of *gimbal*. Gimbals are pivoted rings used for various purposes, such as suspending a ship's compass so that it remains horizontal while the ship rolls. Humpty Dumpty makes clear, however, that the verb *gimble* is here used in a different sense.

21. *Mimsy* is the first of eight nonsense words in *Jabberwocky* that are used again in *The Hunting of the Snark*. It appears in Fit 7, verse 9: "And chanted in mimsiest tones." In Carroll's time, according to the *Oxford English Dictionary, mimsey* (with an *e*) meant "prim, prudish, contemptible." Perhaps Carroll had this in mind.

22. In his preface to the *Snark*, Carroll writes: "The first 'o' in 'borogoves' is pronounced like the 'o' in 'borrow.' I have heard people try to give it the sound of the 'o' in 'worry'. Such is Human Perversity." The word is commonly mispronounced as "borogroves" by Carrollian novitiates, and this misspelling even appears in some American editions of the book.

23. *Mome* has a number of obsolete meanings such as mother, a blockhead, a carping critic, a buffoon, none of which, judging from Humpty Dumpty's interpretation, Carroll had in mind.

24. According to Humpty Dumpty, a *rath* is a green pig but in Carroll's day it was a well-known old Irish word for an enclosure, usually a circular earthen wall, serving as a fort and place of residence for the head of a tribe.

25. "But it fairly lost heart, and outgrabe in despair," *Snark*, Fit 5, verse 10.

26. The Jabberwock is not mentioned in the *Snark*, but in a letter to Mrs. Chataway (the mother of one of his child-friends) Carroll explains that the scene of the *Snark* is "an island frequented by the Jubjub and the Bandersnatch—no doubt the very island where the Jabberwock was slain."

When a class in the Girls' Latin School, Boston, asked Carroll's permission to name their school magazine *The Jabberwock*, he replied:

Mr. Lewis Carroll has much pleasure in giving to the editors of the proposed magazine permission to use the title they wish for. He finds that the Anglo-Saxon word "wocer" or "wocor" signifies "offspring" or "fruit." Taking "jabber" in its ordinary acceptation of "excited and voluble discussion," this would give the meaning of "the result of much excited discussion." Whether this phrase will have any application to the projected periodical, it will be for the future historian of American literature to determine. Mr. Carroll wishes all success to the forthcoming magazine.

27. The Jubjub is mentioned five times in the *Snark*: Fit 4, verse 18, and Fit 5, verses 8, 9, 21, and 29.

28. ". . . those frumious jaws," *Snark*, Fit 7, verse 5. In the *Snark*'s preface Carroll writes:

For instance, take the two words "fuming" and "furious." Make up your mind that you will say both words, but leave it unsettled which you will say first. Now open your mouth and speak. If your thoughts incline ever so little towards "fuming," you will say "fuming-furious"; if they turn, by even a hair's breadth, towards "furious," you will say "furious-fuming"; but if you have that rarest of gifts, a perfectly balanced mind, you will say "fruminous." Supposing that, when Pistol uttered the well-known words:

> *Under which king, Bezonian!*
> *Speak or die!*

Justice Shallow had felt certain that it was either William or Richard, but had not been able to settle which, so that he could not possibly say either name before the other, can it be doubted that, rather than die, he would have gasped out "Rilchiam!"?

29. The Bandersnatch is mentioned again in Chapter 7, and in the *Snark*, Fit 7, verses 3, 4, and 6.

30. Alexander L. Taylor, in his book on Carroll, *The White Knight*, shows how to get *vorpal* by taking letters alternately from *verbal* and *gospel*, but there is no evidence that Carroll resorted to such involved techniques in coining his words. In fact Carroll wrote to a child-friend: "I am afraid I can't explain 'vorpal blade' for you—nor yet 'tulgey wood.'"

31. *Manx* was the Celtic name for the Isle of Man, hence the word came to be used in England for anything pertaining to the island. Its language was called Manx, its inhabitants Manxmen, and so on. Whether Carroll had this in mind when he coined *manxome* is not known.

32. *Tum-tum* was a common colloquialism in Carroll's day, referring to the sound of a stringed instrument, especially when monotonously strummed.

33. "The Bellman looked uffish, and wrinkled his brow," *Snark*, Fit 4, verse 1. In a letter to child-friend Maud Standen, 1877, Carroll wrote that "uffish" suggested to him "a state of mind when the voice is gruffish, the manner roughish, and the temper huffish."

34. *Whiffling* is not a Carrollian word. It had a variety of meanings in Carroll's time, but usually had reference to blowing unsteadily in short puffs, hence it came to be a slang term for being variable and evasive. In an earlier century *whiffling* meant smoking and drinking.

35. "If you take the three verbs '*b*leat,' '*mur*-mur,' and 'wa*rble*,'" Carroll wrote in the letter cited above, "and select the bits I have underlined, it certainly *makes* 'burble': though I am afraid I can't distinctly remember having made it in that way." The word (apparently a combination of *burst* and *bubble*) had long been used in England as a variant of *bubble* (e.g., the burbling brook), as well as a word meaning "to perplex, confuse, or muddle" ("His life fallen into a horribly burbled state," the *Oxford English Dictionary* quotes from an 1883 letter of Mrs. Carlyle's). In modern aeronautics *burbling* refers to the turbulence that develops when air is not flowing smoothly around an object.

36. *Snickersnee* is an old word for a large knife. It also means "to fight with a knife." The *Oxford English Dictionary* quotes from *The Mikado*, Act 2: "As I gnashed my teeth, when from its sheath I drew my snicker-snee."

37. "The Beaver went simply galumphing about," *Snark*, Fit 4, verse 17. This Carrollian word has entered the *Oxford English Dictionary*, where it is attributed to Carroll and defined as a combination of *gallop* and *triumphant*, meaning "to march on exultantly with irregular bounding movements."

38. Tenniel's striking illustration for this stanza was originally intended as the book's frontispiece, but it was so horrendous that Carroll feared it might be best to open the book on a milder scene. In 1871 he conducted a private poll of about thirty mothers by sending them the following printed letter:

I am sending you, with this, a print of the proposed frontispiece for *Through the Looking-glass*. It has been suggested to me that it is too terrible a monster, and likely to alarm nervous and imaginative children; and that at any rate we had better begin the book with a pleasanter subject.

So I am submitting the question to a number of friends, for which purpose I have had copies of the frontispiece printed off.

We have three courses open to us:

(1) To retain it as the frontispiece.
(2) To transfer it to its proper place in the book (where the ballad occurs which it is intended to illustrate) and substitute a new frontispiece.
(3) To omit it altogether.

The last named course would be a great sacrifice of the time and trouble which the picture cost, and it would be a pity to adopt it unless it is really necessary.

I should be grateful to have your opinion, (tested by exhibiting the picture to any children you think fit) as to which of these courses is best.

Evidently most of the mothers favored the second course, for the picture of the White Knight on horseback became the frontispiece.

Correspondent Mrs. Henry Morss, Jr., found a striking similarity between Tenniel's Jabberwock and the dragon being slain by Saint George in a painting by Paolo Uccello, in London's National Gallery. For other pictures of monsters that could have influenced Tenniel, see Chapter 8 of Michael Hancher's *The Tenniel Illustrations to the "Alice" Books*.

39. "But oh, beamish nephew, beware of the day," *Snark*, Fit 3, verse 10. This is not a word invented by Carroll. The *Oxford*

English Dictionary traces it back to 1530 as a variant of *beaming*, meaning "shining brightly, radiant."

40. A species of arctic duck that winters in northern Scotland is called the calloo after its evening call, "Calloo! Calloo!"

More likely, as readers Albert L. Blackwell and Mrs. Carlton S. Hyman each point out, Carroll had in mind two forms of a Greek word, *kalos*, meaning beautiful, good or fair. They would be pronounced as Carroll spells them, and would fit well the meaning of the line.

41. *Chortled*, a word coined by Carroll, also has worked its way into the *Oxford English Dictionary*, where it is defined as a blend of *chuckle* and *snort*.

42. Still far from clear is whether "Jabberwocky" is in some sense a parody. Roger Green, in the *London Times Literary Supplement* (March 1, 1957) and more recently in *The Lewis Carroll Handbook* (1962), suggests that Carroll may have had in mind "The Shepherd of the Giant Mountains," a long German ballad about how a young shepherd slays a monstrous Griffin. The ballad had been translated by Carroll's cousin, Manella Bute Smedley, and published in *Sharpe's*

London Magazine (March 7 and 21, 1846). "The similarity cannot be pinned down precisely," writes Green. "Much is in the feeling and the atmosphere; the parody is of general style and outlook."

In *Useful and Instructive Poetry*, written by Carroll when he was thirteen (it was his first book), there is a parody of a passage from Shakespeare's *Henry the Fourth, Second Part*, in which the Prince of Wales uses the word *biggen*. In Carroll's version he explains to the puzzled king that the word "means a kind of woolen nightcap." Later he introduces the word *rigol*.

"What meaneth 'rigol'?" asks the king.

"My liege, I know not," the prince replies, "save that it doth enter most apt into the metre."

"True, it doth," the king agrees. "But wherefore use a word which hath no meaning?"

The prince's answer has a prophetic reference to the nonsense words of "Jabberwocky": "My lord, the word is said, for it hath passed my lips, and all the powers upon this earth cannot unsay it."

For more on "Jabberwocky," including how Carroll's contemporaries responded to the poem and its influence on literature and the law, see Joseph Brabant's *Some Observations on Jabberwocky* (Cheshire Cat Press, 1997).

2

The Garden of Live Flowers

"I should see the garden far better," said Alice to herself, "if I could get to the top of that hill: and here's a path that leads straight to it—at least, no, it doesn't do *that*—" (after going a few yards along the path, and turning several sharp corners), "but I suppose it will at last. But how curiously it twists! It's more like a corkscrew than a path!¹ Well, *this* turn goes to the hill, I suppose—no, it doesn't! This goes straight back to the house! Well then, I'll try it the other way."

And so she did: wandering up and down, and trying turn after turn, but always coming back to the house, do what she would. Indeed, once, when she turned a corner rather more quickly than usual, she ran against it before she could stop herself.

"It's no use talking about it," Alice said, looking up at the house and pretending it was arguing with her. "I'm *not* going in again yet. I know I should have to get through the Looking-glass again—back into the old room—and there'd be an end of all my adventures!"

So, resolutely turning her back upon the house, she set out once more down the path, determined to keep straight on till she got to the hill. For a few minutes all went on well, and she was just saying "I really *shall* do it this time—" when the path gave a sudden twist and shook

1. Corkscrews are mentioned several times in *Through the Looking-Glass.* Carroll knew, of course, that corkscrews are helices, asymmetric three-dimensional curves that spiral the "other way" in the mirror. Humpty Dumpty tells Alice that the "toves" in "Jabberwocky" look something like corkscrews. He recites a poem in which he speaks of using a corkscrew to wake up the fish, and in Chapter 9 the White Queen recalls his coming to her door, corkscrew in hand, looking for a hippopotamus.

itself (as she described it afterwards), and the next moment she found herself actually walking in at the door.

"Oh, it's too bad!" she cried. "I never saw such a house for getting in the way! Never!"

However, there was the hill full in sight, so there was nothing to be done but start again. This time she came upon a large flower-bed, with a border of daisies, and a willow-tree growing in the middle.

"O Tiger-lily!"[2] said Alice, addressing herself to one that was waving gracefully about in the wind, "I *wish* you could talk!"

"We *can* talk," said the Tiger-lily, "when there's anybody worth talking to."

Alice was so astonished that she couldn't speak for a minute: it quite seemed to take her breath away. At length, as the Tiger-lily only went on waving about, she spoke again, in a timid voice—almost in a whisper. "And can *all* the flowers talk?"

"As well as *you* can," said the Tiger-lily. "And a great deal louder."

"It isn't manners for us to begin, you know," said the Rose, "and I really was wondering when you'd speak! Said I to myself, 'Her face has got *some* sense in it, though it's not a clever one!' Still, you're the right colour, and that goes a long way."

"I don't care about the colour," the Tiger-lily remarked. "If only her petals curled up a little more, she'd be all right."

Alice didn't like being criticized, so she began asking questions. "Aren't you sometimes frightened at being planted out here, with nobody to take care of you?"

"There's the tree in the middle," said the Rose. "What else is it good for?"

"But what could it do, if any danger came?" Alice asked.

"It could bark," said the Rose.

"It says 'Bough-wough!'" cried a Daisy. "That's why its branches are called boughs!"

"Didn't you know *that*?" cried another Daisy. And here they all began shouting together, till the air seemed quite full of little shrill voices. "Silence, every one of you!" cried the Tiger-lily, waving itself passionately from side to side, and trembling with excitement. "They know I ca'n't get at them!" it panted, bending its quivering head towards Alice, "or they wouldn't dare to do it!"

"Never mind!" Alice said in a soothing tone, and, stooping down to the daisies, who were just beginning again, she whispered "If you don't hold your tongues, I'll pick you!"

3. Robert Hornback (in an article cited in Chapter 5, Note 6, of *Alice in Wonderland*) suggests that the daisies are varieties of the wild English daisy: "They have ray petals that are white on top and reddish underneath. When these unfold in the morning, the daisies appear to change from pink to white."

4. In addition to the three Liddell girls of whom Carroll was so fond, there were two younger Liddell sisters, Rhoda and Violet. They appear in this chapter as the Rose and Violet—the only reference to them in the *Alice* books.

There was silence in a moment, and several of the pink daisies turned white.[3]

"That's right!" said the Tiger-lily. "The daisies are worst of all. When one speaks, they all begin together, and it's enough to make one wither to hear the way they go on!"

"How is it you can all talk so nicely?" Alice said, hoping to get it into a better temper by a compliment. "I've been in many gardens before, but none of the flowers could talk."

"Put your hand down, and feel the ground," said the Tiger-lily. "Then you'll know why."

Alice did so. "It's very hard," she said; "but I don't see what that has to do with it."

"In most gardens," the Tiger-lily said, "they make the beds too soft—so that the flowers are always asleep."

This sounded a very good reason, and Alice was quite pleased to know it. "I never thought of that before!" she said.

"It's *my* opinion that you never think *at all*," the Rose said, in a rather severe tone.

"I never saw anybody that looked stupider," a Violet[4] said, so suddenly, that Alice quite jumped; for it hadn't spoken before.

"Hold *your* tongue!" cried the Tiger-lily. "As if *you* ever saw anybody! You keep your head under the leaves, and snore away there, till you know no more what's going on in the world, than if you were a bud!"

"Are there any more people in the garden besides me?" Alice said, not choosing to notice the Rose's last remark.

"There's one other flower in the garden that can move about like you," said the Rose. "I wonder how you do it—" ("You're always wondering," said the Tiger-lily), "but she's more bushy than you are."

"Is she like me?" Alice asked eagerly, for the thought crossed her mind, "There's another little girl in the garden, somewhere!"

"Well, she has the same awkward shape as you," the Rose said: "but she's redder—and her petals are shorter, I think."

"They're done up close, like a dahlia," said the Tiger-lily: "not tumbled about, like yours."

"But that's not *your* fault," the Rose added kindly. "You're beginning to fade, you know—and then one ca'n't help one's petals getting a little untidy."

Alice didn't like this idea at all: so, to change the subject, she asked "Does she ever come out here?"

"I daresay you'll see her soon," said the Rose. "She's one of the kind that has nine spikes,[5] you know."

"Where does she wear them?" Alice asked with some curiosity.

"Why, all round her head, of course," the Rose replied. "I was wondering *you* hadn't got some too. I thought it was the regular rule."

"She's coming!" cried the Larkspur. "I hear her footstep, thump, thump, along the gravel-walk!"[6]

Alice looked round eagerly and found that it was the Red Queen. "She's grown a good deal!" was her first remark. She had indeed: when Alice first found her in the ashes, she had been only three inches high—and here she was, half a head taller than Alice herself!

"It's the fresh air that does it," said the Rose: "wonderfully fine air it is, out here."

"I think I'll go and meet her," said Alice, for, though the flowers were interesting enough, she felt that it would be far grander to have a talk with a real Queen.

5. In the first edition of *Through the Looking-Glass* the sentence "She's one of the kind that has nine spikes . . ." read "She's one of the thorny kind." The "spikes" refer to the nine points on the Red Queen's crown. Tenniel's queens all have nine-pointed crowns, and when Alice reaches the eighth square and becomes a queen, her gold crown has nine points as well.

6. Compare with the following stanza from Tennyson's *Maud*:

There has fallen a splendid tear
    From the passion-flower at the gate.
She is coming, my dove, my dear;
    She is coming, my life, my fate;
The red rose cries, "She is near, she
        is near;"
    And the white rose weeps, "She
        is late;"
The larkspur listens, "I hear, I hear;"
    And the lily whispers, "I wait."

7. An obvious allusion to the fact that forward and back are reversed by a mirror. Walk toward a mirror, the image moves in the opposite direction.

8. In his article "*Alice* on the Stage," cited earlier, Carroll wrote:

The Red Queen I pictured as a Fury, but of another type; *her* passion must be cold and calm; she must be formal and strict, yet not unkindly; pedantic to the tenth degree, the concentrated essence of all governesses!

It has been conjectured that the Red Queen was modeled after Miss Prickett, governess for the Liddell children (who called her by the nickname of "Pricks"). Oxford gossip once linked Carroll and Miss Prickett romantically, because of his frequent visits to the Liddell home, but it soon became evident that Carroll was interested in the children, not the governess. In Paramount's motion picture of *Alice* the role of Red Queen was taken by Edna May Oliver.

"You ca'n't possibly do that," said the Rose: "*I* should advise you to walk the other way."

This sounded nonsense to Alice, so she said nothing, but set off at once towards the Red Queen. To her surprise she lost sight of her in a moment, and found herself walking in at the front-door again.

A little provoked, she drew back, and, after looking everywhere for the Queen (whom she spied out at last, a long way off), she thought she would try the plan, this time, of walking in the opposite direction.

It succeeded beautifully.[7] She had not been walking a minute before she found herself face to face with the Red Queen, and full in sight of the hill she had been so long aiming at.

"Where do you come from?" said the Red Queen. "And where are you going? Look up, speak nicely, and don't twiddle your fingers all the time."[8]

Alice attended to all these directions, and explained, as well as she could, that she had lost her way.

"I don't know what you mean by *your* way," said the Queen: "all the ways about here belong to *me*—but why did you come out here at all?" she added in a kinder tone. "Curtsey while you're thinking what to say. It saves time."

Alice wondered a little at this, but she was too much in awe of the Queen to disbelieve it. "I'll try it when I go home," she thought to herself, "the next time I'm a little late for dinner."

"It's time for you to answer now," the Queen said, looking at her watch: "open your mouth a *little* wider when you speak, and always say 'your Majesty.'"

"I only wanted to see what the garden was like, your Majesty—"

9. Eddington, in the concluding chapter of *The Nature of the Physical World*, quotes this remark of the Red Queen in connection with a subtle discussion of what he calls the physicist's "problem of nonsense." In brief, Eddington argues that, although it may be nonsense for the physicist to affirm a reality of some sort beyond the laws of physics, it is as sensible as a dictionary beside the nonsense of supposing that there is no such reality.

"That's right," said the Queen, patting her on the head, which Alice didn't like at all: "though, when you say 'garden'—*I've* seen gardens, compared with which this would be a wilderness."

Alice didn't dare to argue the point, but went on: "—and I thought I'd try and find my way to the top of that hill—"

"When you say 'hill,'" the Queen interrupted, "*I* could show you hills, in comparison with which you'd call that a valley."

"No, I shouldn't," said Alice, surprised into contradicting her at last: "a hill *ca'n't* be a valley, you know. That would be nonsense—"

The Red Queen shook her head. "You may call it 'nonsense' if you like," she said, "but *I've* heard nonsense, compared with which that would be as sensible as a dictionary!"[9]

10. So many memorable passages have been written in which life itself is compared to an enormous game of chess that a sizable anthology could be assembled out of them. Sometimes the players are men themselves, seeking to manipulate their fellow-men as one manipulates chess pieces. The following passage is from George Eliot's *Felix Holt*:

Fancy what a game of chess would be if all the chessmen had passions and intellects, more or less small and cunning; if you were not only uncertain about your adversary's men, but a little uncertain also about your own; if your Knight could shuffle himself on to a new square on the sly; if your Bishop, in disgust at your Castling, could wheedle your Pawns out of their places; and if your Pawns, hating you because they are Pawns, could make away from their appointed posts that you might get checkmate on a sudden. You might be the longest-headed of deductive reasoners, and yet you might be beaten by your own Pawns. You would be especially likely to be beaten, if you depended arrogantly on your mathematical imagination, and regarded your passionate pieces with contempt.

Yet this imaginary chess is easy compared with a game a man has to play against his fellow-men with other fellowmen for his instruments . . .

Sometimes the players are God and Satan. William James dallies with this theme in his essay on *The Dilemma of Determinism*, and H. G. Wells echoes it in the prologue of his fine novel about education, *The Undying Fire*. Like the Book of Job on which it is modeled, Wells's story opens with a conversation between God and the devil. They are playing chess.

But the chess they play is not the little ingenious game that originated in India; it is on an altogether different scale. The Ruler of the Universe creates the board,

Alice curtseyed again, as she was afraid from the Queen's tone that she was a *little* offended: and they walked on in silence till they got to the top of the little hill.

For some minutes Alice stood without speaking, looking out in all directions over the country—and a most curious country it was. There were a number of tiny little brooks running straight across it from side to side, and the ground between was divided up into squares by a number of little green hedges, that reached from brook to brook.

"I declare it's marked out just like a large chessboard!" Alice said at last. "There ought to be some men moving about somewhere—and so there are!" she added in a tone of delight, and her heart began to beat quick with excitement as she went on. "It's a great huge game of chess that's being played—all over the world[10]—if this *is* the world at all, you know. Oh, what fun it is! How I *wish* I was one of them! I wouldn't mind being a Pawn, if only I might join—though of course I should *like* to be a Queen, best."

She glanced rather shyly at the real Queen as she said this, but her companion only smiled pleasantly, and said "That's easily managed. You can be the White Queen's Pawn, if you like, as Lily's[11] too young to play; and you're in the Second Square to begin with: when you get to the Eighth Square you'll be a Queen—" Just at this moment, somehow or other, they began to run.

Alice never could quite make out, in thinking it over afterwards, how it was that they began: all she remembers is, that they were running hand in hand, and the Queen went so fast that it was all she could do to keep up with her: and still the Queen kept crying "Faster! Faster!" but Alice felt she *could not* go faster, though she had no breath left to say so.

The most curious part of the thing was, that the trees and the other things round them never changed their places at all: however fast they went, they never seemed to pass anything. "I wonder if all the things move along with us?" thought poor puzzled Alice. And the Queen seemed to guess her thoughts, for she cried "Faster! Don't try to talk!"

Not that Alice had any idea of doing *that*. She felt as if she would never be able to talk again, she was getting so much out of breath: and still

the pieces, and the rules; he makes all the moves; he may make as many moves as he likes whenever he likes; his antagonist, however, is permitted to introduce a slight inexplicable inaccuracy into each move, which necessitates further moves in correction. The Creator determines and conceals the aim of the game, and it is never clear whether the purpose of the adversary is to defeat or assist him in his unfathomable project. Apparently the adversary cannot win, but also he cannot lose so long as he can keep the game going. But he is concerned, it would seem, in preventing the development of any reasoned scheme in the game.

Sometimes the gods themselves are pieces in a higher game, and the players of this game in turn are pieces in an endless hierarchy of larger chessboards. "And there is merriment overhead," says Mother Sereda, after enlarging on this theme, in James Branch Cabell's *Jurgen*, "but it is very far away."

11. Lily, the White Queen's daughter and one of the white pawns, was encountered by Alice in the previous chapter. In choosing the name "Lily," Carroll may have had in mind his young friend Lilia Scott MacDonald, the eldest daughter of George MacDonald (Chapter 1, Note 2). Lilia was called "My White Lily" by her father, and Carroll's letters to her (after she passed fifteen) contain many teasing references to her advancing age. The statement here that Lily is too young to play chess may well have been part of this teasing.

There is a record (Collingwood's biography of Carroll, page 427) of a white kitten named Lily ("My imperial kitten" the White Queen calls her child in the previous chapter), which Carroll gave to one of his childfriends. This, however, may have been after the writing of *Through the Looking-Glass*.

the Queen cried "Faster! Faster!" and dragged her along. "Are we nearly there?" Alice managed to pant out at last.

"Nearly there!" the Queen repeated. "Why, we passed it ten minutes ago! Faster!" And they ran on for a time in silence, with the wind whistling in Alice's ears, and almost blowing her hair off her head, she fancied.

"Now! Now!" cried the Queen. "Faster! Faster!" And they went so fast that at last they seemed to skim through the air, hardly touching the ground with their feet, till suddenly, just as Alice was getting quite exhausted, they stopped, and she found herself sitting on the ground, breathless and giddy.

The Queen propped her up against a tree, and said kindly, "You may rest a little, now."

Alice looked round her in great surprise. "Why, I do believe we've been under this tree the whole time! Everything's just as it was!"

"Of course it is," said the Queen. "What would you have it?"

"Well, in *our* country," said Alice, still panting a little, "you'd generally get to somewhere else—if you ran very fast for a long time as we've been doing."

"A slow sort of country!" said the Queen. "Now, *here*, you see, it takes all the running *you* can do, to keep in the same place.[12] If you want to get somewhere else, you must run at least twice as fast as that!"

"I'd rather not try, please!" said Alice. "I'm quite content to stay here—only I *am* so hot and thirsty!"

"I know what *you'd* like!" the Queen said good-naturedly, taking a little box out of her pocket. "Have a biscuit?"

Alice thought it would not be civil to say

"No," though it wasn't at all what she wanted. So she took it, and ate it as well as she could: and it was *very* dry: and she thought she had never been so nearly choked in all her life.

"While you're refreshing yourself," said the Queen, "I'll just take the measurements." And she took a ribbon out of her pocket, marked in inches, and began measuring the ground, and sticking little pegs in here and there.

"At the end of two yards," she said, putting in a peg to mark the distance, "I shall give you your directions—have another biscuit?"

"No, thank you," said Alice: "one's *quite* enough!"

"Thirst quenched, I hope?" said the Queen.

Alice did not know what to say to this, but luckily the Queen did not wait for an answer, but went on. "At the end of *three* yards I shall repeat them—for fear of your forgetting them. At the end of *four*, I shall say good-bye. And at the end of *five*, I shall go!"

She had got all the pegs put in by this time, and Alice looked on with great interest as she returned to the tree, and then began slowly walking down the row.

At the two-yard peg she faced round, and said "A pawn goes two squares in its first move, you know. So you'll go *very* quickly through the Third Square—by railway, I should think—and you'll find yourself in the Fourth Square in no time. Well, *that* square belongs to Tweedledum and Tweedledee—the Fifth is mostly water—the Sixth belongs to Humpty Dumpty—But you make no remark?"

"I—I didn't know I had to make one—just then," Alice faltered out.

"You *should* have said," the Queen went on in a tone of grave reproof, " 'It's extremely kind

13. Gerald M. Weinberg, in a letter, makes two interesting observations about the Queen's advice. Because she is instructing Alice on how to behave as a pawn, "Speak in French when you ca'n't think of the English for a thing" could refer to pawns capturing *en passant* (there is no English term for this ploy), and "turn out your toes" could indicate the way pawns capture by forward diagonal moves to the left or right.

14. A glance at the position of the chess pieces, on the diagram in Carroll's preface, shows that Alice (the white pawn) and the Red Queen are side by side on adjacent squares. The first move of the problem now takes place as the Queen moves away to KR4 (the fourth square on the Red King's rook file, counting from the red side of the board. In this notation the squares are always numbered from the side of the piece that is moved).

of you to tell me all this'—however, we'll suppose it said—the Seventh Square is all forest—however, one of the Knights will show you the way—and in the Eighth Square we shall be Queens together, and it's all feasting and fun!" Alice got up and curtseyed, and sat down again.

At the next peg the Queen turned again, and this time she said "Speak in French when you ca'n't think of the English for a thing—turn out your toes as you walk[13]—and remember who you are!" She did not wait for Alice to curtsey, this time, but walked on quickly to the next peg, where she turned for a moment to say "Good-bye," and then hurried on to the last.

How it happened, Alice never knew, but exactly as she came to the last peg, she was gone.[14] Whether she vanished into the air, or whether she ran quickly into the wood ("and she *can* run very fast!" thought Alice), there was no way of guessing, but she was gone, and Alice began to remember that she was a Pawn, and that it would soon be time for her to move.

3

Looking-Glass Insects

Of course the first thing to do was to make a grand survey of the country she was going to travel through. "It's something very like learning geography," thought Alice, as she stood on tiptoe in hopes of being able to see a little further. "Principal rivers—there *are* none. Principal mountains—I'm on the only one, but I don't think it's got any name. Principal towns—why, what *are* those creatures, making honey down there? They ca'n't be bees—nobody ever saw bees a mile off, you know—" and for some time she stood silent, watching one of them that was bustling about among the flowers, poking its proboscis into them, "just as if it was a regular bee," thought Alice.

However, this was anything but a regular bee: in fact, it was an elephant[1]—as Alice soon found out, though the idea quite took her breath away at first. "And what enormous flowers they must be!" was her next idea. "Something like cottages with the roofs taken off, and stalks put to them—and what quantities of honey they must make! I think I'll go down and—no, I wo'n't go *just* yet," she went on, checking herself just as she was beginning to run down the hill, and trying to find some excuse for turning shy so suddenly. "It'll never do to go down among them without a good long branch to brush them

1. A. S. M. Dickins, in his article on the looking-glass chess game (see Chapter 9, Note 1), mentions that the letter *B* (aside from being a favorite of Carroll's) is the symbol for a chess bishop, and that some six hundred years ago the chess bishop was called an elephant. "*Alfil* in Muslim, *Hasti* in Indian, and *Kin or Siang* in Chinese Chess. The Russians still to this day call it *Slon*, which means Elephant. So in this curious paragraph Lewis Carroll does introduce the Bishop into the story, but wrapped up in a very disguised code-name."

In a charming half-nonsense tale called "Isa's Visit to Oxford," written for his child-friend Isa Bowman, who reprints it in her book *The Story of Lewis Carroll* (J. M. Dent, 1899), Carroll speaks of walking with Isa through the gardens of Worcester College. They failed to "see the swans (who ought to have been on the Lake), nor the hippopotamus, who ought not to have been walking about among the flowers, gathering honey like a busy bee."

away—and what fun it'll be when they ask me how I liked my walk. I shall say 'Oh, I liked it well enough—' (here came the favourite little toss of the head), 'only it *was* so dusty and hot, and the elephants *did* tease so!'

"I think I'll go down the other way," she said after a pause; "and perhaps I may visit the elephants later on. Besides, I *do* so want to get into the Third Square!"

So, with this excuse, she ran down the hill, and jumped over the first of the six little brooks.[2]

————————————————————
————————————————————
————————————————————
————————————————————
————————————————————
————————————————————

"Tickets, please!" said the Guard, putting his head in at the window. In a moment everybody was holding out a ticket: they were about the same size as the people, and quite seemed to fill the carriage.

"Now then! Show your ticket, child!" the Guard went on, looking angrily at Alice. And a great many voices all said together ("like the chorus of a song," thought Alice) "Don't keep him waiting, child! Why, his time is worth a thousand pounds a minute!"

"I'm afraid I haven't got one," Alice said in a frightened tone: "there wasn't a ticket-office where I came from." And again the chorus of voices went on. "There wasn't room for one where she came from. The land there is worth a thousand pounds an inch!"

"Don't make excuses," said the Guard: "you should have bought one from the engine-driver." And once more the chorus of voices went on with "The man that drives the engine. Why, the smoke alone is worth a thousand pounds a puff!"[3]

Alice thought to herself "Then there's no use in speaking." The voices didn't join in, *this* time, as she hadn't spoken, but, to her great surprise, they all *thought* in chorus (I hope you understand what *thinking in chorus* means—for I must confess that *I* don't), "Better say nothing at all. Language is worth a thousand pounds a word!"

"I shall dream about a thousand pounds tonight, I know I shall!" thought Alice.

All this time the Guard was looking at her, first through a telescope, then through a microscope, and then through an opera-glass.[4] At last he said "You're traveling the wrong way," and shut up the window, and went away.

"So young a child," said the gentleman sitting opposite to her, (he was dressed in white paper,)[5] "ought to know which way she's going, even if she doesn't know her own name!"

A Goat, that was sitting next to the gentleman in white, shut his eyes and said in a loud voice, "She ought to know her way to the ticket-office, even if she doesn't know her alphabet!"

3. *Jabberwocky* (March 1970) published my query: "Perhaps one of your readers can clear up what for me is one of the biggest mysteries yet unsolved about the *Alice* books. In the railway carriage scene the phrase 'worth a thousand——a——' (with different words where the blanks are) is repeated several times. I feel certain Carroll was referring here to something familiar to his readers then (an advertising slogan?) but I have been unable to discover what it was."

The consensus among respondents, in the next issue, was that the phrase referred to a popular slogan for Beecham's pills: "worth a guinea a box." R. B. Shaberman and Denis Crutch, in *Under the Quizzing Glass*, offer a different theory. They think it echoes a well-known phrase used by Tennyson when he described the freshness of air on the Isle of Wight as "worth sixpence a pint."

Still another conjecture, in a letter from Wilfred Shepherd, ties the thousand pounds to the enormous publicity that surrounded the building of the *Great Eastern*, a British ship that was gigantic for its time (it was launched in 1858). The *Encyclopaedia Britannica* speaks of it as "perhaps the most discussed steamship that has ever been built, and the most historic failure." Shepherd found an account of the affair in a book called *The Great Iron Ship* (1953) by James Duggan. It is filled with references to costs of a thousand pounds—a thousand pounds a foot to launch the ship, an investment on capital of a thousand pounds a day, and so on. Perhaps someone should check the newspaper accounts Carroll would have read to see if there are references to "a thousand pounds a puff."

Frankie Morris, writing on "'Smiles and Soap:' Lewis Carroll and the 'Blast of Puffery,'" in *Jabberwocky* (Spring 1997), writes that the word *puff* was a common Victorian term for the promotion of a product by advertising and personal endorsements. He quotes from E. S. Turner's *The Shocking History of Advertising* (1953, Chapter 3) a pill maker's offer to Dickens of "a thousand pounds for a puff."

4. Tenniel's illustration for this scene may have been a deliberate parody of *My First Sermon*, a famous painting by John Everett Millais. The resemblance in the way the two girls are dressed is remarkable: porkpie hat with feather, striped stockings, a skirt with rows of tucks at the bottom, pointed black shoes, and a muff. A purse beside Alice takes the place of a Bible at the left of the girl in the church pew. In his diary (April 7, 1864) Carroll records a visit to Millais's house, where he met his six-year-old daughter, Effie, the original of the girl in the painting.

Spencer D. Brown was the first to spot the resemblance of Tenniel's Alice in the train to Millais's girl at church. The parallels are even more striking if Tenniel's drawing is taken as a composite of *My First Sermon* and a later picture, *My Second Sermon*, showing the same girl sleeping in the pew.

My First Sermon was widely reproduced in England. In the United States, Currier and Ives sold a copy in black and white (some were hand-colored) titled *Little Ella*. It is an exact replica of the Millais painting except that it is mirror-reversed (Carroll would have been amused) and the girl's face has been altered to make it more doll-like. The date of the Currier and Ives print is unknown, as is the name of the artist who modified it. Nor is it known whether the picture was pirated, or if Currier and Ives obtained permission to copy it. (See the picture below.)

There was a Beetle sitting next the Goat (it was a very queer carriage-full of passengers altogether), and, as the rule seemed to be that they should all speak in turn, *he* went on with "She'll have to go back from here as luggage!"

Alice couldn't see who was sitting beyond the Beetle, but a hoarse voice spoke next. "Change engines—"[6] it said, and there it choked and was obliged to leave off.

"It sounds like a horse," Alice thought to herself. And an extremely small voice, close to her ear, said "You might make a joke on that—something about 'horse' and 'hoarse,' you know."[7]

Then a very gentle voice in the distance said, "She must be labeled 'Lass, with care,'[8] you know—"

And after that other voices went on ("What a number of people there are in the carriage!" thought Alice) saying "She must go by post, as she's got a head on her—"[9] "She must be sent as a message by the telegraph—" "She must draw the train herself the rest of the way—," and so on.

But the gentleman dressed in white paper leaned forwards and whispered in her ear, "Never mind what they all say, my dear, but take a return-ticket every time the train stops."

"Indeed I sha'n't!" Alice said rather impatiently. "I don't belong to this railway journey at all—I was in a wood just now—and I wish I could get back there!"

"You might make a joke on *that*," said the little voice close to her ear: "something about 'you *would* if you could,' you know."[10]

"Don't tease so," said Alice, looking about in vain to see where the voice came from. "If you're so anxious to have a joke made, why don't you make one yourself?"

The little voice sighed deeply.[11] It was *very*

unhappy, evidently, and Alice would have said something pitying to comfort it, "if it would only sigh like other people!" she thought. But this was such a wonderfully small sigh, that she wouldn't have heard it at all, if it hadn't come *quite* close to her ear. The consequence of this was that it tickled her ear very much, and quite took off her thoughts from the unhappiness of the poor little creature.

"I know you are a friend," the little voice went on: "a dear friend, and an old friend. And you wo'n't hurt me, though I am an insect."

"What kind of insect?" Alice inquired, a little anxiously. What she really wanted to know was, whether it could sting or not, but she thought this wouldn't be quite a civil question to ask.

"What, then you don't—" the little voice began, when it was drowned by a shrill scream from the engine, and everybody jumped up in alarm, Alice among the rest.

The Horse, who had put his head out of the window, quietly drew it in and said "It's only a brook we have to jump over." Everybody seemed satisfied with this, though Alice felt a little nervous at the idea of trains jumping at all. "However, it'll take us into the Fourth Square, that's some comfort!" she said to herself. In another moment she felt the carriage rise straight up into the air, and in her fright she caught at the thing nearest to her hand, which happened to be the Goat's beard.[12]

*   *   *   *
*   *   *
*   *   *   *

But the beard seemed to melt away as she touched it, and she found herself sitting quietly under a tree—while the Gnat (for that was the insect she had been talking to) was balancing

Roger Green convinced me that the resemblance of Tenniel's drawing to the two Millais paintings may have been coincidental. He referred me to pictures of the day in *Punch* that show little girls in railway carriages dressed exactly like Alice, with their hands in muffs. Michael Hearn sent a similar picture from Walter Crane's 1869 book *Little Annie and Jack in London*.

Still, the resemblance of Tenniel's Alice to Millais's daughter in church is so striking that it is impossible to believe Tenniel was not at least aware of it. You can form your own opinion by studying the two pictures reproduced below.

5. A comparison of the illustration of the man in white paper with Tenniel's

political cartoons in *Punch* leaves little doubt that the face under the folded paper hat is Benjamin Disraeli's. Tenniel and/or Carroll may have had in mind the "white papers" (official documents) with which such statesmen are surrounded.

6. It is easy to overlook the humor in having a horse passenger call out not "change horses" but "change engines."

7. There *is* an old joke based on this pun. "I'm a little hoarse," a person says, then adds, "I have a little colt."

8. In England, packages containing glass objects are commonly labeled "Glass, with care."

9. *Head* was Victorian slang for a postage stamp. Because Alice has a head, the voices suggest she should be posted. Note the grim suggestion of a post with an enemy's severed head on top.

10. Carroll may have intended this as a quote of the first line of a Mother Goose melody:

I would, if I could,
If I couldn't how could I?
I couldn't, without I could, could I?
Could you, without you could, could ye?
      Could ye? could ye?
Could you, without you could, could ye?

11. In the "Wasp in a Wig" episode (reprinted in this book) the aged Wasp's long sigh may have expressed Carroll's sadness over the gulf time had placed between himself and Alice. George Garcin says in a letter that he thinks the Gnat's sigh carries similar overtones. Time, symbolized by the train, is carrying Alice (his "dear friend, and an old friend") the "wrong way"—toward woman-

itself on a twig just over her head, and fanning her with its wings.

It certainly was a *very* large Gnat: "about the size of a chicken," Alice thought. Still, she couldn't feel nervous with it, after they had been talking together so long.

"—then you don't like *all* insects?" the Gnat went on, as quietly as if nothing had happened.

"I like them when they can talk," Alice said. "None of them ever talk, where *I* come from."

"What sort of insects do you rejoice in, where *you* come from?" the Gnat inquired.

"I don't *rejoice* in insects at all," Alice explained, "because I'm rather afraid of them— at least the large kinds. But I can tell you the names of some of them."

"Of course they answer to their names?" the Gnat remarked carelessly.

"I never knew them do it."

"What's the use of their having names," the Gnat said, "if they wo'n't answer to them?"

"No use to *them*," said Alice; "but it's useful to the people that name them, I suppose. If not, why do things have names at all?"

"I ca'n't say," the Gnat replied. "Further on, in the wood down there, they've got no names— however, go on with your list of insects: you're wasting time."

"Well, there's the Horse-fly," Alice began, counting off the names on her fingers.

"All right," said the Gnat. "Half way up that bush, you'll see a Rocking-horse-fly, if you look. It's made entirely of wood, and gets about by swinging itself from branch to branch."

"What does it live on?" Alice asked, with great curiosity.

"Sap and sawdust," said the Gnat. "Go on with the list."

Alice looked at the Rocking-horse-fly with great interest, and made up her mind that it must have been just repainted, it looked so bright and sticky; and then she went on.

"And there's the Dragon-fly."

"Look on the branch above your head," said the Gnat, "and there you'll find a Snap-dragon-fly. Its body is made of plum-pudding, its wings of holly-leaves, and its head is a raisin burning in brandy."[13]

"And what does it live on?" Alice asked, as before.

"Frumenty[14] and mince-pie," the Gnat replied; "and it makes its nest in a Christmas-box."

"And then there's the Butterfly," Alice went on, after she had taken a good look at the insect

hood, when she will soon be lost to him. This passage of time may be the "shadow of a sigh" in the last stanza of Carroll's prefatory poem.

Fred Madden, writing on "Orthographic Transformations in *Through the Looking-Glass,*" in *Jabberwocky* (Autumn 1985), has an intriguing explanation of why Carroll put a gnat in the railway carriage alongside a goat. In Carroll's game of Doublets, the word *gnat* becomes *goat* by the change of a single letter. Madden supports this contention by referring to a word ladder that actually appears in Carroll's pamphlet *Doublets: A Word Puzzle* (Macmillan, third edition, 1880, page 31), in which Carroll changed GNAT to BITE in six steps: GNAT, GOAT, BOAT, BOLT, BOLE, BILE, BITE.

12. The train's leap completes Alice's move of P-Q4. In Carroll's original manuscript Alice grabbed the hair of an old lady in the carriage, but on June 1, 1870, Tenniel wrote Carroll:

My Dear Dodgson:

I think that when the jump occurs in the railway scene you might very well make Alice lay hold of the goat's *beard* as being the object nearest to her hand—instead of the old lady's hair. The jerk would actually throw them together.

Don't think me brutal, but I am bound to say that the "wasp" chapter does not interest me in the least, and I can't see my way to a picture. If you want to shorten the book, I can't help thinking—with all submission—that *this* is your opportunity.

In an agony of haste,

      Yours sincerely,

        J. TENNIEL

Carroll adopted both suggestions. The old lady and a thirteenth chapter about the wasp were removed.

13. Snapdragon (or flapdragon) is the name of a pastime that delighted Victorian children during the Christmas season. A shallow bowl was filled with brandy, raisins were tossed in, and the brandy set on fire. Players tried to snatch raisins from the flickering blue flames and pop them, still blazing, into their mouths. The burning raisins also were called snap-dragons.

14. Frumenty is a wheat pudding, usually prepared with sugar, spice, and raisins.

with its head on fire, and had thought to herself, "I wonder if that's the reason insects are so fond of flying into candles—because they want to turn into Snap-dragon-flies!"

"Crawling at your feet," said the Gnat (Alice

drew her feet back in some alarm), "you may observe a Bread-and-butter-fly. Its wings are thin slices of bread-and-butter; its body is a crust, and its head is a lump of sugar."

"And what does *it* live on?"

"Weak tea with cream in it."

A new difficulty came into Alice's head. "Supposing it couldn't find any?" she suggested.

"Then it would die, of course."

"But that must happen very often," Alice remarked thoughtfully.

"It always happens," said the Gnat.

After this, Alice was silent for a minute or two, pondering. The Gnat amused itself meanwhile by humming round and round her head: at last it settled again and remarked "I suppose you don't want to lose your name?"

"No, indeed," Alice said, a little anxiously.

"And yet I don't know," the Gnat went on in a careless tone: "only think how convenient it would be if you could manage to go home without it! For instance, if the governess wanted to

call you to your lessons, she would call out
'Come here—,' and there she would have to
leave off, because there wouldn't be any name
for her to call, and of course you wouldn't have
to go, you know."

"That would never do, I'm sure," said Alice:
"the governess would never think of excusing me
lessons for that. If she couldn't remember my
name, she'd call me 'Miss,' as the servants do."

"Well, if she said 'Miss,' and didn't say anything more," the Gnat remarked, "of course
you'd miss your lessons. That's a joke. I wish *you*
had made it."

"Why do you wish *I* had made it?" Alice
asked. "It's a very bad one."

But the Gnat only sighed deeply, while two
large tears came rolling down its cheeks.

"You shouldn't make jokes," Alice said, "if it
makes you so unhappy."

Then came another of those melancholy little
sighs, and this time the poor Gnat really seemed
to have sighed itself away, for, when Alice
looked up, there was nothing whatever to be
seen on the twig, and, as she was getting quite
chilly with sitting still so long, she got up and
walked on.

She very soon came to an open field, with a
wood on the other side of it: it looked much
darker than the last wood, and Alice felt a *little*
timid about going into it. However, on second
thoughts, she made up her mind to go on: "for I
certainly won't go *back*,"[15] she thought to herself,
and this was the only way to the Eighth Square.

"This must be the wood," she said thoughtfully to herself, "where things have no names. I
wonder what'll become of *my* name when I go
in? I shouldn't like to lose it at all—because
they'd have to give me another, and it would be

15. Yossi Natanson, an Israeli correspondent, points out that Alice
knows she can't go back because she
is a pawn and pawns are unable to
move backward.

16. Queen Victoria, Charles Lovett informed me, owned a spaniel named Dash that was well known in England. The queen was often photographed and painted with Dash at her side or on her lap.

17. Alice may be thinking of Lily, the name of the white pawn whose place she has taken, and also of her own last name, Liddell. Perhaps, as readers Josephine van Dyk and Mrs. Carlton Hyman independently proposed, Alice is vaguely recalling the sound of her first name, which seems to begin with an *L*—"*L*-is." Ada Brown supported this conjecture by sending the following lines from "Bruno's Picnic," a chapter in Carroll's *Sylvie and Bruno Concluded*: "What *does* an Apple-Tree begin with, when it wants to speak?" asks Sylvie. The narrator replies: "Doesn't 'Apple-Tree' always begin with 'Eh!'?"

In *Language and Lewis Carroll* (Mouton, 1970), Robert Sutherland points out that the theme of forgetting one's name is common in Carroll's writings. "Who are you?" the Caterpillar asks Alice, and she is too confused to answer; the Red Queen admonishes Alice, "Remember who you are!"; the man in white paper tells her, "So young a child ought to know where she's going, even if she doesn't know her name"; the White Queen is so frightened by thunder that she forgets her name; the Baker forgets his name in *The Hunting of the Snark*, and so does the Professor in *Sylvie and Bruno*. Perhaps this theme reflects Carroll's own confusion over whether he is Charles Dodgson, the Oxford professor, or Lewis Carroll, writer of fantasy and nonsense.

18. Fred Madden (see this chapter's Note 11) observes that Alice, a

almost certain to be an ugly one. But then the fun would be, trying to find the creature that had got my old name! That's just like the advertisements, you know, when people lose dogs—'*answers to the name of "Dash"*:[16] *had on a brass collar*'— just fancy calling everything you met 'Alice,' till one of them answered! Only they wouldn't answer at all, if they were wise."

She was rambling on in this way when she reached the wood: it looked very cool and shady. "Well, at any rate it's a great comfort," she said as she stepped under the trees, "after being so hot, to get into the—into the—into *what*?" she went on, rather surprised at not being able to think of the word. "I mean to get under the— under the—under *this*, you know!" putting her hand on the trunk of the tree. "What *does* it call itself, I wonder? I do believe it's got no name— why, to be sure it hasn't!"

She stood silent for a minute, thinking: then she suddenly began again. "Then it really *has* happened, after all! And now, who am I? I *will* remember, if I can! I'm determined to do it!" But being determined didn't help her much, and all she could say, after a great deal of puzzling, was "L, I *know* it begins with L!"[17]

Just then a Fawn[18] came wandering by: it looked at Alice with its large gentle eyes, but didn't seem at all frightened. "Here then! Here then!" Alice said, as she held out her hand and tried to stroke it; but it only started back a little, and then stood looking at her again.

"What do you call yourself?" the Fawn said at last. Such a soft sweet voice it had!

"I wish I knew!" thought poor Alice. She answered, rather sadly, "Nothing, just now."

"Think again," it said: "that wo'n't do."

Alice thought, but nothing came of it. "Please,

would you tell me what *you* call yourself?" she said timidly. "I think that might help a little."

"I'll tell you, if you'll come a little further on," the Fawn said. "I ca'n't remember *here*."

So they walked on together through the wood, Alice with her arms clasped lovingly round the soft neck of the Fawn, till they came out into another open field, and here the Fawn gave a sudden bound into the air, and shook itself free from Alice's arm. "I'm a Fawn!"[19] It cried out in a voice of delight. "And, dear me! you're a human child!" A sudden look of alarm came into its beautiful brown eyes, and in another moment it had darted away at full speed.

Alice stood looking after it, almost ready to cry with vexation at having lost her dear little fellow-traveler so suddenly. "However, I know my name now," she said: "that's *some* comfort. Alice—Alice—I wo'n't forget it again. And now, which of these finger-posts ought I to follow, I wonder?"

pawn, is here meeting a fawn, and that in Carroll's game of doublets the change of a single letter turns *pawn* to *fawn*. According to Carroll's Dramatis Personae, at the beginning of the book, the fawn is actually a pawn in the chess game. Presumably the two pawns, both white, are now adjacent to each other.

19. The wood in which things have no name is in fact the universe itself, as it is apart from symbol-manipulating creatures who label portions of it because—as Alice earlier remarked with pragmatic wisdom—"it's useful to the people that name them." The realization that the world by itself contains no signs—that there is no connection whatever between things and their names except by way of a mind that finds the tags useful—is by no means a trivial philosophic insight. The fawn's delight in recalling its name reminds one of the old joke about Adam naming the tiger the tiger because it *looked* like a tiger.

20. Reader Greg Stone calls my attention to the way "house" and the names of the Tweedle brothers are left-right reversed on these signs, in keeping with the fact that Carroll intended the brothers to be mirror images of each other.

21. Carroll clearly intended this last clause and title of the next chapter to be a rhymed couplet:

> *Feeling sure that they must be*
> *Tweedledum and Tweedledee.*

It was not a very difficult question to answer, as there was only one road through the wood, and the two finger-posts both pointed along it. "I'll settle it," Alice said to herself, "when the road divides and they point different ways."

But this did not seem likely to happen. She went on and on, a long way, but, wherever the road divided, there were sure to be two finger-posts pointing the same way, one marked "TO TWEEDLEDUM'S HOUSE," and the other "TO THE HOUSE OF TWEEDLEDEE."[20]

"I do believe," said Alice at last, "that they live in the *same* house! I wonder I never thought of that before—But I ca'n't stay there long. I'll just call and say 'How d'ye do?' and ask them the way out of the wood. If I could only get to the Eighth Square before it gets dark!" So she wandered on, talking to herself as she went, till, on turning a sharp corner, she came upon two fat little men, so suddenly that she could not help starting back, but in another moment she recovered herself, feeling sure that they must be[21]

4

Tweedledum and Tweedledee

They were standing under a tree, each with an arm round the other's neck, and Alice knew which was which in a moment, because one of them had "DUM" embroidered on his collar, and the other "DEE." "I suppose they've each got 'TWEEDLE' round at the back of the collar," she said to herself.

They stood so still that she quite forgot they were alive, and she was just going round to see if the word "TWEEDLE" was written at the back of each collar, when she was startled by a voice coming from the one marked "DUM."

"If you think we're wax-works," he said, "you ought to pay, you know. Wax-works weren't made to be looked at for nothing. Nohow!"

"Contrariwise," added the one marked "DEE," "if you think we're alive, you ought to speak."

"I'm sure I'm very sorry," was all Alice could say; for the words of the old song kept ringing through her head like the ticking of a clock, and she could hardly help saying them out loud:—[1]

> *"Tweedledum and Tweedledee*
> *Agreed to have a battle;*
> *For Tweedledum said Tweedledee*
> *Had spoiled his nice new rattle.*

1. In the 1720s there was a bitter rivalry between George Frederick Handel, the German-English composer, and Giovanni Battista Bononcini, an Italian composer. John Byrom, an eighteenth-century hymn writer and teacher of shorthand, described the controversy as follows:

> *Some say, compared to Bononcini*
> *That Mynheer Handel's but a ninny;*
> *Others aver that he to Handel*
> *Is scarcely fit to hold a candle;*
> *Strange all this difference should be*
> *Twixt tweedle-dum and tweedle-dee.*

No one knows whether the nursery rhyme about the Tweedle brothers originally had reference to this famous musical battle, or whether it was an older rhyme from which Byrom borrowed in the last line of his doggerel. (See the *Oxford Dictionary of Nursery Rhymes*, 1952, edited by Iona and Peter Opie, page 418.)

2. Tenniel's Tweedle brothers, in their schoolboy skeleton suits, as they were called, strongly resemble his drawings of John Bull in *Punch*. See the first chapter of Michael Hancher's *The Tenniel Illustrations to the "Alice" Books*.

"First Boy," Everett Bleiler writes in a letter, was a term used in British schools for the brightest boy in a class, or an older boy who served as a sort of class monitor.

Just then flew down a monstrous crow,
    As black as a tar-barrel;
Which frightened both the heroes so,
    They quite forgot their quarrel."

"I know what you're thinking about," said Tweedledum; "but it isn't so, nohow."

"Contrariwise," continued Tweedledee, "if it was so, it might be; and if it were so, it would be; but as it isn't, it ain't. That's logic."

"I was thinking," Alice said very politely, "which is the best way out of this wood: it's getting so dark. Would you tell me, please?"

But the fat little men only looked at each other and grinned.

They looked so exactly like a couple of great schoolboys, that Alice couldn't help pointing her finger at Tweedledum, and saying "First Boy!"[2]

"Nohow!" Tweedledum cried out briskly, and shut his mouth up again with a snap.

"Next Boy!" said Alice, passing on to Tweedledee, though she felt quite certain he would only shout out "Contrariwise!" and so he did.

"You've begun wrong!" cried Tweedledum. "The first thing in a visit is to say 'How d'ye do?' and shake hands!" And here the two brothers gave each other a hug, and then they held out the two hands that were free, to shake hands with her.[3]

Alice did not like shaking hands with either of them first, for fear of hurting the other one's feelings; so, as the best way out of the difficulty, she took hold of both hands at once: the next moment they were dancing round in a ring. This seemed quite natural (she remembered afterwards), and she was not even surprised to hear music playing: it seemed to come from the tree under which they were dancing, and it was done (as well as she could make it out) by the branches rubbing one across the other, like fiddles and fiddle-sticks.

"But it certainly *was* funny," (Alice said afterwards, when she was telling her sister the history of all this,) "to find myself singing '*Here we go round the mulberry bush.*' I don't know when I began it, but somehow I felt as if I'd been singing it a long long time!"

The other two dancers were fat, and very soon out of breath. "Four times round is enough for one dance," Tweedledum panted out, and they left off dancing as suddenly as they had begun: the music stopped at the same moment.

Then they let go of Alice's hands, and stood looking at her for a minute: there was a rather awkward pause, as Alice didn't know how to begin a conversation with people she had just been dancing with. "It would never do to say 'How d'ye do?' *now*," she said to herself: "we seem to have got beyond that, somehow!"

3. Tweedledum and Tweedledee are what geometers call "enantiomorphs," mirror-image forms of each other. That Carroll intended this is strongly suggested by Tweedledee's favorite word, "contrariwise," and by the fact that they extend right and left hands for a handshake. Tenniel's picture of the two enantiomorphs arrayed for battle, standing in identical postures, indicates that he looked upon the twins in the same way. Note that the position of the fingers of Tweedledum's right hand (or is it Tweedledee's?—the bolster was put around the neck of Dee, but the saucepan marks him as Dum) exactly matches the position of his brother's left fingers.

The Tweedle brothers are mentioned in *Finnegans Wake* (Viking, 1959) on page 258.

4. "In composing 'The Walrus and the Carpenter,'" Carroll wrote to an uncle in 1872, "I had no particular poem in my mind. The metre is a common one, and I don't think 'Eugene Aram' [a poem by Thomas Hood] suggested it more than the many other poems I have read in the same metre" (*The Letters of Lewis Carroll*, edited by Morton Cohen, Vol. 1, page 177).

As a check against the tendency to find too much intended symbolism in the *Alice* books it is well to remember that, when Carroll gave the manuscript of this poem to Tenniel for illustrating, he offered the artist a choice of drawing a carpenter, butterfly, or baronet. Each word fitted the rhyme scheme, and Carroll had no preference so far as the nonsense was concerned. Tenniel chose the carpenter.

The boxlike paper hat that Tenniel placed on the carpenter's head is no longer folded by carpenters. However, these hats are still widely used by operators of newspaper printing presses; they fold them from blank sheets of newsprint and wear them to keep the ink out of their hair. J. B. Priestley has written an amusing article on "The Walrus and the Carpenter" (*New Statesman*, August 10, 1957, p. 168) in which he interprets the two figures as archetypes of two kinds of politicians.

"I hope you're not much tired?" she said at last.

"Nohow. And thank you *very* much for asking," said Tweedledum.

"So *much* obliged!" added Tweedledee. "You like poetry?"

"Ye-es, pretty well—*some* poetry," Alice said doubtfully. "Would you tell me which road leads out of the wood?"

"What shall I repeat to her?" said Tweedledee, looking round at Tweedledum with great solemn eyes, and not noticing Alice's question.

"'*The Walrus and the Carpenter*' is the longest," Tweedledum replied, giving his brother an affectionate hug.

Tweedledee began instantly:

> "*The sun was shining—*"

Here Alice ventured to interrupt him. "If it's *very* long," she said, as politely as she could, "would you please tell me first which road—"

Tweedledee smiled gently, and began again:[4]

> "*The sun was shining on the sea,*
>   *Shining with all his might:*
> *He did his very best to make*
>   *The billows smooth and bright—*
> *And this was odd, because it was*
>   *The middle of the night.*
>
> *The moon was shining sulkily,*
>   *Because she thought the sun*
> *Had got no business to be there*
>   *After the day was done—*
> *'It's very rude of him,' she said,*
>   *'To come and spoil the fun!'*
>
> *The sea was wet as wet could be,*
>   *The sands were dry as dry.*

You could not see a cloud, because
 No cloud was in the sky:
No birds were flying overhead—
 There were no birds to fly.⁵

The Walrus and the Carpenter
 Were walking close at hand.⁶
They wept like anything to see
 Such quantities of sand:
'If this were only cleared away,'
 They said, 'it would be grand!'

'If seven maids with seven mops
 Swept it for half a year,
Do you suppose,' the Walrus said.
 'That they could get it clear?'
'I doubt it,' said the Carpenter,
 And shed a bitter tear.

'O Oysters, come and walk with us!'
 The Walrus did beseech.
'A pleasant walk, a pleasant talk,
 Along the briny beach:
We cannot do with more than four,
 To give a hand to each.'

The eldest Oyster looked at him,
 But never a word he said:

5. Richard Boothe notices in a letter that Peter Newell, in his illustration for this scene, violated the poem by putting both birds and clouds in the sky. (See *More Annotated Alice*, page 219.) Newell's Walrus wears a Victorian bathing suit. The key hanging from his neck is for a bathing machine that Newell placed in the background.

6. At Tenniel's suggestion this line was altered from "Were walking hand in hand."

7. *Cabbages and Kings* was the title of O. Henry's first book. The first four lines of this stanza are the best known and most often quoted lines of the poem. In "The Adventure of the Mad Tea Party," the last story in *The Adventures of Ellery Queen*, these lines are an important element in the detective's curious method of frightening a confession out of a murderer.

Jane O'Connor Creed wrote to point out how Carroll's lines echo the following portion of King Richard's speech in Shakespeare's *Richard the Second*, Act 3, Scene 2:

Let's talk of graves, of worms, and epitaphs;
Make dust our paper, and with rainy eyes
Write sorrow on the bosom of the earth.
Let's choose executors and talk of wills;

. . . .

For God's sake, let us sit upon the ground
And tell sad stories of the death of kings.

The eldest Oyster winked his eye,
And shook his heavy head—
Meaning to say he did not choose
To leave the oyster-bed.

But four young Oysters hurried up,
All eager for the treat:
Their coats were brushed, their faces washed,
Their shoes were clean and neat—
And this was odd, because, you know,
They hadn't any feet.

Four other Oysters followed them,
And yet another four;
And thick and fast they came at last,
And more, and more, and more—
All hopping through the frothy waves,
And scrambling to the shore.

The Walrus and the Carpenter
Walked on a mile or so,
And then they rested on a rock
Conveniently low:
And all the little Oysters stood
And waited in a row:

'The time has come,' the Walrus said,
'To talk of many things:
Of shoes—and ships—and sealing-wax—
Of cabbages—and kings—[7]
And why the sea is boiling hot—
And whether pigs have wings'

'But wait a bit,' the Oysters cried,
'Before we have our chat;
For some of us are out of breath,
And all of us are fat!'
'No hurry!' said the Carpenter.
They thanked him much for that.

'A loaf of bread,' the Walrus said,
  'Is what we chiefly need:
Pepper and vinegar besides
  Are very good indeed—
Now, if you're ready, Oysters dear,
  We can begin to feed.'

'But not on us!' the Oysters cried,
  Turning a little blue.
'After such kindness, that would be
  A dismal thing to do!'
'The night is fine,' the Walrus said.
  'Do you admire the view?

'It was so kind of you to come!
  And you are very nice!'
The Carpenter said nothing but
  'Cut us another slice.
I wish you were not quite so deaf—
  I've had to ask you twice!'

'It seems a shame,' the Walrus said,
  'To play them such a trick.
After we've brought them out so far,
  And made them trot so quick!'

8. For Savile Clarke's *Alice* operetta Carroll added an additional verse:

The Carpenter he ceased to sob;
The Walrus ceased to weep;
They'd finished all the oysters;
And they laid them down to sleep—
And of their craft and cruelty
The punishment to reap.

After the Walrus and Carpenter have gone to sleep, the ghosts of two oysters appear on the stage to sing and dance and punish the sleepers by stamping on their chests. Carroll felt, and apparently audiences agreed with him, that this provided a more effective ending for the episode and also somewhat mollified oyster sympathizers among the spectators.

The ghost of the first oyster dances a mazurka and sings:

The Carpenter is sleeping, the butter's on
his face,
The vinegar and pepper are all about the
place!
Let oysters rock your cradle and lull you
into rest;
And if that will not do it, we'll sit upon
your chest!

We'll sit upon your chest! We'll sit upon
your chest!
The simplest way to do it is to sit upon
your chest!

The ghost of the second oyster dances a horn-pipe and sings:

O woeful, weeping Walrus, your tears are
all a sham!
You're greedier for Oysters than children
are for jam.
You like to have an Oyster to give the
meal a zest—
Excuse me, wicked Walrus, for stamping
on your chest!
For stamping on your chest!
For stamping on your chest!
Excuse me, wicked Walrus, for stamping
on your chest!

The Carpenter said nothing but
'The butter's spread too thick!'

'I weep for you,' the Walrus said:
'I deeply sympathize.'
With sobs and tears he sorted out
Those of the largest size,
Holding his pocket-handkerchief
Before his streaming eyes.

'O Oysters,' said the Carpenter,
'You've had a pleasant run!
Shall we be trotting home again?'
But answer came there none—
And this was scarcely odd, because
They'd eaten every one."[8]

"I like the Walrus best," said Alice: "because he was a *little* sorry for the poor oysters."

"He ate more than the Carpenter, though," said Tweedledee. "You see he held his handkerchief in front, so that the Carpenter couldn't count how many he took: contrariwise."

"That was mean!" Alice said indignantly. "Then I like the Carpenter best—if he didn't eat so many as the Walrus."

"But he ate as many as he could get," said Tweedledum.

This was a puzzler.[9] After a pause, Alice began, "Well! They were *both* very unpleasant characters—" Here she checked herself in some alarm, at hearing something that sounded to her like the puffing of a large steam-engine in the wood near them, though she feared it was more likely to be a wild beast. "Are there any lions or tigers about here?" she asked timidly.

"It's only the Red King snoring," said Tweedledee.

"Come and look at him!" the brothers cried, and they each took one of Alice's hands, and led her up to where the King was sleeping.

"Isn't he a *lovely* sight?" said Tweedledum.

Alice couldn't say honestly that he was. He had a tall red night-cap on, with a tassel, and he was lying crumpled up into a sort of untidy heap, and snoring loud—"fit to snore his head off!" as Tweedledum remarked.

"I'm afraid he'll catch cold with lying on the damp grass," said Alice, who was a very thoughtful little girl.

"He's dreaming now," said Tweedledee: "and what do you think he's dreaming about?"

Alice said "Nobody can guess that."

"Why, about *you*!" Tweedledee exclaimed,

(All the above stanzas are quoted from Roger Green's notes to *The Diaries of Lewis Carroll*, Vol. II, pages 446–47.)

9. Alice is puzzled because she faces here the traditional ethical dilemma of having to choose between judging a person in terms of acts or in terms of intentions.

10. This well-known, much-quoted discussion of the Red King's dream (the monarch is snoring on a square directly east of the square currently occupied by Alice) plunges poor Alice into grim metaphysical waters. The Tweedle brothers defend Bishop Berkeley's view that all material objects, including ourselves, are only "sorts of things" in the mind of God. Alice takes the common-sense position of Samuel Johnson, who supposed that he refuted Berkeley by kicking a large stone. "A very instructive discussion from a philosophical point of view," Bertrand Russell remarked, commenting on the Red King's dream in a radio panel discussion of *Alice*. "But if it were not put humorously, we should find it too painful."

The Berkeleyan theme troubled Carroll as it troubles all Platonists. Both *Alice* adventures are dreams, and in *Sylvie and Bruno* the narrator shuttles back and forth mysteriously between real and dream worlds. "So, either I've been dreaming about Sylvie," he says to himself early in the novel, "and this is the reality. Or else I've really been with Sylvie, and this is a dream! Is Life itself a dream, I wonder?" In *Through the Looking-Glass* Carroll returns to the question in the first paragraph of Chapter 8, in the closing lines of the book, and in the last line of the book's terminal poem.

An odd sort of infinite regress is involved here in the parallel dreams of Alice and the Red King. Alice dreams of the King, who is dreaming of Alice, who is dreaming of the King, and so on, like two mirrors facing each other, or that preposterous cartoon of Saul Steinberg's in which a fat lady paints a picture of a thin lady who is painting a picture of the fat lady who is painting a picture of the thin lady, and so on deeper into the two canvases.

clapping his hands triumphantly. "And if he left off dreaming about you, where do you suppose you'd be?"

"Where I am now, of course," said Alice.

"Not you!" Tweedledee retorted contemptuously. "You'd be nowhere. Why, you're only a sort of thing in his dream!"[10]

"If that there King was to wake," added Tweedledum, "you'd go out—bang!—just like a candle!"[11]

"I shouldn't!" Alice exclaimed indignantly. "Besides, if *I'm* only a sort of thing in his dream, what are *you*, I should like to know?"

"Ditto," said Tweedledum.

"Ditto, ditto!"[12] cried Tweedledee.

He shouted this so loud that Alice couldn't help saying "Hush! You'll be waking him, I'm afraid, if you make so much noise."

"Well, it's no use *your* talking about waking him," said Tweedledum, "when you're only one of the things in his dream. You know very well you're not real."

"I *am* real!" said Alice, and began to cry.

"You wo'n't make yourself a bit realler by crying," Tweedledee remarked: "there's nothing to cry about."

"If I wasn't real," Alice said—half-laughing through her tears, it all seemed so ridiculous—"I shouldn't be able to cry."

"I hope you don't suppose those are *real* tears?" Tweedledum interrupted in a tone of great contempt.

"I know they're talking nonsense," Alice thought to herself: "and it's foolish to cry about it." So she brushed away her tears, and went on, as cheerfully as she could, "At any rate I'd better be getting out of the wood, for really it's coming on very dark. Do you think it's going to rain?"

Tweedledum spread a large umbrella over himself and his brother, and looked up into it. "No, I don't think it is," he said: "at least—not under *here*. Nohow."

"But it may rain *outside*?"

"It may—if it chooses," said Tweedledee: "we've no objection. Contrariwise."

"Selfish things!" thought Alice, and she was just going to say "Good-night" and leave them, when Tweedledum sprang out from under the umbrella, and seized her by the wrist.

"Do you see *that*?" he said, in a voice choking with passion, and his eyes grew large and yellow all in a moment, as he pointed with a trembling finger at a small white thing lying under the tree.

"It's only a rattle," Alice said, after a careful examination of the little white thing. "Not a rattle-*snake*, you know," she added hastily, thinking that he was frightened: "only an old rattle—quite old and broken."

"I knew it was!" cried Tweedledum, beginning to stamp about wildly and tear his hair. "It's spoilt, of course!" Here he looked at Tweedledee, who immediately sat down on the ground, and tried to hide himself under the umbrella.

James Branch Cabell, in *Smire*, the last novel of his *Smirt, Smith, Smire* trilogy, introduces the same circular paradox of two persons, each dreaming the other. Smire and Smike confront one another in Chapter 9, each claiming to be asleep and dreaming the other. In a preface to his trilogy, Cabell described it as a "full-length dream story" that attempts "to extend the naturalism of Lewis Carroll."

The Red King sleeps throughout the entire narrative until he is checkmated at the close of Chapter 9 by Queen Alice when she captures the Red Queen. No chess player needs reminding that kings tend to sleep throughout most chess games, sometimes not moving after castling. Tournament games are occasionally played in which a king remains on its starting square throughout the entire game.

11. This remark of Tweedledum's was anticipated by Alice in the first chapter of the previous book where she wonders if her shrinking size might result in her "going out altogether, like a candle."

12. Molly Martin, in a letter, suggests that Tweedledee's "Ditto, ditto" underscores the doubling of twins and the identical forms of objects and their mirror reflections.

13. The broken rattle can be seen on the ground in Tenniel's illustration for this scene. In a letter to Henry Savile Clark (November 29, 1886) Carroll complained about how Tenniel had slyly drawn a watchman's rattle: "Mr. Tenniel has introduced a false 'reading' in his picture of the quarrel of Tweedledum and Tweedledee. I am certain that 'my nice new rattle' meant, in the old nursery-song, a child's rattle not a watchman's rattle as he has drawn it."

In those days a watchman's rattle consisted of a thin wooden strip that vibrated against the teeth of a ratchet wheel when the rattle was whirled, producing a loud clacking noise that sounded an alarm. They are sold today mainly as party noisemakers. As reader H. P. Young pointed out in a letter, they are fragile and easily broken.

In a shrewd analysis of the objects attached to the White Knight's horse in Chapter 8, Janis Lull identifies a large watchman's rattle at the front of the horse. It is visible in three pictures, as well as in the book's frontispiece. Tenniel had earlier drawn such a rattle in the *Punch* cartoon (January 19, 1856) shown below.

Alice laid her hand upon his arm, and said, in a soothing tone, "You needn't be so angry about an old rattle."

"But it *isn't* old!" Tweedledum cried, in a greater fury than ever. "It's *new*, I tell you—I bought it yesterday—my nice NEW RATTLE!"[13] and his voice rose to a perfect scream.

All this time Tweedledee was trying his best to fold up the umbrella, with himself in it: which was such an extraordinary thing to do, that it quite took off Alice's attention from the angry brother. But he couldn't quite succeed, and it ended in his rolling over, bundled up in the umbrella, with only his head out: and there he lay, opening and shutting his mouth and his large eyes—"looking more like a fish than anything else," Alice thought.

"Of course you agree to have a battle?" Tweedledum said in a calmer tone.

"I suppose so," the other sulkily replied, as he crawled out of the umbrella: "only *she* must help us to dress up, you know."

So the two brothers went off hand-in-hand into the wood, and returned in a minute with their arms full of things—such as bolsters, blankets, hearth-rugs, table-cloths, dish-covers, and coal-scuttles. "I hope you're a good hand at pinning and tying strings?" Tweedledum remarked. "Every one of these things has got to go on, somehow or other."

Alice said afterwards she had never seen such a fuss made about anything in all her life—the way those two bustled about—and the quantity of things they put on—and the trouble they gave her in tying strings and fastening buttons—"Really they'll be more like bundles of old clothes than anything else, by the time they're ready!" she said to herself, as she arranged a

14. Tenniel's illustration of this scene seems to show Alice arranging a bolster around Tweedledee's neck, which would make the other brother Tweedledum. But if you look closely you will see a string in both her hands. The twin on the left is Tweedledum, and Alice is tying a pot on his head. As Michael Hancher points out in his book on the Tenniel pictures, the artist apparently made a mistake here in giving the wooden sword to Tweedledee.

bolster round the neck of Tweedledee, "to keep his head from being cut off,"[14] as he said.

"You know," he added very gravely, "it's one of the most serious things that can possibly happen to one in a battle—to get one's head cut off."

Alice laughed loud: but she managed to turn it into a cough, for fear of hurting his feelings.

"Do I look very pale?" said Tweedledum, coming up to have his helmet tied on. (He *called* it a helmet, though it certainly looked much more like a saucepan.)

"Well—yes—a *little*," Alice replied gently.

"I'm very brave, generally," he went on in a low voice: "only to-day I happen to have a headache."

"And *I've* got a toothache!" said Tweedledee, who had overheard the remark. "I'm far worse than you!"

"Then you'd better not fight to-day," said Alice, thinking it a good opportunity to make peace.

"We *must* have a bit of a fight, but I don't care about going on long," said Tweedledum. "What's the time now?"

15. J. B. S. Haldane, in his book *Possible Worlds* (Chapter 2), thinks that the monstrous black crow of the nursery rhyme is a way of describing a solar eclipse:

Every one, for example, has heard of Tweedledum and Tweedledee, whose battle was interrupted by a monstrous crow as big as a tar-barrel. The true story of these heroes is as follows: King Alyattes of Lydia, father of the celebrated Croesus, had been engaged for five years in a war with Cyaxares, king of the Medes. In its sixth year, on May 28, 585 B.C., as we now know, a battle was interrupted by a total eclipse of the sun. The kings not only stopped the battle, but accepted mediation. One of the two mediators was no less a person than Nebuchadnezzar, who in the preceding year had destroyed Jerusalem and led its people into captivity.

Tweedledee looked at his watch, and said "Half-past four."

"Let's fight till six, and then have dinner," said Tweedledum.

"Very well," the other said, rather sadly: "and *she* can watch us—only you'd better not come *very* close," he added: "I generally hit every thing I can see—when I get really excited."

"And *I* hit every thing within reach," cried Tweedledum, "whether I can see it or not!"

Alice laughed. "You must hit the *trees* pretty often, I should think," she said.

Tweedledum looked round him with a satisfied smile. "I don't suppose," he said, "there'll be a tree left standing, for ever so far round, by the time we've finished!"

"And all about a rattle!" said Alice, still hoping to make them a *little* ashamed of fighting for such a trifle.

"I shouldn't have minded it so much," said Tweedledum, "if it hadn't been a new one."

"I wish the monstrous crow would come!" thought Alice.

"There's only one sword, you know," Tweedledum said to his brother: "but *you* can have the umbrella—it's quite as sharp. Only we must begin quick. It's getting as dark as it can."

"And darker," said Tweedledee.

It was getting dark so suddenly that Alice thought there must be a thunderstorm coming on. "What a thick black cloud that is!" she said. "And how fast it comes! Why, I do believe it's got wings!"[15]

"It's the crow!" Tweedledum cried out in a shrill voice of alarm; and the two brothers took to their heels and were out of sight in a moment.

Alice ran a little way into the wood, and stopped under a large tree. "It can never get at me *here*," she thought: "it's far too large to squeeze itself in among the trees. But I wish it wouldn't flap its wings so—it makes quite a hurricane in the wood—here's somebody's shawl being blown away!"

5

Wool and Water

1. By running wildly to QB4, the White Queen arrives on the square directly west of Alice. The fact that queens do a lot of running throughout the story is an allusion to their power of moving an unlimited distance in all directions across the board. With characteristic carelessness the White Queen has just passed up an opportunity to checkmate the Red King by moving to K3. In his article "*Alice* on the Stage" Carroll writes of the White Queen as follows:

Lastly, the White Queen seemed, to my dreaming fancy, gentle, stupid, fat and pale; helpless as an infant; and with a slow, maundering, bewildered air about her just *suggesting* imbecility, but never quite passing into it; that would be, I think, fatal to any comic effect she might otherwise produce. There is a character strangely like her in Wilkie Collins' novel *No Name*: by two different converging paths we have somehow reached the same ideal, and Mrs. Wragg and the White Queen might have been twin-sisters.

The role of the White Queen was played by Louise Fazenda in Paramount's film version.

2. Edwin Marsden recalls in a letter that when growing up in Massachusetts he was taught to whisper "Bread and butter, bread and butter" whenever he was being circled by a

She caught the shawl as she spoke, and looked about for the owner: in another moment the White Queen came running wildly through the wood, with both arms stretched out wide, as if she were flying, and Alice very civilly went to meet her with the shawl.[1]

"I'm very glad I happened to be in the way," Alice said, as she helped her to put on her shawl again.

The White Queen only looked at her in a helpless frightened sort of way, and kept repeating something in a whisper to herself that sounded like "Bread-and-butter, bread-and-butter,"[2] and Alice felt that if there was to be any conversation at all, she must manage it herself. So she began rather timidly: "Am I addressing the White Queen?"

"Well, yes, if you call that a-dressing," the Queen said. "It isn't *my* notion of the thing, at all."

Alice thought it would never do to have an argument at the very beginning of their conversation, so she smiled and said "If your Majesty will only tell me the right way to begin, I'll do it as well as I can."

"But I don't want it done at all!" groaned the poor Queen. "I've been a-dressing myself for the last two hours."

It would have been all the better, as it seemed to Alice, if she had got some one else to dress her, she was so dreadfully untidy. "Every single thing's crooked," Alice thought to herself, "and she's all over pins!—May I put your shawl straight for you?" she added aloud.

"I don't know what's the matter with it!" the Queen said, in a melancholy voice. "It's out of temper, I think. I've pinned it here, and I've pinned it there, but there's no pleasing it!"

"It *ca'n't* go straight, you know, if you pin it all on one side," Alice said, as she gently put it right for her; "and, dear me, what a state your hair is in!"

"The brush has got entangled in it!" the Queen said with a sigh. "And I lost the comb yesterday."

Alice carefully released the brush, and did her best to get the hair into order. "Come, you look rather better now!" she said, after altering

wasp, bee, or other insect. The phrase was intended to keep one from being stung. If this was a custom in Victorian England, it may explain the White Queen's use of the phrase while being pursued by the giant crow.

It is also possible that the Queen, who is running with outstretched arms "as if she were flying," is imagining that she is one of the Bread-and-butter-flies encountered by Alice in Chapter 3. "Bread and butter" seems to be much on her mind. In Chapter 9 she asks Alice: "Divide a loaf by a knife—what's the answer to *that*?" The Red Queen interrupts Alice to answer this problem in division with the reply "Bread-and-butter, of course," meaning that after cutting a slice of bread, you butter it.

In the United States a more common use of *bread and butter* occurs when two people, walking together, are forced to "divide" and go on both sides of a tree, post, or similar obstruction.

Eric Partridge's *Dictionary of Slang and Unconventional English* gives several colloquial meanings of *bread and butter* current in Victorian England. One of them is "schoolgirl-ish"; a girl who acts like a schoolgirl was called a "schoolgirlish miss." The White Queen may be applying the phrase to Alice.

3. In *AA* I completely missed the way Carroll plays on the Latin word *iam* (*i* and *j* are interchangeable in classical Latin), which means "now." The word *iam* is used in the past and future tenses, but in the present tense the word for "now" is *nunc*. I received more letters about this than about any other oversight, mostly from Latin teachers. They tell me that the Queen's remark is often used in class as a mnemonic for recalling the proper usage of the word.

4. In Carroll's *Sylvie and Bruno Concluded* there is a wild episode in which events go backward in time in response to turning the "reversal peg" on the German professor's Outlandish Watch.

Carroll was as fascinated by time reversal as he was by mirror reversals. In *The Story of Lewis Carroll*, Isa Bowman tells of Carroll's fondness for playing tunes backward on music boxes to produce what he called "music standing on its head." In Chapter 5 of Carroll's "Isa's Visit to Oxford," he speaks of playing an orguinette backward. This American device operated with a perforated roll of paper like the roll of a player piano, which could be rotated by turning a handle:

They put one [roll] in wrong end first, and had a tune backwards, and soon found themselves in the day before yesterday. So they dared not go on, for fear of making Isa so young she would not be able to talk. The A.A.M. [Aged Aged Man] does not like visitors who only howl, and get red in the face, from morning to night.

In a letter (November 30, 1879) to child-friend Edith Blakemore, Carroll said he was so busy and tired that he would go back to bed the minute after he got up, "and sometimes I go to bed again a minute *before* I get up."

most of the pins. "But really you should have a lady's-maid!"

"I'm sure I'll take *you* with pleasure!" the Queen said. "Twopence a week, and jam every other day."

Alice couldn't help laughing, as she said "I don't want you to hire *me*—and I don't care for jam."

"It's very good jam," said the Queen.

"Well, I don't want any *to-day*, at any rate."

"You couldn't have it if you *did* want it," the Queen said. "The rule is, jam to-morrow and jam yesterday—but never jam *to-day*."[3]

"It *must* come sometimes to 'jam to-day,'" Alice objected.

"No, it ca'n't," said the Queen. "It's jam every *other* day: to-day isn't any *other* day, you know."

"I don't understand you," said Alice. "It's dreadfully confusing!"

"That's the effect of living backwards," the Queen said kindly: "it always makes one a little giddy at first—"

"Living backwards!" Alice repeated in great astonishment. "I never heard of such a thing!"[4]

"— but there's one great advantage in it, that one's memory works both ways."

"I'm sure *mine* only works one way," Alice remarked. "I ca'n't remember things before they happen."

"It's a poor sort of memory that only works backwards," the Queen remarked.

"What sort of things do *you* remember best?" Alice ventured to ask.

"Oh, things that happened the week after next," the Queen replied in a careless tone. "For instance, now," she went on, sticking a large piece of plaster on her finger as she spoke, "there's the King's Messenger.[5] He's in prison

now, being punished: and the trial doesn't even begin till next Wednesday: and of course the crime comes last of all."

"Suppose he never commits the crime?" said Alice.

"That would be all the better, wouldn't it?" the Queen said, as she bound the plaster round her finger with a bit of ribbon.

Alice felt there was no denying *that.* "Of course it would be all the better," she said: "but it wouldn't be all the better his being punished."

"You're wrong *there,* at any rate," said the Queen. "Were *you* ever punished?"

"Only for faults," said Alice.

"And you were all the better for it, I know!" the Queen said triumphantly.

"Yes, but then I *had* done the things I was punished for," said Alice: "that makes all the difference."

"But if you *hadn't* done them," the Queen said, "that would have been better still; better,

Since Carroll used it, "backward living" has been the basis of many fantasy and science-fiction tales. The best known is F. Scott Fitzgerald's story "The Strange Case of Benjamin Button."

5. The King's Messenger, as Tenniel's illustration makes clear and as we shall see in Chapter 7, is none other than the Mad Hatter of the previous book.

In keeping with the whimsical idea that Tenniel anticipated the face of Bertrand Russell when he drew the Mad Hatter, Peter Heath claims that the picture of the Hatter in prison (left) shows Russell, circa 1918, working on his *Introduction to Mathematical Philosophy* while in a British prison for opposing England's entry into the First World War. Evidently Carroll asked Tenniel to redraw this picture, because a different version of it has survived. It is reproduced below from Michael Hearn's article "Alice's Other Parent: Sir John Tenniel as Lewis Carroll's Illustrator," in the *American Book Collector* (May/June 1983).

Why is the Mad Hatter being punished? It seems to be for a crime he has yet to commit, but behind the mirror time can go either way. Perhaps he has had a stay of execution for "murdering the time"—that is, singing out of rhythm at a concert given by the Queen of Hearts in the previous book (Chapter 7). You will recall that the Queen had ordered him beheaded.

The Queen's remark about the "week after next" is echoed in Chapter 9 when the creature with the long beak, before he shuts a door, tells Alice, "No admittance till the week after next."

AN UNUSED TENNIEL
ILLUSTRATION

and better, and better!" Her voice went higher with each "better," till it got quite to a squeak at last.

Alice was just beginning to say "There's a mistake somewhere—," when the Queen began screaming, so loud that she had to leave the sentence unfinished. 'Oh, oh, oh!" shouted the Queen, shaking her hand about as if she wanted to shake it off. "My finger's bleeding! Oh, oh, oh, oh!"

Her screams were so exactly like the whistle of a steam-engine, that Alice had to hold both her hands over her ears.

"What *is* the matter?" she said, as soon as there was a chance of making herself heard. "Have you pricked your finger?"

"I haven't pricked it *yet*," the Queen said, "but I soon shall—oh, oh, oh!"

"When do you expect to do it?" Alice asked, feeling very much inclined to laugh.

"When I fasten my shawl again," the poor Queen groaned out: "the brooch will come undone directly. Oh, oh!" As she said the words the brooch flew open, and the Queen clutched wildly at it, and tried to clasp it again.

"Take care!" cried Alice. "You're holding it all crooked!" And she caught at the brooch; but it was too late: the pin had slipped, and the Queen had pricked her finger.

"That accounts for the bleeding, you see," she said to Alice with a smile. "Now you understand the way things happen here."

"But why don't you scream *now*?" Alice asked, holding her hands ready to put over her ears again.

"Why, I've done all the screaming already," said the Queen. "What would be the good of having it all over again?"

By this time it was getting light. "The crow must have flown away, I think," said Alice: "I'm so glad it's gone. I thought it was the night coming on."

"I wish *I* could manage to be glad!" the Queen said. "Only I never can remember the rule. You must be very happy, living in this wood, and being glad whenever you like!"

"Only it is so *very* lonely here!" Alice said in a melancholy voice; and, at the thought of her loneliness, two large tears came rolling down her cheeks.

"Oh, don't go on like that!" cried the poor Queen, wringing her hands in despair. "Consider what a great girl you are. Consider what a long way you've come to-day. Consider what o'clock it is. Consider anything, only don't cry!"

Alice could not help laughing at this, even in the midst of her tears. "Can *you* keep from crying by considering things?" she asked.

"That's the way it's done," the Queen said with great decision: "nobody can do two things at once, you know.[6] Let's consider your age to begin with—how old are you?"

"I'm seven and a half, exactly."

"You needn't say 'exactually,'" the Queen remarked. "I can believe it without that. Now I'll give *you* something to believe. I'm just one hundred and one, five months and a day."

"I ca'n't believe *that*!" said Alice.

"Ca'n't you?" the Queen said in a pitying tone. "Try again: draw a long breath, and shut your eyes."

Alice laughed. "There's no use trying," she said: "one *ca'n't* believe impossible things."

"I daresay you haven't had much practice," said the Queen. "When I was your age, I always did it for half-an-hour a day. Why, sometimes

6. Carroll practiced the White Queen's advice. In his introduction to *Pillow Problems* he speaks of working mathematical problems in his head at night, during wakeful hours, as a kind of mental work-therapy to prevent less wholesome thoughts from tormenting him. "There are sceptical thoughts, which seem for the moment to uproot the firmest faith: there are blasphemous thoughts, which dart unbidden into the most reverent souls; there are unholy thoughts, which torture, with their hateful presence, the fancy that would fain be pure. Against all these some real mental work is a most helpful ally."

7. "I believe it," declared Tertullian in an oft-quoted defense of the paradoxical character of certain Christian doctrines, "because it is absurd." In a letter to child-friend Mary MacDonald, 1864, Carroll warned:

Don't be in such a hurry to believe next time—I'll tell you why—If you set to work to believe everything, you will tire out the muscles of your mind, and then you'll be so weak you won't be able to believe the simplest true things. Only last week a friend of mine set to work to believe Jack-the-giant-killer. He managed to do it, but he was so exhausted by it that when I told him it was raining (which was true) he *couldn't* believe it, but rushed out into the street without his hat or umbrella, the consequence of which was his hair got seriously damp, and one curl didn't recover its right shape for nearly two days.

8. The White Queen moves forward one square to QB5.

9. Alice likewise advances one square. This carries her to Q5 alongside of the Queen (now a sheep) again.

10. Williams and Madan, in their *Handbook of the Literature of the Rev. C. L. Dodgson*, reveal (and they reproduce a photograph to prove it) that Tenniel's two pictures of the shop faithfully copy the window and door of a small grocery shop at 83 Saint Aldgate's Street, Oxford. Tenniel was careful, however, to reverse the positions of door and window as well as the sign giving the price of tea as two shillings. These reversals support the view that Alice is not an anti-Alice.

The little shop (shown below) is now called The Alice in Wonderland Shop, and one can buy there books and items of all sorts related to the *Alice* books.

I've believed as many as six impossible things before breakfast.[7] There goes the shawl again!"

The brooch had come undone as she spoke, and a sudden gust of wind blew the Queen's shawl across a little brook. The Queen spread out her arms again, and went flying after it,[8] and this time she succeeded in catching it for herself. "I've got it!" she cried in a triumphant tone. "Now you shall see me pin it on again, all by myself!"

"Then I hope your finger is better now?" Alice said very politely, as she crossed the little brook after the Queen.[9]

* * * *

* * *

* * * *

"Oh, much better!" cried the Queen, her voice rising into a squeak as she went on. "Much be-etter! Be-etter! Be-e-e-etter! Be-e-ehh!" The last word ended in a long bleat, so like a sheep that Alice quite started.

She looked at the Queen, who seemed to have suddenly wrapped herself up in wool. Alice rubbed her eyes, and looked again. She couldn't make out what had happened at all. Was she in a shop? And was that really—was it really a *sheep* that was sitting on the other side of the counter? Rub as she would, she could make nothing more of it: she was in a little dark shop,[10] leaning with her elbows on the counter, and opposite to her was an old Sheep, sitting in an arm-chair, knitting, and every now and then leaving off to look at her through a great pair of spectacles.

"What is it you want to buy?" the Sheep said at last, looking up for a moment from her knitting.

"I don't *quite* know yet," Alice said very

ALICE'S SHOP AS IT
APPEARS TODAY

gently. "I should like to look all round me first, if
I might."

"You may look in front of you, and on both
sides, if you like," said the Sheep; "but you ca'n't
look *all* round you—unless you've got eyes at
the back of your head."

But these, as it happened, Alice had *not* got:
so she contented herself with turning round,
looking at the shelves as she came to them.

The shop seemed to be full of all manner of
curious things—but the oddest part of it all was
that, whenever she looked hard at any shelf, to
make out exactly what it had on it, that particular shelf was always quite empty, though the
others round it were crowded as full as they
could hold.[11]

"Things flow about so here!"[12] she said at last
in a plaintive tone, after she had spent a minute

David Piggins and C. J. C. Phillips,
writing on "Sheep Vision in *Through
the Looking-Glass*" (*Jabberwocky*,
Spring 1994), consider whether the
sheep's spectacles were intended for
close-up vision because she wore
them only when knitting. She does
not have them on when she is in the
boat with Alice. (In Peter Newell's
picture of this scene the glasses
remain.) Research has shown, the
authors write, that sheep eyes lack the
power of accommodation (the ability
to focus); hence the sheep's glasses,
they conclude, make no optical sense.

11. Alice's difficulty in looking
straight at the objects on sale in the
shop has been compared by popular-
izers of quantum theory to the impossible task of pinning down the precise
location of an electron in its path
around the nucleus of an atom. One
thinks also of those minute specks
that sometimes appear slightly off the
center of one's field of vision, and that
can never be seen directly because
they move as the eye moves.

12. Carroll was a great admirer of Pascal's *Pensées*. Jeffrey Stern, writing on "Lewis Carroll and Blaise Pascal" (in *Jabberwocky*, Spring 1983), quotes a passage that Carroll may well have had in mind when he wrote about how things flow about in the Sheep's little shop:

[We are] incapable of certain knowledge or absolute ignorance. We are floating in a medium of vast extent, always drifting uncertainly, blown to and fro; whenever we think we have a fixed point to which we can cling and make fast, it shifts and leaves us behind; if we follow it, it eludes our grasp, slips away, and flees eternally before us. Nothing stands still for us. This is our natural state and yet the state most contrary to our inclinations. We burn with desire to find a firm footing, an ultimate, lasting base on which to build a tower rising up to infinity, but our whole foundation cracks.

13. A teetotum is a small top similar to what in England and the United States is now called a "put-and-take top." It was popular in Victorian England as a device used in children's games. The flat sides of the top are labeled with letters or numbers, and when the top comes to rest, the uppermost side indicates what the player is to do in the game. Early forms of the top were square-shaped and marked with letters. The letter *T*, on one of the sides, stood for the Latin word *totum*, indicating that the player took all.

14. In his prefatory poem to *Alice's Adventures in Wonderland*, Carroll describes the Liddell girls as rowing "with little skill." Perhaps Alice Liddell, on one of Carroll's rowboat excursions, was as mystified as Alice is here by the rowing term *feather*. The Sheep is asking Alice to turn her oar blades horizontally as she moves them back for the next "catch" so

or so in vainly pursuing a large bright thing, that looked sometimes like a doll and sometimes like a work-box, and was always in the shelf next above the one she was looking at. "And this one is the most provoking of all—but I'll tell you what—" she added, as a sudden thought struck her. "I'll follow it up to the very top shelf of all. It'll puzzle it to go through the ceiling, I expect!"

But even this plan failed: the "thing" went through the ceiling as quietly as possible, as if it were quite used to it.

"Are you a child or a teetotum?"[13] the Sheep said, as she took up another pair of needles. "You'll make me giddy soon, if you go on turning round like that." She was now working with fourteen pairs at once, and Alice couldn't help looking at her in great astonishment.

"How *can* she knit with so many?" the puzzled child thought to herself. "She gets more and more like a porcupine every minute!"

"Can you row?" the Sheep asked, handing her a pair of knitting-needles as she spoke.

"Yes, a little—but not on land—and not with needles—" Alice was beginning to say, when suddenly the needles turned into oars in her hands, and she found they were in a little boat, gliding along between banks: so there was nothing for it but to do her best.

"Feather!"[14] cried the Sheep, as she took up another pair of needles.

This didn't sound like a remark that needed any answer: so Alice said nothing, but pulled away. There was something very queer about the water, she thought, as every now and then the oars got fast in it, and would hardly come out again.

"Feather! Feather!" the Sheep cried again,

that the lower edge of the blade will not drag through the water.

15. *Catching a crab* is rowing slang for a faulty stroke in which the oar is dipped so deeply in the water that the boat's motion, if rapid enough, can send the oar handle against the rower's chest with sufficient force to unseat him. This actually happens to Alice later on. "The phrase probably originated," says the *Oxford English Dictionary*, "in the humorous suggestion that the rower had caught a crab, which was holding his oar down under water." The phrase is sometimes used (improperly) for other rowing errors that can unseat the rower.

taking more needles. "You'll be catching a crab[15] directly."

"A dear little crab!" thought Alice. "I should like that."

"Didn't you hear me say 'Feather'?" the Sheep cried angrily, taking up quite a bunch of needles.

"Indeed I did," said Alice: "you've said it very often—and very loud. Please where *are* the crabs?"

"In the water, of course!" said the Sheep, sticking some of the needles into her hair, as her hands were full. "Feather, I say!"

"*Why* do you say 'Feather' so often?" Alice asked at last, rather vexed. "I'm not a bird!"

"You are," said the Sheep: "you're a little goose."

This offended Alice a little, so there was no

more conversation for a minute or two, while the boat glided gently on, sometimes among beds of weeds (which made the oars stick fast in the water, worse than ever), and sometimes under trees, but always with the same tall river-banks frowning over their heads.

"Oh, please! There are some scented rushes!" Alice cried in a sudden transport of delight. "There really are—and *such* beauties!"

"You needn't say 'please' to *me* about 'em," the Sheep said, without looking up from her knitting: "I didn't put 'em there, and I'm not going to take 'em away."

"No, but I meant—please, may we wait and pick some?" Alice pleaded. "If you don't mind stopping the boat for a minute."

"How am *I* to stop it?" said the Sheep. "If you leave off rowing, it'll stop of itself."

So the boat was left to drift down the stream as it would, till it glided gently in among the waving rushes. And then the little sleeves were carefully rolled up, and the little arms were plunged in elbow-deep, to get hold of the rushes a good long way down before breaking them off—and for a while Alice forgot all about the Sheep and the knitting, as she bent over the side of the boat, with just the ends of her tangled hair dipping into the water—while with bright eager eyes she caught at one bunch after another of the darling scented rushes.

"I only hope the boat won't tipple over!" she said to herself. "Oh, *what* a lovely one! Only I couldn't quite reach it." And it certainly *did* seem a little provoking ("almost as if it happened on purpose," she thought) that, though she managed to pick plenty of beautiful rushes as the boat glided by, there was always a more lovely one that she couldn't reach.

"The prettiest are always further!" she said at last, with a sigh at the obstinacy of the rushes in growing so far off, as, with flushed cheeks and dripping hair and hands, she scrambled back into her place, and began to arrange her new-found treasures.

What mattered it to her just then that the rushes had begun to fade, and to lose all their scent and beauty, from the very moment that she picked them?[16] Even real scented rushes, you know, last only a very little while—and these, being dream-rushes, melted away almost like snow, as they lay in heaps at her feet—but Alice hardly noticed this, there were so many other curious things to think about.

They hadn't gone much farther before the blade of one of the oars got fast in the water and *wouldn't* come out again (so Alice explained it afterwards), and the consequence was that the handle of it caught her under the chin, and, in spite of a series of little shrieks of "Oh, oh, oh!" from poor Alice, it swept her straight off the seat, and down among the heap of rushes.

However, she wasn't a bit hurt, and was soon up again: the Sheep went on with her knitting all the while, just as if nothing had happened. "That was a nice crab you caught!" she remarked, as Alice got back into her place, very much relieved to find herself still in the boat.

"Was it? I didn't see it," said Alice, peeping cautiously over the side of the boat into the dark water: "I wish it hadn't let go—I should so like a little crab to take home with me!" But the Sheep only laughed scornfully, and went on with her knitting.

"Are there many crabs here?" said Alice.

"Crabs, and all sorts of things," said the

16. It is possible that Carroll thought of these dream-rushes as symbols of his child-friends. The loveliest seem to be the most distant, just out of reach, and, once picked, they quickly fade and lose their scent and beauty. They are, of course, consciously intended symbols of the fleeting, short-lived, hard-to-keep quality of all beauty.

17. Undergraduates at Christ Church, in Carroll's day, insisted that if you ordered one boiled egg for breakfast you usually received two, one good and one bad. (See *The Diaries of Lewis Carroll*, Vol. I, page 176.)

18. The Sheep's movement to the other end of the shop is indicated on the chessboard by a move of the White Queen to KB8.

19. Note that the Sheep places the egg *upright* on the shelf—not an easy thing to do without adopting Columbus's stratagem of tapping the egg on a table to crack its lower end slightly.

20. The dots show that Alice has crossed the brook by advancing to Q6. She is now on the square to the right of the White King, although she does not meet him until after the Humpty Dumpty episode of the next chapter.

Sheep: "plenty of choice, only make up your mind. Now, what *do* you want to buy?"

"To buy!" Alice echoed in a tone that was half astonished and half frightened—for the oars, and the boat, and the river, had vanished all in a moment, and she was back again in the little dark shop.

"I should like to buy an egg, please," she said timidly. "How do you sell them?"

"Fivepence farthing for one—twopence for two," the Sheep replied.

"Then two are cheaper than one?" Alice said in a surprised tone, taking out her purse.

"Only you *must* eat them both, if you buy two," said the Sheep.

"Then I'll have *one*, please," said Alice, as she put the money down on the counter. For she thought to herself, "They mightn't be at all nice, you know."[17]

The Sheep took the money, and put it away in a box: then she said "I never put things into people's hands—that would never do—you must get it for yourself." And so saying, she went off to the other end of the shop,[18] and set the egg upright on a shelf.[19]

"I wonder *why* it wouldn't do?" thought Alice, as she groped her way among the tables and chairs, for the shop was very dark towards the end. "The egg seems to get further away the more I walk towards it. Let me see, is this a chair? Why, it's got branches, I declare! How very odd to find trees growing here! And actually here's a little brook! Well, this is the very queerest shop I ever saw!"[20]

*   *   *   *

*   *   *

*   *   *   *

So she went on, wondering more and more at every step, as everything turned into a tree the moment she came up to it, and she quite expected the egg to do the same.

6

Humpty Dumpty

1. Neither Tenniel nor Newell, Everett Bleiler points out in a letter, show Humpty sitting with his legs crossed, a position which would make his perch more precarious.

2. Michael Hancher, in his book on Tenniel's art, calls attention to a subtlety in Tenniel's picture of Humpty that shows how extremely narrow the top of the wall is. At the right of the drawing you can see the wall in cross section. It is topped by an almost pointed coping!

However, the egg only got larger and larger, and more and more human: when she had come within a few yards of it, she saw that it had eyes and a nose and mouth; and, when she had come close to it, she saw clearly that it was HUMPTY DUMPTY himself. "It ca'n't be anybody else!" she said to herself. "I'm as certain of it, as if his name were written all over his face!"

It might have been written a hundred times, easily, on that enormous face. Humpty Dumpty was sitting, with his legs crossed like a Turk,[1] on the top of a high wall—such a narrow one that Alice quite wondered how he could keep his balance[2]—and, as his eyes were steadily fixed in the opposite direction, and he didn't take the least notice of her, she thought he must be a stuffed figure, after all.

"And how exactly like an egg he is!" she said aloud, standing with her hands ready to catch him, for she was every moment expecting him to fall.

"It's *very* provoking," Humpty Dumpty said after a long silence, looking away from Alice as he spoke, "to be called an egg—*very*!"

"I said you *looked* like an egg, Sir," Alice gently explained. "And some eggs are very pretty, you know," she added, hoping to turn her remark into a sort of compliment.

"Some people," said Humpty Dumpty, looking away from her as usual, "have no more sense than a baby!"

Alice didn't know what to say to this: it wasn't at all like conversation, she thought, as he never said anything to *her*; in fact, his last remark was evidently addressed to a tree—so she stood and softly repeated to herself:—[3]

"Humpty Dumpty sat on a wall:
Humpty Dumpty had a great fall.
All the King's horses and all the King's men
Couldn't put Humpty Dumpty in his place again."

"That last line is much too long for the poetry," she added, almost out loud, forgetting that Humpty Dumpty would hear her.

"Don't stand chattering to yourself like that," Humpty Dumpty said, looking at her for the first time, "but tell me your name and your business."

"My *name* is Alice, but—"

"It's a stupid name enough!" Humpty Dumpty interrupted impatiently. "What does it mean?"

"*Must* a name mean something?" Alice asked doubtfully.

"Of course it must," Humpty Dumpty said with a short laugh: "*my* name means the shape I am—and a good handsome shape it is, too. With a name like yours, you might be any shape, almost."[4]

"Why do you sit out here all alone?" said Alice, not wishing to begin an argument.

"Why, because there's nobody with me!" cried Humpty Dumpty. "Did you think I didn't know the answer to *that*? Ask another."

"Don't you think you'd be safer down on the ground?" Alice went on, not with any idea of making another riddle, but simply in her

3. The Humpty Dumpty episode, like the episodes about the Jack of Hearts, the Tweedle twins, and the Lion and the Unicorn, elaborates on the incidents related in a familiar nursery rhyme. Another and quite different elaboration will be found in L. Frank Baum's first book for children, *Mother Goose in Prose* (1897). In recent years Mr. Dumpty has been editing a children's magazine (*Humpty Dumpty's Magazine*, published by Parents Institute). I had the privilege of working under him for eight years, as chronicler of the adventures of his son, Humpty Dumpty, Junior. A high point in Paramount's film version of Alice was the portrayal of Humpty by W. C. Fields.

4. Peter Alexander, in his excellent paper "Logic and the Humor of Lewis Carroll" (*Proceedings of the Leeds Philosophical Society*, Vol. 6, May 1951, pages 551–66), calls attention to a Carrollian inversion here that is easily overlooked. In real life proper names seldom have a meaning other than the fact that they denote an individual object, whereas other words have general, universal meanings. In Humpty Dumpty's realm, the reverse is true. Ordinary words mean whatever Humpty wants them to mean, whereas proper names like "Alice" and "Humpty Dumpty" are supposed to have general significance. Mr. Alexander's thesis, with which one must heartily concur, is that Carroll's humor is strongly colored by his interest in formal logic.

5. Molly Martin calls attention, in a letter, to the word "breaking," anticipating Humpty's fall.

6. These remarks of Humpty (note also his frequent use of the word "proud" in the rest of his conversation with Alice) reveal the pride that goeth before his fall.

good-natured anxiety for the queer creature. "That wall is so *very* narrow!"

"What tremendously easy riddles you ask!" Humpty Dumpty growled out. "Of course I don't think so! Why, if ever I *did* fall off—which there's no chance of—but *if* I did—" Here he pursed up his lips, and looked so solemn and grand that Alice could hardly help laughing. "*If* I *did* fall," he went on, "*the King has promised me*—ah, you may turn pale, if you like! You didn't think I was going to say that, did you? *The King has promised me—with his very own mouth*—to—to—"

"To send all his horses and all his men," Alice interrupted, rather unwisely.

"Now I declare that's too bad!" Humpty Dumpty cried, breaking[5] into a sudden passion. "You've been listening at doors—and behind trees—and down chimneys—or you couldn't have known it!"

"I haven't, indeed!" Alice said very gently. "It's in a book."

"Ah, well! They may write such things in a *book*," Humpty Dumpty said in a calmer tone. "That's what you call a History of England, that is. Now, take a good look at me! I'm one that has spoken to a King, *I* am: mayhap you'll never see such another: and, to show you I'm not proud, you may shake hands with me!"[6] And he grinned almost from ear to ear, as he leant forwards (and as nearly as possible fell off the wall in doing so) and offered Alice his hand. She watched him a little anxiously as she took it. "If he smiled much more the ends of his mouth might meet behind," she thought: "and then I don't know *what* would happen to his head! I'm afraid it would come off!"

"Yes, all his horses and all his men," Humpty

Dumpty went on. "They'd pick me up again in a minute, *they* would! However, this conversation is going on a little too fast: let's go back to the last remark but one."

"I'm afraid I ca'n't quite remember it," Alice said, very politely.

"In that case we start afresh," said Humpty Dumpty, "and it's my turn to choose a subject—" ("He talks about it just as if it was a game!" thought Alice.) "So here's a question for you. How old did you say you were?"

Alice made a short calculation, and said "Seven years and six months."

"Wrong!" Humpty Dumpty exclaimed triumphantly. "You never said a word like it!"

"I thought you meant 'How old *are* you?'" Alice explained.

"If I'd meant that, I'd have said it," said Humpty Dumpty.

Alice didn't want to begin another argument, so she said nothing.

"Seven years and six months!" Humpty Dumpty repeated thoughtfully. "An uncomfort-

7. As others have noted, this is the subtlest, grimmest, easiest-to-miss quip in the *Alice* books. No wonder that Alice, quick to catch an implication, changes the subject.

able sort of age. Now if you'd asked *my* advice, I'd have said 'Leave off at seven'—but it's too late now."

"I never ask advice about growing," Alice said indignantly.

"Too proud?" the other enquired.

Alice felt even more indignant at this suggestion. "I mean," she said, "that one ca'n't help growing older."

"*One* ca'n't, perhaps," said Humpty Dumpty; "but *two* can. With proper assistance, you might have left off at seven."[7]

"What a beautiful belt you've got on!" Alice suddenly remarked. (They had had quite enough of the subject of age, she thought: and, if they really were to take turns in choosing subjects, it was *her* turn now.) "At least," she corrected herself on second thoughts, "a beautiful cravat, I should have said—no, a belt, I mean—I beg your pardon!" she added in dismay, for Humpty Dumpty looked thoroughly offended, and she began to wish she hadn't chosen that subject. "If only I knew," she thought to herself, "which was neck and which was waist!"

Evidently Humpty Dumpty was very angry, though he said nothing for a minute or two. When he *did* speak again, it was in a deep growl.

"It is a—*most*—*provoking*—thing," he said at last, "when a person doesn't know a cravat from a belt!"

"I know it's very ignorant of me," Alice said, in so humble a tone that Humpty Dumpty relented.

"It's a cravat, child, and a beautiful one, as you say. It's a present from the White King and Queen. There now!"

"Is it really?" said Alice, quite pleased to find that she *had* chosen a good subject, after all.

"They gave it me," Humpty Dumpty continued thoughtfully, as he crossed one knee over the other and clasped his hands round it, "they gave it me—for an un-birthday present."

"I beg your pardon?" Alice said with a puzzled air.

"I'm not offended," said Humpty Dumpty.

"I mean, what *is* an un-birthday present?"

"A present given when it isn't your birthday, of course."

Alice considered a little. "I like birthday presents best," she said at last.

"You don't know what you're talking about!" cried Humpty Dumpty. "How many days are there in a year?"

"Three hundred and sixty-five," said Alice.

"And how many birthdays have you?"

"One."

"And if you take one from three hundred and sixty-five, what remains?"

"Three hundred and sixty-four, of course."

Humpty Dumpty looked doubtful. "I'd rather see that done on paper," he said.[8]

Alice couldn't help smiling as she took out her memorandum-book, and worked the sum for him:

$$\frac{\begin{array}{r} 365 \\ 1 \end{array}}{364}$$

Humpty Dumpty took the book, and looked at it carefully. "That seems to be done right—" he began.

"You're holding it upside down!" Alice interrupted.

"To be sure I was!" Humpty Dumpty said gaily, as she turned it round for him. "I thought it looked a little queer. As I was saying, that *seems*

8. Humpty Dumpty is a philologist and philosopher skilled primarily in linguistic matters. Perhaps Carroll is suggesting here that such types, exceedingly plentiful both then and now in the Oxford area, are seldom gifted mathematically.

9. In "Humpty Dumpty and Heresy; Or, the Case of the Curate's Egg," in the *Western Humanities Review* (Spring 1968), Wilbur Gaffney argues that Humpty's definition of *glory* may have been influenced by a passage in a book by that egotistical British egghead, philosopher Thomas Hobbes:

Sudden glory, is the passion which maketh those *grimaces* called LAUGHTER; and is caused either by some sudden act of their own, that pleaseth them [such as, obviously, coming out with a nice knock-down argument]; or by the apprehension of some deformed thing in another, by comparison whereof they suddenly applaud themselves. And it is incident most to them, that are conscious of the fewest abilities in themselves; who are forced to keep themselves in their own favour, by observing the imperfections of others.

Janis Lull, in *Lewis Carroll: A Celebration*, observes that the White Knight declares his "knock-down" dispute with the Red Knight in Chapter 8 a "glorious victory."

Remove the *l* from *glory*, Carroll observes at the end of the sixth knot in *A Tangled Tale*, and you get *gory*. An adjective describing the end of a knockdown argument?

10. In his article "The Stage and the Spirit of Reverence," Carroll put it this way: "no word has a meaning *inseparably* attached to it; a word means what the speaker intends by it, and what the hearer understands by it, and that is all. . . . This thought may serve to lessen the horror of some of the language used by the lower classes, which, it is a comfort to remember, is often a mere collection of unmeaning *sounds*, so far as speaker and hearer are concerned."

11. Lewis Carroll was fully aware of the profundity in Humpty Dumpty's

to be done right—though I haven't time to look it over thoroughly just now—and that shows that there are three hundred and sixty-four days when you might get un-birthday presents—"

"Certainly," said Alice.

"And only *one* for birthday presents, you know. There's glory for you!"

"I don't know what you mean by 'glory,'" Alice said.

Humpty Dumpty smiled contemptuously. "Of course you don't—till I tell you. I meant 'there's a nice knock-down argument for you!'"[9]

"But 'glory' doesn't mean 'a nice knock-down argument,'" Alice objected.

"When *I* use a word," Humpty Dumpty said, in rather a scornful tone, "it means just what I choose it to mean—neither more nor less."

"The question is," said Alice, "whether you *can* make words mean so many different things."[10]

"The question is," said Humpty Dumpty, "which is to be master—that's all."[11]

Alice was too much puzzled to say anything; so after a minute Humpty Dumpty began again. "They've a temper, some of them—particularly verbs: they're the proudest—adjectives you can do anything with, but not verbs—however, *I* can manage the whole lot of them! Impenetrability! That's what *I* say!"

"Would you tell me, please," said Alice, "what that means?"

"Now you talk like a reasonable child," said Humpty Dumpty, looking very much pleased. "I meant by 'impenetrability' that we've had enough of that subject, and it would be just as well if you'd mention what you mean to do next, as I suppose you don't mean to stop here all the rest of your life."

"That's a great deal to make one word mean," Alice said in a thoughtful tone.

"When I make a word do a lot of work like that," said Humpty Dumpty, "I always pay it extra."

"Oh!" said Alice. She was too much puzzled to make any other remark.

"Ah, you should see 'em come round me of a Saturday night," Humpty Dumpty went on, wagging his head gravely from side to side, "for to get their wages, you know."

(Alice didn't venture to ask what he paid them with; and so you see I ca'n't tell *you*.)

"You seem very clever at explaining words, Sir," said Alice. "Would you kindly tell me the meaning of the poem called 'Jabberwocky'?"

"Let's hear it," said Humpty Dumpty. "I can explain all the poems that ever were invented— and a good many that haven't been invented just yet."

This sounded very hopeful, so Alice repeated the first verse:—

> "'Twas brillig, and the slithy toves
>   Did gyre and gimble in the wabe:
> All mimsy were the borogoves,
>   And the mome raths outgrabe."

"That's enough to begin with," Humpty Dumpty interrupted: "there are plenty of hard words there. '*Brillig*' means four o'clock in the afternoon—the time when you begin *broiling* things for dinner."

"That'll do very well," said Alice: "and '*slithy*'?"

"Well, '*slithy*' means 'lithe and slimy.' 'Lithe' is the same as 'active.' You see it's like a portmanteau—there are two meanings packed up into one word."[12]

whimsical discourse on semantics. Humpty takes the point of view known in the Middle Ages as nominalism; the view that universal terms do not refer to objective existences but are nothing more than *flatus vocis*, verbal utterances. The view was skillfully defended by William of Occam and is now held by almost all contemporary logical empiricists.

Even in logic and mathematics, where terms are usually more precise than in other subject matters, enormous confusion often results from a failure to realize that words mean "neither more nor less" than what they are intended to mean. In Carroll's time a lively controversy in formal logic concerned the "existential import" of Aristotle's four basic propositions. Do the universal statements "All A is B" and "No A is B" imply that A is a set that actually contains members? Is it implied in the particular statements "Some A is B" and "Some A is not B"?

Carroll answers these questions at some length on page 165 of his *Symbolic Logic*. The passage is worth quoting, for it is straight from the broad mouth of Humpty Dumpty.

The writers, and editors, of the Logical textbooks which run in the ordinary grooves—to whom I shall hereafter refer by the (I hope inoffensive) title "The Logicians"—take, on this subject, what seems to me to be a more humble position than is at all necessary. They speak of the Copula of a Proposition "with bated breath"; almost as if it were a living, conscious Entity, capable of declaring for itself what it chose to mean, and that we, poor human creatures, had nothing to do but to ascertain *what* was its sovereign will and pleasure, and submit to it.

In opposition to this view, I maintain that any writer of a book is fully authorised in attaching any meaning he likes to any word or phrase he intends to use. If I find an author saying, at the beginning of his book. "Let it be understood that by the word '*black*' I shall always mean '*white*', and that by the word '*white*' I shall always mean '*black*'," I meekly accept his ruling, however injudicious I may think it.

And so, with regard to the question whether a Proposition is or is not to be understood as asserting the existence of its Subject, I maintain that every writer may adopt his own rule, provided of course that it is consistent with itself and with the accepted facts of Logic.

Let us consider certain views that may *logically* be held, and thus settle which of them may *conveniently* be held; after which I shall hold myself free to declare which of them *I* intend to hold.

The view adopted by Carroll (that both "all" and "some" imply existence but that "no" leaves the question open) did not finally win out. In modern logic only the "some" propositions are taken to imply that a class is not a null class. This does not, of course, invalidate the nominalistic attitude of Carroll and his egg. The current point of view was adopted solely because logicians believed it to be the most useful.

When logicians shifted their interest from the class logic of Aristotle to the propositional or truth-value calculus, another furious and funny debate (though mostly among non-logicians) raged over the meaning of "material implication." Most of the confusion sprang from a failure to realize that "implies" in the statement "A implies B" has a restricted meaning peculiar to the calculus and does not refer to any causal relation between A and B. A similar confusion still persists in regard to the multivalued logics in which terms such as *and, not*, and *implies* have no common-sense or intuitive meaning; in fact, they have no meaning whatever other than that which is exactly defined by the matrix tables, which

"I see it now," Alice remarked thoughtfully: "and what are '*toves*'?"

"Well, '*toves*' are something like badgers—they're something like lizards—and they're something like corkscrews."

"They must be very curious-looking creatures."

"They are that," said Humpty Dumpty: "also they make their nests under sun-dials—also they live on cheese."

"And what's to '*gyre*' and to '*gimble*'?"

"To '*gyre*' is to go round and round like a gyroscope. To '*gimble*' is to make holes like a gimblet."

"And '*the wabe*' is the grass-plot round a sun-dial, I suppose?" said Alice, surprised at her own ingenuity.

"Of course it is. It's called '*wabe*,' you know, because it goes a long way before it, and a long way behind it—"

"And a long way beyond it on each side,"[13] Alice added.

"Exactly so. Well then, '*mimsy*' is 'flimsy and miserable' (there's another portmanteau for you). And a '*borogove*' is a thin shabby-looking bird with its feathers sticking out all round— something like a live mop."

"And then '*mome raths*'?" said Alice. "I'm afraid I'm giving you a great deal of trouble."

"Well, a '*rath*' is a sort of green pig: but '*mome*' I'm not certain about. I think it's short for 'from home'—meaning that they'd lost their way, you know."[14]

"And what does '*outgrabe*' mean?"

"Well, '*outgribing*' is something between bellowing and whistling, with a kind of sneeze in the middle: however, you'll hear it done, maybe—down in the wood yonder—and, when you've once heard it, you'll be *quite* content. Who's been repeating all that hard stuff to you?"

"I read it in a book," said Alice. "But I *had* some poetry repeated to me much easier than that, by—Tweedledee, I think it was."

"As to poetry, you know," said Humpty Dumpty, stretching out one of his great hands, "*I* can repeat poetry as well as other folk, if it comes to that—"

"Oh, it needn't come to that!" Alice hastily said, hoping to keep him from beginning.

"The piece I'm going to repeat," he went on without noticing her remark, "was written entirely for your amusement."

Alice felt that in that case she really *ought* to listen to it; so she sat down, and said "Thank you" rather sadly.

generate these "connective" terms. Once this is fully understood, most of the mystery surrounding these queer logics evaporates.

In mathematics equal amounts of energy have been dissipated in useless argumentation over the "meaning" of such phrases as "imaginary number," "transfinite number," and so on; useless because such words mean precisely what they are defined to mean; no more, no less.

On the other hand, if we wish to communicate accurately we are under a kind of moral obligation to avoid Humpty's practice of giving private meanings to commonly used words. "*May* we . . . make our words mean whatever we choose them to mean?" asks Roger W. Holmes in his article, "The Philosopher's Alice in Wonderland," (*Antioch Review*, Summer 1959). "One thinks of a Soviet delegate using 'democracy' in a UN debate. May we pay our words extra, or is this the stuff that propaganda is made of? Do we have an obligation to past usage? In one sense words are our masters, or communication would be impossible. In another we are the masters; otherwise there could be no poetry."

12. *Portmanteau word* will be found in many modern dictionaries. It has become a common phrase for words that are packed, like a suitcase, with more than one meaning. In English literature, the great master of the portmanteau word is, of course, James Joyce. *Finnegans Wake* (like the *Alice* books, a dream) contains them by the tens of thousands. This includes those ten hundred-letter thunderclaps that symbolize, among other things, the mighty fall from his ladder of Tim Finnegan, the Irish hod carrier. Humpty Dumpty himself is packed up in the seventh thunderclap:

Bothallchoractorschumminaround

gansumuminarumdrumstrumtrumi-
nahumptadump-waultopoofoolood
eramaunsturnup!

References to Humpty abound in *Finnegans Wake*, from a mention on the first page to a mention on the last.

13. Readers may not be as quick as Alice to catch Humpty's word play. "Wabe" is the beginning of "*way before*" and "*way behind.*" Alice appropriately adds "*way* beyond."

14. "From home," spoken with a dropped *h*, produces the "mome" sound.

15. Neil Phelps sent me a possible inspiration for Humpty's song, a poem called "Summer Days" by a forgotten Victorian poet, Wathen Mark Wilks Call (1817–1870). The poem is anonymous in many Victorian anthologies. The following version is from *Everyman's Book of Victorian Verse* (1982), edited by J. R. Watson:

In summer, when the days were long,
We walked, two friends, in field and
  wood,
Our heart was light, our step was strong,
And life lay round us, fair as good,
In summer, when the days were long.

We strayed from morn till evening came,
We gathered flowers, and wove us
  crowns,
We walked mid poppies red as flame,
Or sat upon the yellow downs,
And always wished our life the same.

In summer, when the days were long,
We leapt the hedgerow, crossed the
  brook;
And still her voice flowed forth in song,
Or else she read some graceful book,
In summer, when the days were long.

And then we sat beneath the trees,
With shadows lessening in the noon;

"*In winter, when the fields are white,
I sing this song for your delight—*"[15]

only I don't sing it," he added, as an explanation.

"I see you don't," said Alice.

"If you can *see* whether I'm singing or not, you've sharper eyes than most," Humpty Dumpty remarked severely. Alice was silent.

"*In spring, when woods are getting green,
I'll try and tell you what I mean:*"

"Thank you very much," said Alice.

"*In summer, when the days are long,
Perhaps you'll understand the song;*

*In autumn, when the leaves are brown,
Take pen and ink, and write it down.*"

"I will, if I can remember it so long," said Alice.

"You needn't go on making remarks like that," Humpty Dumpty said: "they're not sensible, and they put me out."

"*I sent a message to the fish:
I told them 'This is what I wish.'*

*The little fishes of the sea,
They sent an answer back to me.*

*The little fishes' answer was
'We cannot do it, Sir, because—'*"

"I'm afraid I don't quite understand," said Alice.

"It gets easier further on," Humpty Dumpty replied.

"*I sent to them again to say
'It will be better to obey.'*

*The fishes answered, with a grin,
'Why, what a temper you are in!'*"

I told them once, I told them twice:
They would not listen to advice.

I took a kettle large and new;
Fit for the deed I had to do.

My heart went hop, my heart went thump:
I filled the kettle at the pump.

Then some one came to me and said
'The little fishes are in bed.'

I said to him, I said it plain,
'Then you must wake them up again.'

I said it very loud and clear:
I went and shouted in his ear."

Humpty Dumpty raised his voice almost to a scream as he repeated this verse, and Alice thought, with a shudder, "I wouldn't have been the messenger for *anything*!"

     "But he was very stiff and proud:
     He said 'You needn't shout so loud!'"[16]

     And he was very proud and stiff:
     He said 'I'd go and wake them, if—'

     I took a corkscrew from the shelf:
     I went to wake them up myself.

     And when I found the door was locked,
     I pulled and pushed and kicked and knocked.

     And when I found the door was shut,
     I tried to turn the handle, but—"[17]

There was a long pause.

"Is that all?" Alice timidly asked.

"That's all," said Humpty Dumpty. "Goodbye."

This was rather sudden, Alice thought: but, after such a *very* strong hint that she ought to

---

And in the sunlight and the breeze.
We revelled, many a glorious June,
While larks were singing o'er the leas.

In summer, when the days were long,
We plucked wild strawberries, ripe and
    red,
Or feasted, with no grace but song,
On golden nectar, snow-white bread,
In summer, when the days were long.

We loved, and yet we knew it not,
For loving seemed like breathing then,
We found a heaven in every spot,
Saw angels, too, in all good men,
And dreamt of gods in grove and grot.

In summer, when the days are long,
Alone I wander, muse alone;
I see her not, but that old song,
Under the fragrant wind is blown,
In summer, when the days are long.

Alone I wander in the wood,
But one fair spirit hears my sighs;
And half I see the crimson hood,
The radiant hair, the calm glad eyes,
That charmed me in life's summer mood.

In summer, when the days are long,
I love her as I loved of old;
My heart is light, my step is strong,
For love brings back those hours of gold,
In summer, when the days are long.

16. In his book on Tenniel, Michael Hancher calls attention to how closely Tenniel's illustration for these lines resembles a gigantic gooseberry in his *Punch* cartoon of July 15, 1871.

TENNIEL. "THE GIGANTIC
GOOSEBERRY.

THE GIGANTIC GOOSEBERRY

G. G. "HERE'S A PRECIOUS GO,
FROGGY! I THOUGHT BIG
GOOSEBERRIES AND SHOWERS
O'FROGS UD HAVE A HOLIDAY
THIS 'SILLY SEASON,' ANY-
HOW. BUT THE PRECIOUS
TICHBORNE CASE HAVE BEEN
ADJOURNED, AND WE'LL
HAVE TO BE ON DUTY
AGAIN."

FROM *PUNCH.* 15 JULY 1871

17. "This has to be the worst poem
in the *Alice* books," writes Richard
Kelly, in *Lewis Carroll* (Twayne,
1977). "The language is flat and prosaic, the frustrated story line is without interest, the couplets are
uninspired and fail to surprise or
delight, and there are almost no true
elements of nonsense present, other
than in the unstated wish of the narrator and the lack of a conclusion to
the work."

Beverly Lyon Clark, in her contribution to *Soaring with the Dodo*
(Lewis Carroll Society of North
America, 1982), edited by Edward
Guiliano and James Kincaid, calls
attention to how the abrupt endings
of the poem's lines are echoed
in Humpty's abrupt "Good-bye" to
Alice, and Alice's unfinished comment in the chapter's last paragraph:
"Of all the unsatisfactory people I
ever met—"

The Spectator, on September 9,
1995, published the results of Competition No. 1897. Readers were
asked to add eight couplets to
Humpty's poem. *The Bandersnatch*
(October 1995) published two of the
winners:

> The handle bit me on the hand!
> I said, "Now, handle, understand
>
> I mean to get inside this door,
> So open up! Don't be a bore!"

be going, she felt that it would hardly be civil
to stay. So she got up, and held out her hand.
"Good-bye, till we meet again!" she said as
cheerfully as she could.

"I shouldn't know you again if we *did* meet,"
Humpty Dumpty replied in a discontented tone,
giving her one of his fingers to shake:[18] "you're
so exactly like other people."

"The face is what one goes by, generally,"
Alice remarked in a thoughtful tone.

"That's just what I complain of," said
Humpty Dumpty. "Your face is the same as
everybody has—the two eyes, so—" (marking
their places in the air with his thumb) "nose in
the middle, mouth under. It's always the same.
Now if you had the two eyes on the same side of
the nose, for instance—or the mouth at the
top—that would be *some* help."

"It wouldn't look nice," Alice objected. But
Humpty Dumpty only shut his eyes, and said
"Wait till you've tried."

Alice waited a minute to see if he would speak again, but, as he never opened his eyes or took any further notice of her, she said "Good-bye!" once more, and, getting no answer to this, she quietly walked away: but she couldn't help saying to herself, as she went, "Of all the unsatisfactory—" (she repeated this aloud, as it was a great comfort to have such a long word to say) "of all the unsatisfactory people I *ever* met—" She never finished the sentence, for at this moment a heavy crash shook the forest from end to end.[19]

The handle (also proud and stiff)
Produced a most disdainful sniff

And said, "If you will wait till two,
I might then see what I can do."

"Till two?" I cried. "That's hours away!"
The handle said, "Most wait a day.

I once made someone wait a year:
He died just where you stand, I fear.

So patience, please, till two o'clock,
And then don't kick or push, just knock.

Of course, I cannot guarantee . . .
Perhaps, meantime, you'd sing to me?"
                                    —Andrew Gibbons

When nearly half an hour had gone
I saw that it was painted on.

Just then I heard a snicking sound
Behind me, so I turned around

And saw a cousin of the Queen
With twenty trays of nougatine.

"I s'pose there's room for these inside?"
He asked me gravely. I replied,

"That may be so, I cannot say.
The fish are not themselves today."

He wrote this carefully in a book.
'I s'pose I ought to take a look,

Though as a cousin of the Queen
I must forget what I have seen.

Now do you like them boiled or fried?"
He asked, and smiled, and went inside.
                                    —Richard Lucie

18. John Q. Rutherford, Mill Lane, Essex, calls my attention to the unpleasant habit, of some members of the Victorian aristocracy, of proffering two fingers when shaking hands with their social inferiors. In his pride, Humpty carries this practice to its ultimate.

At the end of Chapter 19, in Somerset Maugham's novel *Cakes and Ale*, a character gives the narrator "two flabby fingers to shake."

19. Students of *Finnegans Wake* do not have to be reminded that Humpty Dumpty is one of that book's basic symbols: the great cosmic egg whose fall, like the drunken fall of Finnegan, suggests the fall of Lucifer and the fall of man.

A fourteen-stanza poem titled "The Headstrong Man," written by Carroll when he was thirteen, anticipates Humpty's mighty fall. The poem appeared in Carroll's first book, *Useful and Instructive Poetry,* written for his younger siblings, and published posthumously in 1954. The poem begins:

> There was a man who stood on high,
>   Upon a lofty wall;
> And every one who passed him by,
>   Called out "I fear you'll fall."

A strong wind blows the man off the wall. Next day he climbs a tree, the branch breaks, and he falls again.

In the Pennyroyal edition of *Through the Looking-Glass,* Barry Moser drew Humpty with the face of Richard Nixon. Will some future illustrator give the egg the face of William Jefferson Clinton?

7

The Lion and the Unicorn

The next moment soldiers came running through
the wood, at first in twos and threes, then ten or
twenty together, and at last in such crowds that
they seemed to fill the whole forest. Alice got
behind a tree, for fear of being run over, and
watched them go by.

She thought that in all her life she had never
seen soldiers so uncertain on their feet: they were
always tripping over something or other, and
whenever one went down, several more always
fell over him, so that the ground was soon
covered with little heaps of men.

Then came the horses. Having four feet, these
managed rather better than the foot-soldiers; but
even *they* stumbled now and then; and it seemed
to be a regular rule that, whenever a horse stumbled, the rider fell off instantly. The confusion
got worse every moment, and Alice was very
glad to get out of the wood into an open place,
where she found the White King seated on the
ground, busily writing in his memorandum-
book.

"I've sent them all!" the King cried in a tone
of delight, on seeing Alice. "Did you happen to
meet any soldiers, my dear, as you came through
the wood?"

"Yes, I did," said Alice: "several thousand, I
should think."

1. The two horses are needed in the chess game to provide steeds for the two white knights.

2. Mathematicians, logicians, and some metaphysicians like to treat zero, the null class, and Nothing as if they were Something, and Carroll was no exception. In the first *Alice* book the Gryphon tells Alice that "they never executes nobody." Here we encounter the unexecuted Nobody walking along the road, and later we learn that Nobody walks slower or faster than the Messenger. "If you see Nobody come into the room," Carroll wrote to one of his child-friends, "please give him a kiss for me." In Carroll's book *Euclid and His Modern Rivals*, we meet Herr Niemand, a German professor whose name means "nobody." When did Nobody first enter the *Alice* books? At the Mad Tea Party. "Nobody asked *your* opinion," Alice said to the Mad Hatter. He turns up again in the book's last chapter when the White Rabbit produces a letter that he says the Knave of Hearts has written to "somebody." "Unless it was written to nobody," comments the King, "which isn't usual, you know."

Critics have recalled how Ulysses deceived the one-eyed Polyphemus by calling himself Noman before putting out the giant's eye. When Polyphemus cried out, "Noman is killing me!" no one took this to mean that someone was actually attacking him.

"Four thousand two hundred and seven, that's the exact number," the King said, referring to his book. "I couldn't send all the horses, you know, because two of them are wanted in the game.[1] And I haven't sent the two Messengers, either. They're both gone to the town. Just look along the road, and tell me if you can see either of them."

"I see nobody on the road," said Alice.

"I only wish *I* had such eyes," the King remarked in a fretful tone. "To be able to see Nobody![2] And at that distance too! Why, it's as much as *I* can do to see real people, by this light!"

All this was lost on Alice, who was still looking intently along the road, shading her eyes with one hand. "I see somebody now!" she exclaimed at last. "But he's coming very slowly—and what curious attitudes he goes into!" (For the Messenger kept skipping up and down, and wriggling like an eel, as he came along, with his great hands spread out like fans on each side.)

"Not at all," said the King. "He's an Anglo-Saxon Messenger—and those are Anglo-Saxon attitudes.[3] He only does them when he's happy. His name is Haigha." (He pronounced it so as to rhyme with "mayor.")[4]

"I love my love with an H,"[5] Alice couldn't help beginning, "because he is Happy. I hate him with an H, because he is Hideous. I fed him with—with—with Ham-sandwiches and Hay. His name is Haigha, and he lives—"

"He lives on the Hill," the King remarked simply, without the least idea that he was joining in the game, while Alice was still hesitating for the name of a town beginning with H. "The other Messenger's called Hatta. I must have *two*, you know—to come and go. One to come, and one to go."

"I beg your pardon?" said Alice.

"It isn't respectable to beg," said the King.

"I only meant that I didn't understand," said Alice. "Why one to come and one to go?"

"Don't I tell you?" the King repeated impatiently. "I must have *two*—to fetch and carry. One to fetch, and one to carry."

At this moment the Messenger arrived: he was far too much out of breath to say a word, and could only wave his hands about, and make the most fearful faces at the poor King.

"This young lady loves you with an H," the King said, introducing Alice in the hope of turning off the Messenger's attention from himself—but it was of no use—the Anglo-Saxon attitudes only got more extraordinary every moment,

3. In his references to Anglo-Saxon attitudes Carroll is spoofing the Anglo-Saxon scholarship fashionable in his day. Harry Morgan Ayres, in his book *Carroll's Alice* (Columbia University Press, 1936), reproduces some drawings of Anglo-Saxons in various costumes and attitudes, from the Caedmon Manuscript of the Junian codex (owned by Oxford's Bodleian Library), and suggests that they may have been used as a source by both Carroll and Tenniel. A novel by Angus Wilson, *Anglo-Saxon Attitudes* quotes this passage of Carroll's on the title page.

4. Hatta is the Mad Hatter, newly released from prison, and Haigha, whose name, when pronounced to rhyme with "mayor," sounds like "Hare," is of course the March Hare. In his book *Carroll's Alice*, Harry Morgan Ayres suggests that Carroll may have had in mind Daniel Henry Haigh, a noted nineteenth-century expert on Saxon runes and the author of two scholarly books about the Saxons.

It is curious that Alice fails to recognize either of her two old friends.

Just why Carroll disguised the Hatter and the Hare as Anglo-Saxon Messengers (and Tenniel underscored this whimsy by dressing them as Anglo-Saxons and giving them "Anglo-Saxon attitudes") continues to be puzzling. "In the context of Alice's dream," writes Robert Sutherland in *Language and Lewis Carroll* (Mouton, 1970), "they come like ghosts to trouble scholars' joy."

The presence in Alice's dream of the chessmen, the characters from nursery rhymes, the talking animals, the various more bizarre creatures is easily explained. They either have their counterparts in Alice's waking experience or are the fantastic creations of a little girl's dreaming mind.

But the Anglo-Saxon Messengers! They are not mentioned in the first chapter, where various aspects of the dream are foreshadowed in Alice's drawing-room. Are we to assume on Alice's part a reading of Anglo-Saxon history in her school-books? Or is the presence of the Anglo-Saxon Messengers a gratuitous addition of Carroll's, constituting a minor flaw in the otherwise consistently conceived structure of the book? Is their presence an intrusion of a private joke at the expense of contemporary Anglo-Saxon scholarship, and a reflection of his own interest in British antiquity? The question of Dodgson's intentions in creating the Anglo-Saxon Messengers is a vexed problem which will remain obscure until further information comes to light.

Roger Green (in *Jabberwocky*, Autumn 1971) offers the following guess. Carroll recorded in his diary (December 5, 1863) his attendance at a Christ Church theatrical that included a burlesque skit called "Alfred the Great." Mrs. Liddell was there with her children. Green surmises that the skit included Anglo-Saxon settings and costumes, which may have given Carroll the idea of turning the Hatter and the Hare into Anglo-Saxon Messengers.

5. "I love my love with an A" was a popular parlor game in Victorian England. The first player recited:

I love my love with an A because
     he's———.
I hate him because he's———.
He took me to the Sign of the———.
And treated me with———.
His name's———
And he lives at———.

In each blank space the player used a suitable word beginning with *A*. The second player then repeated the same lines, using *B* instead of *A*, and the game continued in this fashion through the alphabet. Players unable

while the great eyes rolled wildly from side to side.

"You alarm me!" said the King. "I feel faint—Give me a ham sandwich!"

On which the Messenger, to Alice's great amusement, opened a bag that hung round his neck, and handed a sandwich to the King, who devoured it greedily.

"Another sandwich!" said the King.

"There's nothing but hay left now," the Messenger said, peeping into the bag.

"Hay, then," the King murmured in a faint whisper.

Alice was glad to see that it revived him a good deal. "There's nothing like eating hay when you're faint," he remarked to her, as he munched away.

"I should think throwing cold water over you would be better," Alice suggested: "—or some sal-volatile."[6]

"I didn't say there was nothing *better*," the King replied. "I said there was nothing *like* it." Which Alice did not venture to deny.[7]

"Who did you pass on the road?" the King went on, holding out his hand to the Messenger for some more hay.

"Nobody," said the Messenger.

"Quite right," said the King: "this young lady saw him too. So of course Nobody walks slower than you."

"I do my best," the Messenger said in a sullen tone. "I'm sure nobody walks much faster than I do!"

"He ca'n't do that," said the King, "or else he'd have been here first. However, now you've got your breath, you may tell us what's happened in the town."

"I'll whisper it," said the Messenger, putting his hands to his mouth in the shape of a trumpet and stooping so as to get close to the King's ear. Alice was sorry for this, as she wanted to hear the news too. However, instead of whispering, he simply shouted, at the top of his voice, "They're at it again!"

"Do you call *that* a whisper?" cried the poor King, jumping up and shaking himself. "If you do such a thing again, I'll have you buttered! It went through and through my head like an earthquake!"

"It would have to be a very tiny earthquake!" thought Alice. "Who are at it again?" she ventured to ask.

"Why, the Lion and the Unicorn, of course," said the King.

"Fighting for the crown?"

"Yes, to be sure," said the King: "and the best of the joke is, that it's *my* crown all the while! Let's run and see them." And they trotted off, Alice repeating to herself, as she ran, the words of the old song:—[8]

to supply an acceptable word dropped out of the game. The wording of the recitation varied; the lines quoted above are taken from James Orchard Halliwell's *The Nursery Rhymes of England*, a book popular in Carroll's day. It was clever of Alice to start the game with *H* instead of *A*, for the Anglo-Saxon Messengers undoubtedly dropped their *H*'s.

6. "sal-volatile": smelling salts.

7. Taking phrases literally instead of as they are commonly understood is characteristic of the creatures behind the looking-glass, and a basis for much of Carroll's humor. Another good example occurs in Chapter 9, when the Red Queen tells Alice that she couldn't deny something if she tried with both hands.

One of Carroll's most amusing hoaxes furnishes still another instance of his fondness for this variety of nonsense. In 1873, when Ella Monier-Williams (a child-friend) let him borrow her travel diary, he returned the book with the following letter:

MY DEAR ELLA,

I return your book with many thanks; you will be wondering why I kept it so long. I understand, from what you said about it, that you have no idea of publishing any of it yourself, and hope you will not be annoyed at my sending three short chapters of extracts from it, to be published in *The Monthly Packet*. I have not given any names in full, nor put any more definite title to it than simply "Ella's Diary, or The Experiences of an Oxford Professor's Daughter, during a Month of Foreign Travel."

I will faithfully hand over to you any money I may receive on account of it, from Miss Yonge, the editor of *The Monthly Packet*.

Your affect. friend,
C.L. DODGSON.

Ella suspected that he was joking, but began to take him seriously when she received a second letter containing the following passage:

I grieve to tell you that *every word of my letter was strictly true*. I will now tell you more—that Miss Yonge *has not declined* the MS., but she will not give more than a guinea a chapter: Will that be enough?

Carroll's third letter cleared up the hoax:

MY DEAR ELLA,

I'm afraid I have hoaxed you too much. But it really was true. I "hoped you wouldn't be annoyed at my etc.," for the very good reason that I hadn't done it. And I gave no *other* title than "Ella's Diary," nor did I give *that* title. Miss Yonge hasn't declined it—because she hasn't seen it. And I need hardly explain that she hasn't given more than three guineas!

Not for three hundred guineas would I have shown it to *any* one—after I had promised you I wouldn't.

In haste,

Yours affectionately,

C.L.D.

8. According to the *Oxford Dictionary of Nursery Rhymes*, rivalry between the lion and unicorn goes back for thousands of years. The nursery rhyme is popularly supposed to have arisen in the early seventeenth century when the union of Scotland and England resulted in a new British coat of arms on which the Scottish unicorn and the British lion appear, as they do today, as the two supporters of the royal arms.

9. For reasons not clear, the White King, by running to see the Lion and Unicorn fight, violates his slow square-by-square way of moving in a chess game.

"*The Lion and the Unicorn were fighting for the crown:*
The Lion beat the Unicorn all round the town.
Some gave them white bread, some gave them brown:
Some gave them plum-cake and drummed them out of town."

"Does—the one—that wins—get the crown?" she asked, as well as she could, for the run was putting her quite out of breath.[9]

"Dear me, no!" said the King. "What an idea!"[10]

"Would you—be good enough—" Alice panted out, after running a little further, "to stop a minute—just to get—one's breath again?"

"I'm *good* enough," the King said, "only I'm not *strong* enough. You see, a minute goes by so fearfully quick. You might as well try to stop a Bandersnatch!"

Alice had no more breath for talking; so they trotted on in silence, till they came into sight of a great crowd, in the middle of which the Lion and Unicorn were fighting. They were in such a cloud of dust, that at first Alice could not make out which was which; but she soon managed to distinguish the Unicorn by his horn.

They placed themselves close to where Hatta, the other Messenger, was standing watching the fight, with a cup of tea in one hand and a piece of bread-and-butter in the other.

"He's only just out of prison, and he hadn't finished his tea when he was sent in," Haigha whispered to Alice: "and they only give them oyster-shells in there—so you see he's very hungry and thirsty. How are you, dear child?" he went on, putting his arm affectionately round Hatta's neck.

10. If Carroll intended his Lion and Unicorn to represent Gladstone and Disraeli (see Note 13 below), then this dialogue takes on an obvious meaning. Carroll, who was conservative in his political views and did not care for Gladstone, composed two remarkable anagrams on the full name, William Ewart Gladstone. They are: "Wilt tear down *all* images?" and "Wild agitator! Means well." (See *The Diaries of Lewis Carroll*, Vol. II, page 277.)

Hatta looked round and nodded, and went on with his bread-and-butter.

"Were you happy in prison, dear child?" said Haigha.

Hatta looked round once more, and this time a tear or two trickled down his cheek; but not a word would he say.

"Speak, ca'n't you!" Haigha cried impatiently. But Hatta only munched away, and drank some more tea.

"Speak, wo'n't you!" cried the King. "How are they getting on with the fight?"

Hatta made a desperate effort, and swallowed a large piece of bread-and-butter. "They're getting on very well," he said in a choking voice: "each of them has been down about eighty-seven times."

"Then I suppose they'll soon bring the white bread and the brown?" Alice ventured to remark.

"It's waiting for 'em now," said Hatta; "this is a bit of it as I'm eating."

There was a pause in the fight just then, and the Lion and the Unicorn sat down, panting,

11. The White Queen is moving from a square due west of the Red Knight to QB8. She really doesn't have to flee—the Knight could not have taken her, whereas she could have taken him—but the move is characteristic of her stupidity.

while the King called out "Ten minutes allowed for refreshments!" Haigha and Hatta set to work at once, carrying round trays of white and brown bread. Alice took a piece to taste, but it was *very* dry.

"I don't think they'll fight any more today," the King said to Hatta: "go and order the drums to begin." And Hatta went bounding away like a grasshopper.

For a minute or two Alice stood silent, watching him. Suddenly she brightened up. "Look, look!" she cried, pointing eagerly. "There's the White Queen running across the country![11] She came flying out of the wood over yonder—How fast those Queens *can* run!"

"There's some enemy after her, no doubt," the King said, without even looking round. "That wood's full of them."

"But aren't you going to run and help her?" Alice asked, very much surprised at his taking it so quietly.

"No use, no use!" said the King. "She runs so fearfully quick. You might as well try to catch a Bandersnatch! But I'll make a memorandum about her, if you like—She's a dear good creature," he repeated softly to himself, as he opened his memorandum-book. "Do you spell 'creature' with a double 'e'?"

At this moment the Unicorn sauntered by them, with his hands in his pockets. "I had the best of it this time?" he said to the King, just glancing at him as he passed.

"A little—a little," the King replied, rather nervously. "You shouldn't have run him through with your horn, you know."

"It didn't hurt him," the Unicorn said carelessly, and he was going on, when his eye happened to fall upon Alice: he turned round instantly, and stood for some time looking at her with an air of the deepest disgust.

"What—is—this?" he said at last.

"This is a child!" Haigha replied eagerly, coming in front of Alice to introduce her, and spreading out both his hands towards her in an Anglo-Saxon attitude. "We only found it to-day. It's as large as life, and twice as natural!"[12]

"I always thought they were fabulous monsters!" said the Unicorn. "Is it alive?"

"It can talk," said Haigha solemnly.

The Unicorn looked dreamily at Alice, and said "Talk, child."

Alice could not help her lips curling up into a smile as she began: "Do you know, I always thought Unicorns were fabulous monsters, too? I never saw one alive before!"

"Well, now that we *have* seen each other," said the Unicorn, "if you'll believe in me, I'll believe in you. Is that a bargain?"

"Yes, if you like," said Alice.

"Come, fetch out the plum-cake, old man!" the Unicorn went on, turning from her to the King. "None of your brown bread for me!"

"Certainly—certainly!" the King muttered, and beckoned to Haigha. "Open the bag!" he whispered. "Quick! Not that one—that's full of hay!"

Haigha took a large cake out of the bag, and gave it to Alice to hold, while he got out a dish and carving-knife. How they all came out of it Alice couldn't guess. It was just like a conjuring-trick, she thought.

The Lion had joined them while this was going on: he looked very tired and sleepy, and his eyes were half shut. "What's this!" he said, blinking lazily at Alice, and speaking in a deep hollow tone that sounded like the tolling of a great bell.[13]

12. "As large as life and *quite* as natural" was a common phrase in Carroll's time (the *Oxford English Dictionary* quotes it from an 1853 source); but apparently Carroll was the first to substitute "twice" for "quite." This is now the usual phrasing in both England and the United States.

13. Did Tenniel intend the beasts to caricature Gladstone and Disraeli, who often sparred with each other? Michael Hancher, in his book on Tenniel's art, maintains that neither Carroll nor Tenniel had such resemblances in mind. He reproduces one of Tenniel's *Punch* cartoons, showing a Scottish unicorn and a British lion, both drawn almost exactly like those in *Alice*, confronting one another.

"Ah, what *is* it, now?" the Unicorn cried eagerly. "You'll never guess! *I* couldn't."

The Lion looked at Alice wearily. "Are you animal—or vegetable—or mineral?"[14] he said, yawning at every other word.

"It's a fabulous monster!" the Unicorn cried out, before Alice could reply.

"Then hand round the plum-cake, Monster," the Lion said, lying down and putting his chin on his paws. "And sit down, both of you," (to the King and the Unicorn): "fair play with the cake, you know!"

The King was evidently very uncomfortable at having to sit down between the two great creatures; but there was no other place for him.

"What a fight we might have for the crown, *now*!" the Unicorn said, looking slyly up at the crown, which the poor King was nearly shaking off his head, he trembled so much.

"I should win easy," said the Lion.

"I'm not so sure of that," said the Unicorn.

"Why, I beat you all round the town, you chicken!" the Lion replied angrily, half getting up as he spoke.

Here the King interrupted, to prevent the quarrel going on: he was very nervous, and his voice quite quivered. "All round the town?" he said. "That's a good long way. Did you go by the old bridge, or the market-place? You get the best view by the old bridge."

"I'm sure I don't know," the Lion growled out as he lay down again. "There was too much dust to see anything. What a time the Monster is, cutting up that cake!"

Alice had seated herself on the bank of a little brook, with the great dish on her knees, and was sawing away diligently with the knife. "It's very provoking!" she said, in reply to the Lion (she was getting quite used to being called "the Monster"). "I've cut several slices already, but they always join on again!"

"You don't know how to manage Looking-glass cakes," the Unicorn remarked. "Hand it round first, and cut it afterwards."

15. That is, a *lion's share*. The phrase comes from a fable of Aesop's that tells how a group of beasts divided the spoils of a hunt. The lion demanded one-fourth in virtue of his rank, another fourth for his superior courage, a third quarter for his wife and children. As for the remaining fourth, the lion adds, anyone who wishes to dispute it with him is free to do so.

16. Alice advances to Q7.

This sounded nonsense, but Alice very obediently got up, and carried the dish round, and the cake divided itself into three pieces as she did so. "*Now* cut it up," said the Lion, as she returned to her place with the empty dish.

"I say, this isn't fair!" cried the Unicorn, as Alice sat with the knife in her hand, very much puzzled how to begin. "The Monster has given the Lion twice as much as me!"[15]

"She's kept none for herself, anyhow," said the Lion. "Do you like plum-cake, Monster?"

But before Alice could answer him, the drums began.

Where the noise came from, she couldn't make out: the air seemed full of it, and it rang through and through her head till she felt quite deafened. She started to her feet and sprang across the little brook in her terror,[16]

* * * *
  * * *
* * * *

and had just time to see the Lion and the Unicorn rise to their feet, with angry looks at being interrupted in their feast, before she dropped to her knees, and put her hands over her ears, vainly trying to shut out the dreadful uproar.

"If *that* doesn't 'drum them out of town,'" she thought to herself, "nothing ever will!"

8

"It's My Own Invention"

After a while the noise seemed gradually to die away, till all was dead silence, and Alice lifted up her head in some alarm. There was no one to be seen, and her first thought was that she must have been dreaming about the Lion and the Unicorn and those queer Anglo-Saxon Messengers. However, there was the great dish still lying at her feet, on which she had tried to cut the plum-cake, "So I wasn't dreaming, after all," she said to herself, "unless—unless we're all part of the same dream. Only I do hope it's *my* dream, and not the Red King's! I don't like belonging to another person's dream," she went on in a rather complaining tone: "I've a great mind to go and wake him, and see what happens!"

At this moment her thoughts were interrupted by a loud shouting of "Ahoy! Ahoy! Check!" and a Knight, dressed in crimson armour, came galloping down upon her, brandishing a great club. Just as he reached her,[1] the horse stopped suddenly: "You're my prisoner!" the Knight cried, as he tumbled off his horse.

Startled as she was, Alice was more frightened for him than for herself at the moment, and watched him with some anxiety as he mounted again. As soon as he was comfortably in the saddle, he began once more "You're my—" but here another voice broke in "Ahoy! Ahoy! Check!"

1. The Red Knight has moved to K2; a powerful move in a conventional chess game, for he simultaneously checks the White King and attacks the White Queen. The Queen is lost unless the Red Knight can be removed from the board.

2. The White Knight, landing on the square occupied by the Red Knight (the square adjacent to Alice on her east side), absent-mindedly shouts, "Check!"; actually he checks only his own King. The defeat of the Red Knight indicates a move of Kt. X Kt. in the chess game.

Although most Carrollians agree that Carroll intended the White Knight to represent himself, other candidates have been proposed. Don Quixote is an obvious choice, and the parallels are ably defended in John Hinz's "Alice Meets the Don," in the *South Atlantic Quarterly* (Vol. 52, 1953, pages 253–66), reprinted in *Aspects of Alice* (Vanguard, 1971), edited by Robert Phillips.

Charles Edwards wrote to tell me about a passage in Cervantes's novel (Part 2, Chapter 4) in which the Don asks a poet to write an acrostic poem, the initial letters of its lines to spell "Dulcinea del Toboso." The poet finds seventeen letters awkward for a poem with regular stanzas because seventeen is a prime number with no divisors. The Don advises him to work hard on it because "no woman will believe that those verses were made for her where her name is not plainly discerned." "Alice Pleasance Liddell" has twenty-one letters. This made it possible for Carroll, in his acrostic terminal poem, to have seven stanzas of three lines each.

Another candidate for the White Knight is a chemist and inventor who was a friend of Carroll's and is often mentioned in Carroll's diary. See "The Chemist in Allegory: Augustus Vernon Harcourt and the White Knight," by M. Christine King, *Journal of Chemical Education* (March 1983). Other candidates are considered in Chapter 7 of Michael Hancher's *The Tenniel Illustrations to the "Alice" Books*. Because Tenniel in later life had a handlebar mustache

and Alice looked round in some surprise for the new enemy.

This time it was a White Knight.[2] He drew up at Alice's side, and tumbled off his horse just as the Red Knight had done: then he got on again, and the two Knights sat and looked at each other for some time without speaking. Alice looked from one to the other in some bewilderment.

"She's *my* prisoner, you know!" the Red Knight said at last.

"Yes, but then *I* came and rescued her!" the White Knight replied.

"Well, we must fight for her, then," said the Red Knight, as he took up his helmet (which hung from the saddle, and was something the shape of a horse's head) and put it on.

"You will observe the Rules of Battle, of course?" the White Knight remarked, putting on his helmet too.

"I always do," said the Red Knight, and they began banging away at each other with such fury that Alice got behind a tree to be out of the way of the blows.

"I wonder, now, what the Rules of Battle are," she said to herself, as she watched the fight, timidly peeping out from her hiding-place. "One Rule seems to be, that if one Knight hits the other, he knocks him off his horse; and, if he misses, he tumbles off himself—and another Rule seems to be that they hold their clubs with their arms, as if they were Punch and Judy[3]— What a noise they make when they tumble! Just like a whole set of fire-irons falling into the fender! And how quiet the horses are! They let them get on and off them just as if they were tables!"

Another Rule of Battle, that Alice had not noticed, seemed to be that they always fell on

their heads; and the battle ended with their both falling off in this way, side by side. When they got up again, they shook hands, and then the Red Knight mounted and galloped off.

"It was a glorious victory, wasn't it?" said the White Knight, as he came up panting.

"I don't know," Alice said doubtfully. "I don't want to be anybody's prisoner. I want to be a Queen."

"So you will, when you've crossed the next brook," said the White Knight. "I'll see you safe to the end of the wood—and then I must go back, you know. That's the end of my move."

"Thank you very much," said Alice. "May I help you off with your helmet?" It was evidently more than he could manage by himself: however she managed to shake him out of it at last.

"Now one can breathe more easily," said the Knight, putting back his shaggy hair with both hands, and turning his gentle face and large mild eyes to Alice. She thought she had never

(and his nose resembled that of the White Knight), it has been suggested that Tenniel drew the Knight as a caricature of himself. This seems farfetched because at the time that he drew the White Knight he did not wear a mustache.

Tenniel's frontispiece picture of the White Knight in many ways resembles Albrecht Dürer's etching of the Knight in the presence of Death and the Devil. Was this intentional? When I wrote to Michael Hancher for his opinion, he called my attention to Tenniel's cartoon in *Punch* (March 5, 1887), titled "The Knight and His Companion (Suggested by Dürer's famous picture)." The Knight represents Bismarck and his companion is Socialism. "Obviously Tenniel had a copy of the Dürer in front of him when he drew this cartoon," Hancher wrote. "My hunch is that he did not when he drew the *Looking-Glass* frontispiece, but that he called it up out of his remarkable visual memory."

THE KNIGHT AND HIS COMPANION.
[Suggested by Albert Dürer's famous picture.]

"The White Knight," Carroll wrote to Tenniel, "must not have whiskers; he must not be made to look old." Nowhere in the text does Carroll mention a mustache, nor does he indicate the knight's age. Tenniel's handlebar mustache and Newell's bushy mustache were the artists' additions. Perhaps Tenniel, sensing that the White Knight was Carroll, gave him a balding, elderly look to contrast his age with that of Alice.

Jeffrey Stern, in his article "Carroll Identifies Himself at Last" (*Jabberwocky*, Summer/Autumn 1990), describes a game board hand-drawn by Carroll that was recently discovered. The nature of the game is unknown, but on the underside of the cardboard sheet Carroll had written "Olive Butler, from the White Knight. Nov. 21, 1892." "So, at last," Stern comments, "we know for certain that Carroll *did* portray himself as the White Knight."

DÜRER'S KNIGHT

3. Carroll may be suggesting here that the knights, like Punch and Judy, are merely puppets moved by the hands of the invisible players of the game. Note that Tenniel, unlike modern illustrators in his scrupulous following of the text, shows the knights holding their clubs in traditional Punch-and-Judy fashion.

seen such a strange-looking soldier in all her life.[4]

He was dressed in tin armour, which seemed to fit him very badly, and he had a queer-shaped little deal box[5] fastened across his shoulders, upside-down, and with the lid hanging open. Alice looked at it with great curiosity.

"I see you're admiring my little box," the Knight said in a friendly tone. "It's my own invention—to keep clothes and sandwiches in. You see I carry it upside-down, so that the rain ca'n't get in."

"But the things can get *out*," Alice gently remarked. "Do you know the lid's open?"

"I didn't know it," the Knight said, a shade of vexation passing over his face. "Then all the things must have fallen out! And the box is no use without them." He unfastened it as he spoke, and was just going to throw it into the bushes, when a sudden thought seemed to strike him, and he hung it carefully on a tree. "Can you guess why I did that?" he said to Alice.

Alice shook her head.

"In hopes some bees may make a nest in it— then I should get the honey."

"But you've got a bee-hive—or something like one—fastened to the saddle," said Alice.

"Yes, it's a very good bee-hive," the Knight said in a discontented tone, "one of the best kind. But not a single bee has come near it yet. And the other thing is a mouse-trap. I suppose the mice keep the bees out—or the bees keep the mice out, I don't know which."

"I was wondering what the mouse-trap was for," said Alice. "It isn't very likely there would be any mice on the horse's back."

"Not very likely, perhaps," said the Knight; "but, if they *do* come, I don't choose to have them running all about."

"You see," he went on after a pause, "it's as well to be provided for *everything*. That's the reason the horse has all those anklets round his feet."

"But what are they for?" Alice asked in a tone of great curiosity.

"To guard against the bites of sharks,"[6] the Knight replied. "It's an invention of my own. And now help me on. I'll go with you to the end of the wood—What's that dish for?"

"It's meant for plum-cake," said Alice.

"We'd better take it with us," the Knight said. "It'll come in handy if we find any plum-cake. Help me to get it into this bag."

This took a long time to manage, though Alice held the bag open very carefully, because the Knight was so *very* awkward in putting in the dish: the first two or three times that he tried he fell in himself instead. "It's rather a tight fit, you see," he said, as they got it in at last; "there are so many candlesticks in the bag." And he hung it to the saddle, which was already loaded with bunches of carrots, and fire-irons, and many other things.[7]

"I hope you've got your hair well fastened on?" he continued, as they set off.

"Only in the usual way," Alice said, smiling.

"That's hardly enough," he said, anxiously. "You see the wind is so *very* strong here. It's as strong as soup."

"Have you invented a plan for keeping the hair from being blown off?" Alice enquired.

"Not yet," said the Knight. "But I've got a plan for keeping it from *falling* off."

"I should like to hear it, very much."

"First you take an upright stick," said the Knight. "Then you make your hair creep up it, like a fruit-tree. Now the reason hair falls

4. Many Carrollian scholars have surmised, and with good reason, that Carroll intended the White Knight to be a caricature of himself. Like the knight, Carroll had shaggy hair, mild blue eyes, a kind and gentle face. Like the knight, his mind seemed to function best when it saw things in topsy-turvy fashion. Like the knight, he was fond of curious gadgets and a "great hand at inventing things." He was forever "thinking of a way" to do this or that a bit differently. Many of his inventions, like the knight's blotting-paper pudding, were very clever but unlikely ever to be made (though some turned out to be not so useless when others reinvented them decades later).

Carroll's inventions include a chess set for travelers, with holes to hold pegged pieces; a cardboard grill (he called it a Nyctograph) to assist one in writing in the dark; a postage-stamp case with two "pictorial surprises" (see Chapter 6, Note 5, of *Alice's Adventures in Wonderland*). His diary contains such entries as: "The idea occurred to me that a game might be made of letters, to be moved about on a chess-board till they form words" (Dec. 19, 1880); "Concocted a new 'Proportional Representation' scheme, far the best I have yet devised ... Also invented rules for testing Divisibility of a number by 17 and by 19. An inventive day!" (June 3, 1884); "Invented a substitute for gum, for fastening envelopes ... , mounting small things in books, etc.—viz: paper with gum on *both* sides" (June 18, 1896); "Thought of a plan for simplifying money-orders, by making the sender fill up two duplicate papers, one of which he hands in to be transmitted by the postmaster—it contains a key-number, which the receiver has to supply in order to get the money. I think of suggesting this, and my plan for double postage on

Sunday, to the Government" (Nov. 16, 1880).

Carroll's rooms contained a variety of toys for the amusement of his child-guests: music boxes, dolls, windup animals (including a walking bear and one called "Bob the Bat," which flew around the room), games, an "American orguinette" that played when you cranked a strip of punched paper through it. When he went on a journey, Stuart Collingwood tells us in his biography, "each separate article used to be carefully wrapped up in a piece of paper all to itself, so that his trunks contained nearly as much paper as of the more useful things."

It is noteworthy also that, of all the characters Alice meets on her two dream adventures, only the White Knight seems to be genuinely fond of her and to offer her special assistance. He is almost alone in speaking to her with respect and courtesy, and we are told that Alice remembered him better than anyone else whom she met behind the mirror. His melancholy farewell may be Carroll's farewell to Alice when she grew up (became a queen) and abandoned him. At any rate, we hear loudest in this sunset episode that "shadow of a sigh" that Carroll tells us in his prefatory poem will "tremble through the story."

The role of White Knight was taken by Gary Cooper in Paramount's 1933 film, *Alice in Wonderland*.

5. A deal box is a box made of fir or pine wood.

6. "I suggest that when the White Knight said that his horse's anklets were to guard against the bites of sharks, the compositor in his first proof made the very easy substitution of an 'n' for an 'h,' and set Carroll wondering what the bites of

off is because it hangs *down*—things never fall *upwards*, you know. It's a plan of my own invention. You may try it if you like."

It didn't sound a comfortable plan, Alice thought, and for a few minutes she walked on in silence, puzzling over the idea, and every now and then stopping to help the poor Knight, who certainly was *not* a good rider.

Whenever the horse stopped (which it did very often), he fell off in front; and, whenever it went on again (which it generally did rather suddenly), he fell off behind. Otherwise he kept on pretty well, except that he had a habit of now and then falling off sideways; and, as he generally did this on the side on which Alice was walking, she soon found that it was the best plan not to walk *quite* close to the horse.

"I'm afraid you've not had much practice in riding," she ventured to say, as she was helping him up from his fifth tumble.

The Knight looked very much surprised, and a little offended at the remark. "What makes you say that?" he asked, as he scrambled back into the saddle, keeping hold of Alice's hair with one hand, to save himself from falling over on the other side.

"Because people don't fall off quite so often, when they've had much practice."

"I've had plenty of practice," the Knight said very gravely: "plenty of practice!"

Alice could think of nothing better to say than "Indeed?" but she said it as heartily as she could. They went on a little way in silence after this, the Knight with his eyes shut, muttering to himself, and Alice watching anxiously for the next tumble.

"The great art of riding," the Knight suddenly began in a loud voice, waving his right arm as he spoke, "is to keep—" Here the sentence ended as suddenly as it had begun, as the Knight fell heavily on the top of his head exactly in the path where Alice was walking. She was quite frightened this time, and said in an anxious tone, as she picked him up, "I hope no bones are broken?"

"None to speak of," the Knight said, as if he didn't mind breaking two or three of them. "The great art of riding, as I was saying, is—to keep your balance properly. Like this, you know—"

He let go the bridle, and stretched out both his arms to show Alice what he meant, and this time he fell flat on his back, right under the horse's feet.

"Plenty of practice!" he went on repeating, all the time that Alice was getting him on his feet again. "Plenty of practice!"

"It's too ridiculous!" cried Alice, losing all her patience this time. "You ought to have a wooden horse on wheels, that you ought!"

snarks were like . . . wondering until inevitably *The Hunting of the Snark* followed, which is the way such things get written."
—A. A. Milne, *Year In, Year Out* (1952).

7. Janis Lull, in *Lewis Carroll: A Celebration*, argues that Carroll and Tenniel together loaded the steed with objects closely related to things mentioned or pictured elsewhere in the *Alice* books: the wooden sword and the umbrella are similar to the sword and umbrella owned by the Tweedle brothers; the watchman's rattle looks like the rattle over which the brothers fought; the beehive recalls the elephant bees in Chapter 3; the mousetrap stands for the mouse in the first *Alice* book; the candlesticks allude to the candles that go off like fireworks at the end of Chapter 9; the spring bell suggests the two bells on the door in Chapter 9; the fire irons and bellows are like those in Alice's living room below the mirror; the shark anklets could be identified with the sharks in Alice's recitation in Chapter 10 of the previous book; the two brushes are related to the hairbrush with which Alice combs the White Queen's hair in Chapter 5; the plum-cake dish is, of course, the one that the March Hare produces like magic from his small bag when the Lion and Unicorn are fighting for the crown; the carrots may be there as food for the March Hare; and the wine bottle, perhaps empty, suggests the nonexistent wine that the March Hare asked Alice to drink at the Mad Tea Party, as well as the real wine at the feast in Chapter 9.

"The Knight is a sort of property master," Lull summarizes, "whose furniture both recapitulates what has gone before and anticipates what will come."

For more inventions by Carroll's White Knight, see Chapter 9 of my *Visitors from Oz*.

"Does that kind go smoothly?" the Knight asked in a tone of great interest, clasping his arms round the horse's neck as he spoke, just in time to save himself from tumbling off again.

"Much more smoothly than a live horse," Alice said, with a little scream of laughter, in spite of all she could do to prevent it.

"I'll get one," the Knight said thoughtfully to himself. "One or two—several."

There was a short silence after this, and then the Knight went on again. "I'm a great hand at inventing things. Now, I daresay you noticed, the last time you picked me up, that I was looking rather thoughtful?"

"You *were* a little grave," said Alice.

"Well, just then I was inventing a new way of getting over a gate—would you like to hear it?"

"Very much indeed," Alice said politely.

"I'll tell you how I came to think of it," said the Knight. "You see, I said to myself 'The only difficulty is with the feet: the *head* is high enough already.' Now, first I put my head on the top of the gate—then the head's high enough—then I stand on my head—then the feet are high enough, you see—then I'm over, you see."

"Yes, I suppose you'd be over when that was done," Alice said thoughtfully: "but don't you think it would be rather hard?"

"I haven't tried it yet," the Knight said, gravely; "so I ca'n't tell for certain—but I'm afraid it *would* be a little hard."

He looked so vexed at the idea, that Alice changed the subject hastily. "What a curious helmet you've got!" she said cheerfully. "Is that your invention too?"

The Knight looked down proudly at his helmet, which hung from the saddle. "Yes," he said; "but I've invented a better one than that—like a sugar-loaf.[8] When I used to wear it, if I fell off the horse, it always touched the ground directly. So I had a *very* little way to fall, you see—But there *was* the danger of falling *into* it, to be sure. That happened to me once—and the worst of it was, before I could get out again, the other White Knight came and put it on. He thought it was his own helmet."

The Knight looked so solemn about it that Alice did not dare to laugh. "I'm afraid you must have hurt him," she said in a trembling voice, "being on the top of his head."

"I had to kick him, of course," the Knight said, very seriously. "And then he took the helmet off again—but it took hours and hours to get me out. I was as fast as—as lightning, you know."

"But that's a different kind of fastness," Alice objected.

The Knight shook his head. "It was all kinds of fastness with me, I can assure you!" he said. He raised his hands in some excitement as he said this, and instantly rolled out of the saddle, and fell head-long into a deep ditch.

Alice ran to the side of the ditch to look for him. She was rather startled by the fall, as for some time he had kept on very well, and she was afraid that he really *was* hurt this time. However, though she could see nothing but the soles of his feet, she was much relieved to hear that he was talking on in his usual tone. "All kinds of fastness," he repeated: "but it was careless of him to put another man's helmet on—with the man in it, too."

"How *can* you go on talking so quietly, head downwards?" Alice asked, as she dragged him out by the feet, and laid him in a heap on the bank.

8. In Carroll's day refined sugar was formed into conical chunks called sugar loaves. The term *sugar loaf* is commonly applied to cone-shaped hats and hills.

The Knight looked surprised at the question. "What does it matter where my body happens to be?" he said. "My mind goes on working all the same. In fact, the more head-downwards I am, the more I keep inventing new things."

"Now the cleverest thing of the sort that I ever did," he went on after a pause, "was inventing a new pudding during the meat-course."

"In time to have it cooked for the next course?" said Alice. "Well, that *was* quick work, certainly!"

"Well, not the *next* course," the Knight said in a slow thoughtful tone: "no, certainly not the next *course*."

"Then it would have to be the next day. I suppose you wouldn't have two pudding-courses in one dinner?"

"Well, not the *next* day," the Knight repeated as before: "not the next *day*. In fact," he went on, holding his head down, and his voice getting lower and lower, "I don't believe that pudding ever *was* cooked! In fact, I don't believe that pudding ever *will* be cooked! And yet it was a very clever pudding to invent."[9]

"What did you mean it to be made of?" Alice

asked, hoping to cheer him up, for the poor Knight seemed quite low-spirited about it.

"It began with blotting-paper," the Knight answered with a groan.

"That wouldn't be very nice, I'm afraid—"

"Not very nice *alone*," he interrupted, quite eagerly: "but you've no idea what a difference it makes, mixing it with other things—such as gunpowder and sealing-wax. And here I must leave you." They had just come to the end of the wood.

Alice could only look puzzled: she was thinking of the pudding.

"You are sad," the Knight said in an anxious tone: "let me sing you a song to comfort you."

"Is it very long?" Alice asked, for she had heard a good deal of poetry that day.

"It's long," said the Knight, "but it's very, *very* beautiful. Everybody that hears me sing it —either it brings the *tears* into their eyes, or else—"

"Or else what?" said Alice, for the Knight had made a sudden pause.

"Or else it doesn't, you know.[10] The name of the song is called '*Haddocks' Eyes*.'"

"Oh, that's the name of the song, is it?" Alice said, trying to feel interested.

"No, you don't understand," the Knight said, looking a little vexed. "That's what the name is *called*. The name really *is* '*The Aged Aged Man*.'"

"Then I ought to have said 'That's what the *song* is called'?" Alice corrected herself.

"No, you oughtn't: that's quite another thing! The *song* is called '*Ways and Means*'[11] but that's only what it's *called*, you know!"

"Well, what *is* the song, then?" said Alice, who was by this time completely bewildered.

10. In two-valued logic this would be called an example of the law of excluded middle: a statement is either true or false, with no third alternative. The law is the basis of a number of old nonsense rhymes: e.g., There was an old woman who lived on the hill,/And if she's not gone, she is living there still.

11. In his diary (August 5, 1862) Carroll wrote: "After dinner Harcourt and I went to the Deanery to arrange about the river tomorrow, and stayed to play a game of 'Ways and Means' with the children." I am told that Carroll's relatives own a set of rules in Carroll's handwriting, but no one seems to know if the game was invented by Carroll or by someone else.

12. To a student of logic and semantics all this is perfectly sensible. The song is "A-Sitting on a Gate"; it is *called* "Ways and Means"; the *name* of the song is "The Aged Aged Man"; and the name is *called* "Haddocks' Eyes." Carroll is distinguishing here among things, the names of things, and the names of names of things. "Haddocks' Eyes," the name of a name, belongs to what logicians now call a "metalanguage." By adopting the convention of a hierarchy of metalanguages logicians manage to sidestep certain paradoxes that have plagued them since the time of the Greeks. For Earnest Nagel's amusing translation of the White Knight's remarks into symbolic notation, see his article "Symbolic Notation, Haddocks' Eyes and the Dog-Walking Ordinance," in Vol. 3 of James R. Newman's anthology, *The World of Mathematics* (1956).

A less technical but equally sound and delightful analysis of this passage is included in Roger W. Holmes' article, "The Philosopher's *Alice in Wonderland*" (*Antioch Review*, Summer 1959). Professor Holmes (he was chairman of the philosophy department at Mount Holyoke College) thinks that Carroll was pulling our leg when he has the White Knight say that the song *is* "A-sitting on a Gate." Clearly this cannot be the song itself, but only another name. "To be consistent," Holmes concludes, "the White Knight, when he had said that the song *is* . . . , could only have burst into the song itself. Whether consistent or not, the White Knight is Lewis Carroll's cherished gift to logicians."

The White Knight's song also exhibits a kind of hierarchy, like a mirror reflection of a mirror reflection of an object. Carroll's eccentric White Knight, whom Alice couldn't forget, is also unable to forget

"I was coming to that," the Knight said. "The song really is '*A-sitting on a Gate*':[12] and the tune's my own invention."

So saying, he stopped his horse and let the reins fall on its neck: then, slowly beating time with one hand, and with a faint smile lighting up his gentle foolish face, as if he enjoyed the music of his song, he began.

Of all the strange things that Alice saw in her journey Through The Looking-Glass, this was the one that she always remembered most clearly. Years afterwards she could bring the whole scene back again, as if it had been only yesterday—the mild blue eyes and kindly smile of the Knight—the setting sun gleaming through his hair, and shining on his armour in a blaze of light that quite dazzled her—the horse quietly moving about, with the reins hanging loose on his neck, cropping the grass at her feet—and the black shadows of the forest behind—all this she took in like a picture, as, with one hand shading her eyes, she leant against a tree, watching the strange pair, and listening, in a half-dream, to the melancholy music of the song.[13]

"But the tune *isn't* his own invention," she said to herself: "it's '*I give thee all, I can no more.*'" She stood and listened very attentively, but no tears came into her eyes.

> "*I'll tell thee everything I can:*
>   *There's little to relate.*
> *I saw an aged aged man,*
>   *A-sitting on a gate.*
> '*Who are you, aged man?*' *I said.*
>   '*And how is it you live?*'
> *And his answer trickled through my head,*
>   *Like water through a sieve.*

He said 'I look for butterflies
    That sleep among the wheat:
I make them into mutton-pies,
    And sell them in the street.
I sell them unto men,' he said,
    'Who sail on stormy seas;
And that's the way I get my bread—
    A trifle, if you please.'

But I was thinking of a plan
    To dye one's whiskers green,
And always use so large a fan
    That they could not be seen.[14]
So, having no reply to give
    To what the old man said,
I cried 'Come, tell me how you live!'
    And thumped him on the head.

His accents mild took up the tale:
    He said 'I go my ways,
And when I find a mountain-rill,
    I set it in a blaze;
And thence they make a stuff they call
    Rowland's Macassar-Oil[15]—
Yet twopence-halfpenny is all
    They give me for my toil.'

another eccentric with traits that
suggest that he too may be a caricature of Carroll; perhaps Carroll's
vision of himself as a lonely, unloved
old man.

13. The White Knight's song is a
revised, expanded version of this
earlier poem by Carroll, which appeared anonymously in 1856 in a
magazine called *The Train*.

Upon the Lonely Moor

I met an aged, aged man
    Upon the lonely moor:
I knew I was a gentleman,
    And he was but a boor.
So I stopped and roughly questioned him,
    "Come, tell me how you live!"
But his words impressed my ear no more
    Than if it were a sieve.

He said, "I look for soap-bubbles,
    That lie among the wheat,
And bake them into mutton-pies,
    And sell them in the street.
I sell them unto men," he said,
    "Who sail on stormy seas;
And that's the way I get my bread—
    A trifle, if you please."

But I was thinking of a way
    To multiply by ten,
And always, in the answer, get
    The question back again.
I did not hear a word he said,
    But kicked that old man calm,
And said, "Come, tell me how you live!"
    And pinched him in the arm.

His accents mild took up the tale:
    He said, "I go my ways,
And when I find a mountain-rill,
    I set it in a blaze.
And thence they make a stuff they call
    Rowland's Macassar Oil;
But fourpence-halfpenny is all
    They give me for my toil."

But I was thinking of a plan
    To paint one's gaiters green,
So much the colour of the grass
    That they could ne'er be seen.
I gave his ear a sudden box,
    And questioned him again,
And tweaked his grey and reverend locks,
    And put him into pain.

He said, "I hunt for haddocks' eyes
    Among the heather bright,
And work them into waistcoat-buttons
    In the silent night.
And these I do not sell for gold,
    Or coin of silver-mine,
But for a copper-halfpenny,
    And that will purchase nine.

"I sometimes dig for buttered rolls,
    Or set limed twigs for crabs;
I sometimes search the flowery knolls
    For wheels of hansom cabs.
And that's the way" (he gave a wink)
    "I get my living here,
And very gladly will I drink
    Your Honour's health in beer."

I heard him then, for I had just
    Completed my design
To keep the Menai bridge from rust
    By boiling it in wine.
I duly thanked him, ere I went,
    For all his stories queer.
But chiefly for his kind intent
    To drink my health in beer.

And now if e'er by chance I put
    My fingers into glue,
Or madly squeeze a right-hand foot
    Into a left-hand shoe;
Or if a statement I aver
    Of which I am not sure,
I think of that strange wanderer
    Upon the lonely moor.

"Upon the Lonely Moor" was written for Tennyson's son Lionel. Here is Carroll's account of its origin, from an April 1862 entry in his diary. The entry was in a portion of the diary now missing, but Stuart Collingwood quotes it in his biography of Carroll.

But I was thinking of a way
    To feed oneself on batter,
And so go on from day to day
    Getting a little fatter.
I shook him well from side to side,
    Until his face was blue:
'Come, tell me how you live,' I cried,
    'And what it is you do!'

He said 'I hunt for haddocks' eyes
    Among the heather bright,
And work them into waistcoat-buttons
    In the silent night.
And these I do not sell for gold
    Or coin of silvery shine,
But for a copper halfpenny,
    And that will purchase nine.

'I sometimes dig for buttered rolls,
    Or set limed twigs[16] for crabs:
I sometimes search the grassy knolls
    For wheels of Hansom-cabs.[17]
And that's the way' (he gave a wink)
    'By which I get my wealth—
And very gladly will I drink
    Your Honour's noble health.'

I heard him then, for I had just
    Completed my design
To keep the Menai bridge[18] from rust
    By boiling it in wine.
I thanked him much for telling me
    The way he got his wealth,
But chiefly for his wish that he
    Might drink my noble health.

And now, if e'er by chance I put
    My fingers into glue,
Or madly squeeze a right-hand foot
    Into a left-hand shoe,[19]

Or if I drop upon my toe
   A very heavy weight,
I weep, for it reminds me so
Of that old man I used to know—
Whose look was mild, whose speech was slow,
Whose hair was whiter than the snow,
Whose face was very like a crow,
With eyes, like cinders, all aglow,²⁰
Who seemed distracted with his woe,
Who rocked his body to and fro,
And muttered mumblingly and low,
As if his mouth were full of dough,
Who snorted like a buffalo—
That summer evening long ago,
   A-sitting on a gate."

As the Knight sang the last words of the ballad, he gathered up the reins, and turned his
horse's head along the road by which they had
come. "You've only a few yards to go," he said,
"down the hill and over that little brook, and
then you'll be a Queen—But you'll stay and see
me off first?" he added as Alice turned with an
eager look in the direction to which he pointed.
"I sha'n't be long. You'll wait and wave your
handkerchief when I get to that turn in the road!
I think it'll encourage me, you see."

"Of course I'll wait," said Alice: "and thank
you very much for coming so far—and for the
song—I liked it very much."

"I hope so," the Knight said doubtfully: "but
you didn't cry so much as I thought you would."

So they shook hands, and then the Knight rode
slowly away into the forest. "It wo'n't take long
to see him *off*, I expect," Alice said to herself, as
she stood watching him. "There he goes! Right
on his head as usual! However, he gets on again
pretty easily—that comes of having so many

After luncheon I went to the Tennysons,
and got Hallam and Lionel to sign their
names in my album. Also I made a bargain
with Lionel, that he was to give me some
MS. of his verses, and I was to send him
some of mine. It was a very difficult bargain to make; I almost despaired of it at
first, he put in so many conditions—first, I
was to play a game of chess with him; this,
with much difficulty we reduced to twelve
moves on each side; but this made little
difference, as I checkmated him at the
sixth move. Second, he was to be allowed
to give me one blow on the head with a
mallet (this he at last consented to give
up). I forget if there were others, but it
ended in my getting the verses, for which
I have written out "The Lonely Moor"
for him.

" 'Sitting on a Gate' *is* a parody,"
Carroll said in a letter (see *The
Letters of Lewis Carroll*, edited by
Morton Cohen, Vol. 1, page 177),
"though not as to style or metre—but
its plot is borrowed from Wordsworth's 'Resolution and Independ-
ence,' a poem that has always amused
me a good deal (though it is by no
means a comic poem) by the absurd
way in which the poet goes on ques-
tioning the poor old leech-gatherer,
making him tell his history over and
over again, and never attending to
what he says. Wordsworth ends
with a moral—an example I have *not*
followed."

Carroll surely identified himself
with the song's "aged aged man," a
man even further removed in age
from Alice than was the White
Knight. In "Isa's Visit to Oxford,"
Carroll calls himself "the Aged Aged
Man," abbreviating it throughout
the diary as "the A.A.M." Carroll
was then fifty-eight. He often referred
to himself in letters to child-friends as
an aged, aged man.

On the whole, Wordsworth's
poem is a fine poem, and I say this

with awareness of the fact that a portion of it is included in *The Stuffed Owl*, that hilarious anthology of bad verse compiled by D. B. Wyndham Lewis and Charles Lee.

The opening lines of the White Knight's song burlesque Wordsworth's lines "I'll tell you everything I know" and "I'll give you all the help I can" from the original version of one of the poet's less happy efforts called "The Thorn." The line also reflects the title of the song, "I give thee all, I can no more," to the tune of which the White Knight sings about the aged aged man. This song is Thomas Moore's lyric, "My Heart and Lute," which was set to music by the English composer Sir Henry Rowley Bishop. Carroll's song follows the metrical pattern and rhyme scheme of Moore's poem.

"The character of the White Knight," Carroll wrote in a letter, "was meant to suit the speaker in the poem." That the speaker is Carroll himself is suggested by his thoughts on multiplying by ten in the third stanza of the earlier version. It is quite possible that Carroll regarded Moore's love lyric as the song that he, the White Knight, would have liked to sing to Alice but dared not. The full text of Moore's poem follows.

I give thee all—I can no more—
  Though poor the off'ring be;
My heart and lute are all the store
  That I can bring to thee.
A lute whose gentle song reveals
  The soul of love full well;
And, better far, a heart that feels
  Much more than lute could tell.

Though love and song may fail, alas!
  To keep life's clouds away,
At least 'twill make them lighter pass
  Or gild them if they stay.

things hung round the horse—" So she went on talking to herself, as she watched the horse walking leisurely along the road, and the Knight tumbling off, first on one side and then on the other. After the fourth or fifth tumble he reached the turn, and then she waved her handkerchief to him, and waited till he was out of sight.[21]

"I hope it encouraged him," she said, as she turned to run down the hill: "and now for the last brook, and to be a Queen! How grand it sounds!" A very few steps brought her to the edge of the brook.[22] "The Eighth Square at last!" she cried as she bounded across,

*   *   *   *

  *   *   *

*   *   *   *

and threw herself down to rest on a lawn as soft as moss, with little flower-beds dotted about it here and there. "Oh, how glad I am to get here! And what *is* this on my head?" she exclaimed in a tone of dismay, as she put her hands up to something very heavy, that fitted tight all round her head.

"But how *can* it have got there without my knowing it?" she said to herself, as she lifted it off, and set it on her lap to make out what it could possibly be.

It was a golden crown.[23]

And ev'n if Care, at moments, flings
A discord o'er life's happy strain,
Let love but gently touch the strings,
'Twill all be sweet again!

14. Bertrand Russell, in *The ABC of Relativity*, Chapter 3, applies these four lines to the Lorentz-Fitzgerald contraction hypothesis, an early attempt to account for the failure of the Michelson-Morley experiment to detect an influence of the earth's motion on the speed of light. According to this hypothesis, objects shrink in the direction of their motion, but since all measuring rods are similarly shortened, they serve, like the White Knight's fan, to prevent us from detecting any change in the length of objects. The same lines are quoted by Arthur Stanley Eddington in Chapter 2 of *The Nature of the Physical World*, but with a larger metaphorical meaning: the apparent habit nature has of forever concealing from us her basic structural plan.

In Carroll's earlier poem "Upon the Lonely Moor" (reprinted in Note 13), it is "one's gaiters" that are painted green.

15. The *Oxford English Dictionary* describes this oil as "an unguent for the hair, grandilo-quently advertised in the early part of the nineteenth century, and represented by the makers (Rowland and Son) to consist of ingredients obtained from Macassar." In the first canto, stanza 17, of *Don Juan*, Byron writes:

In virtues nothing earthly could
surpass her,
Save thine "incomparable oil,"
Macassar!

The term "antimacassar," for the piece of cloth put on the backs of chairs and sofas to prevent soiling of the fabric by hair oil, had its origin in the popularity of this oil.

16. Limed twigs are twigs that have been smeared with birdlime (or any sticky substance) for the purpose of catching birds.

17. "Hansom-cabs": Covered carriages with two wheels and an elevated seat for the driver in the back. They were the taxicabs of Victorian England.

18. The Menai Bridge, crossing the Menai Straits in North Wales, consisted of two enormous cast-iron tubes through which trains ran. As a child, Carroll had crossed the bridge on a long holiday trip with his family.

19. It is an ancient superstition, reader Tim Healey tells me, that putting one's right foot into a left shoe is an omen of bad luck. He quotes a passage from Samuel Butler's *Hudibras* which speaks of Augustus Caesar making this mistake:

Augustus, having by an oversight
Put on his left shoe for his right,
And like to have been slain that day
By soldiers mutineering for pay.

20. Physicist David Frisch calls my attention to the following lines —the last two lines of stanza 12 in Wordsworth's poem before he revised them for a later printing:

He answer'd me with pleasure
and surprise
And there was, while he spake, a fire
about his eyes.

21. The White Knight has returned to KB5, the square he occupied before capturing the Red Knight.

Because knight moves are L-shaped, the White Knight's move is the "turn in the road" to which he referred a few paragraphs earlier.

This scene, in which Carroll clearly intends to describe how he hopes Alice will feel after she grows up and says good-bye, is one of the great poignant episodes of English literature. No one has written more eloquently about it than Donald Rackin in his essay "Love and Death in Carroll's *Alices*" (in *Soaring with the Dodo: Essays on Lewis Carroll's Life and Art*, edited by Edward Guiliano and James Kincaid): "The fleeting love that whispers through this scene is, therefore, complex and paradoxical: it is a love between a child all potential, freedom, flux, and growing up and a man all impotence, imprisonment, stasis, and falling down."

22. This is the spot where Carroll originally intended to place his episode about the Wasp in a Wig. Although Tenniel, in his letter to Carroll urging that the episode be omitted, called it a chapter, all evidence indicates it was to be a lengthy section in a chapter that even without it became the longest in the book. The complete episode, with my introduction and notes, is reprinted in this book.

23. Alice has leaped the one remaining brook and is now on Q8, the last square of the queen's file. For readers unfamiliar with chess it should be said that when a pawn reaches the last row of the chessboard it may become any piece the player desires. He usually chooses a queen, the most powerful of the chess pieces.

9

Queen Alice

"Well, this *is* grand!" said Alice. "I never expected I should be a Queen so soon—and I'll tell you what it is, your Majesty," she went on, in a severe tone (she was always rather fond of scolding herself), "it'll never do for you to be lolling about on the grass like that! Queens have to be dignified, you know!"

So she got up and walked about—rather stiffly just at first, as she was afraid that the crown might come off: but she comforted herself with the thought that there was nobody to see her, "and if I really am a Queen," she said as she sat down again, "I shall be able to manage it quite well in time."

Everything was happening so oddly that she didn't feel a bit surprised at finding the Red Queen and the White Queen sitting close to her, one on each side:[1] she would have liked very much to ask them how they came there, but she feared it would not be quite civil. However, there would be no harm, she thought, in asking if the game was over. "Please, would you tell me—" she began, looking timidly at the Red Queen.

"Speak when you're spoken to!" the Queen sharply interrupted her.

"But if everybody obeyed that rule," said Alice, who was always ready for a little argument, "and if you only spoke when you were

1. The Red Queen has just moved to the King's square so that Alice now has a queen on each side of her. The White King is placed in check by this move, but neither side seems to notice it.

Ivor Davies, writing on "Looking-Glass Chess" in *The Anglo-Welsh Review* (Autumn 1970), has an explanation of why no one notices that the White King has been placed in check by the Red Queen's move to the King's square. One of the chess books in Carroll's library was *The Art of Chess-Play* (1846) by George Walker. The book's Law 20 states: "When you give check, you must apprize your adversary by saying aloud 'check'; or he need not notice it, but may move as though check were not given."

"The Red Queen did not say 'Check,'" comments Davies. "Her silence was entirely logical because, at the moment of her arrival at King one, she said to Alice ... 'Speak when you're spoken to!' Since no one had spoken to *her* she would have been breaking her own rule had she said 'check.'"

Another informative paper on the book's chess game is "Alice in Fairyland" by A. S. M. Dickins, in *Jabberwocky* (Winter 1976). A world expert on "fairy chess," Dickins analyzes Carroll's game as a mélange of fairy chess rules. He calls attention to

Walker's Law 14, which, incredibly, allows a player to make a series of consecutive moves in one turn provided the opponent doesn't object!

spoken to, and the other person always waited for *you* to begin, you see nobody would ever say anything, so that—"

"Ridiculous!" cried the Queen. "Why, don't you see, child—" here she broke off with a frown, and, after thinking for a minute, suddenly changed the subject of the conversation. "What do you mean by 'If you really are a Queen'? What right have you to call yourself so? You ca'n't be a Queen, you know, till you've passed the proper examination. And the sooner we begin it, the better."

"I only said 'if'!" poor Alice pleaded in a piteous tone.

The two Queens looked at each other, and the Red Queen remarked, with a little shudder, "She *says* she only said 'if—"

"But she said a great deal more than that!" the White Queen moaned, wringing her hands. "Oh, ever so much more than that!"

"So you did, you know," the Red Queen said to Alice. "Always speak the truth—think before you speak—and write it down afterwards."

"I'm sure I didn't mean—" Alice was beginning, but the Red Queen interrupted her impatiently.

"That's just what I complain of! You *should* have meant! What do you suppose is the use of a child without any meaning? Even a joke should have some meaning—and a child's more important than a joke, I hope. You couldn't deny that, even if you tried with both hands."

"I don't deny things with my *hands*," Alice objected.

"Nobody said you did," said the Red Queen. "I said you couldn't if you tried."

"She's in that state of mind," said the White Queen, "that she wants to deny *something*—only she doesn't know what to deny!"

"A nasty, vicious temper," the Red Queen remarked; and then there was an uncomfortable silence for a minute or two.

The Red Queen broke the silence by saying, to the White Queen, "I invite you to Alice's dinner-party this afternoon."

The White Queen smiled feebly, and said "And I invite *you*."

"I didn't know I was to have a party at all," said Alice; "but, if there *is* to be one, I think *I* ought to invite the guests."

"We gave you the opportunity of doing it," the Red Queen remarked: "but I daresay you've not had many lessons in manners yet?"

"Manners are not taught in lessons," said Alice. "Lessons teach you to do sums, and things of that sort."

"Can you do Addition?" the White Queen asked. "What's one and one and one and one and one and one and one and one and one and one?"

"I don't know," said Alice. "I lost count."

"She ca'n't do Addition," the Red Queen interrupted. "Can you do Subtraction? Take nine from eight."

"Nine from eight I ca'n't, you know," Alice replied very readily: "but—"

"She ca'n't do Subtraction," said the White Queen. "Can you do Division? Divide a loaf by a knife—what's the answer to *that*?"

"I suppose—" Alice was beginning, but the Red Queen answered for her. "Bread-and-butter, of course. Try another Subtraction sum. Take a bone from a dog: what remains?"

Alice considered. "The bone wouldn't remain, of course, if I took it—and the dog wouldn't remain: it would come to bite me—and I'm sure *I* shouldn't remain!"

"Then you think nothing would remain?" said the Red Queen.

"I think that's the answer."

"Wrong, as usual," said the Red Queen: "the dog's temper would remain."

"But I don't see how—"

"Why, look here!" the Red Queen cried. "The dog would lose its temper, wouldn't it?"

"Perhaps it would," Alice replied cautiously.

"Then if the dog went away, its temper would remain!" the Queen exclaimed triumphantly.

Alice said, as gravely as she could, "They might go different ways." But she couldn't help thinking to herself "What dreadful nonsense we *are* talking!"

"She ca'n't do sums a *bit*!" the Queens said together, with great emphasis.

"Can *you* do sums?" Alice said, turning suddenly on the White Queen, for she didn't like being found fault with so much.

The Queen gasped and shut her eyes. "I can do Addition," she said, "if you give me time—but I ca'n't do Subtraction under *any* circumstances!"

"Of course you know your ABC?" said the Red Queen.

"To be sure I do," said Alice.

"So do I," the White Queen whispered: "we'll often say it over together, dear. And I'll tell you a secret—I can read words of one letter! Isn't *that* grand? However, don't be discouraged. You'll come to it in time."

Here the Red Queen began again. "Can you answer useful questions?" she said. "How is bread made?"

"I know *that*!" Alice cried eagerly. "You take some flour—"

"Where do you pick the flower?" the White Queen asked. "In a garden or in the hedges?"

"Well, it isn't *picked* at all," Alice explained: "it's *ground*—"

"How many acres of ground?" said the White Queen. "You mustn't leave out so many things."

"Fan her head!" the Red Queen anxiously

2. Is the Red Queen, as conjectured by Selwyn Goodacre and several other correspondents, alluding to the fact that no move in chess can be taken back? Once it is made "you must take the consequences." Modern chess rules are even more strict. If a piece is merely touched, it must be moved.

3. Carroll was particularly fond of Tuesdays. "Spent the day in London," he wrote in his diary on Tuesday, April 10, 1877. "It was (like so many Tuesdays in my life) a very enjoyable day." The joy on this occasion was his meeting of a modest little girl "who is about the most gloriously beautiful child (both face and figure) that I ever saw. One would like to do 100 photographs of her."

interrupted. "She'll be feverish after so much thinking." So they set to work and fanned her with bunches of leaves, till she had to beg them to leave off, it blew her hair about so.

"She's all right again now," said the Red Queen. "Do you know Languages? What's the French for fiddle-de-dee?"

"Fiddle-de-dee's not English," Alice replied gravely.

"Who ever said it was?" said the Red Queen.

Alice thought she saw a way out of the difficulty, this time. "If you'll tell me what language 'fiddle-de-dee' is, I'll tell you the French for it!" she exclaimed triumphantly.

But the Red Queen drew herself up rather stiffly, and said "Queens never make bargains."

"I wish Queens never asked questions," Alice thought to herself.

"Don't let us quarrel," the White Queen said in an anxious tone. "What is the cause of lightning?"

"The cause of lightning," Alice said very decidedly, for she felt quite certain about this, "is the thunder—no, no!" she hastily corrected herself. "I meant the other way."

"It's too late to correct it," said the Red Queen: "when you've once said a thing, that fixes it, and you must take the consequences."[2]

"Which reminds me—" the White Queen said, looking down and nervously clasping and unclasping her hands, "we had *such* a thunderstorm last Tuesday—I mean one of the last set of Tuesdays, you know."[3]

Alice was puzzled. "In *our* country," she remarked, "there's only one day at a time."

The Red Queen said "That's a poor thin way of doing things. Now *here*, we mostly have days and nights two or three at a time, and sometimes in the winter we take as many as five nights together—for warmth, you know."

"Are five nights warmer than one night, then?" Alice ventured to ask.

"Five times as warm, of course."

"But they should be five times as *cold*, by the same rule—"

"Just so!" cried the Red Queen. "Five times as warm, *and* five times as cold—just as I'm five times as rich as you are, *and* five times as clever!"[4]

Alice sighed and gave it up. "It's exactly like a riddle with no answer!" she thought.[5]

"Humpty Dumpty saw it too," the White Queen went on in a low voice, more as if she were talking to herself. "He came to the door with a corkscrew in his hand—"

"What did he want?" said the Red Queen.

"He said he *would* come in," the White Queen went on, "because he was looking for a hippopotamus. Now, as it happened, there wasn't such a thing in the house, that morning."

"Is there generally?" Alice asked in an astonished tone.

"Well, only on Thursdays," said the Queen.

"I know what he came for," said Alice: "he wanted to punish the fish, because—"[6]

Here the White Queen began again. "It was *such* a thunderstorm, you ca'n't think!" ("She *never* could, you know," said the Red Queen.) "And part of the roof came off, and ever so much thunder got in—and it went rolling round the room in great lumps[7]—and knocking over the tables and things—till I was so frightened, I couldn't remember my own name!"

Alice thought to herself "I never should *try* to remember my name in the middle of an accident! Where would be the use of it?" but she did not

4. It is easy to miss the Red Queen's implication here that *rich* and *clever* are opposites, like *warm* and *cold*.

5. "riddle with no answer": such as the Mad Hatter's unanswered riddle about the raven and the writing desk.

6. Alice is recalling Humpty's song (Chapter 6) in which he tells of taking a corkscrew and going to wake up the fish to punish them for not obeying him.

Alice may not have been interrupted in her remark. She may simply be recalling Humpty's poem in Chapter 6 with its inconclusive couplet:

The little fishes' answer was
"We cannot do it, Sir, because—"

7. Molly Martin speculates in a letter that when the White Queen remembers a time when the roof came off and thunder rolled around the room, this might refer to the lid of a chess box being removed and the pieces rattling around in the box as a player starts removing them or dumping them on the table.

8. "papers": papers around which locks of hair are wound for curling.

9. An obvious burlesque of the familiar nursery rhyme, "Hush-a-by baby, on the tree top . . ."

say this aloud, for fear of hurting the poor Queen's feelings.

"Your Majesty must excuse her," the Red Queen said to Alice, taking one of the White Queen's hands in her own, and gently stroking it: "she means well, but she ca'n't help saying foolish things, as a general rule."

The White Queen looked timidly at Alice, who felt she *ought* to say something kind, but really couldn't think of anything at the moment.

"She never was really well brought up," the Red Queen went on: "but it's amazing how good-tempered she is! Pat her on the head, and see how pleased she'll be!" But this was more than Alice had courage to do.

"A little kindness—and putting her hair in papers[8]—would do wonders with her—"

The White Queen gave a deep sigh, and laid her head on Alice's shoulder. "I *am* so sleepy!" she moaned.

"She's tired, poor thing!" said the Red Queen. "Smooth her hair—lend her your nightcap—and sing her a soothing lullaby."

"I haven't got a nightcap with me," said Alice, as she tried to obey the first direction: "and I don't know any soothing lullabies."

"I must do it myself, then," said the Red Queen, and she began:—[9]

> *"Hush-a-by lady, in Alice's lap!*
> *Till the feast's ready, we've time for a nap.*
> *When the feast's over, we'll go to the ball—*
> *Red Queen, and White Queen, and Alice, and all!*

"And now you know the words," she added, as she put her head down on Alice's other shoulder, "just sing it through to *me*. I'm getting sleepy, too." In another moment both Queens were fast asleep, and snoring loud.

"What *am* I to do?" exclaimed Alice, looking about in great perplexity, as first one round head, and then the other, rolled down from her shoulder, and lay like a heavy lump in her lap. "I don't think it *ever* happened before, that any one had to take care of two Queens asleep at once! No, not in all the History of England— it couldn't, you know, because there never was more than one Queen at a time. Do wake up, you heavy things!" she went on in an impatient tone; but there was no answer but a gentle snoring.

The snoring got more distinct every minute, and sounded more like a tune: at last she could even make out words, and she listened so eagerly that, when the two great heads suddenly vanished from her lap, she hardly missed them.

She was standing before an arched doorway, over which were the words "QUEEN ALICE" in large letters, and on each side of the arch there was a bell-handle; one was marked "Visitors' Bell," and the other "Servants' Bell."

"I'll wait till the song's over," thought Alice, "and then I'll ring the—the—*which* bell must I ring?" she went on, very much puzzled by the names. "I'm not a visitor, and I'm not a servant.

10. As Michael Hancher points out in his book, cited so often in previous notes, the Romanesque doorway in Tenniel's picture of this scene is identical with a doorway he drew for the title page of the bound volume of *Punch*, July–December, 1853. Hancher also reproduces the illustration as Tenniel originally drew it, showing Alice with a crinoline skirt that resembles the lower part of chess queens, in keeping with her crown, which is identical with the crowns of the chess pieces.

Carroll, who is on record as saying "I hate crinoline fashion," objected to five pictures by Tenniel that showed Alice in a crinoline skirt after she became a queen. Tenniel complied with Carroll's request by redrawing all five pictures. His original sketches for the five are reproduced in *Alice's Adventures in Wonderland*, by Justin Schiller and Selwyn Goodacre (privately printed, 1990).

The same Norman-arched doorway, Charles Lovett tells me, with its characteristic zigzag pattern, was drawn by Tenniel in his first commissioned book illustrations, the second series of the *Book of British Ballads*. The arch appears in the background of a scene accompanying a ballad called "King Estmere."

In her booklet *Alice's Adventures in Oxford* (1980) Mavis Batey says that the door is "clearly the door of her [Alice's] father's Chapter House"—the house where the business of Christ Church's cathedral is conducted.

There *ought* to be one marked 'Queen,' you know—"

Just then the door opened a little way, and a creature with a long beak put its head out for a moment and said "No admittance till the week after next!" and shut the door again with a bang.

Alice knocked and rang in vain for a long time; but at last a very old Frog, who was sitting under a tree, got up and hobbled slowly towards her: he was dressed in bright yellow, and had enormous boots on.[10]

"What is it, now?" the Frog said in a deep hoarse whisper.

Alice turned round, ready to find fault with anybody. "Where's the servant whose business it is to answer the door?" she began angrily.

"Which door?" said the Frog.

Alice almost stamped with irritation at the slow drawl in which he spoke. "*This* door, of course!"

The Frog looked at the door with his large dull eyes for a minute: then he went nearer and rubbed it with his thumb, as if he were trying whether the paint would come off: then he looked at Alice.

"To answer the door?" he said. "What's it been asking of?" He was so hoarse that Alice could scarcely hear him.[11]

"I don't know what you mean," she said.

"I speaks English, doesn't I?" the Frog went on. "Or are you deaf? What did it ask you?"

"Nothing!" Alice said impatiently. "I've been knocking at it!"

"Shouldn't do that—shouldn't do that—" the Frog muttered. "Wexes[12] it, you know." Then he went up and gave the door a kick with one of his great feet. "You let *it* alone," he panted out, as he hobbled back to his tree, "and it'll let *you* alone, you know."

At this moment the door was flung open, and a shrill voice was heard singing:—[13]

"To the Looking-Glass world it was Alice that said
'I've a sceptre in hand I've a crown on my head.
Let the Looking-Glass creatures, whatever they be
Come and dine with the Red Queen, the White
      Queen, and me!'"

And hundreds of voices joined in the chorus:—

"Then fill up the glasses as quick as you can,
And sprinkle the table with buttons and bran:
Put cats in the coffee, and mice in the tea—
And welcome Queen Alice with thirty-times-three!"

Then followed a confused noise of cheering, and Alice thought to herself "Thirty times three makes ninety. I wonder if any one's counting?" In a minute there was silence again, and the same shrill voice sang another verse:—

TENNIEL'S ORIGINAL DRAWING

11. The Frog has a frog in his throat.

12. Victorian Cockneys had a habit of exchanging initial *ws* for *vs* and *vs* for *ws*. "Wexes" is how Mr. Pickwick's servant Sam Weller pronounces "vexes" in *Pickwick Papers*.

13. This is a parody of Sir Walter Scott's song, "Bonny Dundee," from his play *The Doom of Devorgoil.*

Bonny Dundee

To the Lords of Convention 'twas
      Claver'se who spoke,
'Ere the King's crown shall fall there are
      crowns to be broke;
So let each Cavalier who loves honour
      and me,
Come follow the bonnet of Bonny
      Dundee.

   "Come fill up my cup, come fill up my
      can,
   Come saddle your horses, and call up
      your men;
   Come open the West Port, and let me
      gang free,
   And it's room for the bonnets of Bonny
      Dundee!"

Dundee he is mounted; he rides up the street,
The bells are rung backward, the drums they are beat;
But the Provost, douce man, said, "Just e'en let him be,
The Gude Town is weel quit of that Deil of Dundee."

Come fill up my cup, &c.

As he rode down the sanctified bends of the Bow,
Ilk carline was flyting and shaking her pow;
But the young plants of grace they look'd couthie and slee,
Thinking, "Luck to thy bonnet, thou Bonny Dundee!"

Come fill up my cup, &c.

With sour-featured Whigs the Grassmarket was cramm'd
As if half the West had set tryst to be hang'd;
There was spite in each look, there was fear in each e'e,
As they watch'd for the bonnets of Bonny Dundee.

Come fill up my cup, &c.

These cowls of Kilmarnock had spits and had spears,
And lang-hafted gullies to kill Cavaliers;
But they shrunk to close-heads, and the causeway was free,
At the toss of the bonnet of Bonny Dundee.

Come fill up my cup, &c.

He spurr'd to the foot of the proud Castle rock,
And with the gay Gordon he gallantly spoke;
"Let Mons Meg and her marrows speak twa words or three,
For the love of the bonnet of Bonny Dundee."

Come fill up my cup, &c.

"'O Looking-Glass creatures,' quoth Alice,
'draw near!
'Tis an honour to see me, a favour to hear:
'Tis a privilege high to have dinner and tea
Along with the Red Queen, the White Queen,
and me!'"*

Then came the chorus again:—

"Then fill up the glasses with treacle and ink,
Or anything else that is pleasant to drink:
Mix sand with the cider, and wool with the wine—
And welcome Queen Alice with ninety-times-nine!"

"Ninety times nine!" Alice repeated in despair. "Oh, that'll never be done! I'd better go in at once—" and in she went, and there was a dead silence the moment she appeared.

Alice glanced nervously along the table, as she walked up the large hall, and noticed that there were about fifty guests, of all kinds: some were animals, some birds, and there were even a few flowers among them. "I'm glad they've come without waiting to be asked," she thought: "I should never have known who were the right people to invite!"

There were three chairs at the head of the table: the Red and White Queens had already taken two of them, but the middle one was empty. Alice sat down in it, rather uncomfortable at the silence, and longing for some one to speak.

At last the Red Queen began. "You've missed the soup and fish," she said. "Put on the joint!" And the waiters set a leg of mutton before Alice, who looked at it rather anxiously, as she had never had to carve a joint before.

"You look a little shy: let me introduce you to that leg of mutton," said the Red Queen.

"Alice—Mutton: Mutton—Alice." The leg of mutton got up in the dish and made a little bow to Alice; and Alice returned the bow, not knowing whether to be frightened or amused.

"May I give you a slice?" she said, taking up the knife and fork, and looking from one Queen to the other.

"Certainly not," the Red Queen said, very decidedly: "it isn't etiquette to cut any one you've been introduced to.[14] Remove the joint!" And the waiters carried it off, and brought a large plum-pudding in its place.

"I wo'n't be introduced to the pudding, please," Alice said rather hastily, "or we shall get no dinner at all. May I give you some?"

But the Red Queen looked sulky, and growled "Pudding—Alice: Alice—Pudding. Remove the pudding!", and the waiters took it away so quickly that Alice couldn't return its bow.

However, she didn't see why the Red Queen should be the only one to give orders; so, as an

The Gordon demands of him which way he goes—
"Where'er shall direct me the shade of Montrose!
Your Grace in short space shall hear tidings of me,
Or that low lies the bonnet of Bonny Dundee.

   Come fill up my cup, &c.

"There are hills beyond Pentland, and lands beyond Forth,
If there's lords in the Lowlands, there's chiefs in the North;
There are wild Duniewassals, three thousand times three,
Will cry hoigh! for the bonnet of Bonny Dundee.

   Come fill up my cup, &c.

"There's brass on the target of barken'd bull-hide;
There's steel in the scabbard that dangles beside;
The brass shall be burnish'd, the steel shall flash free,
At a toss of the bonnet of Bonny Dundee.

   Come fill up my cup, &c.

"Away to the hills, to the caves, to the rocks—
Ere I own an usurper, I'll couch with the fox;
And tremble, false Whigs, in the midst of your glee,
You have not seen the last of my bonnet and me!"

   Come fill up my cup, &c.

He waved his proud hand, and the trumpets were blown,
The kettle-drums clash'd, and the horsemen rode on,
Till on Ravelston's cliffs and on Clermiston's lee,
Died away the wild war-notes of Bonny Dundee.

*Come fill up my cup, come fill up my
can,*

*Come saddle the horses and call up the
men,*

*Come open your gates, and let me gae
free,*

*For it's up with the bonnets of Bonny
Dundee!*

14. No Victorian reader would miss
the pun. *To cut* is to ignore someone
you know. *Brewer's Dictionary of
Phrase and Fable* distinguishes four
kinds of cuts: the cut direct (staring at
an acquaintance and pretending not
to know him or her); the cut indirect
(pretending not to see someone);
the cut sublime (admiring something,
such as the top of a building, until an
acquaintance has walked by); and the
cut informal (stooping to adjust a
shoelace).

15. Roger Green thought Alice's dialogue with the pudding might have
been suggested to Carroll by a cartoon in *Punch* (January 19, 1861)
showing a plum pudding standing up
in its dish and saying to a diner,
"Allow me to disagree with you."
Michael Hancher reproduces the
Punch cartoon in his book on Tenniel, and points out the reappearance
of the pudding, its legs in the air, at
the lower left corner of the chapter's
last Tenniel illustration.

experiment, she called out "Waiter! Bring back
the pudding!" and there it was again in a
moment, like a conjuring-trick. It was so large
that she couldn't help feeling a *little* shy with it,
as she had been with the mutton: however, she
conquered her shyness by a great effort, and cut
a slice and handed it to the Red Queen.

"What impertinence!" said the Pudding. "I
wonder how you'd like it, if I were to cut a slice
out of *you*, you creature!"[15]

It spoke in a thick, suety sort of voice, and
Alice hadn't a word to say in reply: she could
only sit and look at it and gasp.

"Make a remark," said the Red Queen: "it's
ridiculous to leave all the conversation to the
pudding!"

"Do you know, I've had such a quantity of
poetry repeated to me to-day," Alice began, a
little frightened at finding that, the moment she
opened her lips, there was dead silence, and all
eyes were fixed upon her; "and it's a very curious
thing, I think—every poem was about fishes in
some way. Do you know why they're so fond of
fishes, all about here?"

She spoke to the Red Queen, whose answer
was a little wide of the mark. "As to fishes," she
said, very slowly and solemnly, putting her
mouth close to Alice's ear, "her White Majesty
knows a lovely riddle—all in poetry—all about
fishes. Shall she repeat it?"

"Her Red Majesty's very kind to mention it,"
the White Queen murmured into Alice's other
ear, in a voice like the cooing of a pigeon. "It
would be *such* a treat! May I?"

"Please do," Alice said very politely.

The White Queen laughed with delight, and
stroked Alice's cheek. Then she began:

" 'First, the fish must be caught.'
That is easy: a baby, I think, could have caught it.
  'Next, the fish must be bought.'
That is easy: a penny, I think, would have bought it.

  'Now cook me the fish!'
That is easy, and will not take more than a minute.
  'Let it lie in a dish!'
That is easy, because it already is in it.

  'Bring it here! Let me sup!'
It is easy to set such a dish on the table.
  'Take the dish-cover up!'
Ah, that is so hard that I fear I'm unable!

  For it holds it like glue—
Holds the lid to the dish, while it lies in the middle:
  Which is easiest to do,
Un-dish-cover the fish, or dishcover the riddle?"[16]

"Take a minute to think about it, and then guess," said the Red Queen. "Meanwhile, we'll drink your health—Queen Alice's health!" she screamed at the top of her voice, and all the guests began drinking it directly, and very queerly they managed it: some of them put their glasses upon their heads like extinguishers,[17] and drank all that trickled down their faces—others upset the decanters, and drank the wine as it ran off the edges of the table—and three of them (who looked like kangaroos) scrambled into the dish of roast mutton, and began eagerly lapping up the gravy, "just like pigs in a trough!" thought Alice.

"You ought to return thanks in a neat speech," the Red Queen said, frowning at Alice as she spoke.

"We must support you, you know," the White Queen whispered, as Alice got up to do it, very obediently, but a little frightened.

16. The answer: an oyster. *The Lewis Carroll Handbook* (1962) reveals (p. 95) that a four-stanza answer to the White Queen's riddle, in the same meter as the riddle, appeared in the English periodical *Fun*, October 30, 1878, p. 175. The answer had been previously submitted to Carroll, who polished up the meter for the anonymous author. The answer's final stanza, as quoted in the *Handbook*, is:

  Get an oyster-knife strong,
Insert it 'twixt cover and dish in the
      middle;
  Then you shall before long
Un-dish-cover the OYSTERS—dish-cover
      the riddle!

17. The reference is to candle extinguishers, small hollow cones used for snuffing out candles to prevent the smoke fumes from circulating around the room.

"Thank you very much," she whispered in reply, "but I can do quite well without."

"That wouldn't be at all the thing," the Red Queen said very decidedly: so Alice tried to submit to it with a good grace.

("And they *did* push so!" she said afterwards, when she was telling her sister the history of the feast. "You would have thought they wanted to squeeze me flat!")

In fact it was rather difficult for her to keep in her place while she made her speech: the two Queens pushed her so, one on each side, that they nearly lifted her up into the air. "I rise to return thanks—" Alice began: and she really *did* rise as she spoke, several inches; but she got hold of the edge of the table, and managed to pull herself down again.

"Take care of yourself!" screamed the White Queen, seizing Alice's hair with both her hands. "Something's going to happen!"

And then (as Alice afterwards described it) all sorts of things happened in a moment. The candles all grew up to the ceiling, looking something like a bed of rushes with fireworks at the top. As to the bottles, they each took a pair of plates, which they hastily fitted on as wings, and so, with forks for legs, went fluttering about in all directions: "and very like birds they look," Alice thought to herself, as well as she could in the dreadful confusion that was beginning.

At this moment she heard a hoarse laugh at her side, and turned to see what was the matter with the White Queen; but, instead of the Queen, there was the leg of mutton sitting in the chair. "Here I am!" cried a voice from the soup-tureen, and Alice turned again, just in time to see the Queen's broad good-natured face grinning at her for a moment over the edge of the tureen, before she disappeared into the soup.[18]

There was not a moment to be lost. Already several of the guests were lying down in the dishes, and the soup-ladle was walking up the table towards Alice's chair, and beckoning to her impatiently to get out of its way.

"I ca'n't stand this any longer!" she cried, as she jumped up and seized the tablecloth with both hands: one good pull, and plates, dishes, guests, and candles came crashing down together in a heap on the floor.

"And as for *you*," she went on, turning fiercely upon the Red Queen, whom she considered as the cause of all the mischief—but the Queen was no longer at her side—she had suddenly dwindled down to the size of a little doll, and was

18. The White Queen has moved away from Alice to QR6; an illegal move in an orthodox chess game because it does not take the White King out of check.

19. This is Alice's capture of the Red Queen. It results in a legitimate checkmate of the Red King, who has slept throughout the entire chess problem without moving. Alice's victory gives a faint moral to the story, for the white pieces are good and gentle characters in contrast to the fierce vindictive temperaments of the red pieces. The checkmate ends the dream but leaves open the question of whether the dream was Alice's or the Red King's.

now on the table, merrily running round and round after her own shawl, which was trailing behind her.

At any other time, Alice would have felt surprised at this, but she was far too much excited to be surprised at anything *now*. "As for *you*," she repeated, catching hold of the little creature in the very act of jumping over a bottle which had just lighted upon the table, "I'll shake you into a kitten, that I will!"[19]

Shaking

She took her off the table as she spoke, and shook her backwards and forwards with all her might.

The Red Queen made no resistance whatever: only her face grew very small, and her eyes got large and green: and still, as Alice went on shaking her, she kept on growing shorter—and fatter—and softer—and rounder—and—

1. The American writer and critic Everett Bleiler, in a front-page article "Alice Through the Zodiac" (*Book World*, August 3, 1997), makes a curious conjecture. Because Carroll stretched his second Alice book to twelve chapters by making this and the next chapter extremely short, is it possible he had the twelve zodiac signs in mind? For example, the Tweedle twins may allude to Gemini, the Lion to Leo, the Sheep to Aries, the Goat to Capricorn, the White Knight to Sagittarius, Humpty to Libra, and so on. Striking though these correlations are, few Carrollians have taken Bleiler's conjecture seriously. They point out that Carroll had no interest in astrology and that he wanted his second *Alice* book to have the same number of chapters as the first.

1. Rose Franklin, one of Carroll's child-friends, recalled in a memoir that Carroll had said to her, "I cannot decide what to make the Red Queen turn into." Rose replied: "She looks so cross, please turn her into the Black Kitten."

"That will do splendidly," Carroll is reported to have said, "and the White Queen shall be the White Kitten."

Recall that in Chapter 1, before she fell asleep, Alice said to the black kitten, "Let's pretend that you're Red Queen."

It really *was* a kitten, after all.[1]

12

Which Dreamed It?

"Your Red Majesty shouldn't purr so loud," Alice said, rubbing her eyes, and addressing the kitten, respectfully, yet with some severity. "You woke me out of oh! such a nice dream! And you've been along with me, Kitty—all through the Looking-glass world. Did you know it, dear?"

It is a very inconvenient habit of kittens (Alice had once made the remark) that, whatever you say to them, they *always* purr. "If they would only purr for 'yes,' and mew for 'no,' or any rule of that sort," she had said, "so that one could keep up a conversation! But how *can* you talk with a person if they *always* say the same thing?"[1]

On this occasion the kitten only purred: and it was impossible to guess whether it meant "yes" or "no."

So Alice hunted among the chessmen on the table till she had found the Red Queen: then she went down on her knees on the hearth-rug, and put the kitten and the Queen to look at each other. "Now, Kitty!" she cried, clapping her hands triumphantly. "Confess that was what you turned into!"

("But it wouldn't look at it," she said, when she was explaining the thing afterwards to her sister: "it turned away its head, and pretended

1. Alice's point is fundamental in information theory, Gerald Weinberg says in a letter. There is no one-value logic—no way to record or transmit information without at least a binary distinction between yes and no, or true and false. In computers the distinction is handled by the on-off switches of their circuitry.

2. Why did Alice think Humpty was Dinah? Ellis Hillman, writing on "Dinah, the Cheshire Cat, and Humpty Dumpty," in *Jabberwocky* (Winter 1977), offers an ingenious theory. "I'm one that has spoken to a King, *I* am," Humpty said to Alice. As we know from the old proverb that Alice quoted in Chapter 8 of the previous book, a cat may look at a king.

Fred Madden, in his article cited in Chapter 3, Notes 11 and 18, points out that when the initials of Humpty Dumpty are reversed, they become D. H., the first and last letters of "Dinah."

not to see it: but it looked a *little* ashamed of itself, so I think it *must* have been the Red Queen.")

"Sit up a little more stiffly, dear!" Alice cried with a merry laugh. "And curtsey while you're thinking what to—what to purr. It saves time, remember!" And she caught it up and gave it one little kiss, "just in honour of its having been a Red Queen."

"Snowdrop, my pet!" she went on, looking over her shoulder at the White Kitten, which was still patiently undergoing its toilet, "when *will* Dinah have finished with your White Majesty, I wonder? That must be the reason you were so untidy in my dream.—Dinah! Do you know that you're scrubbing a White Queen? Really, it's most disrespectful of you!

"And what did *Dinah* turn to, I wonder?" she prattled on, as she settled comfortably down, with one elbow on the rug, and her chin in her hand, to watch the kittens. "Tell me, Dinah, did you turn to Humpty Dumpty?[2] I *think* you did—

however, you'd better not mention it to your friends just yet, for I'm not sure.

"By the way, Kitty, if only you'd been really with me in my dream, there was one thing you *would* have enjoyed—I had such a quantity of poetry said to me, all about fishes![3] Tomorrow morning you shall have a real treat. All the time you're eating your breakfast, I'll repeat 'The Walrus and the Carpenter' to you; and then you can make believe it's oysters, dear!

"Now, Kitty, let's consider who it was that dreamed it all. This is a serious question, my dear, and you should *not* go on licking your paw like that—as if Dinah hadn't washed you this morning! You see, Kitty, it *must* have been either me or the Red King. He was part of my dream, of course—but then I was part of his dream, too! *Was* it the Red King, Kitty? You were his wife, my dear, so you ought to know—Oh, Kitty, *do* help to settle it! I'm sure your paw can wait!" But the provoking kitten only began on the other paw, and pretended it hadn't heard the question.

Which do *you* think it was?

3. The term *queer fish*, meaning someone considered odd, was current in Carroll's day. In stressing fish in this book, was Carroll thinking of all the odd fish it contained? Or that there is something "fishy" about his nonsense? Coincidentally, *fish* is slang in the United States for a mediocre chess player.

A boat, beneath a sunny sky
Lingering onward dreamily
In an evening of July—

Children three that nestle near,
Eager eye and willing ear,
Pleased a simple tale to hear—

Long has paled that sunny sky:
Echoes fade and memories die:
Autumn frosts have slain July.

Still she haunts me, phantomwise,
Alice moving under skies
Never seen by waking eyes.

Children yet, the tale to hear,
Eager eye and willing ear,
Lovingly shall nestle near.

In a Wonderland they lie,
Dreaming as the days go by,
Dreaming as the summers die:

Ever drifting down the stream—
Lingering in the golden gleam—
Life, what is it but a dream?[1]

1. In this terminal poem, one of Carroll's best, he recalls that July 4 boating expedition up the Thames on which he first told the story of *Alice's Adventures in Wonderland* to the three Liddell girls. The poem echoes the themes of winter and death that run through the prefatory poem of *Through the Looking-Glass*. It is the song of the White Knight, remembering Alice as she was before she turned away, with tearless and eager eyes, to run down the hill and leap the last brook into womanhood. The poem is an acrostic, the initial letters of the lines spelling Alice's full name.

Matthew Hodgart wrote from England to suggest that in this stanza of his acrostic poem Carroll was consciously echoing the sentiments of that anonymous canon, well known in England at the time:

> *Row, row, row your boat*
> *Gently down the stream;*
> *Merrily, merrily, merrily, merrily,*
> *Life is but a dream.*

Ralph Lutts, a correspondent who makes the same suggestion, points out that "merrily" in the canon links to the "merry crew" in the prefatory poem of the first *Alice* book.

The real world and the "eerie" state of dreaming alternate throughout Carroll's two *Sylvie and Bruno* books. "Either I've been dreaming about Sylvie," he says to himself in

Chapter 2 of the first book, "and this is reality. Or else I've been with Sylvie, and this is the dream! Is Life itself a dream, I wonder?"

The prefatory poem of *Sylvie and Bruno*, an acrostic on the name of Isa Bowman, conveys the same theme:

> *Is all our Life, then, but a dream*
> *Seen faintly in the golden gleam*
> *Athwart Time's dark resistless*
> *stream?*

Bowed to the earth with bitter woe,
Or laughing at some raree-show,
We flutter idly to and fro.

Man's little Day in haste we spend,
And, from its merry noontide, send
No glance to meet the silent end.

Morris Glazer wonders in a letter if Carroll intended "Alice" to begin the poem's middle line, thus putting her at the center of the poem as she was central in his life.

The Wasp in a Wig

A "Suppressed" Episode of
*Through the Looking-Glass and
What Alice Found There*

Contents

Preface

In 1974 the London auctioneering firm of Sotheby Parke Bernet and Company listed, inconspicuously, the following item in their June 3 catalog:

Dodgson (C.L.) "Lewis Carroll." Galley proofs for a suppressed portion of "Through the Looking-Glass," slip 64–67 and portions of 63 and 68, with autograph revisions in black ink and note in the author's purple ink that the extensive passage is to be omitted.

The present portion contains an incident in which Alice meets a bad-tempered wasp, incorporating a poem of five stanzas, beginning "When I was young, my ringlets waved." It was to have appeared following "A very few steps brought her to the edge of the brook" on page 183 of the first edition. The proofs were bought at the sale of the author's furniture, personal effects, and library, Oxford, 1898, and are apparently unrecorded and unpublished.

The word "apparently" in the last sentence was an understatement. Not only had the suppressed portion not been published, but Carroll experts did not even know it had been set in type, let alone preserved. The discovery that it still existed was an event of major significance to Carrollians —indeed, to all students of English literature. Now, more than one hundred years after *Through the Looking-Glass* was first set in type, the long-lost episode receives its first major publication.

Until 1974 nothing was known about the missing portion beyond what Stuart Dodgson Collingwood, a nephew of Lewis Carroll, had said about it in his 1898 biography of his uncle, *The Life and Letters of Lewis Carroll*. Collingwood wrote:

The story, as originally written, contained thirteen chapters, but the published book consisted of twelve only. The omitted chapter introduced a wasp, in the character of a judge or barrister, I suppose, since Mr. Tenniel wrote that "a *wasp* in a *wig* is altogether beyond the appliances of art." Apart from difficulties of illustration, the "wasp" chapter was not considered to be up to the level of the rest of the book, and this was probably the principal reason of its being left out.

These remarks were followed by a facsimile of a letter, dated June 1, 1870, that John Tenniel had sent to Carroll. (The letter is here reproduced on pages 295–97.) In Tenniel's sketch for the railway carriage scene, Alice sits opposite a goat and a man dressed in white paper while the Guard observes Alice through opera glasses. In his final drawing Tenniel gave the man in the paper hat the face of Benjamin Disraeli, the British prime minister he so often caricatured in *Punch*.

Carroll accepted both of Tenniel's suggestions. The "old lady," presumably a character in the original version of Chapter 3, vanished from the chapter and from Tenniel's illustration, and the Wasp vanished from the book. In *The Annotated Alice* my note on this ends: "Alas, nothing of the missing chapter has survived." Collingwood himself had not read the episode. We know this because he assumed, mistakenly as it turned out, that if the Wasp wore a wig he must have been a judge or lawyer.

Carroll left no record of his own final opinion of the episode or the poem it contained. He did, however, carefully preserve the galleys, and it seems likely that he intended to do something with them someday. It was Carroll himself, remember, who decided to publish his first version of *Alice in Wonderland*, the manuscript he had hand-lettered and illustrated for Alice Liddell. Many of his early poems, printed in obscure periodicals or not published at all, found their way eventually into his books. Even if Carroll had no specific plans for making use of the Wasp episode or its poem, it is hard to believe he would not have been pleased to know it would find eventual publication.

After Carroll's death in 1898 the galleys were bought by an unknown person and—for the present at least—we know little about who owned them until Sotheby's put them up for auction. They are not listed in the 1898 catalogs of Carroll's effects, apparently because they were included in a miscellaneous lot of unidentified items. "The property of a gentleman" is how Sotheby's labeled them in its catalog. Sotheby's does not disclose the identities of vendors who desire to remain anonymous, but they tell me that the galleys had been passed on to the vendor by an older member of his family.

The galleys were bought by John Fleming, a Manhattan rare book dealer, for Norman Armour, Jr., also of New York City. It was Mr. Armour's gracious consent to permit publication of these galleys that makes this book possible. What more need be said in the way of thanks?

Interior of Railway carriage.
(1ˢᵗ Class). Alice on seat
by herself. Man in white
paper. reading, & Goat.
very Shadowy & indistinct
sitting opposite— (with opera glass)
looking in at windows.

My dear Dodgson.

I think that where
the jump occurs in the
Railway Scene you might
very well make Alice lay
hold of the Goat's beard
as being the object nearest
to her hand – instead of
the old lady's hair. The
jerk would naturally
throw them together.
Don't think me brutal. but
I am bound to say that
the 'wasp' chapter doesn't
interest me in the least; &
~~that~~ I can't see my way
to a picture. If you
want to shorten the book.

*I can't help thinking —
with all submission —
that there is your oppor-
tunity.
In an agony of haste
Yours sincerely
J Tenniel.*

*Portsdown Road.
June 1. 1870*

Facsimile of Tenniel's letter to Dodgson, with
a transcription.

My dear Dodgson.

I think that when the *jump* occurs in the Railway scene
you might very well make Alice lay hold of the Goat's *beard*
as being the object nearest to her hand—instead of the old
lady's hair. The jerk would naturally throw them together.

Don't think me brutal, but I am bound to say that the '*wasp*'
chapter doesn't interest me in the least, & I can't see my
way to a picture. If you want to shorten the book, I can't
help thinking—with all submission—that *there* is your
opportunity.

In an agony of haste

Yours sincerely
J. Tenniel.

Portsdown Road.
June 1, 1870

Introduction

Before the Wasp episode came to light, most students of
Carroll assumed that the lost episode was adjacent to, at
least not far from, the railway carriage scene. This was
because Tenniel, in his letter of complaint, seemed to link the
two incidents. In Chapter 3, where Alice leaps the first brook
and the train jumps over the second, Alice encounters a variety of insects, including bees the size of elephants. Was it not
appropriate that she would meet a wasp in this region of the
chessboard?

That Carroll did not intend Alice to come upon the Wasp
so early in the chess game is evident at once from the numbers on the galleys, and from what Alice thought when the
Wasp told her how his ringlets used to wave. "A curious idea
came into Alice's head. Almost every one she had met had
repeated poetry to her, and she thought she would try if the
Wasp couldn't do it too." The first person to recite poetry to
Alice is Tweedledee, and the second is Humpty Dumpty. The
lost episode, therefore, had to occur later than Chapter 6.

The incomplete first line of the galleys leaves no doubt
that Sotheby's catalog correctly indicates where Carroll had
intended the Wasp episode to go. (The spot is shown by the
arrow in the reproduction of page 183 of the first edition of
Through the Looking-Glass, here printed on page 308.) Alice
has just waved her final farewell to the White Knight, then
gone down the hill to leap the last brook and become a
Queen. "A very few steps brought her to the edge of the
brook." Instead of a period there was a comma. The sentence
continued as at the top of the first galley: "and she was just

going to spring over, when she heard a deep sigh, which seemed to come from the wood behind her."

Both Tenniel and Collingwood called the episode a "chapter," but there are difficulties with this view. The galleys give no indication that they are anything but an excerpt from Chapter 8, and it seems unlikely that Carroll would have wanted his second *Alice* book to have thirteen chapters when the first book had twelve. It is Morton Cohen's belief that Tenniel, writing "in an agony of haste," used the word "chapter" when he meant episode. Collingwood's remarks are easily explained as elaborations of how he interpreted Tenniel's letters. (There must have been at least one other Tenniel letter available to him, because the remark of Tenniel's that he quotes about a wasp in a wig being "beyond the appliances of art" does not appear in the letter he reproduces in facsimile.)

One might argue that had the Wasp episode belonged to the White Knight chapter, the chapter would have been uncommonly long, and would not Tenniel have written that the episode should be removed to "shorten the chapter" rather than "shorten the book"? On the other hand, the fact that the chapter was too long may have been another reason why Carroll was willing to excise the episode. Unfortunately no other galleys for the book are known to have survived, so we are forced to rely on indirect evidence for deciding which view is correct.

Edward Guiliano favors the view that Tenniel had "episode" in mind. He supports the arguments already presented, and also feels that the incidents of the episode would have added thematic unity to the White Knight chapter. After conversing with the White Knight, an upper-class gentleman still in his vigor, Alice meets a lower-class worker in his declining years.* She waves good-bye to the White

---

*The White Knight, so far as Carroll's text alone is concerned, could have been a young man in his twenties. Tenniel, with Carroll's approval, drew him as an elderly gentleman, though certainly not as old as the "aged aged man" about whom the Knight sings.

Knight with a handkerchief; the Wasp has a handkerchief around his face. The White Knight talks about bees and honey; the Wasp thinks Alice is a bee and asks her if she has any honey. Even the pun about the comb, Guiliano believes, is not quite so feeble in the context of the chapter as originally planned. These and other incidents in the Wasp episode link it to the White Knight chapter in ways that suggest it was not intended to stand alone.

Was the Wasp episode worth preserving? It was, of course, eminently worth saving for historical reasons, but that is not what I mean. Does it have intrinsic merit? Tenniel said it did not interest him in the least, and many who have recently read the episode agree that it is not (in Collingwood's words) "up to the level of the rest of the book." Peter Heath feels that one reason the episode lacks the vivacity of other parts of the book is that it repeats so many themes that occur elsewhere. Alice had a previous conversation with an unhappy insect, the Gnat, in Chapter 3. In the chapter following the Wasp episode Alice converses with another elderly lower-class male, the Frog. The Wasp's criticisms of Alice's face are reminiscent of Humpty Dumpty's criticisms. Alice's attempts to repair the Wasp's disheveled appearance parallel her attempts to remedy the untidyness of the White Queen in Chapter 5. There are other echoes of familiar themes that Professor Heath has noted. "It's as if Carroll's inventiveness was flagging a bit," he writes in a letter, "and the momentum of the narrative had temporarily been lost."

All this may be true, but I am convinced that if the episode is read carefully, then reread several times on later occasions, its merit will steadily become more apparent. First of all it is unmistakably Carrollian in its general tone, its humor, its wordplay, and its nonsense. The Wasp's remark "Let it stop there!" and his observation that Alice's eyes are so close together (compared with his own, of course) that she could have done as well with one eye instead of two are both pure Carroll. The wordplay may not be up to Carroll's best, but we must remember that he frequently had a book set in type long before he began to work in earnest on revisions. If the

Wasp episode was removed from the book before Carroll began to polish the galleys, that would explain why the writing seems cruder at times than elsewhere in the book.

Two features of the episode impress me as having special interest: the extraordinary skill with which Carroll, in just a few pages of dialogue, brings out the personality of a waspish but somehow lovable old man, and Alice's unfailing gentleness toward him.

Although Alice is usually kind and respectful toward the curious creatures she meets in her two dreams, no matter how unpleasant the creatures are, this is not always the case. In the pool of tears she twice offends the Mouse, by telling him that her cat chases mice and that a neighbor's dog likes to kill rats. A short time later, after the Caucus-race, she forgets herself again and insults the assembled birds by remarking on how much her cat likes to eat birds. And remember Alice's sharp kick that sends Bill, the Lizard, out the chimney? ("There goes Bill!")

In *Through the Looking-Glass*, Alice (now six months older) is not quite so thoughtless, but there is no episode in the book in which she treats a disagreeable creature with such remarkable patience. In no other episode, in either book, does her character come through so vividly as that of an intelligent, polite, considerate little girl. It is an episode in which extreme youth confronts extreme age. Although the Wasp is constantly critical of Alice, not once does she cease to sympathize with him.

Need I spell it out? We are told how much Alice, the white pawn, longs to become a Queen. We know how easily she could have leaped the final brook to occupy the last row of the chessboard. Yet Alice does not make the move when she hears the sigh of distress behind her. When the Wasp responds crossly to her kind remarks, she excuses his ill-temper with the understanding that it is his pain that makes him cross. After she has helped him around the tree to a warmer side, his response is "Can't you leave a body alone?" Unoffended, Alice offers to read to him from the wasp newspaper at his feet.

Although the Wasp continues to criticize, when Alice leaves him she is "quite pleased that she had gone back and given a few minutes to making the poor old creature comfortable." Carroll surely must have wanted to show Alice performing a final deed of charity that would justify her approaching coronation, a reward that Carroll, a pious Christian and patriotic Englishman, would have regarded as a crown of righteousness. Alice comes through as such an admirable, appealing little girl that Professor Guiliano discovered to his surprise that reading the episode altered a bit his response to the entire book.

The old man, with his waspish temper and his aching bones, is also, of course, a genuine insect. Female wasps (queens and workers) prey on other insects, such as caterpillars, spiders, and flies, which they first paralyze by stinging them. With their strong mandibles they remove the victim's head, legs, and wings; then the body is chewed to a pulp to give as food to their larvae. It may not be accidental that Carroll's insect belongs to a social structure that includes fierce, powerful queens, like the queens of chess and many former queens of England.

In contrast, male wasps (drones) do not sting. In some species the male, if you seize him in your hand, will try to frighten you into dropping him by going through all the movements of stinging. (John Burroughs likened this bluffing to a soldier in battle who tries to frighten the enemy by firing blank cartridges.) Male wasps, like Carroll's Wasp, although they look formidable, resemble the kings of chess. They are amiable, harmless creatures.

Except for a few hibernating queens, wasps are summer insects and do not survive the winter. During the hot months they work furiously to provide for their offspring; then they stiffen and die with the approach of autumn's cold winds. This is how Oliver Goldsmith phrases it in his marvelous, now-forgotten *History of the Earth and Animated Nature:*

While the summer heats continue, they [wasps] are bold, voracious, and enterprising; but as the sun withdraws, it seems to rob them of their courage and activity. In proportion as the cold increases, they are seen to become more domestic; they seldom leave the nest, they make but short adventures from home, they flutter about in the noon-day heats, and soon after return chilled and feeble. . . . As the cold increases they no longer find sufficient warmth in their nests, which grow hateful to them, and they fly to seek it in the corners of houses, and places that receive an artificial heat. But the winter is still insupportable; and, before the new year begins, they wither and die.

Like so many elderly people, the Wasp has happy memories of a childhood when his tresses waved. In five stanzas of doggerel he tells Alice about his terrible mistake of allowing friends to persuade him to shave his head for a wig. All his subsequent unhappiness is blamed on this foolish indiscretion. He knows his present appearance is ridiculous. His wig does not fit. He fails to keep it neat. He resents being laughed at. The Wasp is Oliver Wendell Holmes's "last leaf," enduring the community's ridicule as he clings "to the old forsaken bough."

Although the Wasp pretends not to want Alice to help him in any way, his spirits are lifted by her visit and the opportunity to tell his sad tale. Indeed, before Alice leaves he has become animated and talkative. When she finally says goodbye he responds with "Thank ye." It is the only thanks Alice gets from anyone she meets on the mirror's other side.

The fashion of wearing wigs reached absurd heights in France and England in the seventeenth and eighteenth centuries. During Queen Anne's reign almost every upper-class man and woman in England wore a wig, and one could instantly tell a man's profession by the kind of wig he sported. Some male wigs hung below the shoulders to cover both back and chest. The craze began to fade under Queen Victoria. In Carroll's time it had all but vanished, except for the ceremonial wigs of judges and barristers, the wigs of actors, and the wearing of wigs to conceal baldness. The Wasp's wig is clearly a mark of his advanced age even though he started wearing it when young.

Why a yellow wig? If the Wasp's ringlets were yellow it would be natural for him to substitute a yellow wig, but Carroll seems to emphasize the color for other reasons. He calls it "bright yellow." And when Alice first meets the Wasp his wig is covered by a yellow handkerchief tied around his head and face.

Both *Alice* books contain inside jokes about persons the real Alice, Alice Liddell, knew. It is possible, I suppose, that Carroll's Wasp pokes fun at someone, perhaps an elderly tradesman in the area, who sported an unkempt yellow wig that resembled seaweed.

Another theory has to do with the yellow color of many wasps in England. The American term *yellow-jackets*, for a large class of social insects that were (and are) called hornets, may have been in Carroll's mind. The term had spread to England, and numerous varieties of British wasps have bright yellow stripes circling their black bodies. Wasp antennae are composed of tiny joints that also could be called ringlets. A young wasp's antennae would certainly wave, curl, and crinkle, as the poem has it. If cut off, perhaps they would not grow again.

There may have been wasps in Oxford, familiar to Carroll and Alice Liddell, with black heads circled by a yellow stripe that would look for all the world like a yellow handkerchief tied around the insect's face. Even aside from a yellow stripe, a wasp's face does resemble a human face done up in a hand-kerchief, the knot's ends sticking up from the top of the head like two antennae.* Professor Heath recalls having had just such thoughts himself when he was a child in England.

A third theory is that the Wasp, with his yellow handkerchief above a yellow wig, parallels Alice after she becomes a queen—the gold crown on top of her flaxen hair.

A fourth theory (of course these theories are not mutually

---

*Lewis Carroll's library at the time of his death included a book by John G. Wood called *A World of Little Wonders: or Insects at Home*. The chapter on wasps describes a common variety of social wasp as having antennae with a first joint that is "yellow in front."

exclusive) is that Carroll chose yellow because of its long association in literature and common speech with autumn and old age. Yellow is the complexion of the elderly, especially if they suffer from jaundice. It is the color of fall leaves, of ripe corn, of paper "yellowed with age." "Sorrow, thought, and great distress," wrote Chaucer (in *Romance of the Rose*), "made her full yellow."

Shakespeare frequently used yellow as a symbol of age. Professor Cohen reports that Carroll, at least twice in his letters, quotes the following remark from *Macbeth*: "My way of life is fallen into the sere, the yellow leaf." These lines from Shakespeare's Sonnet 73 are particularly apt:

> *That time of year thou mayst in me behold*
> *When yellow leaves, or none, or few, do hang*
> *Upon those boughs which shake against the cold . . .*

Through the Looking-Glass opens and closes with poems that speak of winter and death. The dream itself probably occurs in November, while Alice sits in front of a blazing fire and snow is "kissing" the windowpanes. "Autumn frosts have slain July" is how Carroll puts it in his terminal poem, recalling that sunny July 4 boating trip on the Isis when he first told Alice the story of her trip to Wonderland.

Although Carroll was not yet forty when he wrote his second *Alice* book, he was twenty years older than Alice Liddell, the child-friend he adored above any other. In the book's prefatory poem he speaks of himself and Alice as "half a life asunder." He reminds Alice that it will not be long until the "bitter tidings" summon her to "unwelcome bed," and he likens himself to an older child fretting at the approach of the final bedtime.

Carroll scholars believe that Carroll intended his White Knight—that awkward, inventive gentleman with the mild blue eyes and kindly smile who treated Alice with such uncharacteristic courtesy for someone behind the mirror—to be a parody of himself. Is it possible that Carroll regarded his Wasp as a parody of himself forty years later? Professor Cohen has convinced me that it is not possible. Carroll prided himself on being a Victorian gentleman. Under no circumstances would he have associated himself with a lower-class drone. Nonetheless, it seems to me that Carroll could not have written this episode without being acutely aware of the fact that the chasm of age between Alice and the Wasp resembled the chasm that separated Alice Liddell from the middle-aged teller of the story.

I am persuaded that Carroll, perhaps not consciously, spoke through his Wasp like a ventriloquist talking through a dummy when he has the Wasp exclaim—in a way that seems strangely out of place in the dialogue—"Worrity, worrity! There never was such a child!"

Where Carroll intended the episode to appear
(reproduction of first edition).

comes of having so many things hung round the
horse——" So she went on talking to herself,
as she watched the horse walking leisurely along
the road, and the Knight tumbling off, first on
one side and then on the other. After the
fourth or fifth tumble he reached the turn, and
then she waved her handkerchief to him, and
waited till he was out of sight.

"I hope it encouraged him," she said, as
she turned to run down the hill: "and now
for the last brook, and to be a Queen! How
grand it sounds!" A very few steps brought
her to the edge of the brook. "The Eighth
Square at last!" she cried as she bounded across,

.   .   .   .   .   .

.   .   .   .   .   .

.   .   .   .   .   .

and threw herself down to rest on a lawn as
soft as moss, with little flower-beds dotted about
it here and there. "Oh, how glad I am to get
here! And what *is* this on my head?" she

The Wasp in a Wig

. . . And she was just going to spring over, when she heard a deep sigh, which seemed to come from the wood behind her.

"There's somebody *very* unhappy there," she thought, looking anxiously back to see what was the matter. Something like a very old man (only that his face was more like a wasp) was sitting on the ground, leaning against a tree, all huddled up together, and shivering as if he were very cold.

"I don't *think* I can be of any use to him," was Alice's first thought, as she turned to spring over the brook:—"but I'll just ask him what's the matter," she added, checking herself on the very edge. "If I once jump over, everything will change, and then I can't help him."[1]

So she went back to the Wasp—rather unwillingly, for she was *very* anxious to be a Queen.

"Oh, my old bones, my old bones!" he was grumbling as Alice came up to him.

"It's rheumatism, I should think," Alice said to herself, and she stooped over him, and said very kindly, "I hope you're not in much pain?"

The Wasp only shook his shoulders, and turned his head away. "Ah, dreary me!" he said to himself.

"Can I do anything for you?" Alice went on. "Aren't you rather cold here?"

"How you go on!" the Wasp said in a peevish

1. The abrupt changes of scenery that take place whenever Alice leaps a brook resemble the changes that occur in a chess game whenever a move is made, as well as the sudden transitions that occur in dreams.

2. *Worrit* was a slang noun in Carroll's time for worry or mental distress. The *Oxford English Dictionary* quotes Mr. Bumble (in Dickens's *Oliver Twist*): "A porochial life, ma'am, is a life of worrit and vexation and hardihood." *Worrity* was another form of the noun commonly used by British lower classes.

3. If any insect had a newspaper it would be the social wasp. Wasps are great paper makers. Their thin paper nests, usually in hollow trees, are made from a pulp which they produce by chewing leaves and wood fiber.

4. "brown sugar": Wasps are fond of all kinds of man-made sweets, especially sugar. Morton Cohen points out that the Wasp's preference for brown sugar is characteristic of Victorian lower classes, who found it cheaper than the refined white.

5. "Engulph" was a common spelling of "engulf" in the sixteenth and seventeenth centuries. It was occasionally seen in Carroll's time, and the Wasp may be voicing Carroll's personal dislike of the spelling. Perhaps it is Alice's incorrect pronunciation, "en-gulph-ed" (three syllables instead of two), that the Wasp finds so outlandish. Donald L. Hotson suggests that Carroll may here be playing on a university slang expression of the time. According to *The Slang Dictionary* (Chatto & Windus, 1974), *gulfed* (sometimes spelled "gulphed") was "originally a Cambridge term, denoting that a man is unable to enter for the classical examination from having failed in the mathematical. . . . The expression is common now in Oxford as descriptive of a man who goes in for honours, and only gets a pass."

tone. "Worrity, worrity! There never was such a child!"[2]

Alice felt rather offended at this answer, and was very nearly walking on and leaving him, but she thought to herself "Perhaps it's only pain that makes him so cross." So she tried once more.

"Won't you let me help you round to the other side? You'll be out of the cold wind there."

The Wasp took her arm, and let her help him round the tree, but when he got settled down again he only said, as before, "Worrity, worrity! Can't you leave a body alone?"

"Would you like me to read you a bit of this?" Alice went on, as she picked up a newspaper which had been lying at his feet.[3]

"You may read it if you've a mind to," the Wasp said, rather sulkily. "Nobody's hindering you, that *I* know of."

So Alice sat down by him, and spread out the paper on her knees, and began. "*Latest News. The Exploring Party have made another tour in the Pantry, and have found five new lumps of white sugar, large and in fine condition. In coming back—*"

"Any brown sugar?" the Wasp interrupted.

Alice hastily ran her eye down the paper and said "No. It says nothing about brown."

"No brown sugar!" grumbled the Wasp. "A nice exploring party!"[4]

"*In coming back,*" Alice went on reading, "*they found a lake of treacle. The banks of the lake were blue and white, and looked like china. While tasting the treacle, they had a sad accident: two of their party were engulphed—*"

"Were *what*?" the Wasp asked in a very cross voice.

"En-gulph-ed," Alice repeated, dividing the word into syllables.[5]

"There's no such word in the language!" said the Wasp.

"It's in this newspaper, though," Alice said a little timidly.

"Let it stop there!" said the Wasp, fretfully turning away his head.

Alice put down the newspaper. "I'm afraid you're not well," she said in a soothing tone. "Can't I do anything for you?"

"It's all along of the wig,"[6] the Wasp said in a much gentler voice.

"Along of the wig?" Alice repeated, quite pleased to find that he was recovering his temper.

"You'd be cross too, if you'd a wig like mine," the Wasp went on. "They jokes at one. And they worrits one.[7] And then I gets cross. And I gets cold. And I gets under a tree. And I gets a yellow handkerchief.[8] And I ties up my face—as at the present."

Alice looked pityingly at him. "Tying up the face is very good for the toothache," she said.[9]

"And it's very good for the conceit," added the Wasp.

Alice didn't catch the word exactly. "Is that a kind of toothache?" she asked.

The Wasp considered a little. "Well, no," he said: "It's when you hold up your head—*so*—without bending your neck."

"Oh, you mean stiff-neck,"[10] said Alice.

The Wasp said "That's a new-fangled name. They called it conceit in my time."

"Conceit isn't a disease at all," Alice remarked.

"It is, though," said the Wasp: "wait till you have it, and then you'll know. And when you catches it, just try tying a yellow handkerchief round your face. It'll cure you in no time!"

He untied the handkerchief as he spoke, and

6. "all along of": all because of. Another lower-class expression of the day.

7. "worrits": The word was also vulgarly used as a verb. "Don't worrit your poor mother," says Mrs. Saunders in Dickens's *Pickwick Papers*. The Wasp's speech marks him clearly as a drone in the wasp social structure.

Carroll not only identified his cantankerous aged man with a creature universally feared and hated, he also made him lower class, in sharp contrast to Alice's upper-class background—facts that make her kindness toward the insect all the more remarkable.

8. A yellow silk handkerchief, colloquially called a "yellowman," was fashionable in Victorian England.

9. Tying a handkerchief around the face, with a poultice inside, was in Carroll's time believed around the world to provide relief from a toothache. Persons who considered themselves good-looking must have frequently been seen in this condition, and their appearance surely would not have strengthened their conceit.

10. A stiff neck is a bodily ailment as well as the bearing of a haughty, proud, or conceited person. Perhaps the Wasp is warning Alice of the danger of becoming a haughty Queen, as stiff-necked as an ivory chess queen. Indeed, as soon as Alice finds the gold crown on her head she walks about "rather stiffly" to keep the crown from falling off. In the last chapter she commands the black kitten to "sit up a little more stiffly" like the Red Queen she fancied the kitten to have been in her dream. Compare also with the "proud and stiff" messenger in Humpty Dumpty's poem.

Professor Cohen observes that the Wasp reverses history when he calls *stiff-neck* a newfangled name. It is a much older word than *conceit*. "You are a stiff-necked people," the Lord commanded Moses to tell the Israelites (Exodus 33 : 5).

11. "bright yellow": The phrase is used again by Carroll in Chapter 9, where it is also associated with advanced age. A "very old frog" is dressed in "bright yellow."

12. "comb": another pun. Note that if Alice is a bee, she is about to become a Queen bee.

13. Is this poem, like so many of the others in both *Alice* books, a parody? Many poems and songs of the time begin "When I was young . . ." but I could find none that seemed a probable basis for this poem. Carroll may have been aware that the phrase "ringlets waved" occurs in John Milton's beautiful description of the naked Eve (*Paradise Lost*, Book 4):

She, as a veil down to the slender waist,
Her unadorned golden tresses wore
Dishevelled, but in wanton ringlets waved
As the vine curls her tendrils . . .

And there is the following line from Alexander Pope's "Sappho":

No more my locks, in ringlets, curled . . .

However, since ringlets always curl and wave, the parallels may be coincidental.

It may be worth pointing out that the word *ringlets* usually refers not to short curls but to long locks in helical form, like the vines mentioned by Milton. As a mathematician Carroll knew that the helix is an asymmetrical structure which (in Alice's words) "goes the other way" in the mirror.

As mentioned earlier, it is no acci-

Alice looked at his wig in great surprise. It was bright yellow like the handkerchief,[11] and all tangled and tumbled about like a heap of seaweed. "You could make your wig much neater," she said, "if only you had a comb."

"What, you're a Bee, are you?" the Wasp said, looking at her with more interest. "And you've got a comb.[12] Much honey?"

"It isn't that kind," Alice hastily explained. "It's to comb hair with—your wig's so *very* rough, you know."

"I'll tell you how I came to wear it," the Wasp said. "When I was young, you know, my ringlets used to wave—"

A curious idea came into Alice's head. Almost every one she had met had repeated poetry to her, and she thought she would try if the Wasp couldn't do it too. "Would you mind saying it in rhyme?" she asked very politely.

"It ain't what I'm used to," said the Wasp: "however I'll try; wait a bit." He was silent for a few moments, and then began again—

"*When I was young, my ringlets waved*[13]
    And curled and crinkled on my head:
  And then they said 'You should be shaved,
    And wear a yellow wig instead.'

But when I followed their advice,
    And they had noticed the effect,
  They said I did not look so nice
    As they had ventured to expect.

They said it did not fit, and so
    It made me look extremely plain:
  But what was I to do, you know?
    My ringlets would not grow again.

So now that I am old and gray,
    And all my hair is nearly gone,

They take my wig from me and say
  'How can you put such rubbish on?'

And still, whenever I appear,
  They hoot at me and call me 'Pig!'[14]
And that is why they do it, dear,
  Because I wear a yellow wig."

"I'm very sorry for you," Alice said heartily: "and I think if your wig fitted a little better, they wouldn't tease you quite so much."

"*Your* wig fits very well," the Wasp murmured, looking at her with an expression of admiration: "it's the shape of your head as does it. Your jaws ain't well shaped, though—I should think you couldn't bite well?"

Alice began with a little scream of laughter, which she turned into a cough as well as she could.[15] At last she managed to say gravely, "I can bite anything I want."[16]

"Not with a mouth as small as that," the Wasp persisted. "If you was a-fighting, now—could you get hold of the other one by the back of the neck?"

"I'm afraid not," said Alice.

"Well, that's because your jaws are too short," the Wasp went on: "but the top of your head is nice and round." He took off his own wig as he spoke, and stretched out one claw towards Alice,[17] as if he wished to do the same for her, but she kept out of reach, and would not take the hint. So he went on with his criticisms.

"Then your eyes—they're too much in front, no doubt. One would have done as well as two, if you *must* have them so close—"[18]

Alice did not like having so many personal remarks made on her, and as the Wasp had quite recovered his spirits, and was getting very talkative, she thought she might safely leave him. "I

dent that the second *Alice* book is filled with references to mirror reversals and asymmetric objects. The helix itself is mentioned several times. Humpty Dumpty compares the toves to corkscrews, and Tenniel drew them with helical tails and snouts. Humpty also speaks in a poem about waking up fish with a corkscrew, and in Chapter 9 the White Queen recalls that Humpty had a corkscrew in hand when he was looking for a hippopotamus. In Tenniel's pictures the unicorn and the goat have helical horns. The road that leads up the hill in Chapter 3 twists like a corkscrew. Carroll must have realized that the young (perhaps then conceited?) Wasp, admiring himself in a mirror, would have seen his ringlets curl "the other way."

Any way you look at it, the poem itself is a strange one to appear in a book for children, though no more so, perhaps, than the inscrutable poem recited by Humpty in Chapter 6. The cutting off of hair, like decapitation and teeth extraction, is a familiar Freudian symbol of castration. Interesting interpretations of the poem by psychoanalytically oriented critics are possible.

14. In the Pig and Pepper chapter of *Alice in Wonderland*, Alice at first thinks that "Pig!," shouted by the Duchess, is addressed to her. It turns out that the Duchess is hurling the epithet at the baby boy she is nursing, who soon turns into an actual pig. The use of "pig" as a derisive name for a person, says the *OED*, was common in Victorian England. Surprisingly, even then it was an epithet often used against police officers. An 1874 slang dictionary adds: "The word is almost exclusively applied by London thieves to a plain-clothes man."

J. A. Lindon, a British writer of comic verse, suggests that it is the Wasp's baldness (cf. the baldness of the Duchess's baby) that prompts the epithet; and he recalls the association of pig and wig in "piggywiggy," which the *OED* says is applied to both a little pig and a child. In "The Owl and the Pussycat," Edward Lear writes:

And there in a wood a Piggy-wig stood,
With a ring at the end of its nose.

15. Alice changed her "little scream of laughter" at the Wasp to a discreet cough. A short time before she had tried unsuccessfully to hold back a "little scream of laughter" at the White Knight. We cannot be sure, of course, that all parallels such as this were in the original text. After removing the Wasp episode, Carroll may have borrowed some of its phrases and images for use elsewhere when he polished the rest of the galleys.

16. Alice once frightened her nurse by shouting in her ear; "Do let's pretend that I'm a hungry hyæna, and you're a bone!" (*Through the Looking-Glass*, Chapter 1).

17. This somewhat terrifying scene, a large wasp reaching out a "claw" to remove Alice's hair, recalls three other episodes in the book. The White Knight, mounting his horse, steadies himself by holding Alice's hair. The White Queen grabs Alice's hair with both hands in Chapter 9. And, in a reversal of ages, Carroll planned to have Alice seize the hair of an old lady sitting near her when the railway carriage jumps the second brook, as we know from Tenniel's letter.

think I must be going on now," she said. "Good-bye."

"Good-bye, and thank-ye," said the Wasp, and Alice tripped down the hill again, quite pleased that she had gone back and given a few minutes to making the poor old creature comfortable.

18. Unlike Alice, wasps have bulbous compound eyes on the sides of their heads and large strong jaws. Like Alice's, their heads are "nice and round." Other Looking-glass creatures (the Rose, the Tiger lily, the Unicorn) size up Alice in similar fashion, in the light of their own physical attributes.

Tenniel, at the age of twenty, lost the sight of one eye in a fencing bout with his father. The button accidentally dropped from his father's foil, and the blade's tip flicked across his right eye with a sudden pain that must have felt like a wasp's sting. One can understand why Tenniel might have been offended by the Wasp's remark; if so, it could have colored his attitude toward the episode.

Original Pencil Sketches by Tenniel

The pencil drawings in
the book are the original
sketches – done by me.
John Tenniel.

A Note about Lewis Carroll Societies

The Lewis Carroll Society of North America is a nonprofit organization that encourages the study of the life, work, times, and influence of Charles Lutwidge Dodgson. The society was founded in 1974 and has grown from several dozen members to several hundred, drawn from across North America and from abroad. Current members include leading authorities on Carroll, collectors, students, general enthusiasts, and libraries. The society is making a concerted professional effort to become the center for Carroll activities and studies.

The society meets twice a year, usually in the fall and in the spring, at the site of an important Carroll collection in the eastern United States. Meetings have featured distinguished speakers and outstanding exhibitions.

The society maintains an active publications program, administered by a distinguished committee interested in publishing and assisting in the publication of materials dealing with the life and work of Lewis Carroll. Members receive the society's newsletter (the *Knight Letter*), chapbooks in the society's series (*Carroll Studies*), and other special publications. *The Wasp in a Wig* was first published as part of this series.

Further information can be obtained by writing to The Secretary, Ellie Luchinsky, Lewis Carroll Society of North America, 18 Fitzharding Place, Owings Mill, Maryland 21117.

England's older Lewis Carroll Society was founded in 1969. It publishes a periodical—*The Carrollian* (formerly titled *Jabberwocky*), edited by Anne Clark Amor—and *Bandersnatch*, a newsletter. For information write to The Secretary, Sarah Stanfield, Acorns, Dargate, near Faversham, Kent, England ME13 9HG.

The Lewis Carroll Society of Canada publishes *White Rabbit Tales*, a newsletter edited by Dayna McCausland, Box 321, Erin, Ontario, Canada N0B 1T0.

The Lewis Carroll Society of Japan issues a newsletter in both English and Japanese. The society's secretary is Katsuko Kasai, 3–6–15 Funato, Abiko 270–11, Japan. Carroll has a large following in Japan, with about sixty Japanese editions of the *Alice* books in print.

Selected References

By Lewis Carroll

Alice's Adventures in Wonderland. 1865. Carroll arranged for the first edition of two thousand copies to be published on July 4 to commemorate the date of the boating trip, three years earlier, on which he first told the story of Alice. This edition was recalled by Carroll and Tenniel because they did not like the quality of the printing. Unbound sheets were then sold to the New York firm of Appleton, who issued a thousand copies with a new title page printed at Oxford and dated 1866. This was the second issue of the first edition. The third issue was the remaining batch of 952 copies, carrying a title page printed in the United States. Carroll had little interest in the quality of his U.S. printings. "I fear it is true that there are no children in America," he wrote in his diary (Sept. 3, 1880) after meeting an eight-year-old New York girl of whose behavior he did not approve.

An Elementary Treatise on Determinants. 1867.

Through the Looking-Glass, and What Alice Found There. 1871.

The Hunting of the Snark, An Agony in Eight Fits. 1876.

Euclid and His Modern Rivals. 1879; reprint, 1973.

Alice's Adventures Under Ground. 1886; reprint, 1965. A facsimile of the original manuscript, which Carroll hand-lettered and crudely illustrated as a gift for Alice Liddell. It is a little more than half the length of *Alice's Adventures in Wonderland.*

Sylvie and Bruno. 1889; reprint, 1988.

The Nursery "Alice." 1889; reprint, 1966. A rewritten and short-ened version of the first *Alice* book, for very young readers "from Nought to Five." The illustrations are Tenniel's, enlarged and colored.

Sylvie and Bruno Concluded. 1893.

The Lewis Carroll Picture Book. Edited by Stuart Dodgson Collingwood. 1899; reprint, 1961. A valuable collection of miscellaneous short pieces by Carroll, including many of his original games, puzzles, and other mathematical recreations.

Further Nonsense Verse and Prose. Edited by Langford Reed. 1926.

The Russian Journal and Other Selections from the Works of Lewis Carroll. Edited by John Francis McDermott. 1935; reprint, 1977. Includes Carroll's diary record of his trip to Russia in 1867 with Canon Henry Liddon.

The Complete Works of Lewis Carroll. Introduction by Alexander Woollcott. 1937. The title is something of a fraud for the book is far from complete even when one excludes (as this book does) the many books published under the name of Charles Dodgson. It continues, however, (as a Modern Library book), to be the most easily obtained collection of Carroll's prose and verse.

The Diaries of Lewis Carroll. 2 volumes. Edited by Roger Lancelyn Green. 1953. Indispensable for any student of Carroll, though one regrets that Green's excisions include "mathematical and logical formulae and minor problems," and "long accounts of how he [Carroll] saw children on the shore at Eastbourne, but failed to cultivate their friendship." An excellent review by W. H. Auden appeared in the *New York Times Book Review*, February 28, 1954.

Symbolic Logic and the Game of Logic. Reprint, 1958. Single-volume reprint of Carroll's two books on logic, both intended for children.

Pillow Problems and a Tangled Tale. Reprint, 1958. Single-volume reprint of Carroll's two books of problems in recreational mathematics.

The Rectory Umbrella and Mischmasch. Reprint, 1971. A reprint of two early manuscripts by Carroll.

The Oxford Pamphlets, Letters, and Circulars of Charles Lutwidge Dodgson. Edited by Edward Wakeling. 1993.

Lewis Carroll's Diaries. Edited by Edward Wakeling. Vol. 1 (1993), Vol. 2 (1994), Vol. 3 (1995), Vol. 4 (1997).

Phantasmagoria. Edited by Martin Gardner. 1998. A reprint of Carroll's comic ballad about a ghost.

Annotated Editions of the Alice Books

Alice in Wonderland and Through the Looking-Glass. Edited by Roger Lancelyn Green. 1971.

Alice in Wonderland. Edited by Donald J. Gray. 1971.

The Philosopher's Alice. Edited by Peter Heath. 1974.

Alice's Adventures in Wonderland and Through the Looking-Glass. 2 volumes. Edited by James R. Kincaid. 1982–83.

Alice in Wonderland and Through the Looking-Glass. Edited by Hugh Haughton. 1998.

Illustrated Editions of Alice

More than a hundred artists have illustrated the *Alice* books. For a checklist, see *The Illustrators of Alice in Wonderland,* edited by Graham Ovenden, with an introduction by Jack Davis. Published in 1972 by Academy Editions in England and here by St. Martin's Press. This handsome volume reproduces numerous illustrations, some in full color.

Letters of Lewis Carroll

A Selection from the Letters of Lewis Carroll to His Child-Friends. Edited by Evelyn M. Hatch. 1933.

The Letters of Lewis Carroll, 2 volumes. Edited by Morton N. Cohen. 1979.

Lewis Carroll and the Kitchins. Edited by Morton N. Cohen. 1980.

Lewis Carroll and the House of Macmillan. Edited by Morton N. Cohen and Anita Gandolfo. 1987.

Lewis Carroll's Letters to Skeffington. Edited by Anne Clark Amor. 1990.

Theatrical Productions of Alice

Alice on Stage. Charles C. Lovett. 1990.

Biographies of Lewis Carroll

The Life and Letters of Lewis Carroll. Stuart Dodgson Collingwood. 1898. A biography by Carroll's nephew; the primary source of information about Carroll's life.

The Story of Lewis Carroll. Isa Bowman. 1899; reprint, 1972. Recollections of Carroll by one of the actresses who played Alice in Savile Clarke's stage musical and who became one of Carroll's leading child-friends.

Lewis Carroll. Walter de la Mare. 1932.

The Life of Lewis Carroll. Langford Reed. 1932.

Carroll's Alice. Harry Morgan Ayres. 1936.

Victoria through the Looking-Glass. Florence Becker Lennon. 1945; reprint, 1972.

Lewis Carroll: Photographer. Helmut Gernsheim. 1949; revised 1969. Includes excellent reproductions of sixty-four photographs by Carroll.

The Story of Lewis Carroll. Roger Lancelyn Green. 1949.

Lewis Carroll. Derek Hudson. 1954; revised 1977.

Lewis Carroll. Roger Lancelyn Green. 1960.

The Snark Was a Boojum. James Plasted Wood. 1966.

Lewis Carroll. Jean Gattégno. 1974.

Lewis Carroll. Richard Kelly. 1977; revised 1990.

Lewis Carroll. Anne Clarke. 1979.

Lewis Carroll. Graham Ovenden. 1984.

Lewis Carroll: Interviews and Reflections. Edited by Morton N. Cohen. 1989.

Lewis Carroll in Russia. Fan Parker. 1994.

Lewis Carroll. Morton N. Cohen. 1995.

Lewis Carroll. Michael Bakewell. 1996.

Lewis Carroll in Wonderland. Stephanie Stoffel. 1996.

Lewis Carroll. Donald Thomas. 1998.

Reflections in a Looking Glass. Morton N. Cohen. 1998. Beautiful reproductions of Carroll's photographs, including the four surviving nude portraits of little girls.

Carroll Criticism

Carroll's Alice. Harry Morgan Ayres. 1936.

The White Knight. Alexander L. Taylor. 1952.

Charles Dodgson, Semiotician. Daniel F. Kirk. 1963.

Alice's Adventures in Wonderland. Edited by Donald Rackin. 1969.

Language and Lewis Carroll, Robert D. Sutherland. 1970.

Aspects of Alice. Edited by Robert Phillips. 1971.

Play, Games, and Sports: The Literary Works of Lewis Carroll. Kathleen Blake. 1974.

The Raven and the Writing Desk. Francis Huxley. 1976.

Lewis Carroll Observed. Edited by Edward Guiliano. 1976.

Soaring With the Dodo. Edited by Edward Guiliano and James R. Kincaid. 1982.

Lewis Carroll: A Celebration. Edited by Edward Guiliano. 1982.

Modern Critical Reviews: Lewis Carroll. Edited by Harold Bloom. 1987.

Alice's Adventures in Wonderland and Through the Looking-Glass. Donald Rackin. 1991.

Semiotics and Linguistics in Alice's World. R. L. F. Fordyce and Carla Marcello. 1994.

The Literary Products of the Lewis Carroll–George MacDonald Friendship. John Docherty. 1995.

The Making of the Alice Books: Lewis Carroll's Use of Earlier Children's Literature. Ronald Reichertz. 1997.

Lewis Carroll: The Alice Companion. Jo Elwyn Jones and J. Francis Gladstone. 1998.

The Art of Alice in Wonderland. Stephanie Lovett Steffel. 1998.

Psychoanalytic Interpretations of Carroll

"Alice in Wonderland Psycho-Analyzed." A. M. E. Goldschmidt. *New Oxford Outlook* (May 1933).

"Alice in Wonderland: the Child as Swain." William Empson. In *Some Versions of Pastoral.* 1935. The U.S. edition is titled *English Pastoral Poetry.* Reprinted in *Art and Psychoanalysis.* Edited by William Phillips. 1957.

"Psychoanalyzing Alice." Joseph Wood Krutch. *The Nation* 144 (Jan. 30, 1937): 129–30.

"Psychoanalytic Remarks on *Alice in Wonderland* and Lewis Carroll." Paul Schilder. *The Journal of Nervous and Mental Diseases* 87 (1938): 159–68.

"About the Symbolization of *Alice's Adventures in Wonderland*." Martin Grotjahn. *American Imago* 4 (1947): 32–41.

"Lewis Carroll's Adventures in Wonderland." John Skinner. *American Imago* 4 (1947): 3–31.

Swift and Carroll. Phyllis Greenacre. 1955.

"All on a Golden Afternoon." Robert Bloch. *Fantasy and Science Fiction* (June 1956). A short story burlesquing the analytic approach to Alice.

On Carroll as Logician and Mathematician

"Lewis Carroll as Logician." R. B. Braithwaite. *The Mathematical Gazette* 16 (July 1932): 174–78.

"Lewis Carroll, Mathematician." D. B. Eperson. *The Mathematical Gazette* 17 (May 1933): 92–100.

"Lewis Carroll and a Geometrical Paradox." Warren Weaver. *The American Mathematical Monthly* 45 (April 1938): 234–36.

"The Mathematical Manuscripts of Lewis Carroll." Warren Weaver. *Proceedings of the American Philosophical Society* 98 (October 15, 1954): 377–81.

"Lewis Carroll: Mathematician." Warren Weaver. *Scientific American* 194 (April 1956): 116–28.

"Mathematical Games." Martin Gardner. *Scientific American* (March 1960): 172–76. A discussion of Carroll's games and puzzles.

The Magic of Lewis Carroll. Edited by John Fisher. 1973.

Lewis Carroll: Symbolic Logic. William Warren Bartley, III. 1977; revised 1986.

Lewis Carroll's Games and Puzzles. Edited by Edward Wakeling. 1982.

The Mathematical Pamphlets of Charles Lutwidge Dodgson and Related Pieces. Edited by Francine Abeles. 1994.

Rediscovered Lewis Carroll Puzzles. Edited by Edward Wakeling. 1995.

The Universe in a Handkerchief. Edited by Martin Gardner. 1996.

On Alice Liddell

The Real Alice. Anne Clark. 1981.
Lewis Carroll and Alice: 1832–1982. Morton N. Cohen. 1982.
Beyond the Looking Glass: Reflections of Alice and Her Family.
    Colin Gordon. 1982.
The Other Alice. Christina Bjork. 1993.

Bibliographies

The Lewis Carroll Handbook. Sidney Herbert Williams and
    Falconer Madan. 1931. Revised by Roger Lancelyn Green,
    1962; further revised by Dennis Crutch, 1979.
Alice in Many Tongues. Warren Weaver. 1964. On translations of
    the Alice books.
Lewis Carroll: An Annotated International Bibliography 1960–77.
    Edward Guiliano. 1980.
Lewis Carroll: A Sesquicentennial Guide to Research. Edward
    Guiliano. 1982.
*Lewis Carroll's Alice: An Annotated Checklist of the Lovett
    Collection*. Charles and Stephanie Lovett. 1984.
Lewis Carroll: A Reference Guide. Rachel Fordyce. 1988.

On Nonsense

"A Defence of Nonsense," Gilbert Chesterton. In *The Defendant*.
    1901.
"Lewis Carroll" and "How Pleasant to Know Mr. Lear." Gilbert
    Chesterton. In *A Handful of Authors*. 1953.
The Poetry of Nonsense. Emile Cammaerts. 1925.
"Nonsense Poetry." George Orwell. In *Shooting an Elephant*.
    1945.
The Field of Nonsense. Elizabeth Sewell. 1952.
Nonsense. Susan Stewart. 1980.

On Tenniel and Other Illustrators

Enchanting Alice! Black-and-white
Has made your charm perennial;
And nought save "Chaos and old Night"
Can part you now from Tenniel.

— from a poem by Austin Dobson

Creators of Wonderland. Marguerite Mespoulet, 1934. The book argues that Tenniel was influenced by the French artist J. J. Grandville.

Sir John Tenniel. Frances Sarzano. 1948.

"The Life and Works of Sir John Tenniel." W. C. Monkhouse. *Art Journal* (Easter Number, 1901).

The Illustrators of Alice in Wonderland and Through the Looking-Glass. Graham Ovenden. 1973; revised 1979.

The Tenniel Illustrations to the "Alice" Books. Michael Hancher. 1985.

"Peter Newell." Michael Patrick Hearn. In *More Annotated Alice.* Edited by Martin Gardner. 1990. This book reproduces Newell's eighty illustrations for the two *Alice* books.

Sir John Tenniel: Alice's White Knight. Rodney Engen. 1991.

Sir John Tenniel: Aspects of His Work. Roger Simpson. 1994.

SIR JOHN TENNIEL. A SELF-PORTRAIT, 1889

Alice on the Screen

David Schaefer, a Carroll scholar who lives in Silver Spring, Maryland, owns a great collection of *Alice*-related films. He has kindly provided the following listings.

Newsreel

1932 *Alice in U.S. Land*. Paramount News. Newsreel of Mrs. Alice Liddell Hargreaves, eighty, arriving for the hundredth-anniversary celebration of Carroll's birth. Talks of her trip down the river with "Mr. Dodgson." Her son, Caryl Hargreaves, and her sister Rhoda Liddell, are identifiable. Filmed aboard the Cunard Line's *Berengeria* in New York Harbor, April 29, 1932. Running time: seventy-five seconds.

Feature Films

1903 *Alice in Wonderland*. Produced and directed by Cecil Hepworth. Filmed in Great Britain. Alice is played by May Clark. The very first *Alice* film. Alice shrinks and grows. The film has sixteen scenes, all from *Alice's Adventures*. Running time: ten minutes.

1910 *Alice's Adventures in Wonderland (A Fairy Comedy)*. Produced by the Edison Manufacturing Company, Orange, New Jersey. Alice is played by Gladys Hulette. The film has fourteen scenes, all from *Alice's Adventures*. Running time: ten minutes (one reel). The film was made in the Bronx. Gladys Hulette later became a Pathé star.

1915 *Alice in Wonderland*. Produced by Nonpareil Feature Film

Company directed by W. W. Young, "picturized" by Dewitt C. Wheeler: Alice is played by Viola Savoy. Most of the scenes were filmed on an estate on Long Island. The film as originally made contained scenes from *Alice's Adventures* and *Through the Looking-Glass*. Running time: fifty minutes (five reels).

1931 *Alice in Wonderland*. Commonwealth Pictures Corporation. Screen adaptation by John F. Godson and Ashley Miller. Produced at the Metropolitan Studios, Fort Lee, New Jersey. Directed by "Bud" Pollard. Alice played by Ruth Gilbert. All scenes are from *Alice's Adventures*. The first sound *Alice*. The thump of the camera can often be heard.

1933 *Alice in Wonderland*. Paramount Productions. Produced by Louis D. Leighton, directed by Norman McLeod, screenplay by Joseph J. Mankiewicz and William Cameron Menzies. Music by Dimitri Tiomkin. Alice played by Charlotte Henry. An all-star cast of forty-six includes: W. C. Fields as Humpty Dumpty, Edward Everett Horton as the Mad Hatter, Cary Grant as the Mock Turtle, Gary Cooper as the White Knight, Edna May Oliver as the Red Queen, May Robson as the Queen of Hearts, and Baby LeRoy as the Deuce of Hearts. Scenes from *Alice's Adventures* and *Looking-Glass*. Running time: ninety minutes. In looking-glass fashion Charlotte Henry started her movie career as the star of this film and worked her way down to lesser roles.

1948 *Alice au pays des merveilles (Alice in Wonderland)*. Produced in France at Victorine Studios by Lou Bunin. Directed by Marc Maurette and Dallas Bowers; script by Henry Myers, Edward Flisen, and Albert Cervin. Marionette animation by Lou Bunin. Alice played by Carol Marsh. Voices for puppets by Joyce Grenfell, Peter Bull, and Jack Train. The prologue, which shows Lewis Carroll's life at Christ Church, has Pamela Brown as Queen Victoria and Stanley Baker as Prince Albert. Color: Produced in French and English versions. Exclusive of the prologue, all the characters are puppets except Alice, who is a live adult. Disney tried to stop production, distribution, and display of the film.

1951 *Alice in Wonderland*. Walt Disney Production. Production Supervisor, Ben Sharpsteen. Alice's voice by Kathryn Beaumont. Animation. Color. Sequences from *Alice's Adventures* and *Looking-Glass*. Running time: seventy-five minutes.

Poorly received when produced, but has made a great deal of money for Disney since.

1972 *Alice's Adventures in Wonderland*. Executive Producer, Joseph Shaftel. Producer, Derek Home. Director, William Sterling. Musical Director, John Barry. Lyricist, Don Black. Alice played by Fiona Fullerton. Peter Sellers is the March Hare, Dame Flora Robson is the Queen of Hearts, Dennis Price is the King of Hearts, and Sir Ralph Richardson is the Caterpillar. Color. Wide screen. A lavish production, visually beautiful, slow moving. The Tenniel illustrations were faithfully followed. Sequences from *Alice's Adventures* and *Looking-Glass*. Running time: ninety minutes.

1985 *Dreamchild*, The 80-year old Alice (Alice Hargreaves) is played by Coral Browne. Her young paid companion by Nicola Cowper. The young Alice by Amelia Shankley and Lewis Carroll by Ian Holm. A fictional story inspired by Alice's visit to the United States in 1932.

1976 *Alice in Wonderland, an X-Rated Musical Comedy*. Alice is played by Kristine DeBell.

1988 *Neco z Alenky*. Directed and written by Jan Svankmajer of Czechoslovakia.

Alice Sequences in Other Feature Films

1930 *Puttin' on the Ritz*. Produced by John W. Considine, Jr., directed by Edward H. Sloman. Music and lyrics by Irving Berlin. Joan Bennett is in a six-minute *Alice in Wonderland* dance sequence from this film.

1938 *My Lucky Star*. 20th Century Fox. Sonja Henie is an Alice on skates along with many other characters from the book, all on the ice. Approximately ten-minute sequence.

Cartoons

1933 *Betty in Blunderland*. Cartoon directed by Dave Fleischer. Animation by Roland Crandall and Thomas Johnson. Betty Boop follows *Wonderland* and *Looking-Glass* characters from a jigsaw puzzle via subway station down the rabbit hole. Running time: ten minutes.

1936 *Thru the Mirror*. Walt Disney Productions. A brilliant Mickey Mouse cartoon based on *Through the Looking-Glass*.

1955 *Sweapea Thru the Looking Glass*. King Features Syndicate cartoon. Executive Producer, Al Brodax. Directed by Jack Kinney. Color. Sweapea goes through a looking glass and falls down a golf hole into the "Wunnerland Golf Club."

1971 *Zvahlar aneb Saticky Slameného Huberta*. Produced by Katky Film, Prague. Screenplay, design, and direction by Jan Svankmajer. This animation begins with a reading of "Jabberwocky." "Sequence of images composed of seemingly nonsense activities." Color. Running time: fourteen minutes.

Made for Television

1950 *Alice in Wonderland*. Television production staged at the Ford Theatre in December 1950. Alice is played by Iris Mann and the White Rabbit by Dorothy Jarnac.

1965 *Curly in Wonderland*. The Three Stooges in animation.

1966 *Alice in Wonderland, or What's a Nice Kid Like You Doing in a Place Like This?* Hanna-Barbera Productions. Book by Bill Dana. Music and lyrics by Lee Adams and Charles Strauss. Color. Animation. Alice's voice by Janet Waldo, Cheshire Cat by Sammy Davis, Jr., White Knight by Bill Dana, Queen by Zsa Zsa Gabor. Running time: fifty minutes. Alice follows her dog through a television tube.

1966 *Alice Through the Looking Glass*. Shown November 1966. Script by Albert Simmons, lyrics by Elsie Simmons, music by Moose Charlap. Its cast includes Judi Rolin as Alice, Jimmy Durante as Humpty Dumpty, Nanette Fabray as the White Queen, Agnes Moorehead as the Red Queen, Jack Palance as the Jabberwock, The Smothers Brothers as Tweedledum and Tweedledee, Ricardo Montalban as the White King. Running time: ninety minutes.

1967 *Alice in Wonderland*. BBC television production. Directed by Jonathan Miller. Presentation of Wonderland as a Victorian social commentary. Grand production with a star cast: Sir John Gielgud as the Mock Turtle, Sir Michael Redgrave as the Caterpillar, Peter Sellers as the King, Peter Cook as the

Hatter, Sir Malcolm Muggeridge as the Gryphon, Anne-Marie Mallik, a young schoolgirl, as Alice.

1967 *Abbott and Costello in Blunderland.* Hanna-Barbera Productions. An animation.

1970 *Alice in Wonderland.* O.R.T.F. (French television) production. Directed by Jean-Christophe Averty. Burlesque with stunning visual and auditory overlay. Alice Sapritch and Francis Blanche as the King and Queen.

1973 *Through the Looking-Glass.* BBC television production. Produced by Rosemary Hill, adapted and directed by James MacTaggart. Twelve-year-old Sarah Sutton as Alice, Brenda Bruce as the White Queen, Freddie Jones as Humpty Dumpty, Judy Parfitt as the Red Queen, and Richard Pearson as the White King.

1985 *Alice in Wonderland and Through the Looking Glass.* Produced by Irwin Allen. Songs by Steve Allen. Natalie Gregory as Alice, with a cast of stars including Jayne Meadows, Robert Morley, Red Buttons, and Sammy Davis, Jr.

1999 *Alice in Wonderland.* Three-hour production directed by Nick Willing. There were 875 postproduction digital effects. Robert Halmi, Sr., and Robert Halmi, Jr., were the executive producers, and Peter Barnes wrote the script. Tina Majorino is Alice; Whoopi Goldberg, the Cheshire Cat; Martin Short, the Mad Hatter; Ben Kingsley, the Caterpillar; Christopher Lloyd, the White Knight; Peter Ustinov, the Walrus; Miranda Richardson, the Queen of Hearts; and Gene Wilder, the Mock Turtle. Robbie Coltrane and George Wendt are Tweedledum and Tweedledee. The first *Alice* with extensive computer enhancement.

Educational

1972 *Curious Alice.* Written, designed, and produced by Design Center, Inc., Washington, D.C. Made for the National Institute of Mental Health. Color. Part of a drug course for elementary school children. A live Alice has a journey among animated characters. The Caterpillar smokes marijuana, the Mad Hatter takes LSD, the Dormouse uses barbiturates, and the March Hare pops amphetamines. The White Rabbit is a leader already into drugs. The Cheshire Cat is Alice's conscience. Running time: approximately fifteen minutes.

1978 *Alice in Wonderland: A Lesson in Appreciating Differences.* Walt Disney Productions. Live action at beginning and end with the lesson in appreciating differences brought home by a showing of the flower sequence from the Disney feature and a discussion about how badly the flowers treated Alice simply because she was different.